MURDER on the PAGE

Kensington books by Daryl Wood Gerber:

The Literary Dining Mystery series

Murder on the Page

The Fairy Garden Mystery series

A Sprinkling of Murder

A Glimmer of a Clue

A Hint of Mischief

A Flicker of a Doubt

A Twinkle of Trouble

DARYL
WOOD GERBER

MURDER on the PAGE

Kensington Publishing Corp.
www.kensingtonbooks.com

KENSINGTON BOOKS are published by

Kensington Publishing Corp.
900 Third Avenue
New York, NY 10022

All Kensington titles, imprints and distributed lines are available at special quantity discounts for bulk purchases for sales promotion, premiums, fund-raising, educational or institutional use. Special book excerpts or customized printings can also be created to fit specific needs. For details, write or phone the office of the Kensington Special Sales Manager: Kensington Publishing Corp., 900 Third Avenue, New York, NY, 10022. Attn. Special Sales Department. Phone: 1-800-221-2647.

KENSINGTON and the KENSINGTON COZIES teapot logo Reg. US Pat & TM Off.

Library of Congress Control Number: 2024939441

ISBN: 978-1-4967-4817-1

First Kensington Hardcover Edition: November 2024

ISBN: 978-1-4967-4819-5 (ebook)

10 9 8 7 6 5 4 3 2 1

Printed in the United States of America

To Mom, thank you for taking me to the library on a weekly basis.
Also thanks for introducing me to Nancy Drew. When I got the measles and you gave me your entire set of books to read, I fell in love with reading, and my world changed forever.

Cast of Characters

Allie Catt, caterer
Brendan Bates, detective
Candace Canfield, Quinby's wife
Celia Harrigan, neighbor of Marigold's
Chloe Kang, bookshop clerk
Dennell Watkins, Tegan's friend
Evelyn Evers, head of the Community Theater Foundation
Fern Catt, Allie's mother
Frank Fitzwilliam, private detective
Graham Wynn, game store owner
Helga, housekeeper and cook at the Blue Lantern
Jamie Catt, Allie's father
J.J., pawnshop owner
Katrina Carlson, brewery bartender
Lillian Bellingham, owner of Puttin' on the Glitz
Marigold Markel, bookshop owner
Ms. Ivey, bank manager
Ms. Richards, Realtor
Mr. Tannenbaum, estate attorney
Noeline Merriweather, owner of the Blue Lantern
Oly Olsen, owner of the Brewery
Piper Lowry, junior-college teacher
Quinby Canfield, landscaper
Rick O'Sheedy, financial consultant
Stella Burberry, accountant
Tegan Potts, Marigold's niece
Upton Scott, Katrina's ex-boyfriend
Vanna Harding, Marigold's other niece
Wallis, waitress at the Brewery
Winston Potts, Tegan's husband
Yvonne, local actress
Zach Armstrong, crime investigation detective

CHAPTER 1

"I am only resolved to act in that manner, which will, in my own opinion, constitute my happiness, without reference to you, or to any person so wholly unconnected with me."

—Elizabeth Bennet, in Jane Austen's *Pride and Prejudice*

Clippety-clop-*splat*. My shoes struck the rain-soaked sidewalk at a brisk pace. Clippety-clop-*splat*.

"Careful, Allie," I muttered to myself. The rain had stopped, but the pavement was still slick. "Slow down."

But I couldn't. Why was I rushing on foot to Dream Cuisine, the pristine ghost kitchen that I rented on a month-to-month basis? Because Marigold Markel, one of my favorite people in the whole world, the woman who owned Feast for the Eyes, a darling bookshop, had hired me to make and serve a midmorning tea tomorrow for the Bramblewood Community Theater Foundation, and she'd put in an additional request. Driving to the store down the street to purchase the few extra items seemed senseless. But now I was late getting started. I hated being late for anything.

Clippety-clop-*splat*. Skid!

"Honestly, Allie, get a grip," I said as I veered right onto Main Street. "You'll get it all done."

Would I? Making six dozen mini mince pies, five dozen tea sandwiches, four dozen icebox sugar cookies, and a pound of chocolate caramel fudge would not be a snap.

"Breathe," I said.

Dutifully, I inhaled and exhaled, adjusted the two reusable bags filled with groceries that I was carrying, and refocused on the sound of the narrator reading my latest foray into Sherlock Holmes stories, *The Sign of the Four,* via my earbuds.

Reading—even audible reading—calmed me. At one time in my life, I was destined to become an English teacher. And why not? I'd spent most of my childhood days reading books while dreaming about any host of heroes and heroines. In high school, my passion for fiction swelled. At Davidson College, it became an obsession. I graduated eager to alter young minds. I also graduated foolishly thinking that getting engaged to a handsome, intriguing banker was a good idea.

At the age of twenty-one, reality hit me hard. Number one: Not all prospective English teachers got hired right off the bat . . . or at all. Number two: Bankers were not intriguing, and fiancés were not worth the effort. Case in point: When I became aware that my beloved was leaving me for a younger woman, I was devastated. I mean, how much younger could he find without robbing the cradle? Needless to say, a week later, I hawked my engagement ring for a gold Celtic knot necklace. I had Celtic heritage on my mother's side, primarily those that settled in the British Isles who identified more with the talkative Irish nature than the direct and economical English personality.

A month after the breakup, I gave up trying to launch a career as a teacher, moved home to Bramblewood, a serene town in the Blue Ridge Mountains northwest of Asheville, North Carolina, and decided to try my hand as a caterer and baker. Why a caterer? Because while waiting for a teaching position to open up in Charlotte, I'd worked as an assistant caterer for a popular diner known as the Eatery and discovered I was good at it. Why wouldn't I be? I'd learned to cook at the tender age of five. I'd had to, out of sheer necessity. My mother, a mathematics teacher who was easily distracted in the kitchen, burned everything.

Now, four years after starting my business, thanks to a devoted clientele and a little pluck—pluck that I drummed up by mimicking all my favorite fictional characters—I was still catering, as well as working as a personal chef and supplying goods to local bakeries. Six clients were demanding twice-weekly deliveries of my scones, cupcakes, and cookies. Three others regularly ordered my fruit or chocolate tarts. Could I use more business? Sure. Couldn't everybody? I certainly needed more money in my coffers to buy all the books I wanted to read.

"Allie, stop!" someone yelled, and batted my arm.

I glanced over my shoulder at Tegan Potts, née Merriweather, my best friend since kindergarten, who was hauling back to assault me again. "Hey. Stop hitting me."

"Haven't you heard me calling you? I've been chasing you for blocks." Her cheeks were pink with exertion.

"Sorry. Can't talk now. I'm running behind."

"Cool your jets. You're your own boss. Time is irrelevant."

"Not to me. Your aunt expects me to deliver the goods." Marigold was Tegan's aunt.

I jammed a key into the lock on the front door of Dream Cuisine, twisted, and pushed the door open. The alarm system started to bleat. I hurried inside and tapped 6-4-6-3 on the keypad, the reciprocal numbers for *m-i-n-e.* The code didn't register correctly. The panel started to bleat faster. "Stop, stop," I grumbled at the idiot box while reentering the digits. Last week, I'd had a techie tweak the darned thing so this wouldn't happen. That worked well. *Not.* Finally the code took, and the system announced almost gleefully that it was now off.

"Bully for you," I snarled at the smug, inanimate object.

I wiped the soles of my shoes on the mat and tossed my key ring on the desk to the right of the door. Then I switched off my audiobook, pocketed my cell phone and earbuds, and unloaded the groceries on the granite counter. I slipped my light-weight tote off my shoulder and set it beside the bags. Light-weight was a misnomer. It weighed a ton, mainly because of the recipe cards, business cards, utility knife, ongoing grocery list, to-do list, paperback book, and Kindle it held. I would be lost without it. My mother told me I wasn't doing my body any favors carrying the entirety of my life around with me, but I rarely heeded what she said.

Tegan entered behind me.

"Whoa! Stop right there!" I pointed at the doormat. She needed to clean her wet shoes, too. I prided myself on keeping the kitchen as clean as a whistle.

She stamped her feet with a grunt.

I shrugged off my peacoat—the air in April could be chilly—and shoved the tails of my white button-down shirt back into my black jeans. Then I started to unpack items: flour, sugar, chocolate, nuts, and more.

Tegan closed the door and jammed her fists into her hips. "Give me your full attention, Allie Catt. Or else." Clad in her puffy, knee-length white parka, all five-feet-three of her looked about as intimidating as the Stay Puft Marshmallow Man. The cute one, not the supersized monster in *Ghostbusters.*

"Or else what?"

"I'll meow!"

"You wouldn't dare."

Don't get me wrong. I liked the name Allie, and I even liked my surname. The earliest reference to Catt was Catford, a name of medieval English origins, which initially meant a ford frequented by wildcats. I considered myself pretty wild, so the name fit. But how many jokes could one girl endure in a life-time?

What do you get when you cross a baby chick with an alley cat? A peeping Tom.

Why don't alley cats play poker in the jungle? Too many chee-tahs.

Kids could be cruel; adults too.

On the other hand, my world-traveling parents—they rarely came to the States for longer than a day's visit—could have named me Pussy, which would have been way worse. So there you have it. I was Allie Catt, a five-foot-six, almost-twenty-six-year-old caterer who escaped into books or presided over book clubs when not making food for a client, which I aimed to do right now.

"Here, kitty, kitty." Tegan meowed.

I whirled around. "Honestly, I don't have time to play today." I tapped my big-faced cat watch and motioned to the white corkboard to my right. Dozens of future orders were tacked to it, as well as a floor plan of the bookshop.

"Whew! You're busy," Tegan said.

Thanks to the parties that people liked to throw in Bramble-wood, as well as Asheville and its ritzy enclave, Montford, I stayed regularly employed—that is, unless Vanna Harding, Tegan's older half sister and premier caterer, didn't get the gig first. Why Marigold hadn't hired her to serve tomorrow's tea was beyond me. A smirk tweaked the corners of my mouth. Maybe my food was simply better, or perhaps Marigold realized how out of touch with the common folk her snobby niece was. Vanna thought molecular gastronomy was chic. To me, it tasted like soap bubbles.

"Nice layout," Tegan said, tapping the floor plan. "Very organized."

"Thanks." On the floor plan, as I did for any event I catered, I'd drawn the specs for every aspect of the location. That way, I could formulate where I'd stage the savory foods and sweets. It was like a flowchart, the flow being the attendees. Tomorrow I would set the savory food table in front of the sales counter and the sweets tables by the endcaps of each aisle.

"Why are you here?" I pulled mixing bowls from the wire racks that also held pots and pans. A half-dozen mixers stood on a shelf beneath the island. Knives and utensils hung on a magnetic strip affixed to two of the walls. Floor-to-nearly-ceiling shelves held my designer pastry boxes, serving trays, and more. "Why aren't you at the bookstore?"

"Auntie gave me a two-hour lunch break so she could close the shop and hold a meeting for the theater foundation board." Tegan clerked at Feast for the Eyes. She was a terrific salesperson. She'd always been a good conversationalist.

"Why didn't I know about it?"

"No food required. Beverages only."

"Well, don't bug me," I said. "Go do something fun."

For those unfamiliar with Bramblewood, it was a delicious locale that consisted of a primary boulevard named Main Street, as well as Mountain Road, which crossed Main Street in the middle and led into the mountains. There were a number of offshoots, too. The town brimmed with art galleries, shops, and restaurants. All the buildings were uniform red clapboard with white trim. Because the town wasn't flat, there were charming terraced courtyards connecting the streets, each with additional shops at the crest. Tourism and second-home property owners kept the economy hopping.

Most of the homes, bed-and-breakfast inns, apartments, and condos were within walking distance of Main Street. In addition, there was a modest lake, which was north of town, a nine-hole golf course, and plenty of hiking trails. A stone's throw away was the burgeoning metropolis of Asheville, which boasted the splendiferous Biltmore Hotel and the University of North Carolina Asheville.

In summer, the weather was spectacular. During the fall, leaf peepers descended upon the town to witness the changing colors. In winter, tourists enjoyed a variety of seasonal sports. In the spring, like right now, tulips and daffodils were in bloom, as were redbud trees and dogwoods.

I said, "I know what you can do. Ride a kayak on the French

Broad. You're dressed warmly enough." The river was one of the oldest in the world and one of two in the United States that flowed north. "Or check out the bazaar." The town's year-round bazaar, which was housed in a series of old abandoned buildings that artists had revitalized at the turn of the twenty-first century, offered lots of handmade goods for sale.

"Can't. I've got errands to run." Tegan smoothed her white-blond braids. "Why is it every time I visit, you're busier than a beaver?"

"I've got to make ends meet."

"No, it's because you're selfish," she jibed with mock seriousness. "Selfish, selfish, selfish. Am I surprised? No, I am not. Do you know why? Because you're an only child."

"Blame Fern and Jamie," I said.

Yes, I was an only child. A *surprise* only child. My parents—Fern and Jamie, not Mom and Dad—had been shocked to become parents and hadn't even considered stocking the pond with another guppy after my birth. During my early years, they were cool to me. Their lack of compassion was another reason I'd lost myself in the world of books. Now that I was grown, they were kinder but not warmer.

"Speaking of parents, how is your mother?" I fetched two dozen eggs from the walk-in refrigerator. "Any good prospects on the dating scene?"

"She's seeing someone new."

"Is he nice?"

"How would I know? I haven't met him," she said with a bite.

"Then don't judge a book by its cover . . . or lack of one."

"Spare me." My pal flopped melodramatically onto a stool by the counter, crossed her legs, and bounced one tiny foot. If I didn't know better, she was getting ready to audition for a Tennessee Williams play. But I did know better. Though she could be chatty one-on-one with customers, she hated putting herself in the public eye.

Me? I'd performed in a lot of plays growing up. I wasn't a ham, but I didn't shy away from the spotlight. "Did they meet online?" I asked.

"Ugh, no! They met the old-fashioned way, after bumping into one another, literally, in a grocery aisle."

Tegan's mother, Noeline Merriweather, was the proud owner of the Blue Lantern, a bed-and-breakfast in Montford. Twice a widow, she had pieced herself together after her second husband, Tegan's father, the true love of her life, passed away from a rare blood disease. Recently she'd rejoined the dating pool. Clearly, Tegan was not happy about it. She didn't believe her mother had grieved long enough, but even I knew people grieved differently. Time was not a measure. Shakespeare wrote, "Grief makes one hour ten." I might not have lost a husband, but the demise of my engagement had left me hurting and wondering if I would ever find someone to love.

"What does Vanna think of him?" I asked.

Tegan rubbed her finger under her nose. "She says he's okay. I bet if I had a brother, he wouldn't be so happy about it."

I had brothers. Guy friend "brothers" who wanted to take care of me. Protect me. My best guy friend from high school had hated my first boyfriend. My best guy friend from college had abhorred my second boyfriend. And my best guy friend from my just-out-of-college days had despised my fiancé. According to him, no one was good enough for me. Period. I wasn't sure why I attracted guys who treated me like a younger sister. I wasn't the girl-next-door type. I had ample curves, and according to my mother, my curly red hair was saucy, bordering on scandalous. She didn't have a clue where I'd gotten it. Not from her or my father—their hair was stick straight and dark brown—and no one in their lineage had red hair or even a red beard. In addition to my aforementioned attributes, my ex-fiancé said my sage-green eyes were smoldering. *Definitely not* girl-next-doorish. Maybe my guy friends had latched on to me because my smile was bright and cheery, with no hint of a sirenlike come-on. Also, I wasn't a prude, but I didn't wear anything that showed off my cleavage. I liked sporty, fitted clothing. For catering and deliveries, I wore the basics: white shirt or white sweater and black slacks, leggings, or jeans, like I was wearing today.

"Look, I'm sorry to intrude on your work time," Tegan said. "I know you need to focus. It's just . . ." She burst into tears and flailed her arms. "My cheating ratfink husband wants a divorce."

"Oh, honey." I ran to her and attempted a hug. Her down coat prevented me from getting a good grip. "Why didn't you start with that?" I had lots of compassion for women who had been dumped like me. At least, I hadn't married the guy.

"I did. I said I needed to talk, but you didn't hear me. When you're on a mission . . ." She waved her hand.

She was right. I could be single-minded. My mother said it was my fatal flaw. I begged to differ. Being single-minded made it possible for me to accomplish anything I aimed to do. Well, almost anything.

"Whoa!" Tegan exclaimed.

I gazed in the direction she was pointing and moaned. "Oh, no!" A long trail of ants was marching across the floor from the pantry to the rear door. "No, no, no!"

"It's a satellite colony," Tegan said.

"A what?"

"A group of ants that didn't go into hibernation in the winter because they found a warm spot, like a kitchen." All of her young life, Tegan had enjoyed studying science and anything computer-related. It wasn't until high school that she fell in love with the magical world of books.

"Crud." I couldn't bake in a place where I'd have to spray

ant killer solution. The natural way to get rid of ants was water and vinegar, but that wouldn't work fast enough. "Grab this." I shrugged into my peacoat, snatched up my keys, rebagged the items on the counter, and shoved them into Tegan's arms. "Let's go."

"Where?"

"To my house."

"But your kitchen is small."

"I can make it work." I wasn't Wonder Woman. I couldn't move at warp speed. But I wouldn't let Marigold down. I had twenty-four hours to complete the task.

I lived around the corner from Dream Cuisine, but I almost always drove because I needed my Ford Transit for deliveries. We stowed the bags in the rear of the van and climbed in. "Buckle up."

I sped lickety-split to my mountain retreat, which was located at the far end of a cul-de-sac. Actually, the house wasn't mine. It belonged to my parents. I was renting from them. I called it *mine* because I had no fear they would want it back. They would never return to town to live. When they turned sixty, they decided Bramblewood was too pedantic for their tastes.

On the way there, I phoned the pest company that serviced Dream Cuisine and put them on alert for ants. They had their own key and promised they'd solve the problem before the end of the day. I warned them about the four-digit security code sometimes not taking on the first try. They assured me they could deal with it.

I skidded up the rain-slick gravel driveway, parked beneath the carport, hurried to the porch, and pushed through the front door. The aroma of knotty pine wafted to me. *Heaven.* I removed my coat and hurled it, as well as my tote bag, onto the leather couch in the living room. In addition to the living room, there was a parlor, two modest bedrooms, two-and-a-half baths, a laundry room, an attic for storage, a dining nook, and the aforementioned kitchen. Thirty years ago, my parents had bought the place furnished and hadn't updated a thing. Luckily, the owner before them had good taste. They'd liked shabby chic and comfy when it came to seating, plus they'd installed a double oven, side-by-side refrigerator, granite counters, petite island, and pantry large enough to store my trays, mixers, and whatnot. The rest of the décor was *getaway cabin* in flavor. A few skylights. An easy-to-light gas fireplace. A lovely south-facing bay window by the kitchen dining area with a sitting bench. To make the house even homier, I'd added a rocking chair, throw pillows, and a number of plaques with sassy literary sayings, my favorite being: *A book lover never goes to bed alone.* Upkeep on the house was a challenge. A month ago, the roof had a leak. Six months ago, the porch needed shoring up. Before that, the washing machine overflowed and soaked the floor. Thankfully, my parents agreed to pay for all repairs.

"Put the groceries on the table in the dining nook." I tossed my key ring on the foyer table. *A creature of habit is a creature of comfort,* my mother often said; to which, I'd snarkily retort, *A creature of habit is a creature.*

Tegan obeyed. "Don't you lock your door?"

"Why? Crime isn't an issue in Bramblewood."

Tegan slipped off her parka and tugged down the sleeves of her Demon Slayer anime T-shirt. In addition to enjoying books of every genre, she was a fangirl of movies, music, and video games. Plus she collected vintage comic books. "What the heck is this?" She picked up the key ring and twirled it on her finger.

"The same kind of key ring your aunt has." I'd recently swapped out all my keys for the quick-release, pull-apart kinds. Too often over the past year, I'd needed to give a key to a workman, and my nails had suffered the consequence.

"Clever," she said, pulling one off and letting it snap into place via the magnet.

I removed my to-be-read pile of books from the rustic dining table and plunked them on the colorful woven rug next to my tower of already-read-but-saved-to-be-savored-again books. "Darcy! Here, kitty." I made kissing sounds. Yes, I'd named my cat Darcy. I'd dubbed my childhood cat Darcy as well. Once smitten . . . twice bitten. Darcy One was now in kitty heaven. Fortunately, my former fiancé wasn't named Darcy or Fitzwilliam or any variation of Fitzwilliam Darcy of *Pride and Prejudice* fame, or I might have fought harder to keep him and been stuck to the man for life. "Where are you, boy?"

My tuxedo cat slinked from behind my stack of Jane Austen books. I swear, he could read. Of all things, he had a particular fondness for *Pride and Prejudice.* Often I found him lying on the book, opened to a new page. He trotted to me and begged for a scratch under his chin. I obliged. Then he scampered to Tegan. She picked him up and showered him with kisses. Her husband was allergic to cats, so whenever she saw Darcy, she pretended he was hers. She put the cat on the floor, and he scampered to his barrel-shaped llama, a cat-scratching station near the dining table, and disappeared into the belly of the beast.

"Come with me," I said.

I moved into the kitchen, Tegan followed, and I closed the floor-to-ceiling Plexiglas door. Darcy was pretty much hypoallergenic. I groomed him often enough to remove his undercoat, which earned me a good Cottage Food Operator health rating so that on the rare occasion when I couldn't bake at Dream Cuisine, I could do so at home. To comply with the rating, I'd installed the see-through door to keep the kitchen separate from the rest of the house, and I fed Darcy in the dining nook. He wasn't allowed to enter the kitchen ever.

I washed my hands, dried them on a cat-themed tea towel,

slipped on my mesh-style chef's cap to keep my hair in tow, and tied on a checkered apron. "Now tell me what's going on with you and Winston." I fetched all the mixing bowls I had in stock. I made a mental note to purchase more, plus another stand mixer for just such emergencies. I could store them in the attic, if needed. "I can listen while I'm baking. He cheated on you?"

Winston Potts was a computer geek in the bourgeoning tech industry in Asheville. He and Tegan met in high school. They'd both been seriously into coding back then, and they'd both been in the band. She'd played the clarinet, and he'd played the snare drum. Even though he went off to Duke and she enrolled at UNC Chapel Hill, she always felt they were destined to be together. *Perhaps not.*

"He admitted he's been having affairs ever since we got married," Tegan said.

"Are you kidding?"

"Auntie joked that I thought I married Mr. Darcy, when in actuality I married Mr. Wickham."

"He should have come with a warning label," I said.

She tried to laugh at my joke, but a sob caught in her throat. "Am I as dumb as a rock?"

"You were hopelessly in love." I washed my hands and dried them with paper towels.

"I'm thinking of creating a Dear Jane group with the other women he dumped so we can commiserate. Either that or a murder club."

"Bad idea on both fronts."

"For now, I think I'll stay at my mother's inn until we get everything sorted."

"You could stay here."

"I don't want to inconvenience you. Besides, I'll be served two delicious meals a day there." Tegan couldn't make ice in a freezer.

My cell phone jangled in my tote. "Get that, would you?"

Tegan rifled through my bag. "I can hear it, but I can't find it."

"Outside pocket," I said. "By the logo."

She retrieved the cell phone. "It's Aunt Marigold calling."

"Answer it."

"Hello, Miss Catt's personal assistant." She did a curtsy to mock me.

I stuck out my tongue while I cracked two eggs into one of the bowls.

"What? Auntie! Auntie, it's me, Tegan. Can you repeat that? Auntie!" Tegan gawked at me. "I think she's choking."

CHAPTER 2

*"I declare after all there is no enjoyment like reading!
How much sooner one tires of anything than of a book!"*

—Caroline Bingley, in Jane Austen's *Pride and Prejudice*

I snatched my cell phone from Tegan. "Marigold, it's Allie. Are you okay?" I heard a *thud* through the line. "Oh, no! She must have fallen. Tegan, wasn't anyone at the bookstore when you left?"

"Uh-uh. Auntie was gearing up for her meeting and wanted privacy."

"Let's go."

I removed my cap, raced out of the kitchen, grabbed my peacoat and threw Tegan her parka, and we hightailed it to the Ford Transit.

Like Dream Cuisine, the bookstore was located on Main Street but closer to Mountain Road. I parked in the public parking on Holly Street and raced to the shop. Tegan slogged behind me, panting heavily. It wasn't the altitude affecting her. Bramblewood was no more than two thousand feet above sea level, but some people, like Tegan, who wasn't a jogger, let alone a runner, could suffer.

"Slow down if you have to," I said. "I've got this." I took extensive hikes weekly and tried to run at least two miles every other day. A caterer needed to keep fit.

I jammed toward Feast for the Eyes. Posters for the upcoming Celtic Festival were everywhere. Unlike Asheville's festival, which was held in the winter, our Celtic Festival occurred in the spring, both indoors and outdoors at the Bramblewood Park and Rec Center, which abutted the park. Posters, such as *Get in touch with your Celtic roots! Dress up!* and *Immerse yourself in the history!,* abounded. Tegan and I had discussed joining in the fun. Over the years, we'd attended many Renaissance fairs and other costumed occasions.

The CLOSED sign on the bookshop was visible, but the door was ajar, not locked as I'd expected it to be. "Marigold!" I called upon entering. I dashed past the year-round book tree decorated with miniature book ornaments and yelled again.

The floor plan of the shop included four aisles to the right and three to the left, plus a reading nook fitted with an L-shaped couch, an assortment of beanbags, and midcentury modern upholstered chairs. A display island was positioned in front of the sales counter. The stockroom and office were beyond it.

I peered down the first aisle to my left, its shelves packed with books. Marigold wasn't lying on the floor. She hadn't fallen off the rolling ladder. "Marigold!"

No answer.

I peeked down all of the other aisles and into the reading nook. Empty. I checked inside the customer bathroom beyond the nook. It was vacant.

"Tegan, where's Chloe?" I asked. She was the other clerk. "Didn't she come in today?"

"Yes, but she left for a dental appointment."

"Marigold!" I yelled again.

Maybe she was in the office. It was visible from the main shop, although the blinds on the picture window were drawn.

Someone moaned. I peeked past the island of books and caught sight of feet in black ballet slippers jutting from behind the sales counter.

"Oh, no!"

I darted to Marigold and bent down. She was lying faceup, eyes open, mouth agape. Her wispy silver hair haloed her aging face. The diamond pendant she always wore was askew. Her aqua-blue painter's smock was bunched around her black trousers. Pencils and Post-it notepads had spilled from the smock's pockets.

I took her hand and patted it. "Marigold, it's me, Allie." Having catered at the Eatery, I'd seen my fair share of people passed out from overdrinking alcohol, overeating, and the like. I was trained in CPR. I was familiar with how to check for a victim's responsiveness and other life-threatening conditions. And I knew enough to turn a victim struggling for breath onto her back. Fortunately, I didn't have to in this case.

Marigold's eyes blinked open. She focused on my face.

"Are you all right?" I asked.

"Mm-hmm," she murmured. "I think so, dear."

"Allie!" Tegan yelled. "Where are you?"

"Over here." I kept my focus on Marigold. "What happened?"

"I'm not exactly sure." She licked her parched lips. "I must have fainted."

"Is it possible you had an episode?"

"I don't think so. I never have."

Her eyes were moist. I checked her pulse. It was weak.

"Auntie!" Tegan rounded the counter, chest heaving. "Is she okay?"

I nodded. "Marigold, smile." She did. "Raise both arms." She complied. "Say 'I love books.'" She repeated the words. *Phew.* She hadn't had a stroke. I said, "Have you been drinking enough water?" People often forgot to keep hydrated.

"I had tea."

"I've told you before, that doesn't count. I know others have warned you, too."

"You're too bossy," she said, and winked.

"I'm cautious." The manager at the Eatery had required us to take hours upon hours of emergency training. The instructor who'd led my group reminded us often that tea, coffee, and soda were never substitutes for water. "Tegan, stay with her. Hold her hand."

Tegan obeyed.

I raced into the mini kitchen in the stockroom, filled a glass with water from the faucet, and returned just as a middle-aged woman was entering through the front door.

"Wow, what a place!" the woman raved as she spun in a circle and took in the shop. "Such high ceilings and so many books. And the entryway on the street is so whimsical"—she twirled a finger—"all fitted out with plaster-of-Paris book pages. Very clever. Oh, gee! Is that entire section devoted to classic mysteries? I love Dorothy L. Sayers."

"Sorry, ma'am, we're closed!" I yelled.

"But the door was ajar."

"Closed for a medical emergency," Tegan explained. "Come back tomorrow. Thank you."

I returned my focus to Marigold and asked if she could sit up. She said she could. I carefully slid an arm around her slender torso and propped her in a sitting position against the counter. "Any bruises? Broken bones? Twinges?"

"No. I think I slumped. I didn't crash."

I'd heard a pretty substantial *thud* over the cell phone and doubted a slump could've caused the noise, but I didn't press. She seemed alert. I held the water to her lips and she sipped. "I should call Noeline."

"No, don't bother her." Marigold had confided once that when she and her sister were growing up, she, being the eldest, had acted like a mother hen to Noeline. Heaven forbid the tables turn and Noeline baby her.

"What's going on?" a woman hooted. I recognized the voice. It was Vanna, Tegan's older half sister. No one else on earth had such a piercing tone, something akin to a crow squawking or a crane whooping. "Auntie? What happened?"

She rushed toward us, the tautness of her silver-gray pencil skirt preventing her from taking long strides. The matching peplum jacket didn't help. How she moved around a kitchen in clothing like that was beyond me. Perhaps this was the outfit she wore to pitch her business to local shops. With her strawberry-blond hair secured in a fashionable knot, her eyes outlined heavily in black, and her lips daubed with ruby-red lipstick, she reminded me of an exotic bird. I couldn't remember the last time I'd put on lipstick. I was a lip-gloss kind of girl.

"Out of the way, Allie." Vanna tried to gracefully lower herself to the floor, but her four-inch heels threw her off-balance.

Honestly, four-inch heels? The town's sidewalks were brick and uneven. I steadied her by the shoulder.

Vanna thanked me curtly and said, "Let's get you to your feet, Auntie." She seized her aunt's wrist.

"No!" I restrained her. "Your aunt needs to remain seated to get her bearings."

"Isn't that exactly like you, Allie, forcing your will upon others?" Vanna sniffed and rose to her full height.

I flashed on one of my least favorite characters in all of literature, the eldest Bingley sister from *Pride and Prejudice*. She was persnickety and rude.

"Hello?" a woman said from the front of the store. "What's all the hoopla? Isn't the tea tomorrow, or did I mess up on the calendar? Is it today?"

I peeked around the counter. Noeline Merriweather sauntered to us, wrapped in a belted white coat and matching boots. She wore a handsome indigo-blue scarf looped around her long neck and was sporting a new hairdo. A bob. All my life, I'd only seen her with long, wavy hair. The shorter hairdo suited her. It was flirty.

"You didn't mess up, Noeline," I said. "It's tomorrow, Saturday, but your sister had an incident."

"An incident?" Noeline skirted the sales counter. "Sis!"

"She's fine," I said.

"Don't worry about me. I'm dehydrated, that's all," Marigold said, accepting my diagnosis.

"Tegan." Noeline was a warm, caring woman with a gentle voice and easy demeanor. "Why didn't you call 911?"

Vanna said snottily, "I was going to ask the same thing."

"We just got here," Tegan said. "I was on a break, visiting Allie. When Auntie telephoned, we rushed right over. Auntie, I'm going to cancel your meeting with the donors."

"Yes, do that, dear." Marigold struggled to her feet. "What are you doing here, Noeline?"

"I was taking a morning stroll."

Marigold said, "Liar. You hate walks. You came to check on me."

"Did not."

"You think I'm withering in my old age. You think I won't be able to balance the books," Marigold said. She was seventy; Noeline was ten years younger.

"That's not true." Noeline owned a quarter of the bookshop, a gift from Marigold, although she was a silent partner, since she had her hands full with the bed-and-breakfast. "And you know it."

"Do I?" Purposely, Marigold pulled a prunish face, then laughed.

Noeline chuckled, too, in the identical throaty way.

Their laughter wasn't their only likeness. They had the same fine features and inquisitive eyes, and now their hairdos were similar, although Noeline continued to dye hers blond.

"Mother," Vanna said. "I was at the mayor's house going over a menu and thought I'd stop in and check on Auntie." She couldn't help dropping names of Bramblewood's high and mighty. "Good thing I did."

Good thing, indeed, I reflected.

"Noeline, sweetheart." A handsome, silver-haired gentleman, with prominent cheekbones and an easy smile, came into view. "Is everything okay?"

"Yes." Noeline grabbed hold of his hand.

"Who are you?" Tegan asked abruptly.

"Rick O'Sheedy," he replied.

Noeline beamed. "Rick is a—"

"A financial consultant for Alta Barlow Hospital," Marigold cut in, her tone sharp. Evidently, she had rebounded. Did she disapprove of Rick's being an advisor or of him personally?

Rick nervously smoothed the silk tie that lay beneath his pin-striped suit and pocketed his key ring. I noticed the key ring had a red fob on it and tamped down a giggle. I'd seen comparable ones on dog collars of dogs whose persons who walked their furry pets in the dark. Did Rick get lost often?

Tegan gave me a curious look, probably wondering why I was pressing my lips together.

Noeline said, "Rick is prepping the hospital so they can issue bonds to raise money."

The Alta Barlow Hospital was a newer concern and more like an emergency clinic, consisting of three floors with approximately one hundred beds. It was situated north of the police station and fire department on Mountain Road. Its sister facility in Asheville was much larger. Each of the rotating staff was top-notch.

"Rick has been meeting with the finance teams to ensure a good rating," Noeline added, signaling him to continue.

"We're allowed to temporarily issue thirty million a year in tax-exempt, bank-qualified bonds," he said. "These deals not only expand a hospital's credit power, but because we can bring them about quickly, they take as few as sixty days to close—"

"Rick," Noeline cut in. "Don't get technical. Broad strokes."

He petted her cheek fondly. "Of course. They're good for the hospital. Enough said."

"You two are certainly spending a lot of time together," Vanna said.

"Togetherness is important if you want to get to know someone," Noeline replied with an alluring lilt.

I glanced at Tegan, who was sizing up Rick. The shop's phone rang. She moved to answer it.

Noeline approached Marigold. "Sweetie, truth. What happened? Were you overexerting yourself? I told you no one cares if you change the shop's décor. It's perfect the way it is."

"No, I wasn't," Marigold said tartly.

I rose and let the two of them rehash the scenario. Marigold reiterated my diagnosis: *dehydration.* Noeline huffed as if that was the lamest excuse she had ever heard. Vanna mimicked her mother. I leveled her with a look. She wrinkled her nose in defiance.

"Help me, Rick," Noeline said to her date, and the two of them guided Marigold into the chair behind the sales counter.

"Marigold," I said, "you're in good hands. I have to get back to work."

"Don't forget the tasting cups of custard, dear," Marigold reminded me.

"I wouldn't dare." Okay, I had forgotten about the custard, but I had plenty of staples at home to make it. I hurried to Tegan, who was hanging up the shop's phone. I spied a compendium of Dashiell Hammett's works on the desk behind the sales counter, which included *Red Harvest, The Glass Key,* and *The Thin Man.* I didn't see a note assigning it to a customer. "Who do you think that's for?"

"Got me."

"Hold it for me if no one else claims it."

She agreed.

On my way to the door, I nearly rammed into Lillian Bellingham, a contemporary of Tegan's and mine, and owner of

Puttin' on the Glitz, the clothing and accessories shop next door that tailored to high-end buyers. Recently I'd provided a week's worth of personalized meals for Lillian and her bestie from college. Like Tegan, Lillian couldn't cook, but she sure did know how to dress. Today, in her baby-blue Coach trench coat, black rain boots, and black leather gloves, she looked like a million bucks. I clasped her elbow and tried to prevent her from entering.

"Hi, sugar. Is the shop open? The Closed sign is hanging on the door." Her voice was a breathy mix of Marilyn Monroe meets Sharon Stone, with a tinge of a Southern accent. For a brief moment, she'd lived in Hollywood and had starred in a couple of B movies. I hadn't seen either of them. I preferred watching classics. She tired quickly of beating the pavement and, like me, moved back to the Asheville area. With her family's help, she opened her business. In her off-hours, to keep active in the arts, she helped make and organize costumes at the community theater.

I said, "Marigold had an incident."

"Poor thing. She can be so clumsy." Lillian wriggled from my grasp. "Why, last month, I saw her fall off the ladder and twist her ankle. It was the itty-bitty three-rung ladder, but a woman her age . . ." She *tsk*ed. "Who's tending to her?"

"Her sister."

"Noeline. A lovely woman. Good, good. I've sent many clients to her bed-and-breakfast. Charming place. Hi, Marigold!" Lillian flitted a finger. "I have a few books to purchase for my nieces. I'll come another time. I can't wait for tomorrow's tea."

Marigold didn't respond. She was glancing between Noeline and Vanna as if weighing how to deal with them.

I said, "I think that would be a good idea, Lillian," and once again clasped her elbow.

"Are you kidding me!" Vanna shouted at the top of her lungs.

"Vanna, hush," Noeline said.

"I won't hush. Auntie hired Allie to cater the tea?" Vanna leveled me with a vile look and turned to her aunt. "How could you? I'm the best in town. Everyone knows that."

I couldn't catch Marigold's response, but it must have incensed Vanna.

"Give me a break!" She threw her arms wide. "No one bakes better cookies than I do!"

For the record, my cookies, every last one of them, were excellent. I paid extra special attention to insure they were. I adored cookies.

Noeline jutted her head for me to leave and gestured that she would fix things, but I didn't have a chance to reach the door before Vanna came flying at me.

"Don't move, Allie!"

Tegan reached for her sister but missed.

Lillian rasped, "Gotta go," and raced out of the shop.

Chicken, I thought.

"For your information, Miss Catt," Vanna continued, "I can throw a better tea party than you any day. Any. Day." Her shrill tone could have shattered crystal.

A quote from my high-school English teacher came to me: "Deflect to conquer when confronted by a bully."

I said, "I'm sure you can, Vanna. You're a wonderful caterer."

"But Auntie hired *you.*"

"Because I know the clientele. I come to book clubs and special events and—"

"Big deal. I can memorize people's names."

"Plus I think she wanted to do me a favor. You know, to pad my pockets so I can buy myself a birthday present. I will turn twenty-six in a few weeks." I'd been born on Mother's Day. What a thorn that must have been in Fern's side! "Marigold thought—"

"Stuff it." Vanna wagged a pointy fingernail in my direction. If it had been any sharper, she'd have to register it as a weapon. "In the future, don't say yes to any offers from my aunt."

"Or what?" I asked.

Tegan joined me and repeated the question. "Or what?"

I elbowed her to keep quiet. I didn't need Vanna more riled than she already was.

"Or Dream Cuisine"—Vanna gave me and my pal a withering look—"might earn some bad reviews."

"Are you saying you'll damage my reputation?" I asked, truly appalled by the threat.

"That's libel," Tegan added.

"Libel, *schmibel*. Beware." Vanna aimed two fingers from her eyes to ours. "I'm watching you."

CHAPTER 3

"Follies and nonsense, whims and inconsistencies do divert me, I own, and I laugh at them whenever I can."

—Elizabeth Bennet, in Jane Austen's *Pride and Prejudice*

Seething, I returned to my house, and over the course of the next few hours, with jazz music blasting, I baked dozens of cookies, made batches of fudge, and piped fifty custards into pretty floral tasting cups. Throughout, I dwelled on Vanna. Was it possible she'd discovered, earlier than at the bookshop, that Marigold had offered me the gig? Did she sabotage Dream Cuisine by bringing in ants? Each time I mulled over the possibility, I convinced myself I was wrong. Vanna wasn't vindictive, just snappish.

On the other hand, the French poet Anatole France said, "It is well for the heart to be naïve and the mind not to be."

Somebody rapped on the front door and pushed it open. Quickly I grabbed a spatula, as if that would be a good weapon, and raced through the Plexiglas door.

"Hello? Anybody home?" Zach Armstrong poked his head into the house, with a twinkle in his eye, a lock of his lustrous brown hair dangling on his forehead, and a wicked grin that carved a long dimple down the right side of his handsome face.

I lowered the spatula, bellowed to my artificially intelligent virtual assistant to stop the music, and tucked a loose hair beneath my headband. How did I look? Did I have flour on my face or on my *Martha Stewart doesn't live here* apron?

"Are you going to make me beg?" Zach asked.

"For what?"

"I caught a whiff of cookies as I was getting in an afternoon run." Zach stepped inside. At thirty-four, he looked lean and virile in his snug-fitting tracksuit. "You know I'm a cookie hound."

"Actually, no, I didn't know that. We've had coffee at Ragamuffin Coffeehouse, let me see, two times? Each time you ate a scone." Ragamuffin was one of my best clients. They requested scones with regularity. They were also the chief buyer of my cream cheese muffins.

"Nah. No way. Scones are for sissies."

"Take that back." I aimed the spatula at him.

Zack raised both hands. At six-foot-four, he dwarfed me. Prior to being recently sworn in as the crime investigative detective for the Bramblewood Police Department, he had served in the army. His stint had helped pay for the criminal justice degree he earned in college.

"What are you making?" He padded to me as if heavy footsteps might damage my creations.

"Sugar cookies."

"Yum."

Darcy sprinted from the llama to Zach and circled his ankles. The cat's tail twitched with curiosity. Zach bent to pet him, giving him a good stroke beneath his chin. Satisfied that he'd dominated the human, Darcy sprang onto the llama's head and resumed his nap. On Zach's and my first date, which wasn't really a date—he'd stopped by to say he was going for coffee; did I want to come?—Zach revealed he was an animal person. He'd had a menagerie growing up: cats, dogs, turtles, rabbits. His mother, who had been raised on a farm, couldn't say no to any of them.

I pushed open the door to the kitchen. "Come with me."

He did.

The door swung shut. I washed my hands, as I always did, and asked Zach to do the same. Then I grabbed an undecorated cookie and offered it to him. "Here you go. How's it going, Mr. Detective?"

"Good." He ate the cookie in two bites and asked for another.

"I can only spare a few."

"A few will have to do." He leaned against the counter and crossed one ankle over the other. "Gee, you look pretty today."

"*Pfft.*"

"Your cheeks are glowing."

"Because it's hot in here." Not because I was lusting after this man. *Uh-uh, not that.*

"Hey, I heard there's going to be a concert tomorrow night in Asheville. A sing-along. Want to go?"

"I'm pretty booked up."

"It's right after your party at Feast for the Eyes. If I help you clean up the dishes . . ."

Feast for the Eyes was where he and I had met. I'd seen him around town before, but he'd come across as aloof. Not *disdainful* aloof. Simply *reserved* aloof, as if weighing his responses. At the bookshop, we hadn't exchanged names or telephone numbers until the day when each of us was browsing the self-help section. He'd been looking for a book to explore his inner child. I'd been searching for a book for Fern. No, it wasn't a spiteful gift. When not reading about quantum physics or obscure concepts like the Fibonacci sequence, my mother devoured self-help *whatever.* Over chatter about whether *The Self-Love Experiment* might be good for her, Zach admitted that he also liked reading thrillers, and I said I enjoyed traditional mysteries, as well as the classics like *Jane Eyre* and *The Great Gatsby.* Standing at the checkout register, he happened to mention that he could barbecue a mean steak. He hadn't invited me over yet to test the veracity of that claim.

I heard the front door to my house open. Seconds later, Tegan appeared outside the kitchen door, a shopping bag in each hand. I allowed her to enter.

"Auntie booted me out of the shop again. She's fine. She thought you might need extra supplies. Oh—" She caught sight of Zach. "Well, hello there."

He smiled. "Hi."

Tegan tilted her head and snapped her fingers. "Gee, you look familiar. Are you a movie star?"

"Ha-ha! Yeah, I get that a lot, Tegan. Allie . . ." He tattooed the counter. "I should be going."

"Not on my account," Tegan said.

"Absolutely not. I could chat with you all day." He winked at her, the flirt. "No, I've got to meet with the chief of police."

I didn't know Zach well enough to guess whether he aspired to becoming the chief one day, but I'd bet he'd be good at it.

"See you after tomorrow's tea, Allie. Remember, I'll dry." He swiped one more cookie and strolled out of the kitchen, chuckling.

"He'll dry?" Tegan placed her bags on the floor as the front door clacked shut. "Explain."

"He'll dry dishes after the tea."

"*Ooh-la-la.* I'd say, my sweet friend, that he is clearly smitten with you."

"Get out. He's a guy friend."

Tegan smirked. "You and your 'guy' friends." She mimed quotation marks. "Do you know how many of them wanted to make an honest woman of you?"

"None."

"All." She thwacked her chest with her palm. "I was the shoulder they cried on."

"Get out of here."

"No lie." She crossed her heart. "But this one. Zach? You have the hots for him. He's a keeper."

I glanced toward the door, thinking he truly might be. He was direct yet warm, authoritative yet conversational, but ever since my breakup with my fiancé, I'd been gun-shy on relationships, so I wasn't pressing for more with Zach. *Yet.* I pushed thoughts of him aside and said, "Enough about me. Let's discuss your jerk of a husband."

"Uh-uh. I don't want to talk about him." She washed and dried her hands. "I'm too worried about Aunt Marigold."

"She's fine."

"She was mumbling something about her neighbor yesterday. She wishes he'd get his act together."

"That says a lot about her. She cares."

"She seems concerned about something else, too. Sales have been down."

"That's true for every business in early spring. Let it go. She'll get her much-needed rest, and all will be right with the world in the morning."

While I tootled around the kitchen, decorating cookies and packing them into white pastry boxes with sage-green labels— sage green was my signature color—Tegan perched on the stool by the island and, to distract herself, chatted about the theater foundation people coming to the tea. She was keen on what each liked to read. *Mrs. So and So preferred romance. Mr. So and So relished sports and nonfiction.* In college, after giving up on becoming a computer geek because she'd fallen in love with literature, Tegan considered becoming a librarian. She earned her undergraduate degree in library arts, but when she started working for her aunt at Feast for the Eyes, on a temporary basis until she found a librarian position, she fell in love with book selling and scrapped the career as a librarian.

When I was cleaning up, Tegan said, "How about I treat you to a burger and a beer at the Brewery?"

"Sounds good." The Brewery was one of my favorite haunts. Tegan's and her aunt's, too. Like many restaurants in Bramble-wood, it served craft beer, as well as cider, and it had an extensive burger list, as well as hearty mountain food like potatoes verde drenched in chile verde sauce and cotija cheese. *Drinking food,* I called it. "You don't have to ask me twice." I checked Darcy's food bowl—he'd eaten every bite—made sure his water was fresh, and off we went. "Shall we invite your aunt?"

"Yes." Tegan texted her and received an instant response. She showed it to me. "She wrote, 'Not up to it. Next time.'"

"Staying home is smart," I said. "She has to be sharp for the fund-raising event tomorrow."

Whenever Tegan and I went to the Brewery, we liked to belly up to the bar. Not only did it have six comfortable swivel chairs, but Katrina Carlson, the main bartender, was good to people of the female persuasion. Pretty and freckly, with long curls that she tied off her face, she had a curvy body, a full-bodied laugh, and a saucy sense of humor. All the waitstaff wore crisp white shirts tucked into black pants. However, each was allowed to wear one piece of jewelry. Katrina always chose bracelets. On a previous visit, I'd admired a thick silver bangle studded with fake gems. She said she couldn't resist buying it when she'd seen it in the window at Fair Exchange, the pawn-shop on Holly Street. It was a one-of-a-kind beauty.

"What'll it be?" Katrina asked, slipping a cocktail napkin onto the bar in front of each of us. Tonight's bracelet, one I hadn't seen before, made a jangling sound. "Spruce Goose? Buzz Lightbeer? Audrey Hopburn?"

Behind the bar, a dozen taps were affixed to the wall. Like a flight of wines, the variety of beers went from dark to light, left to right. Most had ridiculously silly names.

As much as I wanted to eat something super salty, I knew I'd regret it in the morning, seeing as I had to be up bright and early. I shrugged out of my coat, slung it over the back of the

swivel chair, ordered a simple burger and Oly's pale ale—
Oliver "Oly" Olsen was the owner of the Brewery and the
craftsman. He didn't show up often. When he did, he made
sure he said hello to everyone. Tegan requested a cheeseburger
and an Ugly Pig, which was a dark ale with an edge.

While we waited, I spun in my chair to see if I recognized
anyone. The place wasn't big. There were only three rectangular bar-style tables fitted with stools, each sitting eight, and two
more for diners who liked to stand, but the noise was loud.
High ceilings plus stone floors amplified the acoustics. A couple of TVs hanging on poles attached to the rafters were
broadcasting basketball games. I caught sight of Lillian, who
was seated with a twenty-something actress I recognized from
a theater production I'd attended. I waved and Lillian responded in kind. The petite blond waitress named Wallis was
tending to them.

"Where's your aunt?" Katrina asked Tegan as she set our
beers on the counter.

"She's under the weather. She'll join us next time."

"That's too bad. I was hoping to pick her brain about what I
should read next."

Because she worked nights, Katrina didn't attend book club
events, but I'd seen her name on numerous stacks of sold
books at the bookshop. She had a penchant for historical romance and the occasional mystery.

"New jewelry?" I asked, nodding to the bracelet.

"You like?" Katrina lifted her wrist. "They're charms
shaped like cocktails. Isn't it adorbs? Sounds like bells, right?"
She wiggled her arm.

"Adorbs," I repeated. To be honest, the constant *clink-clink*
would drive me nuts, but it was noisy enough in the bar that
most customers wouldn't notice.

"Your burgers will be up soon. Enjoy." She moved to another customer.

Tegan swiveled to face me and toasted her glass to mine. She sipped and sighed. Not with contentment.

"Want to talk about Winston now?" I asked, her husband's name tasting vile on my tongue. "I'm all ears." How many nights had Tegan and I spent chatting until the wee hours about boys, school, parents, and our dreams? She knew all my secrets, and I was pretty sure I was hip to all of hers. Winston's infidelity sure had come as a surprise, though.

"No," Tegan said. "I was thinking about Auntie again. She was so . . . so . . . fragile."

"Dehydration can make a person fuzzy."

"Yesterday she was frowning like she was working through some idea she couldn't form into words. And the other day, Mom asked her what was wrong, but Auntie wouldn't say and told her not to mother her." Tegan laughed. "That's like calling the kettle black. Vanna heard us talking and barged in, demanding to know what was up. Man, she's a bull in a china shop."

I listened attentively, even though I'd heard it all before. She and her half sister had never gotten along. Perhaps it was the six years between them. Possibly it was because Vanna hadn't taken after Noeline's side of the family. I didn't know much about Vanna's father. He'd died in a climbing accident, leaving Noeline a widow at twenty-nine. But my guess was, female members of the Harding clan had similarly irritable personalities.

We stopped talking about family and directed our attention to books. She'd recently read a new bestseller but didn't think highly of it, saying the heroine dwelled on her problems non-stop and the story never went anyplace. I told her about a mystery I'd read, but I refused to reveal the ending, promising if she checked it out, we could compare notes.

Two hours later, after a delicious meal, we went back to my place. By ten, Tegan was yawning so deeply that I worried she wouldn't be able to drive to the B&B. I offered her the guest room. She agreed and texted her mother so Noeline wouldn't worry.

Around three a.m., I heard her pacing and muttering to herself. Clearly, she had to see a professional about her marriage. I would broach the delicate subject over a cup of coffee.

At six thirty a.m., careful not to wake my pal, I fed Darcy and then stowed the trays with all my baked goods on a rolling cart. I telephoned Marigold and told her I was running on time. Sounding breathy, she said she was already at the shop and looked forward to seeing me soon.

At eight, I knocked on the guest bedroom door, knowing Tegan would want to change before heading to the bookshop. I was surprised to find her gone. When had she slipped out? Why hadn't she left me a note? Deciding she'd driven to the B&B, after all, I texted her but got no response. I tried not to worry. I understood how a breakup could disturb one's sleep. I'd see her at the bookshop soon enough.

At nine, I threw a raincoat on over my white shirt and skinny black jeans and, after filling my van with the goodies, drove to Feast for the Eyes. When I arrived, I wasn't surprised to see a huge knot of people lining up outside. Being a tourist town, Bramblewood lured plenty of visitors, as well as locals, who enjoyed reading on a hike, at their mountain retreats, or at one of the many coffee shops or cafés. But I was surprised that the front door wasn't propped open. Maybe it was because the temperature was a brisk forty-two degrees. At the head of the line, I spotted Noeline and her new friend, Rick. Why hadn't they entered? Was Marigold running behind?

I parked in a space not far from the shop and opened the van's rear door. I lowered the trolley to street level, locked up the van, and pushed the cart to the shop. I set the foot brake and weaved through the throng to Noeline. She was wearing a camel-hair coat, tan boots, and matching purse. A red dress peeked from beneath the hem of the coat. Rick's hair was mussed and his striped shirt, jacket, and trousers were rumpled, as if he'd thrown on his clothes in a hurry. *Oho!* Had he and Noeline been, um, messing around this morning and lost track of time?

Stop, Allie. Not your business.

"What's going on?" I asked Noeline. "Why isn't the shop open?"

"Marigold must be running late. Tegan too. I've tried calling them, but neither is answering. I'm worried. We all are."

Rick knocked on the shop's door. "Marigold! Hello! Are you in there?"

"Will you stop doing that?" Noeline snapped. "It's plain to see no one's inside."

"I saw Marigold leave her house this morning around six," Graham Wynn said. He was Marigold's neighbor, a forty-year-old, baby-cheeked man, with thinning hair, sad eyes, and a partiality for clerical fiction. That preference surprised me, I was ashamed to say, seeing as he owned GamePlay, a store that sold video games, collectibles, and comic books. Not that a game-loving guy couldn't enjoy religious-themed stories, but it didn't seem a natural fit. At one of our book club meetings, Graham shared that he fancied himself as a preacher in another life. "She was climbing into her car to come here and had forgotten her coat," he went on. "I reminded her to fetch it."

"She should have reminded *you,*" Piper Lowry teased. Dark-haired and willowy, she was a popular junior-college teacher and a do-gooder who volunteered at the Y, the blood bank, the theater foundation, and the hospital. Primarily, she read historical fiction, but she also perused mysteries. We had often found ourselves browsing the same aisle at the shop.

"Yeah, no coat. What an idiot, right?" Graham cupped his hands and blew into them. His sweater sleeves slithered up his forearms, revealing a wealth of tattoos on his right arm and a wide bandage on his left. New ink, I decided. Why hadn't he put on a jacket or gloves? Hadn't he consulted a weather app? "I didn't want to be late."

"Please tell me winter is not going to return." Piper stamped her feet and tightened the belt of her coat. "I really love springtime."

Many in the group agreed about the temperature. Had they forgotten that a month ago it was at least ten degrees cooler?

"When did you arrive?" I asked a woman I didn't recognize to my right. She was carrying a map of the town and a couple of tourist brochures.

"Five minutes ago."

Piper said, "I got here a few minutes before that." Though she wasn't a beauty, she had a ballerina's grace. I asked her once if she'd danced, and she said she'd hoped to, but her parents had forbidden it. "When did you get here, Graham?" She turned and fluttered her thick eyelashes to great effect.

"Right before you," he said, blushing.

Noeline eyed me. "My sister is never late."

I said, "When I spoke to her earlier, she said she was already here. That was around six thirty."

The stockroom light was on, but the rest of the shop was dark. The sales counter was empty of the stacks of books that were piled on it yesterday. The rolling ladder was repositioned at the end of the left aisle, nearest the window.

Noeline sighed. "You don't think she's had another fainting spell, do you, Allie?"

A frisson of concern skittered down my spine. Was Marigold's condition something worse than dehydration?

"Oh, if only I had my keys," Noeline said. "I left them at home. I didn't think—" She poked Rick's arm. "Can you pick the lock?"

He laughed uncomfortably. "I'm skillful, sweetness, but that's one talent I lack."

"You said you're a whiz at all things technical."

" 'Technical' is the operative word."

If only Marigold had given me a key to the shop. I'd suggested it once, saying that way I could set up earlier for teas and she could sleep in, but she'd pooh-poohed the idea.

"Do you know where Tegan is, Allie?" Noeline asked.

"She wasn't at the B and B this morning?"

"No. She texted me last night to say she was staying with you." Her face paled. "I hope she didn't go home. What if she got into a fight with Winston?"

"You know about the problem with their marriage?"

"Yes."

I rested a hand on her arm. "I'm sure she's just running late, thinking her aunt has this covered."

"Except she doesn't."

"Everything's going to be fine," I said, though a twinge of worry for my pal nipped me in the gut. Tegan always responded to texts in a timely manner. So, why hadn't she this morning? Was she all right?

"Everyone, move away from the door, please." Chloe Kang, the twenty-something junior clerk at the shop, who possessed the vim of the Energizer Bunny, beat a path through the crowd while waving her key chain. Her almond-shaped eyes sparkled with joy. The outfit she had on—plaid poncho, red dress, and Sherlock Holmes–style hat—made her look like a character on a Nancy Drew book cover. "Where's Marigold?"

"We don't know," Noeline said.

Chloe cupped her hands and peered through the window. "This reminds me of *The Secret of the*—"

"Not now, Chloe," Noeline said.

Chloe could rattle off tidbits about every novel she'd ever read. She'd never held a job that wasn't in a bookstore or library.

"Open up," Noeline demanded. "We're freezing."

"Here we go." Chloe, always chipper, inserted her key into the lock, twisted, and pushed the door open. She switched on a single light. "Give me a sec. I'll make it brighter." She bustled toward the panel of light switches at the rear of the store, rounded the sales counter, and screamed.

CHAPTER 4

"Importance may sometimes be purchased too dearly."

—Elizabeth Bennet, in Jane Austen's *Pride and Prejudice*

"Marigold has fallen again!" Chloe cried.

I cut around the other patrons and spotted Marigold lying faceup on the floor. My breath snagged. Blood had pooled beneath her head. Her face was blue. But that was all I could see of her. The rest was buried beneath a pile of coffee-table books, cookbooks, and hardcover fiction. I bent to clear them.

"Oh, my!" Noeline whimpered.

I glanced over my shoulder at her. The knuckles of her right hand were pressed to her lips. Though my insides were chugging with adrenaline, I shouted like a trained paramedic, "Everyone, back up! You too, Noeline." I started pushing books off Marigold. "Give us room. Chloe, call 911."

"On it," Chloe said.

"Marigold! It's me, Allie." I cleared the top half of her and saw she was clutching *Pride and Prejudice* in her arms. "Marigold! Wake up." There was no rise and fall beneath her V-neck sweater. I pressed my fingers above the chain of her pendant to detect a pulse on her neck, but there wasn't one. Not even a faint one. "She's . . ." My throat clogged with emotion. "She's dead."

Noeline wailed and began clawing at the remaining books. "Help me get her out from under these. Sis! Wake up!"

"Stop." I rested a hand on her shoulder. "Don't. The police will need to photograph the scene."

"The police?"

"Looks like an accident to me," Rick said.

I glowered at him. "Are you kidding? She did not pull all of these tomes on top of herself."

"All I meant was—"

"Maybe she tripped," Noeline said, cutting Rick off. "Or she had another spell."

"That doesn't explain the pile of books," I argued.

Noeline said, "Teetering, she reached for the edge of the counter." She mimed the action. "The books toppled."

"And she smothered," someone said from behind her.

I doubted lack of oxygen killed Marigold. Her mouth and nose had remained uncovered. I noticed a small bruise no bigger than a quarter on her neck, not far from her right ear, and supposed the heft of the books might have knocked her to the floor and nicked her, making her bang her head. Death by blunt force trauma.

Brushing Marigold's bangs off her face, I eyed the novel in her hands. Had someone startled her as she was opening the shop? Had she hoped to fend off whoever it was, as Elizabeth Bennet would, with biting remarks? Was the book her shield? I didn't see her cell phone anywhere, but a legal-looking envelope, the kind with lace ties to secure it, lay facedown near her shoulder. Pinching the upper-left corner, I flipped it over. The front read: *Private and Confidential.* I peeked inside. Empty. Had Marigold intended to insert something into it, or had her assailant—I was almost certain she'd been attacked—taken the contents?

"Let's clear the space," I said, rising to my feet. Like a restaurant manager, a caterer needed to be in command. I could use my big voice when necessary. "Rick, would you lead everyone out of the store?" He interacted with teams of people at a hospital. He'd have the ability to oversee a concerned crowd. "Everyone, please remain outside. The police might want to question you." Who knew what anyone would remember? Hints to clues, as I'd absorbed over the course of reading mysteries, came from many directions and multiple sources. "Graham, you saw Marigold at six, so I'm sure the police will want to talk to you, too. Stick around."

Rick squeezed Noeline's shoulder, whispered, "I'm so sorry," and he dutifully led the charge outside.

Noeline mewled. I looped an arm around her shoulder as I scanned the shop. The front door had been locked. Did Marigold let her killer inside, or had the killer sneaked in through the stockroom door?

"Mom!" Tegan yelled as she burst into the shop, struggling with Rick, who was trying to hold her at bay. "Let. Me. Go." She wrenched free and cut across the carpet. "What's going on? Why are the books on the—" She gagged. "Is that Auntie?"

I blocked her. "Tegan, your aunt is dead."

"Dead?"

"Don't move. This is a crime scene."

"A crime—" Like her mother, Tegan choked back a sob.

Noeline said, "Maybe she was dehydrated and passed out and hit her head."

"I doubt that's what happened," I responded. "Not after the scare she had yesterday." An empty bottle of water stood on the sales counter. An untouched cup of tea sat beside it, as well as stacks of books that hadn't tumbled to the floor. The pegboard behind the desk, which held the shop's computer, was neat and tidy, nothing askew. The screen of the computer swirled with a screensaver of magical books. The wall clock with the phrase *So many books, so little time* was correct as to the hour. "I think she was murdered."

Tegan gasped. "Why would anyone kill Auntie?" She was wearing the same clothes she'd been wearing last night, meaning she hadn't gone home to change between when she'd left my place and now. So where had she been? "Auntie was beloved by all. A stellar member of the community. She didn't have an evil bone in her body. It makes no sense."

I'd read enough murder mysteries to know that in the end the murder did make sense, but at first it was hard to piece the clues together. "You need to cancel the tea, Tegan." My pulse was racing, yet I sounded as calm as a seasoned detective. How was that possible? "Alert the attendees."

Tegan started toward the sales counter. I held her at bay. "Don't use the shop's phone. That's out of bounds. Go over by the window. Use your cell."

"I don't have the complete list of attendees."

"I do," Chloe said, and flashed her mobile at Tegan. Tears were pooling in the young woman's eyes.

I felt them brimming in mine and willed them to stay put. I needed to keep my wits about me.

"Marigold sent it to me last night," Chloe added.

Why would Marigold have done that? Did she have a premonition of her demise? Why not send it to Tegan, too?

I said, "Chloe, share your info with Tegan." I regarded Marigold again. Where was her purse? Most likely, she'd stowed it and her phone in the office.

A siren bleated outside. A fire truck double-parked in front of the shop. A pair of burly emergency medical technicians leaped from it and raced inside.

"The owner," I said to them, pointing. "She's dead. Her name is Marigold Markel. Age seventy."

One knelt to inspect her; the other was already communicating with the police. Within minutes, a squad car pulled up behind the fire truck. Seconds later, Zach Armstrong strode into the shop clad in jeans, white turtleneck, and smoke-gray jacket. Bramblewood detectives weren't required to wear uniforms. His partner, Detective Brendan Bates, who was as tall as an NBA player, gave off a jazz-club vibe with his tight Afro, neatly trimmed goatee, and black-on-black outfit. Like Zach, Bates was a reader. I'd met him last year at a book club featuring noir fiction. That book club was the reason for my new-found appreciation for Dashiell Hammett, Ross Macdonald, and Raymond Chandler.

Zach and Bates crossed to the EMTs, who provided a quick update. Then Bates started taking photos with his cell phone to document the crime scene, and Zack returned to me.

"What are you doing here?" I asked.

"It was our turn in the rotation. Are you okay?" His voice was gentle but firm. "Ever seen a dead body before?"

"*Mm-hmm.*" I'd never forget the day I stumbled across the chef at the Eatery after he'd suffered a heart attack. His skin had been gray, his eyes as blank as buttons.

"What do you think happened here?" Zach asked.

I explained my theory of Marigold being startled by an intruder. I added that the front door was locked when we all arrived, which was unusual, since she had been expecting a crowd. "No one had a key until Chloe"—I pointed her out—"arrived and unlocked the door and went to turn on the lights." I indicated the panel of switches. "She saw Marigold and screamed. I took over at that point." A shiver coursed through me. "I couldn't detect a pulse, and with the blood pooling under her head . . ." My voice cracked. "I think there was a struggle and someone pushed her. I noted a small bruise on the right side of her neck." My finger rose to my own neck automatically.

"Or she could've suffered a heart attack, stumbled, toppled the books herself, and one of them struck her," Zach proposed.

Most of the books were in the same state as when I'd pushed them off Marigold, although the EMTs had tossed a few to one side, causing them to splay open. Seeing them like that, their spines cracked, made my head hurt.

"She's clutching a copy of *Pride and Prejudice*," I stated.

"Do you think that's significant?" Zach asked.

"It was her favorite book, but it seems an odd one to use for protection."

"If she was trying to protect herself," he countered.

"There were plenty of other books to choose from." I motioned to the ones on the floor. "Large coffee-table books, for example." One, a thick tome about the history of costumes in theater, held a sticker with Lillian's name on it. She often boned up on theater-related nonfiction. The latest Lee Child thriller had been tagged with Zach's name. A bundle of YA books tied with rattan held a Post-it note that read: *Piper.*

"Armstrong," Bates called over his shoulder. "Take a look." He was on one knee and pointing to Marigold's neck.

In the flurry, I hadn't realized a uniformed female officer had arrived. She'd placed a large canvas carryall on the floor and was marking items with yellow crime-scene cones.

Zach left me, hitched his jeans up a tad, and crouched beside Bates. He glanced over his shoulder at me and returned his focus to Marigold's neck. Was he inspecting the bruise? Now would he agree with me that she'd struggled with the killer?

Zach said something to Bates, who rose to his feet to make a call on his cell phone. Bates asked someone a question. He listened. Then he shook his head at Zach, who grumbled and crossed to me.

"What's wrong?" I asked.

"The traffic cameras aren't working in this area. The storm last week damaged them."

Meaning the police wouldn't be able to review footage to see if anyone came or went from the bookshop between six thirty a.m., when I'd last spoken to Marigold, and when she died. *Swell.*

"You should check the stockroom door," I said, being proactive. "If it's unlocked—"

"We will."

"You can't leave through the rear without securing the deadbolt," I added. "It's a safeguard Marigold put in place. She didn't want to accidentally lock herself out. There could be fingerprints on the knob."

He didn't respond.

"Have you found her keys?" I asked.

A smile tugged the corners of his mouth and quickly vanished. "When would I have had time to search?"

"Right, of course. I'm a dolt. An idiot." I was blathering. I hated to blather. Out of nowhere, it dawned on me that our date for the sing-along in Asheville—if he'd intended it to be an official date—would need to be postponed, and I wanted to kick myself for having such a selfish, aimless thought. "I'm not thinking straight," I said, and apologized. Tears stung my eyes. My heart ached as though cinched with metal bands.

"Do you have a key to the shop?" he asked.

"No. I'm not an employee. Tegan and Chloe have them."

Noeline had joined Tegan in a huddle. She was saying something that seemed to be unnerving my pal. Tegan was shaking her head in denial.

"Allie?" Zach said softly to make me refocus.

"Noeline has keys, too. She mentioned that she left them at home."

"Noeline?"

"Noeline Merriweather, Marigold's younger sister." I motioned to her. "She's part owner of the bookshop and runs the Blue Lantern bed-and-breakfast."

"In Montford."

"That's the one."

Zach shifted his weight and pulled a notepad and pen from his hip pocket. "Tell me about the others who were waiting to enter when you arrived."

"Do you think the murderer might be one of them?"

His face gave away nothing.

But taking that as a maybe, I proceeded to explain who Rick O'Sheedy was, before moving on to Piper Lowry, Graham Wynn, and the other few patrons of the shop that I recognized from book clubs. I described each one by height and clothing. Zach took in the crowd on the sidewalk, as if memorizing names and faces.

"There are a few tourists, too," I added.

"Got it."

"By the way, Graham is Marigold's neighbor," I said. "He saw her at six this morning. Outside her house. I spoke to her around six thirty. She was already here. What if the killer . . ."

Zach tapped the nib of his pen on his notepad. "Uh-uh. Do not speculate. You are not a trained detective. I don't care how many murder mysteries you've read or watched."

"How about all the real crime podcasts I've listened to?" I asked, and instantly regretted the sassy quip. "I don't see Marigold's things. Her purse. Her phone. I suppose they could be in the office, or the killer might have stolen them. And that envelope marked 'Private and Confidential' . . ." Bates had left it in place. A yellow cone stood beside it. "It's empty."

"You touched it?"

"Um, one corner."

"Okay. In the future, don't touch anything at a crime scene."

In the future, I would not see another crime scene.

"Would you please ask Marigold's sister to talk with me?" he asked.

I crossed to her. "Noeline, Detective Armstrong would like to speak with you."

Mascara-stained tears streaked her cheeks. With a wadded tissue in her fist, she slinked to him. He asked a question. She responded. He asked another. She fished in her purse and pulled out her cell phone. She opened it with her fingerprint and handed it to him. He scrolled through something, messages I supposed, and gave it back.

Tegan sidled to me. "What's he doing?"

"Checking your mother's communications with Marigold is my guess."

"I can't believe Auntie was . . . was . . . murdered," Tegan sputtered.

The word "murdered" stuck in my throat. Why kill Marigold? Why end the life of one of the nicest people in the world? Was this a random attack, or was the killer someone Marigold knew? Both possibilities made me shudder. "Tegan, were you able to contact all of today's attendees?"

"Yes. They are beyond upset. A few asked what would happen to the bookstore. I said I didn't know. I imagine Auntie left her estate to my mother. Do you think she'll keep it open? The B and B is requiring all her energy."

"We'll see. Was that what you and your mom were talking about? You seemed concerned."

"No. She was telling me where she was this morning. It was odd, like she wanted to prove that she didn't do this, as if I'd think she could have. *Ever.*"

"Suspects blurt alibis all the time. They get jittery, and the weirdest things pop out of their mouths."

"She said she was at the B and B."

"Of course she was. She serves breakfast. She greets the guests."

"Right. So there will be plenty of people to confirm that."

"Maybe she was telling you her alibi because, in truth, she wanted to know where you were." I waited a beat for her to offer an answer. When she didn't, I said, "So, where were you? Why didn't you return my text earlier?"

Tegan folded her arms across her chest. "I—"

The door to the shop flew open and Vanna stormed inside,

the tails of her white-checked scarf flying behind her. Rick chased her, unable to prevent her from advancing.

"What the heck!" Vanna shrieked. A hurricane couldn't have entered with less subtlety. "You did this!" She rushed at Tegan. "You!"

Tegan's cheeks burned pink. "What are you talking about?"

"If Auntie's been murdered, like everyone outside is saying"—Vanna thrust an arm in the direction of the crowd—"then you killed her. *You!*"

All sound ceased in the shop. Zach and Bates pivoted and stared in our direction.

I wrapped an arm around my friend and said to her vicious half sister, "Stop it this instant. What has gotten into you?"

"They're saying Auntie is dead," Vanna wailed. "She was murdered."

"It's true," I said. At least, the dead part. Not necessarily the murdered part.

"Then Tegan killed her." Vanna's voice could have cut ice. Honestly, at times I marveled that she had been born with any of Noeline's genteel genes.

"I did not kill Auntie, Vanna." Tegan wrenched free of me and balled her hands into fists. "Take it back."

Zach strode to us. "What's going on, ladies?"

"My aunt left her portion of the bookstore to my half sister," Vanna blurted. "That's motive. Tegan, where were you this morning?"

"How dare you!" Tegan squawked.

I glowered at Vanna. She truly believed Tegan was capable of murder? She wasn't just jabbering?

"Where were you?" Vanna repeated, smugly smoothing the front of her silk dress.

"Auntie did not leave the shop to me," Tegan said, avoiding answering the question. "Where did you hear such a thing?"

"I . . ." Vanna faltered, but recovered and raised her chin. "I saw a letter Auntie wrote. It was on her desk at home when I visited the other day. It wasn't there this morning."

"Why did you go to her house this morning?" I asked.

"I saw her after she closed the shop last night. Her car was sputtering like a sick dog. I thought she might need a ride today."

I narrowed my gaze. "What were you doing hanging around here after closing?"

"If you must know, I had an appointment nearby. The Bramblewood Inn was asking about my services." The inn was located around the corner, on Mountain Road. "I decided to stretch my legs before going home. I swung through the alley and saw Auntie in her car."

An alley ran behind the shops on the north side of Main Street to make deliveries easier and keep the thoroughfare free of overly large trucks. "Anyway, Auntie wasn't home when I arrived this morning at eight."

"No," I said, "she was at the shop already. So, why did you go into her house?"

"I needed to use the loo," Vanna continued. "That's when I noticed the letter was gone. She must've mailed it or something."

I scoffed.

"What did the letter say?" Zach asked.

"That Tegan, a great lover of books, would be a fine bookshop owner, one that Auntie would entrust with her life's work." Vanna whirled on Tegan. "You saw the letter. I know you did."

"I did not." Tegan eyed Zach. "I swear I didn't." She glowered at her sister. "Why are you here, anyway?"

"I saw a crowd out front." Vanna harrumphed. "If only Auntie had hired me to do the catering for the tea, instead of Allie, she wouldn't have died, because I would have been here at the crack of dawn, and no killer would have been able to get past me."

"But she didn't hire you," Tegan said acidly. "Do you know why? Because she didn't like your food. Oh, sure, you've got a fine reputation, and you've got clients, but your food is too frou-frou. Auntie didn't like it, and that's why she hired Allie. My friend makes down-to-earth, good-tasting food that sticks to your ribs, and cookies that taste like cookies, not flowers."

Zach cleared his throat "Ladies, if you don't mind, I'd like to speak to each of you individually."

Vanna huffed. "Fine."

"Fine," Tegan said.

"Let's start with you, Tegan," he said, gently guiding her toward the rear of the store. "Tell me your whereabouts for this morning."

Tegan gasped. "You don't think . . . You can't think . . ." She glanced over her shoulder at me, and her eyes told the story. She'd balked when Vanna had demanded her alibi, because it was as flimsy as wet cardboard.

CHAPTER 5

"Do you prefer reading to cards?" said he; "that is rather singular."

—Mr. Hurst, in Jane Austen's *Pride and Prejudice*

I trucked after my friend, earning a caustic stare from Zach. "Does she need a lawyer?"

"Not if she has nothing to hide," he replied.

"I d-don't," Tegan said, but she didn't sound certain.

Zach waited for me to leave, but I held my ground. Sighing, he said, "Okay, Tegan, fill me in."

Beyond Zach, I noticed Bates and the female officer eyeing the empty water bottle and sniffing the cold cup of tea. The tech took photos of each, bagged the water bottle, and then pulled a glass container from her carryall and placed the teacup, including the liquid, into it.

"I was at Allie's until . . ." Tegan paused.

Until three a.m., I reflected. After that, it was anybody's guess.

"Around three," she said, stating the truth.

I breathed easier.

"I couldn't sleep because Auntie had a scare yesterday. She fainted, and I was worried sick, and—"

"Wait," Zach cut in. "She fainted?" He regarded me. "You neglected to mention that."

"It slipped my mind. Sorry."

"Go on, Tegan," he said.

She licked her lips. "I got restless, so I left and walked home." Tegan and Winston lived about ten blocks from me. Not too far, but strolling at that time of night was not the safest thing to do. And slipping into her house after three, when she and her husband were on the outs, didn't sound like the wisest idea.

"Did anyone see you?" Zach asked.

"A man with a leashed puppy relieving itself and the janitor at the mini mart. But neither of them would recognize me," she said. "I was bundled up."

"They'd remember your coat," I suggested. "It's puffy and white and knee-length. It makes her look like a roly-poly bug."

"It does not," Tegan said, taking umbrage.

Where's her coat now, seeing as she hadn't changed the rest of her outfit?

"I left the coat at home," she said, answering my unasked question. "I knew I'd be inside here all day." She blinked rapidly. Was she trying to signal me to keep quiet? Why not come clean? She hadn't killed her aunt—of that, I was certain.

"Didn't your husband see you?" Zach pressed.

"He's traveling. On business."

That was easily verifiable. Was it true or false?

"What did you do when you arrived home?" Zach asked.

"The usual. Brushed my teeth. Read for a few minutes. Slept."

Sleep must have been the only thing she'd done. She hadn't showered. Hadn't run a comb through her hair. Hadn't put on a stitch of new makeup.

"Did any of your neighbors see you?" Zach asked.

She shook her head. "Their houses were dark."

That was probably true. Mostly older people populated her block. Marigold, who had been the executrix for an elderly female friend, had privately negotiated the sale of the friend's house when the woman passed away in debt. Marigold had even made the down payment for Tegan and Winston. To be fair, she'd helped Vanna buy her first house, too.

I studied Vanna, off to one side, arms folded, her tongue working the inside of her cheek, and decided she should thank her lucky stars she could cook. Otherwise, with her rancid personality, no one would hire her.

"Allie," Zach said.

I refocused on him. "Yes?"

"Did you hear Tegan leave your place?"

"Yes. I mean, no. I heard her rummaging around at three. I figured she'd settle down sooner or later, so I went back to sleep."

"Your cat didn't startle when she left the house?"

"Darcy? He's the rare cat that can sleep through a lightning storm."

Zach posed a few more questions to Tegan, about her relationships with Marigold and her mother, as well as the duties of her job. He asked if she donated time to the theater foundation, like her aunt did. She said no, but she volunteered at the blood bank. All seemed like pointless questions, but I got the feeling Zach was trying to take the measure of her. After all, he didn't know her well. He'd merely interacted with her as the shop's clerk. Perhaps he was trying to trip her up. Before he released her, he asked her for her alibi again. She reiterated what she'd said earlier, not changing a word. Had she rehearsed it?

Zach clasped my elbow and whispered, "Allie, stay close to a phone in case I need you."

On any other day, that request might have sent goose bumps, the good kind, down my spine, but not today. It sent chills.

Tegan bid her mother good-bye, I left my Ford Transit parked on the street, and she and I strolled to Ragamuffin. I needed a scone. Yes, it would be one of the six dozen scones I'd delivered yesterday, but I was willing to pay for it. I was starving.

Ragamuffin, which was located in one of the connecting

courtyards between Holly Street and Elm, was packed with customers. I'd never seen the place lacking in attendance. Its proprietary small-batch, free-trade coffee was the best. The baristas were gifted when it came to adding all sorts of unique syrups to their coffee beverages, like lavender, honey-maple, Irish cream, and more. Their green teas were fabulous, as well, with additions of cinnamon, ginger, and mint. An apple cider vinegar concoction was decidedly delicious. The exterior patio held a half-dozen bistro tables, but it was too cool to sit out, so I left Tegan at the teensy bar, which was standing room only, and moved to the register to order. I peered into the pastry case that held butterscotch cookies, gluten-free ricotta cake, cinnamon buns, and lemon scones. I ordered a cinnamon bun for Tegan and a scone for me, plus two lattes.

I carried my purchases to where Tegan was standing and un-packed our treats. Rhythmic reggae music played through speakers, but I sure didn't feel like dancing.

"You really didn't know about the inheritance?" I nibbled the scone. The extra lemon zest I'd added gave it a real zing.

"Not a whit." She sipped her coffee, flinching from the heat. "I mean, Auntie might have mentioned it, but I thought she was kidding. After all, she shared the shop with Mom. I fig-ured if she died, she'd leave her portion to my mother and let her figure out, you know, if she even wanted to keep it. Mom's been so busy at the inn, she's taken no interest in the book-shop." She took a bite of her cinnamon bun and hummed her approval. "*Mmm.* Moist. You should make these."

"I'll test out a few recipes." I popped the lid on my coffee to let it cool. "Where did you go this morning? What's your alibi? And don't lie. I can read you like a book. A memorized book. And is Winston really out of town on a trip? Zach can verify that."

"He is on a trip. I didn't lie about that."

"But you didn't go home."

She picked up a crumb of cinnamon bun with her fingertip and sucked it off. "No. I visited a friend."

"A friend?" I was stunned. How could she be seeing someone so soon after learning of Winston's deceit? "What's his name?"

"Not a guy friend. A girlfriend."

"Golly! Why didn't you tell Zach that? She can vouch for you."

"No, she can't."

"Why not?" I asked. "What's the big secret?"

"I can't say. Please don't make me. Just believe me when I say I was with her until eight forty-five." She slumped as if the weight of the world had landed on her.

I patted her shoulder. "Okay, for now, I won't press. You were somewhere. With someone. That's good." I took another bite of my scone and sipped the latte.

"Who killed my aunt?" Tegan said, her voice crackling with sadness.

My insides wrenched. My sorrow couldn't be as poignant as hers, but I'd lost a good friend, a fellow bibliophile. "Your guess is as good as mine."

"Auntie didn't like Rick."

"He didn't kill her. He barely knew her."

"She was edgy around him."

"She would have been prickly around any of your mother's boyfriends. She loved your father. She thought he and your mother were the perfect pair. Who else?"

"Auntie was always complaining about her neighbor Graham."

"He's the one you were referring to yesterday. She wanted him to get his act together."

She hummed.

"What was the problem?" I asked. "Did he throw loud parties?"

"No. He watched her."

"Like a stalker?"

"Not exactly. More like he kept an eye on her. He watched other neighbors, too. He doesn't trust anyone."

"That reminds me of the neighbor who lived across the street from Samantha in *Bewitched*. Remember her?"

"Gladys Kravitz!" Tegan cried. As girls, we'd watched reruns in the afternoons and had tried in vain to twitch our noses. We'd failed miserably.

"Yes, her." I polished off my scone and brushed my fingertips on the napkin provided with the treats. "Did you see the envelope near your aunt's head?"

Tegan opened her eyes wide. "No."

"It was a legal envelope about yea big." I gestured with my hands. "With the words 'Private and Confidential' on it. It was empty."

"What do you think was inside?"

"She might have kept records in it or notes for books that were reserved." Neither of those seemed like something worth stealing.

"How did the killer get in?"

"Not sure." At one point, Bates had gone to the stockroom. He and Zach must know by now whether the door had been locked or unlocked. "Do you have your key?"

"Sure do. I don't leave home without it."

"Your mother left hers at the B and B."

"Understandable. She doesn't open the shop. Her key is purely a backup."

"Why do you think your aunt was holding *Pride and Prejudice*?" I asked.

"Conceivably, she was reading it for the umpteenth time when the killer showed up. It was her favorite book. She could quote every passage." Tegan dumped the remainder of her cinnamon bun into the carry bag and wadded her napkin. "She once told me that if she was reincarnated, she wanted to return as Elizabeth Bennet because Lizzie was smart yet tender, and she adored her silly family." She smiled whimsically. "I guess that was her way of saying she thought we were silly."

"Not you." I patted my friend's hand. "Not your mother, either." *Possibly Vanna,* I reflected, but didn't say it aloud.

Tegan rotated the bag with one finger. "Do you think the police will find clues? Fingerprints? DNA evidence? That kind of thing?"

"Let's hope." Before leaving the bookshop, I'd heard Bates requesting that another technician come to the site.

"When do you think they'll let me in?" She sighed. "There will be so much to do."

"As soon as they have everything they need. I'd guess around twenty-four hours."

Had someone from the Office of the Chief Medical Examiner shown up yet? The OCME investigated all deaths due to injury or violence.

"Do you know if your mother will hold a funeral?" I asked.

"Auntie wanted to be cremated."

That surprised me. I would have thought Marigold would have preferred a traditional burial. "You know what we should do to honor her, then?" I polished off my latte. "We should host a memorial tea, and we should center it around *Pride and Prejudice.* I can make food from the era, and we could ask everyone to dress up in costumes. I'm sure Lillian, with her connections at the theater, could get her hands on a variety of Regency Era getups. They've done plays from that time period. Or she could design some." I remembered admiring the clothes she'd made for *Sense and Sensibility*, in particular the bonnets.

"What a wonderful idea! Auntie would love that." She clapped a hand to her chest. "We could have a string quartet playing music from that era, too."

"If you want, we could even make it a book club–type event. We could read passages from the book."

"Yes." Tears leaked down Tegan's cheeks. "That's perfect. When?"

"Saturday, two weeks from now. That should give us plenty of time to prepare."

"I'll alert my mother, and we'll clue in the bookshop customers and Auntie's friends and the theater foundation folks." She squinched up her face. "I can't believe Vanna thinks—"

"You didn't kill your aunt, and your sister knows it. If your aunt really did write a letter, like Vanna says, she's feeling maligned. We'll get her on board. You'll see."

"I need to be with my mother."

"Go. I'll dispose of our trash."

Needing a project so I wouldn't dwell on Marigold's demise and sink into a dark emotional abyss, I delivered all the goods in the van to a nearby women's shelter—I didn't want to throw it all out—and then I drove to Dream Cuisine to deal with the decimated ants. By now, the pest company would've sprayed, but they wouldn't have cleaned up. Most importantly, I had to figure out where the critters had entered. If Vanna hadn't instigated the attack, and to be honest, I doubted she was smart enough to have dreamed it up, caulking might be in order.

After opening the door and tapping in the security code, I hurried to my teensy office, where I disrobed, wriggled into a one-piece jumper I kept on hand, slipped into a pair of clogs, and headed to the kitchen. When baking, I used my scrubbed, bare hands to decorate cookies and cakes and to arrange fruit in tarts and such, but when cleaning, I always covered up. Disposable latex-free gloves were one of those items I kept in stock at all times. I opened a new box, pulled on a pair, and scoured the corners of my specialty kitchen.

The project did not stop my mind from rehashing what I'd seen at the bookshop: Marigold beneath the books. The bruise on her neck. The *Private and Confidential* envelope. If I asked

Zach, would he fill me in on his investigation? Doubtful. Would he and his partner uncover the truth? I hoped so. But even I wasn't foolish enough to think all cases were solved. Some went cold.

"There you are," I said when I found the offending spot where most of the pesticide had been applied. Right by the water heater. Like Tegan said, a perfectly cozy spot for a satellite colony of ants.

On hands and knees, I peeked beneath the tank. I checked for any holes or gaps in the wall behind it in case the ants had figured out how to hide while the pest guys were applying their death serum. Finding none, I dosed the area with vinegar. I was one of the few people I knew who didn't find the odor offensive.

Then, to honor Marigold, I decided to eliminate the smell by baking her favorite cookies. She had delighted in the combination of butterscotch and chocolate. I did, too. I'd keep them for myself. To eat in solace.

Tears sprang to my eyes. I brushed them aside and opened a classical musical playlist on my cell phone, and as I listened to Ignace Pleyel's Violin Concerto in D Major, a favorite during the Regency Era, I preheated the oven and arranged all the ingredients on the counter. The sugar, butterscotch, and chocolate morsels to the left, and dry ingredients to the right.

In a matter of minutes, I made the dough. While dropping oversized spoonfuls of the luscious goodness onto baking sheets, which I'd lined with parchment paper, the shocking image of Marigold lying on the floor of the bookshop popped into my head. My breath caught in my chest as I realized I would never see her again. Never speak to her. Never get her insight as to which book I should read next. Never hear her lead another book club. I recalled one of her favorite quotes from Pablo Neruda: "Absence is a house so vast that inside you will pass through its walls and hang pictures on the air."

Yes, that was exactly how I felt. Exactly.

Why had Marigold been holding a copy of *Pride and Prejudice*? Had she picked it up for a reason? To signal who might have killed her?

My cell phone jangled. It was Zach. I answered.

"Hey," he said softly. "How are you holding up?"

"I'm okay. Did you find out who did this?"

"Not yet. The wheels of justice do not move as swiftly as TV detectives make out. But we will."

"Did the medical examiner determine she died from hitting her head on the floor?"

"Look, I know you said you'd seen a dead body before, but . . ." He paused. "But seeing the body of a person you knew—"

"Loved."

"Isn't easy. Believe me, you don't want to go over it again and again. Try to erase the memory from your mind. We're on the case."

I slid the baking trays into the preheated oven and set the timer.

"Do you want company?" he asked.

"Rain check?"

"Sure. Is that Haydn playing in the background?"

"Pleyel."

"Never heard of him."

"He was one of Jane Austen's favorite composers. I'll educate you sometime." I took a butterscotch morsel from the bag and plunked it into my mouth. "Were you able to finish up at the bookstore? Will Tegan be able to get in tomorrow? There will be so much to do."

"Yes. Bates contacted her and gave her the green light."

I wondered if Noeline had reached out to the executor for Marigold's estate. Wouldn't there have to be some kind of forensic accounting of the business? How would Marigold have divvied up the proceeds?

"Did you find Marigold's personal items?" I asked. "Her purse? Her phone?"

"Allie—"

"It was a simple question. That kind of info certainly can't be proprietary."

He clicked his tongue, hesitating, then said, "We found both."

"Was everything intact?"

"She had a bunch of receipts and lots of loose change in her purse, but her wallet was empty. We think this was a robbery gone wrong."

"If it was, why didn't the thief steal her diamond pendant?"

CHAPTER 6

"If a woman conceals her affection with the same skill from the object of it, she may lose the opportunity of fixing him; and it will then be but poor consolation to believe the world equally in the dark."

—Charlotte Lucas, in Jane Austen's *Pride and Prejudice*

"Zach, that piece of jewelry is worth a lot of money. A long-lost lover gave it to her."

I explained that the lover, the man she was supposed to marry, had been a bibliophile, like Marigold. He died before they could wed and was the reason she was independently wealthy. Sadly, like his father and his uncle, he had a weak heart. None lived past the age of twenty-five. In preparation for their nuptials, however, he rewrote his will and bequeathed her his sizable estate.

"So," I continued, "why wouldn't the *thief*"—I stressed the word—"steal the necklace?"

Zach didn't answer or even give me the satisfaction of a grunt.

"Okay, okay," I said. "I won't badger you. Thank you for revealing what you could. I'll talk to you soon."

I ended the call, finished baking, packed up my goods, cleaned the kitchen, and headed home. Darcy was waiting for me at the door, his tail upright and curled, as if he, too, had lots of questions and needed answers. I cradled him in my arms and stroked his chin as fresh tears trickled down my cheeks. I wanted justice for Marigold, but I would be useless if I didn't sleep.

The next morning, I awoke to the jangle of my cell phone. Darcy, lying at the foot of my bed, complained with a yowl. No wonder. It was Sunday. I didn't have any baking on the schedule, and I didn't have deliveries to make. I shushed him and answered.

"Allie," Tegan said, her voice carrying sharply through the speaker. "Come to the shop now. We need to talk."

"It's early."

"Please."

"Put on a pot of coffee. I need caffeine."

In a matter of minutes, I fed the cat, packed a half-dozen scones in a Dream Cuisine pastry box, threw on a pair of jeans, a navy sweater, ankle boots, and peacoat, and drove to the shop. After parking on the street, I swathed my lips with gloss and lightly dusted my cheeks with rouge. Tegan wouldn't care if I donned makeup, but in case I ran into a client or bookshop customer, I wanted to look my best.

Tentatively I approached Feast for the Eyes, treats in hand. The CLOSED sign faced out, but the door was unlocked. I reached for the knob. At the same time, the bells from the nearby Congregational church pealed. The sound jolted me. I shimmied off the tension and entered. The aroma of coffee wafted to me.

"Tegan!" I yelled.

She emerged from the storage room beyond the sales counter, her hair swooped sloppily into a clip, messy tendrils cupping her cheeks. Even her makeup looked slapdash. The thigh-length sweater she'd thrown on over leggings—the sweater's design was a defeated anime woman—appeared three sizes too big. The cuffs hung way past her fingertips. It must have been an impulse buy. Whenever she fell into a funk, she bought something new.

"Chloe's in the stockroom," Tegan said. "She'll bring out coffee when it's brewed."

I wrinkled my nose.

"Don't worry," she said. "I made it." Though Tegan couldn't cook, she could make a good pot of coffee. Chloe scorched it. She looped her hand around my elbow and drew me to the sales counter. "I'll get to those," she said, referring to the books that were stacked willy-nilly on the counter. How well she knew me. My first instinct was to organize them. "For now, I simply wanted them off the floor. There was dust— fingerprint dust, I'm pretty sure—on a lot of them, so they'll need to be cleaned."

"I can help, if you like."

"No. I'll do it. I—" She plucked at the sleeves of the sweater. "The file cabinets in the office were hanging open. I suppose the police went through all of the records for our customers. One might be a suspect."

"That would make sense."

A small moan escaped her lips. She lifted a hand to her mouth to stifle another. I'd never seen her look so fragile. I wanted to hug her but worried she'd crumble.

"Do you know what your mother wants to do with the shop?" I asked.

"We haven't spoken about it. She was crushed last night and went to bed with a migraine." Idly she lifted the *Bramblewood Art District* coffee-table book from the pile on the counter and set it down. "How am I going to come in, day after day, and stand here, right where my aunt died, and sell books?"

The notion made me squirrely, too. I moved to the other side of the counter, where I would normally wait to make a purchase, and put the pastry box down. Then I perched on one of the two ladder-back chairs.

"This was Auntie's baby," Tegan went on. "She was the glue that held it all together. She did the heavy lifting."

I opened the seal on the box and flipped the lid. "She would want you to press on."

"But what if I'm terrible at it? What if it all unravels?" Tegan removed a scone and called, "Chloe, bring napkins when you come!"

"What did you need to talk to me about?" I asked. "It sounded urgent."

"I really like your idea of having a memorial tea for Auntie. She would be so pleased."

I gawked at her. "That's it? You couldn't have said as much over the phone? I'd hoped the police had given you some news. Perhaps a hint as to the killer's identity."

"No. Nothing. I . . . I needed to see your cheery face."

I was pretty sure my face wasn't remotely cheery. I mustered a weak smile.

"Did I hear you say we're having a memorial tea?" Chloe asked, putting a tray prepared with three cups of coffee on the counter. "That's a good idea. Tea is so soothing." Though her fitted dress was chic, black was not a good color for her. Retro styles in shades of red were her usual go-to choices. "Cream and one sugar for you, Allie."

"Thanks."

Tegan placed her scone on a napkin and pushed it aside. "Allie suggested we make the tea a tribute to my aunt by focusing it on *Pride and Prejudice*. We'll serve foods from the Regency Era, like pies and tarts and assorted scones. Allie will cater it."

"Will you serve white soup?" Chloe asked.

"Yes." I'd never made white soup, but I'd always wanted to try. "I think I'll pass on making Scotch collops." They were akin to veal scallopini and too heavy for an afternoon tea. "Poached salmon might be a better fit."

Tegan's eyes brimmed with tears. "We'd like everyone to dress in costume. We're going to ask Lillian to facilitate that."

Chloe said, "I can just imagine the gown your aunt would have worn. All lace and ribbons. And she'd have pinned on that gorgeous brooch. The one with all the diamonds." She fluttered her fingers. "Super glitzy."

"I briefly mentioned the idea to Mom last night," Tegan said. "She'll send out invitations. Auntie had tons of friends. They'll all want to come. Money is no object."

The notion of money made me wonder again about who would be the executor of Marigold's estate. It also made me recall Zach saying her wallet was empty. She'd loathed using a credit card. She'd invariably had cash on hand. How much had she been carrying? When had she last withdrawn money from the bank? Would there be an accounting, so the police might guess how much had been stolen? I paused as a new thought occurred to me. What if Marigold had filled the *Private and Confidential* envelope with the shop's weekly earnings with the intention of going to the bank to deposit it, but the thief—the killer—stole it?

I explained my theory about the wallet and envelope to Tegan and Chloe.

Tegan said, "The week's take was not in the envelope. I made the deposit Friday, after Auntie's fainting spell. Do you know what was in the envelope, Chloe?"

"Nope. I saw it on the counter the night before she—" She choked back a gasp.

"Died." I gave her a supportive look. "We're going to have to get used to saying the word."

Chloe bobbed her head. "I didn't think to ask her what was in it." She looked heartsick that she hadn't. "What if it was a secret dossier?"

Tegan scoffed. "Are you suggesting Auntie worked for the government?"

"No. But what if—"

"You read too many spy novels."

Chloe hitched a shoulder. "What's not to love about Jason Bourne?"

"His lack of a memory, for one," Tegan quipped. "Although I'd like to lose all my memories of my soon-to-be ex."

"Your what?" Chloe squealed.

Tegan filled her in. "As for what Auntie had in her wallet, I don't have a clue."

"It's probably not vital to the investigation," I said.

Chloe disappeared and returned with three fresh copies of *Pride and Prejudice,* as well as the CliffsNotes versions. "These might help you plan for the memorial." Marigold had stocked a lot of guides because students at UNC Asheville, as well as Bramblewood Junior College, often needed help organizing their thoughts. "What do you think about putting quotes from the book around the shop for the memorial? They could be decoration."

"Good idea," Tegan said. "We could also download photos from the television series starring Colin Firth."

At the same time, Chloe and I whispered, "Colin Firth." When he was young, he had been drop-dead gorgeous. He was still a handsome man.

"By the way," Tegan continued, "I scoured my house last night for the letter Vanna claims she saw. There was nothing anywhere. Not in new mail. Not in old mail. I even went through my recycling bin, in case I accidentally tossed it, but nada. Zilch. And Auntie didn't send me any kind of email, so . . ." She wrapped her arms around her torso. "If the police find the letter, will it incriminate me?"

"No," I stated, as if I was an authority. "You didn't know about the inheritance."

"And I have an alibi," she stated.

I threw her the side-eye. "Which you won't elaborate on."

She frowned but stayed mum.

"Let's contact the estate attorney," I said. "Do you know who it is?"

"Mom is handling that."

"Okay. In the meantime—"

"Who killed Marigold?" Chloe cried.

"Vanna!" Tegan blurted.

I frowned. "Your sister did not kill your aunt."

"Of course not. Believing Auntie didn't want her to inherit the bookshop, she'd have done everything to keep her alive so she could sweet-talk her into changing her mind. No, you misunderstood me." Tegan propped an elbow on the sales counter. "I'm going to ask Vanna to help with the memorial. Maybe that will earn me some Brownie points with her."

"Good luck with that," I murmured.

"You're right. She hates me." She wrinkled her nose. "She's always been my enemy. Mom told me stories about how Vanna reacted when I showed up six years after she was born. She was always saying, 'Baby, be gone.' 'Baby, go away.' 'I hate baby.' "

"No," Chloe said.

"Yes."

Tegan had told me the story years ago, adding she intended to put the memories behind her. She'd failed. I took a sip of coffee.

"I mean, c'mon," Tegan went on, "was it my fault that Mom and Dad had sex?"

I spit out the coffee. Luckily, it didn't hit any of the books. I would hate to have marred a book with spewed liquid. Or any liquid, for that matter. I was dedicated to the beauty of books. I'd never even dog-eared a page. "You want to make nice and woo her?"

"Woo-woo." Chloe twirled fingers by her ears. "Marigold always said Vanna was a little nutty."

We all laughed. Good old Marigold, ever present in our thoughts.

"Time to get serious," Tegan said.

"Call your sister," I suggested.

"Are you crazy? She'll rip me to shreds when I tell her you're the caterer. I'll text." Tegan pulled her cell phone from her pocket, typed a message, and pressed Send. She stared at the phone. "No response."

"Maybe she's serving a hoity-toity brunch for the mayor," Chloe said.

"Or I could be wrong about her innocence, and the police are questioning her a second time," Tegan said conspiratorially. "By the way, have you talked to Detective Armstrong, Allie?"

"Briefly." I told her how the police were considering this a robbery gone wrong.

"No way." Chloe sniffed.

"I don't buy it, either," I said.

"Oh, Tegan," Chloe continued, "I almost forgot to tell you. Piper stopped by earlier, before you arrived. She wanted consoling. She's a sensitive soul, isn't she? She was sobbing as if Marigold was her best friend and asked to see where she died. It was sort of macabre."

Tegan said, "It's understandable. She worked with Marigold on charitable projects."

The front door opened and Noeline slogged in. Her face was pinched, her eyes swollen from crying. She crossed to where we were, shrugged out of her coat, slung it on the other ladder-back chair, and slumped onto the seat. The ends of the bow on her black silk blouse wafted as she did. She pulled her black skirt down over her knees.

I stewed for a moment. Tegan and Chloe had dressed in black, as well. Should I have donned a black shirt with my black jeans, or was it okay to wear navy when mourning?

"Mom." Tegan hurried to her. "Where are you off to?"

"Church. You left so early, I was hoping I'd find you here. Do you want to go with me?"

"Where's Rick?" Tegan asked.

"He has a business meeting."

On a Sunday? I wondered, but silenced my suspicious mind. Hospitals operated 24/7. Their financial gurus probably kept the same hours.

"Yes, I'll go with you," Tegan said. "We can say a prayer for Auntie. Chloe, will you hold down the fort and start cleaning the books? Keep the Closed sign in place. We're not open today, out of respect."

Chloe saluted.

"I'll stick around and help with the books," I said.

"Thanks." Tegan threw her arms around me. "I appreciate you more than you know."

A minute after Noeline left with Tegan, Lillian opened the front door while rapping on the frame. "May I come in?"

"We're closed," Chloe said.

"Yes, I know, but I saw you milling about. I'm not here to purchase anything."

"Lock the door after you," Chloe said.

Lillian did and removed her trench coat, revealing a sparkly sweater dress. She never wore casual clothes to work. She claimed she had to present a vibrant image to her customers. "I can't believe Marigold's gone." She draped her coat over one arm and ambled toward the sales counter, dragging a fingertip fondly over the books on the endcaps as she went.

"Neither can we." Chloe's voice cracked.

"The police stuck around all day yesterday," Lillian said. "They were in and out of the bookshop. Wandering in the alley. Doors opening and slamming. They must have put out twenty of those yellow thingies that mark evidence."

Had they found anything worth preserving? Or did they tag everything so they could later rule out stuff that was inconsequential? Other than what I read in books or saw on film, I had no idea what the police did. Would Zach educate me?

"People were pausing to peer inside the shop all day, too," Lillian went on. "The police tape kept them off the sidewalk, but they stopped and gawked." She hung her coat on a ladder-back chair, as Noeline had. "*Ooh,* Allie, did you bring the scones?"

"Help yourself."

She selected one, took a bite, and let out a delighted sigh.

Chloe hitched her chin and mouthed, *Ask her.*

"Lillian," I said, "we'd like to have a memorial tea for Marigold featuring her favorite book."

"*Pride and Prejudice,*" Lillian chimed. "What a great idea. I can't tell you how many times she and I discussed that story."

I told her about the menu that was cycling through my head, which would include soup, tarts, salmon, and tea sandwiches.

She said, "You absolutely have to serve trifle."

"Of course. We're also thinking that everyone who wants to do so should dress in costume for the occasion. Would you—"

"Provide them?" She clasped her hands as if in prayer. "Yes. I'm totally on board. Marigold would be so pleased to be honored in that fashion. The community theater will be more than happy to help us out, too. She was, after all, the foundation's chair."

I'd gone to the theater with Marigold and Tegan a few times. Marigold would light up whenever she was around actors. When asked if she had a secret ambition to perform onstage, she dismissed the notion. *Actors,* she said, *are fearless. I, on the other hand, quake at leading a book club.* That was baloney. She had been as intrepid as they come, but she'd never boasted.

"By the way," Lillian said around a mouthful of scone, "one of my regular customers came in late yesterday for a fitting. Celia Harrigan. Do you know her? I don't think she's much of a reader. She lives on Marigold's street in a yellow Craftsman with white trim. Anyway, Celia saw someone in a hoodie sneaking around Graham Wynn's house a week ago Saturday, during the day. She wasn't sure if it was a man or a woman. The reason I mention it is because she said the person was acting sketchy, and she wondered if, in view of what happened to Marigold, the person might have been staking out Marigold's house, since, you know, she lived across the street from Graham."

"That's a leap," I said.

"Perhaps." She polished off her scone. "You know about Marigold's jewelry collection, don't you?"

Marigold was wealthy, but she'd never lavished herself with gifts or spent her wealth on cruises. However, she'd loved antique jewelry. Invariably, she would wear her prized diamond necklace, but over the years she'd invested in rings and bracelets and brooches. At dinner parties, she would show off her jewelry, like the Bulgari serpent bracelet she'd found at an estate sale or a Georgian-style trembling floral brooch—the one Chloe had referred to earlier—which featured over a hundred hand-cut diamonds. As far as I knew, Marigold stored all of her jewelry in a safety-deposit box at the bank, not at home. I thought of what Celia Harrigan told Lillian. What if the lurker had actually been Graham in disguise, and he was spying on Marigold? What if he had been keeping watch, waiting for a time when she might go to the bank to retrieve her jewelry? And what if he saw her slip a valuable piece into the envelope marked *Private and Confidential*?

CHAPTER 7

"I must learn to brook being happier than I deserve."

—Captain Frederick Wentworth, in Jane Austen's
Persuasion

I was walking into my house when my cell phone jangled. I tossed my keys on the foyer table and pulled my phone from my purse. Zach was calling.

"Caught the killer?" I asked.

"Not yet," he said. "I was hoping you might want to go on a hike with me."

"Don't you have to work?"

"I need to clear my head."

"Sure, okay. Have you eaten lunch? Are you hungry?"

"Always."

"I'll pack a picnic. You bring a blanket. Give me a half hour." I didn't need to change anything but my shoes. For a dash of color, I threw on the sage-green scarf Marigold had given me for Christmas. Then I put together a picnic and stuffed it into a backpack.

Thirty minutes later, Zach knocked on the door. I liked a man who was punctual. My ex-fiancé always ran fifteen minutes late. Tegan told me it meant he wasn't committed to the relationship. How true that had proven to be.

Zach looked ruggedly handsome in a plaid shirt over a burgundy Henley, jeans, and hiking boots. "Ready?"

"Yep." I told Darcy I'd return in a few hours, hoisted the backpack, and off we went in Zach's silver Jeep Wrangler.

Bramblewood Hill Park Trail was located north of town and boasted one of the most beautiful views of the mountains. We walked in companionable silence until we neared the pinnacle. The ground was damp, but it wasn't slippery. The scent of white pines was heady. The blossoms on the redbuds and dogwoods were incredible in varying shades of pink, red, and white. There were other hikers in front of and behind us, but no one spoke above a reverent whisper.

When we found a spot, Zach spread out a waterproof blanket, and I pulled out pita wraps filled with salami, Swiss cheese, and chopped veggies, as well as paper plates and napkins. "For dessert, chocolate butterscotch cookies." I jiggled a baggie holding four of the cookies I'd baked yesterday.

"Can I start with dessert?" He grinned.

Oh, that dimple. "I won't say no." I offered him a cookie, took one for myself, and crossed my legs, comfortable in his presence.

He bit into the cookie and swallowed. "Wow, so good."

"You are definitely a cookie guy."

"Team Cookie all the way. Don't get me wrong. I like pie—in particular, pumpkin pie—but cookies travel well, and when I need a pick-me-up, cookies do in a pinch."

I smiled. My fiancé had eschewed anything sweet. That might have been why he was such a sourpuss. I took a bite of cookie and brushed crumbs off my lips with my pinky. "I know it's only been a little over twenty-four hours, but is there anything new in the investigation?"

"We're canvassing the shops near Feast for the Eyes. It being Sunday, very few are open. Bates is following up with some of Marigold's friends, like people in the theater foundation, her bridge group, and such."

"Did you go through the customer list at the shop?"

He arched an eyebrow.

"Tegan was pretty sure the police riffled through the filing cabinets."

"We did," he admitted.

"And the shop's computer, et cetera?"

He nodded.

"You should poll Marigold's neighborhood, too." I told him what Lillian had said about the suspicious activity at Graham's house a week ago.

"Why didn't Miss Bellingham tell us when we questioned her?"

"She didn't know. One of her customers lives near Marigold, a woman named Celia Harrigan. She came into Lillian's shop for a fitting late yesterday."

"Gossip," he muttered.

"Marie Curie said, 'Be less curious about people and more curious about ideas.'"

"Wise woman." He polished off his cookie and took another.

"Tegan said Marigold was muttering about Graham the other day, wishing he'd get his act together."

Zach tilted his head. "The two don't seem to equate."

"I thought I'd loop you in on what I heard. Also you should know Marigold owned other jewelry, in addition to the pendant." I outlined my theory about her going to the bank and the killer, possibly Graham or someone hanging outside his house, stalking her to steal it.

"I'll consider that angle." His mouth quirked up on one side and his awe-inspiring dimple appeared. "Are you going to be looping me in a lot?"

"You know, caterers and bakers have an eye for detail. I also have a steel-trap memory when it comes to books, as well as remembering things people say."

"Modesty becomes you." He chuckled and tapped his cookie

to mine as a toast. "You know, you left the bookshop pretty fast yesterday, once I was done with Tegan."

"Wasn't I supposed to?"

"I wanted to ask you a few things."

Worry swelled in me like a hot balloon. Was that what this was? An interrogation, not a date? Suddenly my interest in him waned. If he was going to be a sneaky Pete . . .

Testily I said, "Fire away."

"Tell me about your timeline Saturday morning."

"Mine?" I uncrossed and recrossed my legs in the other direction. "Am I a suspect because I was the last one to speak to Marigold?"

"No," he replied, but he didn't say it with conviction.

"Fine." I recapped my mundane morning. Getting up. Feeding the cat. Packing up the food. Loading the van. Calling Marigold. "At eight, I went to wake Tegan, but she wasn't there."

"Once you got to the shop, what happened?"

I replayed those movements. Parking the van. Noticing the crowd. Wedging through the throng to the front door. Seeing Piper and Graham, as well as Noeline and her boyfriend. "Everyone was concerned. I told you, Graham spied Marigold in their neighborhood earlier, didn't I?"

"You did. Did you believe his account?"

"He didn't seem to be lying, but I'm not a human polygraph." As much as I might like to be. I hated when people lied to me. Did Zach's ruse of going on a hike constitute one? "Look, I loved Marigold. I would never—"

He held a fingertip to my lips. "*Shh.* I know. I just wanted you to repeat your account, to make sure I hadn't misunderstood any of it. In the early stages of an investigation, we have to pay attention. Stories change. Alibis fluctuate."

Needing to cool my jets—he didn't really suspect me, did he?—I downed another cookie. After a long silence, I said,

"Tegan and I are going to have a memorial tea for Marigold. That's okay, isn't it?"

"You can have a memorial anytime."

"You're invited, by the way. It'll be at Feast for the Eyes. Two weeks from yesterday." I told him our plan to honor Marigold's favorite book by serving food appropriate to the Regency Era and that we'd be asking attendees to wear costumes.

"Unique idea."

We sat in reverent silence for a moment.

"Why was she holding *Pride and Prejudice*?" I murmured, my voice rife with emotion. Not knowing the answer was driving me nuts. "It's got to be significant. There were all those other books to choose from."

"How are Tegan and her sister and mother?" he asked, avoiding my question.

"Half sister," I corrected. "They're managing. Tegan and Noeline went to church." I set the pita wraps on paper plates and pushed one in his direction. "Did you find fingerprints on the books that buried Marigold?"

He cocked his head. "Are you trying to wheedle information from an officer of the law?"

"You aren't naïve enough to believe I'd go on a hike with you and not ask questions."

Another smile pulled at the corners of his mouth, but he tamped it down.

"Did you?" I pressed. "You dusted the books. There was gunk on them. Did you dust the door handles? Was everything wiped clean?"

"We think the killer used gloves."

"Of course. So you didn't find any telltale DNA."

He hummed.

"Or did you? From the struggle? Did Marigold scratch the killer?"

He didn't answer.

I twisted the pita wrap on my plate but didn't pick it up. "How did the killer get in? Through the rear entrance?"

"Both doors were locked."

"A closed-room murder," I said, a touch of awe in my tone. I enjoyed reading closed-room murders. There were plenty written during the Golden Age of Detective Fiction by authors like Christie, Sayers, and Marsh, but my latest favorite was a present-day mystery titled *Under Lock and Skeleton Key*, about a female magician who moved home to help her father. His construction company built secret staircases.

"It wasn't necessarily a closed-room murder," Zach said. "If the murderer had a key to the shop—"

"Tegan did not kill her aunt!" I didn't mean to sound so shrill, but I had to defend my friend. "Sorry."

"You care. I get it."

"Noeline didn't do it, either. Or Chloe. Those are the only people who have keys."

"What about the cleaning crew?"

"Yes, I suppose they'd have one," I conceded. "Which means there could be others that have access, like a pest control company," I said, recalling that mine had a key to Dream Cuisine. "Or the alarm company. Or the IT guy who overhauled the shop's computer system last month."

"For your information, we found Marigold's set of keys."

"Meaning the killer didn't take them."

I recalled an event a couple of weeks ago when Marigold was searching for her key ring. She always hung it on a hook on the pegboard behind the desktop computer. Mumbling that she never misplaced anything—*never, never, never*—she scrounged through drawers, in the wastebasket, under the counters. Frustrated to the point of breaking, she wondered aloud if she was losing her mind. When she cried, "Here they are!"—they were stuffed into a remote corner of the shallow pencil-and-pen drawer and hard to see upon first glance—I laughed along with her and told her how many times I'd lost a measuring cup or cookie cutter to a remote corner of a kitchen drawer.

"What about the empty envelope?" I asked. "Do you have any idea what was inside it? Like money or jewelry or a document? Could whatever it was be crucial to the investigation?"

"The techs are studying it."

"I noticed they bagged the empty water bottle and the teacup filled with tea."

"They procured a lot of things."

He took a big bite of his sandwich, I nibbled the corner of mine, and the two of us fell quiet again. For a long while, we listened to the sound of birds chirping in the trees.

When a squirrel skittered up the trunk of a nearby redbud, I dared to pose another question. "Lillian said your people were searching the alley behind the shop. Did they find any clues, like footprints or, I don't know, dirt deposits, or . . ." I twirled the hand holding the wrap.

He frowned.

"C'mon. Give me something." I dropped the wrap on my plate. "How about the bruise on Marigold's neck? Did the coroner determine if it was caused by a book nicking her?"

Zach took another bite of his sandwich and pointed to his mouth, meaning *too full to speak.*

I narrowed my gaze, sensing I'd landed on something. "Okay, a book didn't do it. What else might have caused it? Did the killer inject her with something, like a heart-stopping poison or a sedative, so he or she could overpower her? Done hastily, that might leave a dime-sized bruise. The last time I had blood drawn at the blood bank, the volunteer was in such a hurry that she poked me too hard, and the crook of my elbow turned black and blue."

"It's a bruise," he said. "Nothing more, nothing less."

"That's it? That's all you're going to give me?"

He swallowed hard and set his wrap aside. "Look, you've known Tegan since you were a girl. Does she have a knack for science?"

I squinted. What an odd question. "Um, yes, she won the science fair in her freshman year of high school, and she—" I halted as dread crawled up my esophagus. "Marigold was poisoned, wasn't she? It was murder." I held up a hand. "Tegan didn't do it. She gave up science and computers and everything geeky when she fell in love with the written word." Booklovers could be geeks, too, but that was beside the point. "Plus she has an alibi."

"Which she won't divulge."

My appetite vanished. I packed up my pita wrap and stowed it in the backpack. "She was with a girlfriend."

"Name?"

"I don't know."

"Sounds lame."

It did, but I didn't want to give voice to my own doubts. The cool air cut through my clothes. I began to shiver.

"Let's go," Zach said. "I'm chilly, too." He held out a hand to help me off the blanket.

The scent of him, all rugged and leathery, made me want to grasp the collar of his plaid shirt and pull him close, but I held myself in check. Right now, he was the enemy of my friend.

"Want to grab a beer at the Brewery?" he asked.

"You're not mad at me for prying?"

"Like you said, I expected you to ask questions. I simply can't provide more answers."

"At least tell me whether or not Marigold was poisoned," I said, batting my eyelashes as Piper had at Graham yesterday morning—and hating myself for it. I was not an eyelash-batting kind of girl.

"Yes."

"With what? Arsenic? Strychnine? Cyanide?" No, none of those. They would have made her vomit.

"With tetrahydrozoline."

"Never heard of it."

"It's a decongestant used to relieve red itchy eyes, readily available over the counter. It can come in nasal spray and eye drop forms." Then he gravely added, "I'm warning you if that information gets out, I'll know you're the source. We haven't looped in the media."

On the drive to the pub, I gazed out the window, drinking in the waning sun, the wisps of clouds striating the sky, and the distant skyline of Asheville. I had enjoyed living in and near Charlotte, but I was so glad I'd moved home. I loved Bramble-wood. The Blue Ridge Mountains. The beauty. The art scene. The local flavor. Our town was large enough to be designated a city but small enough for me to know just about everyone I ran into.

We entered the Brewery and found two swivel chairs at the bar. Katrina was tending, but her typically flashy smile was missing in action. By now, I imagined she'd heard about Marigold's death and was in mourning, like the rest of us. However, the moment she spotted Zach, she perked up.

"Hello, handsome," she said in typically sassy fashion. She wiped down the counter in front of us as we sat, tossed the towel in the sink behind the bar, and set down two cocktail napkins. "Long time no see."

"I've been working a few cases," Zach said.

So the Brewery was one of his hangouts, too. We obviously came in on different nights of the week. Otherwise, I would have noticed him.

"Allie, I'm sorry about Marigold," Katrina said. "I heard you were there. At the shop. You found her. That had to be awful. Is that why you two are hanging out?" She gazed between us, as if trying to figure out if we were on a date. "Are you swapping stories? Can you share any details?"

"No," Zach and I said at the same time.

Katrina threw up both hands. "Okay. No prob. I care, you know. Marigold was good people. I was never a reader before going to Feast for the Eyes. I'd like to see justice served."

"Wouldn't we all," I muttered.

Zach ordered a Spruce Goose for each of us. I wasn't hungry, but he requested a hot soft pretzel with spicy mustard, saying he'd share if my appetite returned.

After setting our drinks down, Katrina said, "I have to leave in thirty. This is my one early shift a week. So, if you don't mind, I'll ask you to settle up."

I reached for my purse.

Zach said, "I've got this."

He paid the thirty-dollar charge with a couple of twenties and told her to keep the change. Big tipper, I noted. She thanked him with a wink.

Both of us swung around on our chairs and nursed our beers while watching a Charlotte Hornets basketball game on one of the TV screens. There wasn't any sound. Closed captions were turned on.

"Do you like basketball?" Zach asked.

"I do. I was a point guard in high school." A player in that position was expected to run a team's offense by controlling the ball and making sure it got to the right teammate.

"Ha! I would have thought you'd devoted all your time to reading."

I smiled. "A girl likes to run. And a bossy girl likes to be in charge."

He chuckled. "Did your dad play?"

I nearly did a spit take with my beer. "My father? He has never worked up a sweat. He is a dollars-and-cents guy." All his life, Jamie Catt had relished working with numbers. After graduating college with a master's in economics, he became a venture capitalist and ranked right up there with the best. That was how he and Fern had earned enough money to become world travelers. "No, a guy friend in junior high taught me moves."

"I'll bet he did."

I punched his arm.

Katrina brought the pretzel with three choices of mustard and told us Wallis would be tending bar when she left.

Wallis had a winsome smile but was reserved in a dainty kind of way, reminding me of Jane Bennet in *Pride and Prejudice*. Jane was modest and sweet-tempered and quick to defend someone when Elizabeth suspected them of having shortcomings. Even Wallis's delicate cameo necklace made me think of jewelry Jane might wear.

"Need anything?" she asked as she swapped out our cocktail napkins for new ones.

"I'll take another Spruce Goose," Zach said.

"One's my limit," I answered.

Wallis pulled a tap and filled a new glass with the golden liquid. She brought it to Zach, checked over her shoulder, and leaned in, voice hushed. "You're handling the murder, right?"

Zach's eyes widened. "I'm off duty."

"Yes, but you're it. The lead guy."

"Why?"

"I really liked Marigold."

"We all did," he said.

"Well, Marigold and Katrina argued last week."

"What about?"

"I'm not exactly sure, but I heard Marigold say, 'Don't be catty,' and Katrina said, 'If anyone finds out, I'll know it was you who told them.'"

I shuddered, recalling the warning Zach had given me at the end of our hike.

Wallis worked her teeth over her lower lip. "I don't usually talk out of school, and I really like Katrina, but she seemed steamed. Later on, she was in the staff room slamming doors right and left."

If anyone finds out what? Did Marigold discover a secret that Katrina would have killed to keep quiet?

CHAPTER 8

*"All this she must possess, and to all this she must yet add
something more substantial, in the improvement of her mind
by extensive reading."*

—Fitzwilliam Darcy, in Jane Austen's *Pride and Prejudice*

Working at home with the kitchen door closed, I prepared a variety of doughs and batters and finally slogged to bed at half past eleven. But who could sleep? I tossed all night thinking about Tegan and why she was being circumspect with me. If she was innocent—of course, she was innocent!—she knew she could tell me anything. She couldn't have been stalking her soon-to-be ex if he was out of town. Was she embarrassed about whatever she'd been up to? Wasn't she more concerned about being considered the number one suspect in her aunt's murder? I also couldn't stop mulling over what Wallis had told me and Zach. Had Marigold stumbled onto Katrina's secret, or had Katrina confessed to Marigold, hoping she would give her advice and take the secret to her grave? The notion made me shiver.

At five a.m., Darcy picked up on my frazzled mood and crawled up the comforter to my face. He nuzzled my nose with his.

"Yes, sir, it's time to rise and shine," I said. "Mondays wait for no one."

He meowed.

"Of course I'll feed you." I chuckled. The cat was like a teenager with a hollow leg. He never gained weight, even though he ate twice as much as my previous cat.

I scrambled out of bed, my feet instantly chilled by the wood floor. I slipped on my fifteen-year-old moccasins—I'd never replace them if I could help it—fed Darcy, did my ablutions, and took twenty minutes to perform my stretches, a habit bred in me by my high-school basketball coach. I'd jog in the afternoon if I could fit in the time. Then I slipped on black leggings and a white V-neck sweater and packaged up all the baked goods.

At seven a.m., I was out the door. At nine, after all the deliveries were made, I went to the grocery store to pick up supplies so I could test out a few of the recipes for the memorial, and I proceeded to Dream Cuisine. I emptied everything onto the granite counter. Herbs and veggies to the right, meats and liquids to the left. I made a pot of coffee at the Cuisinart beverage center and switched on music.

While sipping coffee and listening to Haydn's Symphony No. 94, "Surprise," a lilting air with occasional cymbal clashes, I began preparing the veal stock for the white soup. Making stock wasn't for the faint of heart. It could take hours. The recipe I'd stumbled upon asked for three pounds of veal chops, one small chicken, a bunch of vegetables and herbs, and twelve whole cloves. To allow the stock's flavor to mature, after removing and shredding the cooked meat to save for later, the recipe instructed me to let the stock sit refrigerated overnight. I'd be adding cream, almond milk, and breadcrumbs to the recipe tomorrow.

While I chopped and diced vegetables, I ran through the clues Zach had revealed so far.

"Tetrahydrozoline." I processed thoughts better when I said

them out loud. "It's found in nasal sprays and over-the-counter eye drops."

I recalled Zach asking whether Tegan was good at science. Would an amateur chemist like her know the drug's effect? How would it have been administered? What if the killer held Marigold steady with one hand, thus causing the bruise, and shoved her backward? She hit her head on the counter, which dazed her. While she was incapacitated, the killer lowered her to the floor and poured the poison into her mouth.

I gasped as another scenario took shape. "The empty water bottle," I said aloud. "What if the killer laced Marigold's water with poison? Does it have a taste? I don't have a clue. What if she drank it, with the killer present, and suddenly realized she'd been poisoned? Panicking, she groped for balance and knocked books to the floor. In her last-ditch effort, she seized *Pride and Prejudice.*"

I texted the theory to Zach. To my surprise, he responded within seconds with a frowning-face emoji. Did that mean I was on the wrong track, or that he was upset with me for touching base? I pushed the latter notion aside and pondered another angle.

"How did the killer get inside the shop?" I murmured. "Did Marigold let him . . . or *her* . . ." I paused on that notion. Which was it? "Did she let him or her in, or did the killer have a key?"

Again I recalled the incident when Marigold had searched for her keys, only to find them stuffed at the rear of a cluttered drawer. Was it possible the killer swiped, copied, and replaced the shop's keys, accidentally putting them in the wrong spot, and then waited until Saturday to use them? Who would have had access to her key ring? I supposed a customer could have easily nabbed it off the hook where it hung on the pegboard behind the desktop computer.

I bundled sage, bay leaves, rosemary, and thyme in cheesecloth and added the bundle to the soup. "If I'm right, that means Marigold didn't die at the hands of a robber. It was, indeed, planned."

I poured myself a second cup of coffee and queued up another piece, Beethoven's "Sunset, The Return to Ulster." A renowned Beethoven historian once said of Beethoven's Irish folk song arrangements that they had a sophisticated artlessness. I would agree.

I resumed stirring the soup, and my musings about the poison continued. "A robber wouldn't have come armed with tetrahydrozoline. A knife or a gun would have done the job faster. On the other hand, a person who knew about Marigold's valuables, and had been staking out her house in order to follow her, might have known about her dehydration issue."

Needing more than my own agreement to work through the clues, I phoned Tegan to see if she could break free from the shop for a bit. She said when customer traffic died down, she would come over, but at the moment, the place was overrun with people wanting to know where the murder happened. She couldn't leave Chloe on her own.

"Why do you want to see me?" she asked.

"I was wondering if you, your mother, or the bank might have a record of valuables Marigold kept in her safety-deposit box."

She didn't.

"Also would you bring a list of Feast customers who might be doctors or scientists or even food-safety experts?"

"Are you investigating?" Tegan asked.

"I'm thinking outside the box."

Seconds after I ended the call, my cell phone jangled. I glanced at the readout, expecting it to be Tegan saying she couldn't make it, but it was my mother.

I pressed Accept. "Hi, Fern. Is everything okay?" My parents seldom telephoned me. They texted photos of their adventures. "Is Jamie okay?"

"Your father is fine. You worry too much."

I did, because I'd had to grow up faster than other kids. When I turned five, my parents encouraged me to make adult-type decisions. I established my own eating and sleeping schedules. I created menus. I cooked dinners.

"What about you, Allie?" Fern asked. "We read the news about the murder."

Be still, my heart! My mother never wanted to know how I was doing. And since when did she and my father read the news? All my life, they'd acted like ostriches, keeping their heads in the sand as it pertained to world events. Oh, sure, Jamie read articles about economic trends, and Fern received direct feeds from journals that would inform her about statistical physics, combinatorics, and other mathematical break-throughs. She didn't want to be distracted by *real* news.

"Are you all right?" she asked. "Marigold Markel owned that bookstore you love."

My head started to spin. My mother actually remembered which bookstore I patronized?

"I'm fine," I replied, "but we're all heartbroken. Marigold was so lovely. She didn't deserve—" My voice trembled.

"Tell me what happened. You were there. What did you see? Will you solve the mystery?"

I gulped. Had she mentally picked up on my morning musings? No way. She did not have ESP. She disdained all things magical or paranormal. "Me? Solve it? Get real."

"Cookie, c'mon."

That was the one endearing phrase she had ever called me. Never "sweetie" or "honey." I had to admit that I liked the nickname. Although my parents had granted me a lot of lee-way growing up, they had put their feet down when it came to eating anything sugary. A cookie a week had been their one in-dulgence. Odd, wasn't it, that my baking skills became my strong suit?

"You were never good at math, Allie. You could barely grasp

the square root of anything. But you've always been a mystery buff."

Hello. Was that a compliment?

"Do you remember when you were a girl and you wanted to grow up to be Nancy Drew or Judy Bolton?"

Or Trixie Belden, I added to the list, a famous teenaged detective who'd struggled with math, as I had; although chemistry, which was akin to baking, I'd grasped. Go figure.

"What are you trying to say, Fern?"

"Don't trust the police to do their job. They never have and never will. Solve this murder yourself."

Yes, my parents had a beef with the police, because twenty years ago, someone stole my father's prized chess set, and the culprit was never apprehended. The chessmen, rare collectibles from Thailand, never showed up on the open market, either, suggesting a collector must have swiped them.

"That's not true, Fern," I said. "The police get it right ninety-five percent of the time." I happened to know, because I'd viewed BPD's statistics when I'd checked out Zach on the police forum. Yep, the moment I met him, I'd wanted to know more.

"All I'm saying, Allie, is she was your friend. Your mentor. And Tegan's aunt." Tegan was the only friend my mother had ever liked. "You have every right to investigate."

"Okay, thanks, Fern. Say hi to Jamie. Um, where are you?"

"Timbuktu."

"No, really."

"Really. We've visited the Djinguereber, Sankoré, and Sidi Yahya mosques. They're from Timbuktu's Golden Age. And we've viewed so many ancient manuscripts I'm starting to speak Korya Chinni. That's a Songhay variety."

Good to know. Not.

"Plus we visited the Grand Marché. That's their bazaar. Jamie is an incredible haggler. He negotiated for a Tuareg knife and paid half the asking price. I purchased a *unique* bangle." She stressed the word, meaning it was not in the least rare, implying the vendor had tried to snooker her, but she'd been on to him. "You cannot get one-of-a-kind anything for ten American dollars, but it's pretty."

I considered Katrina's bracelet fetish and wondered if that could have anything to do with her secret. What if she'd stolen a bracelet? What if she was a kleptomaniac and had lifted other things?

"You know, a fair rule of thumb," my mother continued, "is to offer about a third of the first price they quote. That way, when they haggle, you counteroffer and wind up paying half."

She'd shared this advice in the past, but I would never need it. I had no desire to go to a market and barter for anything. I'd wind up paying double.

The front door opened and Tegan strode in.

"Fern, I've got to go. Tegan's here."

"Tell her hello."

I blew a kiss. She didn't blow one back. I stuck out my tongue as I pressed End.

"Let me guess, your mother?" Tegan asked.

"Yep." I loved Fern, but she could rattle me.

"Here are the things you requested." Tegan handed me a cluster of three-by-five cards bound with a rubber band. "Man, Auntie was old school when it came to her records. Card catalogues. Rolodex. All of which she duplicated on the computer." She shrugged out of her jacket to reveal a T-shirt featuring an angry-looking Pokémon Pikachu. My guess? She'd worn it to convey her inner feelings. *"Mmm."* Her nostrils flared. "That smells fragrant. What is it?"

"My first attempt at white soup. I want it to be perfect for the memorial."

"I'm detecting a hint of cloves."

"More than a hint."

"Where are your parents this time?"

I told her.

"Who the heck goes there?" She threw her arms wide. "Isn't it dangerous?"

"So is Bramblewood. In our sweet little town, we have murder."

"Allie, how . . . how Bingley sister of you. That was insensitive." Tears sprang to her eyes and leaked down her cheeks. She mopped them with her fingers and licked them off her lips. "Honestly!"

"Sorry." I rounded the counter and clasped her in a hug. "You're right. It was crude and thoughtless. Forgive me." I was testy because of the conversation with Fern. Was my mother right? Would the police mess up the investigation? Did I have to intercede? I released my pal and sorted through the packet of three-by-five cards. "Do you know the customers personally?"

"Every one of them. I can't imagine any is a killer. I work with two of the nurses at the blood bank. One of the doctors delivers babies. The other one is a psychiatrist who treats PTSD. They're all good souls. Why did you ask for their names?"

"It's a hunch." I couldn't tell her about the tetrahydrozoline or the fact that Zach had been asking about Tegan's science skills. He'd made me swear. "Look, this morning, I've been going over the clues the police have so far."

She shuffled to the tuxedo-cat cookie jar I'd added to my work kitchen for a touch of home, reached in, and withdrew a sugar cookie. She downed it in two bites, then fetched an *I Love Bramblewood* mug, one with a cute Deco image of the town's buildings, and poured herself a cup of coffee from the Cuisinart beverage center.

"It's cold," I warned. I'd switched off the machine after my second cup. "Use the single-serve option on the right."

"You have a microwave." She zapped her mug for one

minute, pulled it out, and took a swig. "*Aah.* So much better than the crud Chloe made this morning. I swear, why can't she measure properly?"

"She probably has a pod-style machine at home and never has to."

Tegan perched on a stool and wrapped both hands around the mug. "Talk. Why do you know which clues the police have so far?"

"Zach invited me on a hike, and—"

"*Ooh.*" She waggled her eyebrows in comic fashion. "You and Zach went on another date?"

"Don't get ahead of your skis. It wasn't a date. He cajoled me into it in order to question me."

"The devil. He doesn't think you're guilty, too, does he?"

"No. And because I'm crafty, I was able to pry a few tidbits out of him."

"Like . . ."

I filled her in on the ones I could share. That gloves were used, meaning the killer left no prints. That the techs were studying the empty envelope. "Maybe they'll find something on the envelope that will prove the killer's identity." I told her about the police locating Marigold's keys and that both doors of the shop had been locked.

She bobbed her head. "The police asked me for names of services Auntie might have given her keys to. There were four. Did you learn anything else?"

"No," I said, hating that I couldn't spill the tea. "We went to the Brewery later on."

"That's definitely a date!" She thrust a finger at me.

"Possibly. I don't know." I pulled items from the pantry so I'd be ready to make my baked goods, once I was done with the meat stock. "While we were enjoying our beer, Katrina left for the night, and Wallis took over the bar shift." I recapped Wallis's account.

"What do you think Marigold discovered?" Tegan asked.

"No idea. The police will question Katrina." I wondered if Zach had followed up on that yet.

"Mom chatted with the estate attorney. He said he'll present Auntie's will tomorrow morning at ten a.m. He'll meet us at Feast for the Eyes. Will you come? I don't think I'll be able to handle Vanna with only Mom as backup."

"I'd be glad to support you."

"FYI, my lovely sister sent a scathing response to my text about the memorial. She's such a diva."

It was to be expected, I supposed.

"Did you tell Zach what Lillian's customer said about seeing something suspicious at Graham Wynn's house?" she asked.

"I did."

"And?"

"He'll be checking that out, too."

Tegan glanced at her watch. "You know, I have time before I have to relieve Chloe. Can your stock sit?"

"It needs to simmer for two hours."

"Perfect. I've got an idea. Come with me. I'm driving." Tegan didn't wait for me. She slipped on her jacket and raced out the door.

"Be there in a sec," I called after her.

Rather than leave the stock on the stove with an untended gas flame, I transferred it to a slow cooker and set it on low with a two-hour timer. I snatched my coat and scarf and zipped after my pal.

She'd parked her MINI Clubman, a black-and-white version that suited her, in the driveway.

"You added a new sticker," I said.

"Yep." The rear bumper was plastered with clever sayings she'd purchased online, like *Only ugly people tailgate* and *I brake for goth girls*. The newest read: *Equality is not rocket science.* "Auntie always told me to make a statement, so I do."

"Where are we going?" I buckled my seat belt.

"To my aunt's neighborhood. I want to see for myself what Celia Harrigan saw."

Marigold had lived in a charming home on Oak Knoll Lane, north of Main Street. Most of the houses in the area were Queen Anne style architecture. Many boasted wraparound porches and steeply pitched roofs. Marigold's was a simple pale blue with white trim.

"That's Graham's house." Tegan parked and pointed across the street.

It was anything but subtle. Though it was white, the trim was a mishmash of pink, blue, lavender, and yellow. The steps leading to the front door were painted a bright bold coral.

"He once told Auntie that he finds color stimulating. His store, GamePlay, is painted ten different colors."

Each to their own, I mused.

"Look!" Tegan exclaimed. "There's the letter carrier. Let's ask him if he's noticed anything weird lately. In particular, a week ago Saturday." She bounded from her car.

The letter carrier, an older guy with a weathered face and thinning hair, was on foot, a mailbag slung across his hefty torso. His truck was parked at the far end of the street.

"Sir!" Tegan waved as she approached. "Do you have a minute?"

"You bet I do." He grinned. "Wait a sec. I've seen you around here. You're Marigold's niece."

"That's right."

"Aw, what a shame. I liked her a lot. She was good to everyone except—" He balked. "Nope. Nope. I won't speak out of turn."

Tegan exchanged a look with me and refocused on the man. "C'mon, who wasn't she good to? You can tell us."

He shifted feet. "Well, see, it was Graham Wynn who was the object of your aunt's disapproval. Why, the other day, she was going at him something fierce. Finger wagging. Stomping her foot."

I couldn't see Marigold ever stomping her foot, but if she was having a heated argument, she might have. She'd told Tegan she hoped Graham would get his act together. "What did they argue about?" I asked. "Did she accuse him of spying on her?"

"Don't know."

"Did he throw loud parties? Did he use the wrong color palette for his house? Did he leave his trash cans by the curb too long?" I had a neighbor who despised when people did that, claiming it made the neighborhood look bad.

"I was too far away to overhear."

"Could she have been upset about the loiterer?" Tegan asked.

"What loiterer?"

"Celia Harrigan saw someone in a hoodie hanging around Graham Wynn's house a week ago Saturday. She thought the person might have been staking out my aunt's place."

"Haven't seen anyone in a hoodie." He scratched his stubbly chin. "But I've got a regular schedule. If Celia Harrigan saw someone before or after my shift, I could've missed them. Why don't you ask her? Celia!" He waved to a woman strolling down the street. There were no sidewalks, just gravelly dirt berms that could make walking on them treacherous. "Hiya, Celia." He winked at us. "We all go by first names around here." He raised his hand in greeting again. "Ma'am, these young ladies have a question for you." He bid us good day and proceeded on his route.

Celia Harrigan, a full-figured woman in a knee-length coat and exquisite boots, reminded me of Darcy's pompous aunt in *Pride and Prejudice*. Lifting her chin, she approached us with a skeptical gaze. "Who are you, and what is your need of me?" Even the tone of her voice matched what I thought Lady Catherine would sound like.

Tegan explained our purpose.

"That's correct. The person had on a gray hoodie," Celia replied. "Whoever it was also wore nondescript boots. You know the kind. Unisex, I think they're called." She sounded dismissive of the term. "However, I can't affirm that the person was watching your aunt's house. It was a supposition. Perhaps the individual was checking out the street action before sneaking to the rear of Graham's house."

"Why would you presume that?" I asked.

"Because I've seen others stealing to the rear yard, always during the day, some very early in the morning. I can't say for certain"—she tapped a finger along the side of her fleshy cheek—"but Graham has been acting strangely. Lately those beady eyes of his dart this way and that. I've been wondering if drugs might be involved. I happen to know his business has been suffering. Perhaps he's a dealer."

That was a huge leap.

"If drugs are involved," Celia went on, "then it's possible the person in the hoodie had nothing to do with Marigold."

CHAPTER 9

"There is a stubbornness about me that never can bear to be frightened at the will of others. My courage always rises at every attempt to intimidate me."

—Elizabeth Bennet, in Jane Austen's *Pride and Prejudice*

On the way back to Dream Cuisine, Tegan and I discussed what we'd discovered. Not much, truthfully. Was Graham Wynn taking or dealing drugs? If so, what kind? Anxiety meds to keep him calm, or more serious drugs that had made him a slacker in his business? Did Marigold find out about the drugs? Did she threaten to turn him in? If that was the case, why didn't he kill her at home? Did he worry that the police would suspect her neighbors? What if, instead, he followed her to the shop that morning and killed her after I spoke to her, and then he mingled with the crowd, hoping his presence might be considered proof that he was innocent?

Tegan pulled in front of my kitchen. Her lip was quivering. "Auntie didn't deserve to . . ." She hiccupped.

I rested a hand on her shoulder. "Breathe, pal. We're going to figure this out."

"Will you tell Zach what we've dug up?"

"You bet. Go to work. Occupy your mind. And tonight, binge-watch musicals with your mother. You two love musicals. Find that one starring Gene Kelly and Leslie Caron."

"An American in Paris."

"Yes! I'll see you tomorrow at ten."

She swiveled in her seat and threw her arms around me. "Thank you."

When I entered the kitchen, the aroma in the place was incredible. I did love the scent of cloves, and when mixed with fresh herbs, divine. I turned off the slow cooker, removed the veal chops and chicken from the pot, and set them on a cutting board fitted with a juice groove. When they'd cooled for ten minutes, I cut away the meat from the bones, shredded it, and stored it in a glass food container.

An hour later, when the temperature of the stock had reduced enough, I covered the pot, arranged it on a trivet in the refrigerator, made three dozen scones and two dozen muffins—Tuesday's orders were minimal—and headed home.

When I walked in, Darcy was on his cat-scratching llama station. He gave me an annoyed look as if to say, *Where the heck have you been?*

I stroked him under the chin. "Life got in the way."

He heaved a sigh and twitched his tail, signaling he was ready for our game of Pounce.

"Uh-uh," I warned. "No."

He trilled, *Please?*

"Okay, one time." I took the mouselike catnip toy off the llama, threw it beneath the living-room couch, and stared at my cat. I held his gaze for a full ten seconds before lifting my chin and nodding abruptly.

Responding to the command, Darcy flew off the llama and tackled the toy. Prey conquered, he leaped to the top of the llama and dropped it proudly at his feet.

"Good boy! My turn for a little exercise."

I took a late-afternoon run and felt revitalized.

An hour later, after showering and changing into my comfy

pajamas, I fed Darcy his favorite tuna and decided it was time to feed myself. I'd skipped breakfast and lunch, but I wasn't very hungry, so I threw together a batch of my go-to comfort food, mac 'n' cheese. Using three to five cheeses made the difference. Then, taking my advice to Tegan, I carried my dinner to the living room, nestled on the couch, and switched on the TV. I couldn't find *An American in Paris,* but I spotted *Singin' in the Rain* in the On Demand list and clicked on it. Humming along with Gene Kelly and Debbie Reynolds, I ate a bowlful of my cheesy goodness. By eleven p.m., I felt like I'd been knocked in the head with a sledgehammer and crawled into bed.

Tuesday morning, following my deliveries, I went to Dream Cuisine to finish up the white soup. I added breadcrumbs and fresh herbs bundled in cheesecloth to the pot of refrigerated veal stock, set the soup on the stove to simmer, and decided to test out a recipe for the traditional English tart Maids of Honor, which consisted of a puff pastry shell filled with sweetened cheese curds, but I'd use locally-sourced strawberry jam in my rendition.

While the pastries baked, I tasted the white soup. It was nice and savory. Hurrah! I switched off the heat and let it cool and retreated to the office to throw on the black slacks, smoky-gray silk sweater, and black short-cropped jacket, which I'd brought along. I figured if I was going to meet an attorney, I should dress appropriately.

When the pastries had cooled, I boxed them up, covered the soup pot, and arranged it on a trivet in the refrigerator, freshened my makeup, and drove to Feast for the Eyes.

Noeline Merriweather was waiting outside the shop when I arrived. I bussed her cheek. She'd been crying. How I wished I could comfort her better, but I was feeling forlorn, too.

"Why are you standing here?" I asked. "Didn't you remember to bring your keys today?"

"I did, but . . ." She dabbed her eyes with a tissue. "I didn't want to go in alone."

"Tegan and Chloe aren't here yet?"

She shook her head, removed a key chain from her purse, and unlocked the front door.

I went in first. There was definitely an emotional gloom in the shop. I placed the box of pastries on the sales counter, flipped on the lights, and kicked on the heater. I went to the audio system, as Marigold had been inclined to do, and queued up some classical music. The lyrical strains of Bach's Cello Suite No. 1 in G Major, "Prélude," started playing through speakers mounted above the desk. It was a beautiful rendition. Yo-Yo Ma's notes were pure, his dynamics exquisite.

Tegan, clad in a thigh-length black sweater over black jeans and boots, rushed in a few minutes later. "Mom, you're early!"

"You know me," Noeline said. "I hate to be late."

"Like Allie." Tegan gave her mother a hug. The two stood that way for a long time before releasing one another.

"Nice getup, pal," I said. Give her a cowboy hat and a gun in a holster, and she could have been the villain in a shoot-out.

"You should talk. You look like you work for a mortician." The instant the words flew out of her mouth, she gagged. "Oh, oh, oh. I'm so sorry. I'm a horrible human being."

"Gallows humor," I said. "It's to be expected."

"Where's Chloe?" Noeline asked as Tegan tossed her purse under the sales counter.

Tegan checked her watch. "She usually arrives closer to ten." Store hours were ten to six. "Are those treats, Allie?" She motioned to the box of pastries.

"Maids of Honor."

"Yum." She helped herself to one and cooed her approval. "Best ever. Auntie would be as pleased as punch." She offered one to Noeline, but her mother declined.

Vanna swept into the shop next. "What are you doing here,

Allie?" she demanded, her imperious attitude intact. She adjusted the fake-zebra tote, which was wedged beneath her arm. It clashed with her leopard-skin dress and rhinoceros-studded belt, unless, of course, she was going for the full-on, tasteless-tourist, African-safari look. The way she was glowering at me made me flash on the snake, Kaa, in *The Jungle Book*. That character had scared the bejesus out of me when I'd read the story, and I would never forget its sibilant, silky voice in the Disney movie version. I'd had nightmares for days.

"I'm moral support," I said.

"You're not welcome."

"I invited her, Vanna. Cool your jets," Tegan said, displaying more backbone than usual.

You go, girl.

"Please, everyone." Noeline sighed. "Let's be civil."

Chloe bustled into the shop at five to ten and said she'd make coffee. Tegan winced but didn't argue. Beneath her overcoat, Chloe was wearing another black dress as formfitting as the one she'd worn on Sunday. At least, she'd donned her signature red boots and a red-themed silk scarf to add a pop of color.

At exactly ten, Mr. Tannenbaum, a thin sixty-something man in a pin-striped, three-piece suit, strode through the front door. He introduced himself. Tegan informed him that I would be sitting in. He didn't quibble.

"Where shall we meet?" he asked.

"In the conference room," Tegan said.

It was hardly a conference room. No bigger than eight feet by eight feet, it was the space where Marigold would bring buyers interested in viewing rare books and first editions. Those books were kept in the office in a polyurethane-painted wood case lined with acid-free paper. The temperature in the office was a steady sixty-five degrees, and a dehumidifier kept the room free of moisture.

"This way," Tegan said, leading everyone through the archway into the stockroom.

The space had the delicious aroma of hardcover and paperback books and held the promise of adventure. Unopened boxes were stacked on top of one another and lined one wall. New books, as well as returns—books that would revert to publishers because they didn't sell—filled two floor-to-ceiling shelves. A beverage station, small table with two chairs, refrigerator, and microwave abutted the remaining wall. Marigold's office was to the right. The conference room lay to the left.

Tegan pushed the door open and let everyone file in first. In the center of the room was a blond oak table surrounded by six chairs.

"Please sit," Tannenbaum instructed, taking a chair. He set his briefcase on the table, popped it open, and pulled a folder from it. Then he leaned forward on his elbows, fingers interlaced. "Now, then, I'm sorry about the loss of your sister," he addressed Noeline, "and your aunt," he said to Tegan and Vanna. "She was a lovely woman and will be greatly missed. I remember many times coming to this bookshop and discussing what I should read next. She certainly had her opinions." His smile was genuinely warm, and I could see why he was good at his profession. It couldn't be easy drawing up wills, finalizing trusts for people, and conveying the news to those who'd lost loved ones.

"To the business at hand," he went on, opening the folder. "I'll start at the top. It's all straightforward. First of all, Marigold leaves her house to Vanna and Tegan."

"Her house?" Tegan said almost reverently. "But Mom—"

"Sweetheart, these are your aunt's wishes," Noeline said. "Go on, Mr. Tannenbaum."

"If neither of you want to buy the home from the other, it will be sold at fair market value, and the proceeds split evenly."

Next he outlined the division of the personal property.

Marigold stated that Noeline had everything she'd ever need, so the furniture, books, and household items would be divided equally between Vanna and Tegan.

Chloe traipsed in, pushing a food cart that held a pot of coffee, mugs, sugar, cream, napkins, glasses filled with ice water, and the Maids of Honor, which she'd arrayed on a plate. She positioned the cart against the far wall. "If you need anything else—"

"Leave." Vanna flicked her fingers.

Chloe glowered at her but politely closed the door as she exited.

I proceeded to pour coffee, taking requests for sugar and cream. Tegan passed them around and set the plate of pastries in the middle of the table.

Vanna said, "What do you think you're doing? Take these away. We don't want to get jam on any of the documents."

Tegan threw her the evil eye as she bussed the goodies back to the cart.

"Now, to the matter of her savings accounts and jewelry," Tannenbaum went on.

"About her jewelry," I said, wondering again if Marigold might have been carrying a piece in the empty envelope. "Did she store it all—"

"Hush, Allie!" Vanna ordered. "No one gave you permission to talk."

"Darling, please," Noeline said.

"Don't 'darling' me, Mother. Someone's got to take control here or things could get out of hand."

Noeline drew in a sharp breath. Tegan moaned. I gritted my teeth.

"Proceed," Vanna said to Tannenbaum.

Before he could, the door to the room opened, and Zach stepped inside. "Good morning." He looked more formal than I'd ever seen him, in a blazer, shirt, and slacks.

"Detective Armstrong," Noeline said, "do you know Mr. Tannenbaum?"

"We've met," Zach said. "I'm sorry to meet you again under these circumstances." He made eye contact with each of us. I couldn't decide if he was pleased to see me or not. His expression was unreadable.

Maybe he tracked me down to talk about my water bottle theory, I thought hopefully, but quickly revised the notion. No one but the people present knew I was here.

"What brings you in, Detective?" Noeline asked.

"I was summoned."

"By whom?" Noeline arched an eyebrow.

"By your daughter Vanna." Zach pulled a white envelope from the inside of his jacket pocket. "She left this letter on my desk, with a note that I'd find her here and to come at once."

"What's in the letter?" Noeline asked, her voice crackling with tension.

"As your elder daughter intimated the other day, it is a letter from Marigold to your younger daughter stating that she will inherit a portion of the bookstore."

"No way!" Tegan's eyelashes flickered. "I never received any such letter."

"Oh, but you did," Vanna said with a bite. "Because I found it at your house between your trash bin and your desk."

"What were you doing rooting around my things?"

"I didn't believe you when you said Auntie never sent you the letter. I saw it with my own two eyes in her home office. And it was stamped. I knew she must have sent it, and, voilà, she did."

"I . . . I . . ." Tegan sputtered. "You planted it."

"I did no such thing."

"You must have. You're a . . . a . . ."

"Tegan, chill." I reached over and patted my pal's arm. "Take a breath." I regarded her half sister. "Vanna, was the letter opened or was it sealed?" She didn't respond. "Is it possible it fell to the floor and Tegan never saw it?"

Vanna squirmed.

Zach cocked his head. "Ms. Harding, did you open this without your sister's permission?"

"I knew what it was," Vanna said in her defense.

Noeline clicked her tongue in disapproval.

"This is nuts," Tegan said. "I did not kill Auntie to inherit the bookshop. Detective"—she pushed away from the table and scrambled to her feet—"I'm telling the truth. I never read that letter. Never even saw it. And Auntie never said anything to me. *Ever.*"

Vanna scoffed.

Tannenbaum said, "Shall I continue?"

"Yes," Noeline said.

"No!" Tegan shouted. "I want to know when you broke into my house, Vanna."

"Hello?" Chloe pushed the door open, knocking as she did. "I hate to intrude, but, Tegan, you have a visitor."

"Who?" she asked rather sharply, and immediately blanched. "Sorry, Chloe."

"That's okay. It's—"

"It's me." A frizzy-haired redheaded woman with tired eyes peeped past Chloe. "You asked me to meet you at noon." She had a haunting whiskey voice. "But I have to get to work, and I wondered if you could—" She stopped short, suddenly realizing the room was occupied. Her cheeks blazed with embarrassment. "Oh, gosh. I'll . . ." She hooked her thumb over her shoulder. The sleeve of her green sweater slid up her arm revealing multiple bangles. "I'll wait out here."

"No, Dennell, wait," Tegan said. "Detective, could my friend and I speak with you privately?"

"Now?" Vanna asked. "We're in a meeting."

"Dennell is my alibi for Saturday morning," Tegan said.

"Let's hear it." Vanna folded her arms.

"What she has to say is private and not to be shared with a room full of strangers." Tegan eyed Zach. "Please, Detective. Allie, you come, too. It'll take three minutes. No more."

Tegan ushered Dennell into the stockroom. Zach and I followed.

Standing there, I eyed the knob and dead bolt on the exit door and noted, as I'd remembered, that two keys would have been required to enter from the alley. Did everyone who had keys to the shop have the two, or only a copy of the one to the front door? Was that relevant?

"This is what went down," Tegan said. "Dennell Watkins and her partner make high-end arty jewelry. They sell it online."

Zach stared at Dennell. She began chewing the thumbnail on her left hand. Her other fingers looked raw from similar attacks.

"Her business partner can be very prickly," Tegan went on. "They used to be best friends, but things have gotten sticky. It's not easy to run a business."

I eagle-eyed Tegan, mentally urging her to get to the point, or Vanna was going to blow a gasket.

"Dennell's partner has accused her of stealing from the company coffers," Tegan continued.

"I h-haven't stolen a dime," Dennell rasped. "I'm just not good with numbers. Balancing books is tricky for me. I make mistakes, so there are lots of erasures, and . . ." She cleared her throat, sounding as if she might choke.

I fetched her a paper cup of water. She thanked me and drank the liquid greedily.

"The reason I was with her that morning . . ." Tegan began to explain. "The reason I've kept quiet about it—"

"I'm an alcoholic," Dennell blurted. "Last week, I made a real mess of the books, so I decided Tuesday night to go cold turkey. No more booze ever. By Friday night, I was having the DTs."

"Delirium tremens," Tegan said.

Dennell nodded. "I was shaking and icy cold, but sweating, and I was really confused. I texted Tegan after midnight—"

"At three," Tegan cut in.

"That I needed help. Someone I could trust."

"I went right over," Tegan continued, "because if her partner finds out, she'll end the partnership, like that." She snapped her fingers. "She's an extremely religious person and inserted a temperance and noncompete clause in their partnership contract. She will get the business outright if she finds out Dennell breached it. Dennell could lose everything. That's why I kept quiet."

"I'm planning to ask her to buy me out," Dennell said, "but if she can end our deal without paying me a nickel . . ." She spread her hands. "She's miserly enough to do something like that. Religious or not, to her, money is everything. I was a fool to go into business with her."

"Detective Armstrong," Tegan said, "I contacted Dennell this morning saying we had to talk after the appointment with Mr. Tannenbaum. I wanted to convince her to meet with you. But then, you showed up and she arrived early, so . . ." Tegan rotated a hand. "It's Kismet, right?"

Zach studied Dennell and Tegan. "How do you two know each other?"

Tegan smiled. "Dennell likes any kind of mystery or romantic suspense where jewels are involved. I've been advising her for a couple of years about what she should read. We became friends."

"Good friends," Dennell said.

I'd never spent time with Dennell, and didn't know the extent of their friendship, but Tegan didn't know all my friends, either. Wasn't life funny that way? You could hang out with people, could know them since kindergarten, and, yet, unless you purposely made an effort to introduce one friend to another, they might never meet.

"Is there anyone who saw the two of you together?" Zach asked.

Dennell said, "A delivery guy for Big Mama's Diner brought over really strong coffee and glazed donuts. I had a craving for sugar." Big Mama's was one of my clients. The cream-cheese–filled coffee cakes I sold them were one of their biggest draws. I didn't sell them donuts because, one, I didn't make them, and two, the diner created their own, using an in-house machine. "He might have seen Tegan."

Tegan shook her head. "I'm not so sure. I was in the bathroom at the time. But he might have heard the toilet flush."

"I'll need the guy's name," Zach said to Dennell.

"He's the really skinny one with spiky hair." She gestured to hers, a tad erratically, and quickly tucked her hands under her armpits. "He's twenty or twenty-one, I think."

After a long moment, Zach said, "I hope you'll seek treatment. My ex-brother-in-law is an alcoholic. He's been sober ten years and continues to go to AA meetings."

Ex-brother-in-law? Did that mean the brother of an ex-wife or the husband of a sister? How little I knew about Zach, but wanted to know more.

"I agree," Dennell said. "I'm hoping I can do it as an outpatient."

"I have a contact for you." Zach pulled out his cell phone and texted the information to Tegan. Her mobile pinged. "Get help, and you"—he aimed a finger at Tegan—"work things out with your sister."

CHAPTER 10

"You showed me how insufficient were all my pretensions to please a woman worthy of being pleased."

—Fitzwilliam Darcy, in Jane Austen's *Pride and Prejudice*

Vanna and Noeline were chatting between themselves when Zach, Tegan, and I reentered the meeting room. Mr. Tannenbaum was consulting his cell phone.

"Well?" Vanna demanded.

"Your sister is innocent," Zach said matter-of-factly. "All of you may proceed with the business at hand. If you have any further clues as to who might have killed your aunt, don't hesitate to contact me. We appreciate all tips." He turned to leave.

"Detective, do you have suspects?" Noeline asked, her voice plaintive.

"Ma'am, we'll keep our findings to ourselves, but rest assured, we're doing all we can."

"Zach," I began, hoping to pull him aside and ask about the water bottle theory.

"Not now, Allie," he said. I must have flinched at his curtness, because he said, "Sorry, but I've got to go."

When he closed the door, Tegan and I took our seats, and Tannenbaum resumed, declaring that most of Marigold's jewelry went to Vanna and Tegan.

"Most?" Vanna asked.

"Most," Tannenbaum said with no inflection. "I'll read what

Marigold wrote. 'Noeline, if I do not outlive you, as well I shall not, I know you are well-off and do not need my money or personal items to sustain you. Therefore, in remembrance, I give you my treasured Georgian-style trembling floral brooch. You have always admired it.'"

Noeline moaned and pressed a hand to her chest.

Tannenbaum continued, "'Wear it well and often. And know that I will love you forever.'"

Noeline sucked back a sob.

"There are a few more items to contend with," the lawyer went on. Humming, he flipped a page. "Regarding the cash on hand and in savings—"

"Mr. Tannenbaum," Vanna cut in. "I want to know what happens to the bookshop."

He cleared his throat. "Fine. We'll divert to there." He turned over a few more pages. "As you know, Noeline, your sister owned three-quarters of the bookshop, with you owning the final quarter."

"Yes."

"Your portion remains untouched, per your contract. However, as to her three-quarters ownership, half the bookshop will go to Tegan, and—"

"I told you!" Vanna cried.

Tannenbaum held up a hand. "I quote, 'My niece Tegan is the reader in the family. She will cherish and foster the bookshop and its customers, thus giving my sister, Noeline, freedom to pursue her own dreams.'"

"I read!" Vanna said.

"Cookbooks," Tegan taunted.

Vanna jumped to her feet. "Why, you—"

"Sit!" Noeline ordered. "Girls, listen through the entire presentation, please. Vanna, your aunt has left you a very wealthy young woman, and you will be happy with whatever she doled out to you. She could've disinherited you, but she didn't."

"She wouldn't have."

"She had a mind to. Your acerbic ways were never to her liking. I begged her to be kind."

"Are you . . . *kidding?*" Vanna sputtered, her eyes wide.

Tannenbaum continued where he'd left off. "Half of the bookshop's ownership will go to Tegan, and the remaining quarter—"

"Will go to me," Vanna stated.

"No." The attorney eyed me. "Ms. Catt, I'm glad you're here, because the final quarter will go to you."

"Me?" I squawked. "But I never . . . Marigold needn't . . ." I felt my pulse racing. "I didn't ask for anything."

"She'll own the same percentage as our mother?" Vanna squealed. "That's insane."

"Ms. Catt, Marigold treasured you as a friend and fellow booklover," Tannenbaum went on, nonplussed. "She wrote, and I quote, 'Allie Catt questioned me, challenged me, and drove me to read outside my comfort zone. I hope that becoming part owner of the bookshop she loves so much will bring her great joy.'"

Tegan grasped my hand and squeezed. "Partners."

Vanna jumped to her feet. "This is ridiculous! You killed her, Allie. Admit it!"

"What?" I barked, my blood seething. "You're nuts!"

"She did it." Vanna aimed a finger at me.

Noeline said, "Vanna, hush."

"No, Mother, Auntie was out of her mind. Obviously, she told Allie what she'd written in her will, and Allie took the bull by the horns and—"

I launched to a stand, one fist raised.

Vanna went silent and folded her arms. Her nostrils flared.

It took all my willpower not to blurt a comeback, such as *Were you born this stupid or did you take lessons?*

"Allie, please sit," Noeline said softly.

Rolling the tension from my shoulders, I complied and muttered, "I loved your aunt, Vanna."

She made a dismissive sound—no apology—and resumed her seat.

"Moving on," Tannenbaum said in an effort to rein in the volatile proceedings. "Regarding the cash on hand, Marigold left one hundred thousand dollars to the Bramblewood Community Theater Foundation."

"Whoa, hold on!" Vanna thrust her hand into the air. "That's a lot of money. What if someone who works for the foundation killed her so the funds would get to them sooner rather than later?"

"Vanna!" Noeline scolded. "What a horrid thing to say. Those people adored your aunt. Mind your tongue."

Tannenbaum turned to a previous page. "Whatever cash remains will be equally divided between Vanna and Tegan."

"Well, at least you didn't get any money, Allie," Vanna said nastily.

Tannenbaum closed the document and laid it on the table. "Thus ends the reading of the will of Marigold Markel." He folded his hands. "I've arranged with Ms. Ivey, the manager at Bramblewood Savings and Loan, to review all the assets your aunt held. Here is her card." He handed it to Noeline.

Vanna plucked it out of her mother's hand and took a snapshot with her cell phone.

"If you need anything further, do not hesitate to call." Tannenbaum returned items to his briefcase, nodded to Noeline, Tegan, and me, but he avoided making eye contact with Vanna.

After he exited, Vanna gave her mother the business card, announced that she would be in charge of securing a Realtor to appraise the place, and added that she didn't need a house. Therefore, they would sell it. I wondered how Tegan felt about that. With a divorce imminent, she might want to keep it. Would whatever cash Marigold had bequeathed her be enough to buy out Vanna?

"You handle the bank, Tegan," Vanna said. "Give me a report."

"Oh, now you trust me?" Tegan asked, sarcasm oozing out of her.

"If you're innocent, you're innocent. It's water under the bridge. Forgive me for implying that anything improper occurred."

Tegan shimmied her disgust.

"Regarding the bookshop," Vanna continued, "honestly, Auntie was right. I don't give a darn about it. It's yours and Allie's." She uttered my name as though it was a curse word. "You two can bury yourself with work, while I continue to thrive as the premier caterer in town." She threw the last comment in my direction.

I didn't take the bait. I smiled sweetly at her. As a girl, I'd had years of practice responding to bullies. They'd taunted me about my looks and how old my parents were.

Before Noeline could caution her eldest daughter to cease and desist, Vanna paraded out the door.

"Partners," Tegan said. "We're going to be partners."

I couldn't wrap my head around it. Why me? What did Marigold think I could bring to the table? Sure, I'd led a few book discussions, and yes, I was an avid reader, but why not give all three-quarters of the bookstore ownership to Tegan? My pal and I would have to talk about what she expected of me. I wasn't going to give up my job as a caterer, but I supposed I could devote a day or two, or, at the very least, afternoons, to the enterprise.

When we emerged from the conference room, the bookshop was bustling with customers. Like the Scarecrow in *The Wizard of Oz*, Chloe was standing behind the sales counter jutting her arms right, left, and crosswise giving directions.

Tegan clasped my arm. "This afternoon, will you go to the bank with me? That way, I won't miss anything Ms. Ivey might say. You know me when my brain gets flooded with too much information."

"Sure." She was exaggerating. She could process data as quickly and efficiently as a computer, but I could see she was feeling overwhelmed after the reading of the will.

"I have to admit I'm surprised Vanna didn't demand she take the lead at the bank," she said. "Auntie's house obviously captured her attention. Shiny objects and all that."

I chuckled.

Noeline wrapped Tegan in her arms and petted her hair. "Darling, I know you loved your aunt. I'm sorry that your sister is . . ." She couldn't finish.

"Is a gray sprinkle on a rainbow cupcake?" I quipped.

Tegan cackled, and gave me a high five for coming up with the retort. "Isn't that what you were going to say, Mom?"

"Something like that." Noeline kissed Tegan's cheek. "Call me if you need me for anything." Tears sprang to her eyes.

"Are you going to the B and B?" Tegan asked.

"No, I'm off to have lunch with Rick." She waited for a second, as if hoping Tegan would say, *Have fun,* but Tegan didn't. Mopping the tears with her pinkies, Noeline followed a customer carrying a large Feast for the Eyes tote bag out the front door.

For a few minutes, I lingered at the shop and directed eager readers to the proper aisle, while Tegan and Chloe concluded sales.

When the place quieted down, I drove to Dream Cuisine. I spent the next couple of hours finalizing orders that were due to be delivered tomorrow: two dozen blueberry scones for a startup café; four dozen iced cookies for Jimmy Madison's birthday party; six dozen mini spinach quiches, three dozen mozzarella-stuffed mushrooms, and four dozen bacon-wrapped jalapeño peppers for an office party at Legal Eagles, one of my steadiest gigs. The spicy aromas of the appetizers tickled my salivary glands and made me hungry. While the scones and cakes baked, I noshed on bacon bites, tiny morsels of bacon wrapped around melon and sprigs of rosemary. *Yum.*

While icing the cookies, which I'd made in cowboy boot shapes, seeing as the birthday boy desperately wanted to grow up to be a sheriff with a horse, I mulled over the foods I still wanted to taste test for Marigold's memorial. Tarts. Tea sandwiches. I knew how to make trifle, but I decided I needed to bake at least one pound cake. I hadn't made it in years.

At one p.m., Tegan arrived and said she would drive.

Bramblewood Savings and Loan, one of the first banks established in town, was located on Main Street, east of Mountain Road. Like the other buildings in town, it was red clapboard with white trim. In the main room, customers were waiting in a cordoned-off line for two clerks to attend to them. To the right, small offices were fitted with desks for all advisors. We strode to the manager's reception desk and gave our names. The assistant escorted us into Ms. Ivey's office, a formal room with dark brown furniture, one potted plant, and three filing cabinets.

Ivey rose to greet us and dismissed her assistant. "Ladies." A stately woman, she reminded me of the original Miss Moneypenny in the James Bond novels. Her eyes were cool and quizzical, her demeanor reserved and official.

After Tegan introduced me and explained that I was purely there for moral support, the bank manager led us to the vault of safety-deposit boxes so we could inspect Marigold's container. The room smelled like metal and some kind of cleaning solution. After the gate was locked and we were alone inside, she gave Tegan a key, retaining a duplicate for herself, and together they inserted their matching keys into the locks of Marigold's box and twisted. A *click* was heard. The box jutted out an inch. Ivey slid it from its slot and set it on the felt-topped cabinet in the center of the room.

She lifted the lid and removed a sheaf of papers, which had

been tucked into a clear pocket folder. "This is a list of the contents of the box. I have a duplicate in your aunt's folder on my desk." One by one, she laid the items on the felt and, using a pen, marked them off against the list. "'Tiffany diamond ring, value twenty thousand.' Check. 'Blue antique cushion lab diamond ring, value nineteen thousand.' Check. 'Late-Victorian old-mine diamond cluster ring, value sixteen thousand.' Check."

Tegan gasped. "I had no idea Auntie had so many costly keepsakes. I mean, I knew she appreciated antique jewelry, but all I remember seeing are knickknacks, you know? I thought the mainstay would be funky rings picked up at garage sales and pawnshops."

Ivey added more rings to the collection, reciting each piece's worth. Then she moved on to the bracelets. "'Bulgari serpent bracelet in blue rose gold with sapphires, fifteen thousand. Elizabeth Locke Venetian glass, ten thousand. Hermès *Dans les Nuages* Art Deco bangle, four hundred dollars.'"

Tegan pointed to the latter. "Okay, that's the kind of jewelry I thought she owned. Glitzy, trendy stuff. Why did she have so many items worth thousands? She rarely wore any of them. Wait until Vanna finds out."

"Is anything missing, Ms. Ivey?" I asked, once again picturing the empty envelope at the crime scene.

"No, I don't believe so." She regarded her list and counted again. "Wait. A ring is gone."

"Which one?" Tegan asked.

"'A diamond-and-ruby target ring, circa 1920, value seventy-nine thousand dollars.'"

"I remember that ring," Tegan said. "Auntie told me all about its history. It was worth seventy-nine thousand?"

"At purchase, that was the cost. The value will have gone up by now."

"Did Marigold sign out the ring?" I asked.

"Yes. *Phew.*" The bank manager looked visibly relieved.

"There's a slip I overlooked. She often withdrew jewelry and brought it in a week or so later."

"So it's most likely at her house," Tegan said. "I'll bet Vanna knows where it is. She's a snoop. She'll have gone through all of Auntie's closets and drawers by now."

Why would Marigold have removed that particular ring? Did she plan to have it resized? Or cleaned? Had she intended to wear it to the community foundation tea? It wasn't on her hand the day she died.

"This piece." Tegan indicated the Georgian-style trembling floral brooch that featured dozens of hand-cut diamonds. "It's the one my mother inherits."

I said, "It's gorgeous."

"She'll never wear it," Tegan said. "She'll be too nervous."

"She needn't be," Ivey said, her mouth curving up at the corners. "Each item is insured, and your aunt prepaid the premium for ten years. I'll convey that to your mother."

That meant if the ring was stolen by the killer, Noeline could be compensated. I supposed there was some comfort in that.

"Marigold certainly planned ahead," I said. "When did she pay the premium?"

The bank manager consulted her file. "A month ago."

Again I wondered whether Marigold had foreseen her own demise.

"Let's put everything back in the box," Tegan said. "I'll return with my sister, and we'll go through the items together."

When Ivey completed the task and reinserted the box into its slot, she said, "Follow me."

We retreated to her office, and while she fetched water for us, Tegan and I sat in a pair of chairs facing the desk.

"Can you believe it?" Tegan whispered. "We won't have to worry about sales to keep the bookshop going, and if we have to, we can sell off jewelry to keep afloat for years."

"Not we. *You.*"

"You're my partner now."

"About that . . ."

She held up a hand. "Uh-uh. I will not allow you to give your portion to me or Mom, and I sure as heck won't let you bequeath it to Vanna."

I chuckled. *As if.*

"Auntie wouldn't want me to hawk the jewelry, but if I have to, I will. The bookshop was her baby."

"Here we are." The bank manager laid cocktail napkins on the small table between our chairs and set down the glasses of water. Then she perched on the ergonomic chair behind her desk and opened a folder. "Now I'll fill you in as to the cash on hand, as well as to the significant value of her stocks and bonds."

"Auntie had stocks and bonds?" Tegan pressed three fingers to her lips, thoroughly dumbfounded.

I batted her arm. "You didn't know? Are you saying I knew more about your aunt than you did? She told me she'd invested."

"She told me, too," Tegan said, "but I had no idea they would have a *significant* value. How much are we talking?"

"Over a million dollars," Ivey replied.

Tegan whistled.

"The man Marigold was to marry," I said, to enlighten Ivey, "not only left her his estate, but he was wise in matters of finance and taught her everything he knew." Marigold had regaled me with stories of their blossoming love. Sometimes I'd wondered if she'd embellished their history, merely to keep the spark alive, but after seeing the jewelry and hearing about her portfolio, I realized she hadn't inflated any of it. She'd promised to teach me some of her investment tricks but hadn't gotten around to it. "Your mother must have known your aunt's net worth," I added. "That's why she chided Vanna."

Ivey said, "In addition, she had over seven hundred thousand dollars in cash."

"Seven—" Tegan cut herself off. "Vanna is going to be miffed that she didn't come along on this visit."

Ivey passed an envelope embossed with the bank's logo to Tegan. "I have another for your sister. Pull out the sheet of paper. At the top, you'll see the stocks, starting with Apple and Google."

I craned my head to get a peek at Tegan's list. Ivey hadn't misrepresented anything. Tegan and Vanna were going to be very wealthy women, and if Tegan wanted to buy Vanna out of the house, she would be able to do so.

Tegan muttered, "Crud."

"What's wrong?" I asked.

"I just realized my husband will get half of everything I inherit."

"No, he won't," I said. "In North Carolina, separate property refers to assets or debts owned by one spouse individually."

"Really?"

Ivey nodded.

"Separate property is considered all property," I said, "whether real estate or personal property, that has been acquired by a spouse prior to marriage or attained by gift or inheritance during the marriage. All you have to do is keep anything you inherit in your own account, not a joint account."

"How do you know so much about this?" Tegan asked.

"A customer at the Eatery sheltered his money from his wife, paying for all things household-related from their joint account and giving her a monthly allowance, as if she was an employee. When they divorced, he was able to pay her a flat sum. He was a scoundrel."

"I'd like to be a scoundrel, too." Tegan smiled. "Ms. Ivey, can you make sure I do it correctly?"

"Contact Mr. Tannenbaum. He can advise you," she suggested. "By the way, Marigold withdrew a large amount of cash recently."

"When?"

"Friday, at the end of day."

"After I deposited the weekly take?"

"That's right."

Tegan said, "How much?"

"One hundred thousand dollars."

I gawked. She'd come here after she'd fainted? Was she of clear mind or still dazed? "Ms. Ivey, did she tell you why she needed it?"

"It wasn't my business."

"That's a lot of cash to be carrying around in a purse."

"Oh, she didn't put it in her purse. She asked me to slip it into one of the bank's envelopes, and then she stowed the envelope in the brown leather satchel she'd brought along. I presumed she intended to hand it over to someone."

CHAPTER 11

"My good opinion once lost, is lost forever."

—Fitzwilliam Darcy, in Jane Austen's *Pride and Prejudice*

"Would you come to the bookshop with me?" Tegan asked while shifting her car into gear. "I need time to process this. Why would Auntie withdraw one hundred thousand dollars?"

I buckled my seat belt. "Maybe she wanted to give the theater foundation the money she intended to bequeath to it on Saturday rather than make the foundation wait for her to, you know . . ."

Tegan moaned. "To die."

"Yes . . . No," I said, quickly revising as something niggled at the edges of my mind. "Wouldn't she have consulted Mr. Tannenbaum if she'd decided to do that? And don't you think she would have delivered it in the 'Private and Confidential' envelope Ms. Ivey put it in, which was found empty at the crime scene?"

"Ms. Ivey didn't say anything about a 'Private and Confidential' envelope. She said she put it into a bank envelope, and Auntie slotted the envelope into her satchel."

"You're right! Do you remember seeing your aunt's satchel at the shop?"

"Yes. It was tucked under the sales counter. The police went through it. They didn't find any cash or bank envelope in it."

We both fell silent. Cars whooshed by.

A recent exchange with Marigold came to mind. Last week, when I went to Feast for the Eyes to pick up the Jenn McKinlay mystery I'd preordered, she asked me if I'd read Grisham's *The Firm* or *The Whistler,* or Puzo's *The Godfather.* I said yes, I'd read all three—each of the books had bribery as a theme— but before we could discuss them, a customer entered, desperately in need of a book for her granddaughter's birthday, and I had to depart to deliver lemon-lavender scones to a client.

"Or . . ." I said softly, letting the word hang.

"Or what?" Tegan glanced at me.

"What if someone wanted to blackmail her?"

"No, no, and no. Auntie never did anything wrong in her life. She was as honest as the day is long." Tegan took the turns at too high a speed. She'd never been involved in an accident, so I didn't ask her to slow down, but I gripped the door handle in case she was tempting fate.

A minute later, she pulled into her parking spot in the alley behind the shop, and we hustled through the rear door. The aroma of burned coffee wafted to me.

"Chloe," I muttered, and switched off the coffeepot. "Tegan, it's time you invest in a Keurig. It's not worth the waste . . . or the stench."

"You mean, it's time *we* invest."

My head ached at the thought of partnering with my best friend. Would we face the same kinds of conflicts Dennell was experiencing with her business partner? Maybe it would be better if I was a silent partner, like Noeline. On the other hand, I could instigate some specialty events at the shop and drum up business utilizing my catering skills. Throw a few teas. Even open up a small café in the far-right corner. There was room. What kind of license would we need?

We weaved between a new shipment of book boxes, and I said, "I've got an idea. Let's go through your aunt's email and texts and see who she was communicating with. She might have mentioned the cash."

"The police confiscated her phone, and they browsed the shop's computer, as well as her personal one."

"Okay, but how thoroughly?"

She threw me a sideways glance. "You read too many mysteries."

"Get with the times, girlfriend. Fresh eyes on the prize . . . or, in this case, clues."

We passed through the arch to the bookshop and came to a halt. Lots of people were browsing books in the aisles. A line of customers was waiting at the sales counter ready to check out. Chloe was trying furiously to keep up. Her red scarf was askew. Her usually smooth black hair looked as if she'd combed it with an eggbeater. Evidently, one person managing the bookshop that was overrun with traffic was not enough manpower.

"Oh, good, you're here," Lillian Bellingham said to Tegan. She was standing on the other side of the sales counter. In her tailored 1940s-style suit, with its broad shoulders, tapered waist, and large lapels, she looked like she could be cast in *Witness for the Prosecution.* All she'd need was a fancy fascinator hat to complete the ensemble. "I have sample costumes for the memorial." She'd draped a travel dress bag over one ladder-back chair and had stacked a bunch of hatboxes on the other.

"In a sec," Tegan said, and sidled next to Chloe to tend to customers. "Allie, would you bag the books?"

I saluted.

Lillian said, "Your aunt would be so happy you're having the memorial for her. How she treasured the theater, and she lived for afternoon tea."

Minutes later, when the line of customers had dwindled to one, Tegan rounded the counter and splayed her hands. "Show us what you brought, Lillian."

"What do you think of this little number?" Lillian unzipped the dress bag and pulled out a lacy sage-green gown with empire bodice, puff sleeves, and an elegant train.

"Ooh," Tegan said. "Pretty, but not for me. It's perfect for Allie, though it might need altering. This green is her favorite color. Got anything in blue?"

"Of course, but nothing with anime characters," Lillian teased.

"Ha ha."

"Check out the hats I brought, too." She gestured to the stack of boxes. "Open the top one."

Tegan did and pulled out a baby-blue boater. "Love it."

Lillian said, "It's made of sinamay, with matching ribbon and feathers. I call it the Juliet fascinator."

Tegan positioned it at a jaunty tilt on her head and coyly curled her fingers beneath her chin. "What do you think?"

"Your aunt would approve." Lillian pulled a sage-green bonnet from the second box and handed it to me. "This should look perfect on you."

I placed it on my head, tied the sassy bow, and instantly felt swept away to the Regency Era.

"Why, Elizabeth Bennet, you look ravishing!" Tegan said to me.

"My dear Jane," I said, taking on the persona she'd granted me, "you are a breath of fresh air, but whatever will the men say? Papa would be shocked by the cost."

"Nonsense. Papa will grant us whatever we wish."

The two of us giggled and quickly sobered, realizing we were making sport of costumes meant for a memorial. Tears sprang to our eyes. Tegan removed her hat. I took off mine. And the two of us hugged fiercely.

"Could someone help me?" a woman with blond-streaked hair asked as she approached the sales counter.

"I'd be happy to." I replaced the bonnet in its box and joined her. "What do you need, ma'am?"

"I'm looking for three different things. My daughter wants a YA murder mystery, but it can't be too gory. My ten-year-old son wants something with dragons." She wrinkled her nose. "And my husband wants the latest best-selling thriller."

"Follow me." I'd roamed the bookshop aisles so often that I knew where every genre was located. Marigold had tagged many of the books with BOOKSELLER RECOMMENDS labels, which made it much easier to help the woman. Within minutes, she and I returned to the sales counter with a James Patterson novel for her husband, *How to Train Your Dragon* for her son, and *A Good Girl's Guide to Murder* for her daughter. I'd helped at the register on previous occasions, so I rang her up.

"Now for the men," Lillian was saying to Tegan as my customer was leaving. "I've got all sorts of ideas. Tailcoats, waistcoats, ruffled shirts, cravats. Anyone who wants to dress up should call me, and I'll accommodate them."

The door swung open, and Stella Burberry, another of my private home-meals clients, sauntered in, her gaze taking in the books on the endcaps.

"Hi, Stella," I said.

She was wearing a lavender trench coat, and beneath that, a lavender knit sweater. Her trousers were lavender, too. I bit back a smile. I couldn't remember a time when I hadn't seen Stella outfitted in a single color. Blue one day. Red the next. At a book club event, she confided that dressing in a single color made life easier. She wasn't a fashion guru and trying to assemble outfits taxed her brain. An accountant, she added, was a black-and-white, no-frills kind of person. Tegan once wisecracked that Stella reminded her of a human Crayola. Even the way she piled her lavender-streaked hair on top of her head gave her a pointy look.

Two teenaged girls in raggedy denim jackets and jeans trailed Stella, but I didn't think they were accompanying her. Stella didn't have children. Graham Wynn tramped in after them and shut the door with a *clack*. His nose was red and raw, as though he was fighting a cold. He covered his mouth with a handkerchief. He coughed into it and tucked the handkerchief into the pocket of his dark blue running suit.

"Swell," Tegan whispered. "If he's sick, why doesn't he stay home?"

"Because he's hoping to glean information about the murder," I said.

"Or"—Chloe lowered her voice—"he's returning to the scene of the crime."

"Eww." Tegan wriggled her nose.

Chloe went to help Stella, and Tegan moved to assist the girls.

Slapping on a smile, I approached Graham. "What brings you in?"

"You work here now?" he asked.

"I'm filling in."

He peered past me, as if visualizing where Marigold died.

I clicked my tongue to redirect his attention. Ghouls were unwelcome. Lookie-loos too. How I wished I could wave a magic wand to make all the people who were coming into the shop expressly to see *where it happened* disappear. *Poof!*

"Need a book?" Remembering his penchant for clergy-themed mysteries, I said, "Have you read Julia Spencer-Fleming's *In the Bleak Midwinter*?"

"I have not."

"It's about the first female priest of an Episcopal church in upstate New York. A former army pilot, she locks horns with the members of her congregation, as well as the chief of police until she winds up solving mysteries with him, and they find themselves attracted to each other."

I led the way to the mystery section, pulled a copy of Spencer-Fleming's book off the shelf, and handed it to him. "You live across the street from Marigold, don't you?"

"That's correct." He scanned the book's blurb.

"I was there with Tegan yesterday and ran into your neighbor Celia Harrigan. She thought she saw someone suspicious hanging around your house a week ago Saturday. Did you notice anyone?"

"Nope, can't say I did." He fixed his gaze on mine. "Between you and me, that old biddy should mind her own business."

"I think she was concerned about you."

"Ha!" He tilted his head, assessing me. "She's never been concerned about anyone but herself."

"I think she was also worried that whoever it was might have been spying on Marigold or the neighborhood, in general."

He raised his handkerchief and coughed into it. "Sorry, allergies."

Maybe so. It was April, after all, when everything was starting to bloom. "Also your letter carrier said—"

"What were you doing questioning him?" he demanded.

"Tegan and I were checking out her aunt's house. It's going up for sale." It was a decent dodge. "He was quite friendly and let slip that you and Marigold argued recently."

"We didn't argue. We chatted."

The letter carrier was adamant about the severity of their set-to, so I pressed. "What did you chat about?"

He hesitated, as if framing an answer. "Marigold didn't like the way I cut the hedges."

"Really?" I threw him a skeptical look. "How unlike her to get upset about something so trivial, especially since your house doesn't abut her property."

"She said I was letting the neighborhood down. If you

don't mind, I'm going to check out." He tucked the book under his arm.

To keep him talking, I tapped him on the shoulder, a technique I'd learned years ago when trying to become a teacher. It was a gentle way to refocus a person and regain the lead. "You'll like the book. The character is strong and forthright."

"Like you."

"I suppose." I offered a self-deprecating smile. "By the way, I was wondering why you were out so early last Saturday. You said you saw Marigold around six."

"That's right. I was on my way to work. Like anyone who owns a shop, I have to accept shipments. Restock. That sort of thing." His gaze skated down and to the left. He wasn't scanning the book, so I presumed again that he was trying to formulate a better answer. "Why the twenty questions? Aren't you a baker, or did you recently join the police force?"

"Ha ha. Funny man."

"Some think so."

"While we're on the subject of your business, how's it going at GamePlay? Are you busy? I know café and bookstore sales can be slow until after spring break."

"I get folks all year round. Gamers are dedicated." He marched to the checkout desk, dismissing me.

Lillian was there, reinserting the costumes she'd shown us into the dress bag. She said something to Graham. I heard the word "memorial." He nodded, and she pulled a waistcoat from the bag. She turned it this way and that on its hanger. He appraised it and bobbed his head again, apparently agreeing to rent something like it from her, making me think he intended to attend the memorial. *Interesting.*

The front door burst open.

"Tegan!" a man with wild, curly hair yelled as he stormed into the shop. He was waving a book in the air. "Tegan!"

Tegan left her customers in the YA aisle and rushed into view, eyes wide with alarm. When she saw who was hailing her, her face relaxed. "Mr. Canfield, welcome," she said cheerily.

Canfield. I knew that name. Then it came to me. I'd seen a woman named Candace Canfield playing guitar and singing folk songs at one of the coffeehouses I delivered to. At the time, I'd figured she had to be related to the owner, because she had a shy, reserved voice. Without a microphone, she could barely be heard. Perhaps she was this man's wife. She'd looked the approximate age.

"I've told you, it's Quinby," the man said. "Just Quinby."

"Quinby," Tegan said even more sunnily. "Is your better half Candace with you?" she asked, confirming my suspicion that the singer was his wife.

"No."

I'd never seen Quinby Canfield before. Angular, with jaw-bones that could cut ice, he had a feral look in his eye, like he was itching for a fight, but Tegan seemed steady and unwor-ried.

"I didn't like the beginning of this book," Quinby said. "I want to return it." He shoved it at her.

Tegan inspected it. "The spine is broken."

"Not my fault."

"It was intact when you purchased it."

"Says who?" He balled a fist.

My shoulders tensed. Would I need to intervene? I was big-ger and stronger than my petite pal.

Tegan remained calm and continued to scan the book. After a long moment, she said, "Okay, then. I'll give you a refund. Get in line."

Ugh. Was the customer always right? Would the book now go on the discounted table? How was Tegan staying so non-chalant? I wanted to punch the bully in his pointy nose.

Chloe approached the desk with Stella, who was carrying an

armload of cozy mysteries. From the spines, I could see one was a Honeychurch Hall mystery and another was a Paws & Claws Mystery. I'd read both of the delightful books and couldn't wait for new releases in the series. Stella lined up behind Quinby.

Sotto voce, but loudly enough for all to hear, Quinby said to Graham, "If you ask me, that raven-haired she-wolf Piper Lowry killed Marigold."

I gasped. That was some accusation and some description— yes, Piper had dark hair, but she wasn't at all predatory. In fact, she struck me as a docile woman with a kind word for everyone. Did Quinby know Graham personally, or was he spouting off because he felt Graham was a kindred spirit?

"She's a bad influence on the young," Quinby continued. "She taught my son squat. He had to do an extra year at the JC in order to better his grades before he could get accepted at UNC Asheville. She thinks we all have money to burn."

"Quinby Canfield, that's not true," Stella said. "I know Piper very well. She would never make anyone do an extra year unless he or she needed it. She's devoted to her students."

I'd have to agree. Once when I was browsing the bookstore, I'd spotted Piper with a small group of students she'd brought in on a field trip. She was teaching them in the nook area. Her manner was excellent and enthralling. Each of her students was paying rapt attention.

"Bah, Stella!" Quinby sliced the air with a hand. "Keep your trap shut."

"Do you two know each other?" I asked.

"I'm Quinby's accountant," Stella said. "And I'm Piper's neighbor."

Small world. But, then, Bramblewood's population was a mere nine thousand. Six degrees of separation was a real thing here.

Graham finalized his purchase, threw me a curious look upon exiting, and Quinby stepped forward.

"Piper Lowry is bad news," Quinby continued, palm out, ready for his refund. "That's all there is to it, and I'll make sure the police know it."

"Quinby," Tegan said, "for your edification, Piper and my aunt got along famously. They could wax rhapsodic about any kind of fiction or nonfiction, and Piper is always up-to-date on the latest books her students might enjoy."

"Well," he said, "I don't like talking out of turn . . ."

Sure you do, I thought.

"But I saw her sneaking around the bookshop a few days before the murder, peeking in the windows after hours. Why was she doing that? Not to get ideas for the classroom, that's for sure. My guess? She was trying to find a secret way in."

A niggling sensation ran down my spine as I recalled Chloe saying Piper had seemed more than curious about the murder—so curious, in fact, that she'd come into the shop Sunday under the pretense of needing consoling and asked to see exactly where Marigold died. Was I wrong about her? Did a killer lurk beneath the surface of her sweet personality?

"Quinby, there's no way she killed Marigold," Stella said. "No way."

I hoped she was right.

"Why, I saw—"

"Shut it, Stella!" Quinby said sharply.

The bookshop went deadly quiet. Tegan handed Quinby Canfield his money. He didn't thank her and left with a huff.

When the door banged closed behind him, we all heaved a collective sigh.

"What a tornado!" I exclaimed.

"He's always been like that," Lillian said. "He has a beef against everyone and everything."

"FYI," Stella said, "his kid is a slacker. I know that's not nice to say, but he won't apply himself."

"How does Quinby make a living?" Lillian asked. "I mean, I know he's a landscaper, but I don't know how he makes a go of it. Everything he plants dies."

"He lives frugally." Stella paid for her items, accepted a bag from Chloe, and waved good-bye.

When the door swung shut, Tegan said, "Why would Quinby lash out against Piper? So what if he saw her in the area? Lots of people roam these streets."

Lillian said, "Well, to be truthful, Piper can be secretive."

Being secretive didn't make her a killer. We all kept secrets. The diaries that were wedged between my mattress were filled with them, like the time I'd downed a dozen donuts one Sunday morning at the age of ten, or having a crush on Finn Parker in sixth grade, or making a death wish in tenth grade for Heather What's-her-name. To this day, I couldn't remember her last name. I'd hated her because she told lies about me. The list went on. I was no saint. And I was definitely no angel. But I wasn't a killer.

"Lillian, how is Piper secretive?" Tegan asked as she started to ring up Stella's books.

Lillian zipped the dress bag. "Well, I was making a home delivery in her neck of the woods the other day, a really lovely ensemble that her neighbor ordered for a theater event, and I saw Piper with a younger man. They were standing just inside her front door. Hugging. When she saw me glancing her way, she closed the door."

"How much younger?" Tegan asked.

"Over sixteen but under twenty-one. Her arms were around him."

"He was most likely one of the students she tutors," Tegan reasoned. "I'll bet she was comforting him because he got a bad grade or something."

Lillian clucked her tongue. "It didn't look like a mercy hug to me, but what do I know?"

Uh-uh. I wouldn't go there. Piper was not having an affair with a student, even an of-age student. On the other hand, I swallowed hard. If she was and Marigold found out, would Piper have killed her to keep the secret?

CHAPTER 12

"Books—oh! no. I am sure we never read the same, or not with the same feelings."

—Elizabeth Bennet, in Jane Austen's *Pride and Prejudice*

I couldn't stand it. I liked Piper Lowry. I had to find out the truth. After Lillian and Stella left the bookshop, I pulled up Piper's contact in the Rolodex by the computer and dialed her using the landline.

"Hello? Who is this?" Piper answered breathlessly.

"It's Allie Catt."

"Oh, hi." She whispered my name to someone nearby.

"Piper, I'll be direct. I heard you came into Feast for the Eyes on Sunday."

"Why does it matter to you?" she snapped, then said quickly, "I'm sorry. That was rude. I . . . I miss Marigold. I know you do, too. I can't believe she's dead. I hope the police will find the killer. Do you know anything about how the investigation is going?"

"That's sort of why I'm calling. You see, Tegan is a person of interest." *Was* a person of interest. She wasn't any longer. Zach had cleared her. "She's my best friend. I can't stand for her to be a suspect. So I'm sort of looking into Marigold's murder to clear Tegan's name."

"Aren't the police doing their job?"

"Of course they are. Detective Armstrong is a good cop, but as Hercule Poirot said, 'Suddenly confronted with the possibility of being tried for murder, the most innocent person will lose his head and do the most absurd things.'" I juddered. Who had taken over my body, and why was I spouting famous lines from *Murder on the Orient Express*?

"Are you saying Tegan is acting strangely?"

"Not at all, but I want her to feel confident that no stone has been left unturned."

Piper whispered again to whomever she was with. "Listen, Allie, I've been thinking about Marigold's murder a lot, too, but I'm sort of busy. Can I call you at another time? We can bat around theories. Thanks for understanding. Bye." She hung up.

I stared at the phone wondering why she'd ended the call so abruptly but decided that was not evidence of guilt. She'd sounded as grief-stricken as Chloe had made out. Grappling with the loss of a beloved friend was difficult.

Chloe said, "Everything okay, Allie?"

"Uh-huh."

Tegan sagged against the sales counter, a fresh glass of water in hand. "Is everyone going to have an opinion about who killed Auntie?"

"It's only natural," I said. "Curiosity shows interest, plus we all want resolution."

Chloe ran her fingers through her tousled hair. She turned pale. "Oh, golly, am I a mess?"

"You look a tad harried," Tegan said tactfully.

Chloe stepped into the stockroom to consult the mirror on the other side of the archway and gasped. In seconds, she returned. "Better?"

"Much," Tegan said.

"It's been nonstop today." Chloe resumed organizing books

that customers had brought to the sales counter but hadn't purchased.

Tegan's cell phone pinged. "It's Vanna." She read the message and talked to us as she typed a response. "I'm telling her to come here so I can bring her up to speed about what we discovered from Ms. Ivey, and she can update us about Auntie's house and whether she found any valuable items."

"What did you learn at the bank?" Chloe asked.

Tegan rattled off our findings.

"You and your sister are going to be rich," Chloe said. "Are you sure she didn't kill your aunt?"

"Chloe!" Tegan exclaimed.

Chloe propped a fist on one hip. "She thought *you* did."

"Because of the letter," Tegan replied. "FYI, you should know Allie will be inheriting one-quarter of the bookshop."

Chloe whistled.

Tegan rushed to add, "I'm sure Auntie would have included you in her will, Chloe, if she'd been certain you'd commit to running the shop as your career."

Chloe batted the air. "Don't worry. I won't take offense. I'll come into plenty of money one day. My family's well-off. They've established a trust fund. Besides, I don't want to own anything. I want to be free to go wherever the wind blows me."

"From bookstore to bookstore," Tegan said.

"Well, duh." Chloe pulled a face. "Marigold knew this about me, and besides, she's known Allie forever."

One of my fondest memories of Marigold was when she'd joined Tegan and me for a tea party to celebrate Tegan's birthday. I was eight and attended in pink shoes with satin bows and my prettiest dress, a pink frilly one I'd begged my mother to buy. Marigold gushed about my sense of style. Later, when Tegan opened my gift and saw it was a copy of *A Wrinkle in Time*—would any child ever forget how scary yet exhilarating that story was?—her aunt praised me for being so considerate.

Reading, she said, developed one's mind. After that, Tegan fell in love with fantasy stories.

"I'm excited to have you on board," Chloe said, and hugged me. When she released me, tears sprang to her eyes. "I really loved Marigold. She is going to be missed. She was so wise and, well, you know, so . . . so . . ."

"So Marigold," I finished.

Chloe covered her mouth and fled into the stockroom.

Tegan's cell phone pinged again. "It's Vanna. She can't make it. She'll touch base tomorrow."

The door to the shop opened. Noeline strolled in. Rick followed. Each was holding a to-go cup from Ragamuffin.

"Darling," Noeline said to Tegan. "I stopped by to tell you all the memorial invites have gone out via email, and nearly everyone has responded yes. I've sent you and Allie emails as well, with a head count. I think it's about a hundred."

"A hundred?" I whistled. I'd have to enhance my menu and freeze some baked goods along the way so I'd have enough for everyone. Luckily, I had plenty of time before the event. "The bookshop will be crowded," I said.

"I could apply for an ordinance to allow tables outside," Tegan suggested.

"You'll need to rent heaters."

"Nah. People around here can handle the cool spring weather," she said. "We're cold-blooded."

"Oh, my," Noeline responded.

"Not cold-blooded in *that* way, Mother. Not in the murder-mystery kind of way."

Noeline said, "At least, we can rest assured knowing everyone we're inviting isn't a murderer."

Rick said, "How can you be certain?"

Tegan blinked. "He's right. One might be. Allie, you and I have to keep coming up with suspects."

Noeline gawked. "You two are discussing this?"

"Allie is investigating." Tegan hooked her thumb in my direction. "I'm her sounding board."

I swatted her. "I am not investigating. Not officially. But I am trying to come up with theories that I can share with the police."

Noeline frowned. "The last I knew, neither of you attended the police academy."

"Mo-om," Tegan carped, stretching out the word. "We want answers."

"We all do, darling. Even so, that's no reason for you to put yourselves in harm's way."

"Relax, sweetheart," Rick said. "They're bright young women. They'll be fine." He slung an arm around her and gave her a supportive squeeze. "I'm going to use the restroom in back. I'll be right out. Then let's go to Mosaic. You said there's something you wanted to see there."

Mosaic was a fine-arts shop down the street.

"Yes, let's."

For the next minute, Tegan filled her mother in on what we'd learned at the bank. Noeline wasn't surprised by the value of Marigold's estate. She and her sister had regularly discussed finances.

After she and Rick left, I opened the email Noeline had sent the two of us, and the idea that I'd raised in the car resurfaced. "We need to check your aunt's messages and such."

"I told you, the police took her iPhone."

"Do you know if she was set up for iCloud services? If so, her messages will be stored in the cloud, meaning we can see them on any device."

"You're right. Follow me." She led me to the office, which was fitted with a desk; a metal storage bin; two oak cabinets, which held Marigold's antiquated card catalogue files; a hermetically-designed bookshelf filled with rare books; a pegboard for receipts; and a whiteboard for orders.

On the desk stood Marigold's laptop computer, a Rolodex, and an in-and-out box for orders. I sat in the chair and awakened the computer. I sighed when I realized I needed a password to access it. I asked Tegan if she knew it.

"Type prejudice." She spelled out. *"P-r-e-j-u-d-i-c-e."*

"Really?" I gawked. "Her password is 'prejudice'?"

Tegan said, "Would you have guessed it?"

"Nope."

I typed it in, and the computer came to life. I clicked her email browser, which did not require a password. She had a few new messages—all spam—but I was surprised to learn she had no cache of previous messages. Had she erased them? I was not in the habit of deleting mine. Oh, sure, I eliminated junk, but if I wanted to see a previous message, I stored it in a file I'd named as Future to Keep. Her similarly named file was empty.

"Did she have a computer at home, too?" I asked.

"Nope. She left this one here so she could devote her time to reading at home and wouldn't be tempted to go online." I studied the screen. There were opened documents. "Do you mind if I view these files? I have a bee in my bonnet."

"Be-e-e my guest." Tegan *buzzed.*

I clicked on the Mission Control app. The Calendar page, Browser page, Contacts page, and two Word documents appeared. One of the Word documents was a letter-in-progress addressed to the Bramblewood Community Theater Foundation donors. It laid out Marigold's plan for the year, detailing events and how its funds would be spent. It wasn't complete. It ended midparagraph regarding expenditures, which explained why the document would've been open.

The other file read like the beginning of a mystery novel. It was new and hadn't been saved. It didn't have a title.

"Tegan, look at this."

Chapter One
Heart pounding, Josephine Bellamy stood beneath the
gaslight at Broadway and 34th, the hem of her plaid silk
dress dusting the street. She peered into the dim night.
Which way to go? Where to turn? The killer's threats had
been real, she had no doubt. She knew the truth, but she
dare not tell anyone. She couldn't. If she did, her family
would be a target. Josephine was barely eighteen, but she
knew things other girls her age didn't. Elizabeth Bennet
would have liked her. She observed. She spoke out of turn.
She was always underestimated.

A whisper of fear crawled down my spine.

Tegan whistled. "It's not bad."

"Did she tell you she was writing a book?"

"I didn't have a clue."

To preserve the file, I saved it with a simple title, Marigold_book_draft, and then clicked on the Google browser page. In the search line was the word "gaslight." The initial website listing was the dictionary definition of the word, both noun and verb. As widely as Marigold read, I imagined she knew what gaslighting meant in present-day lingo. Thanks to the classic movie *Gaslight,* with Ingrid Bergman, to gaslight meant to use psychological methods that made a person question his or her own sanity. I guessed Marigold also knew when gaslighting was introduced in New York, so why would she need to research the term? I scrolled down to view other links, all of which pertained to the film.

Wondering what else Marigold might have delved into, I opened her search history and was surprised to see that, except for the current page, it had been cleared out the day she died. Had she done so, or had someone else? Why?

"Who else had the password to your aunt's computer?" I asked.

"Me, Chloe. That's it."

"Then explain this." I pointed to the date when the history had been wiped clean.

She yelled, "Chloe, c'mere!"

Chloe rushed in.

"Did you erase the Internet search history on this computer?" Tegan asked.

"I never touch that computer," Chloe said. "I mean, I can open it, but I never do. Marigold said it was private, and I should only access it in an emergency. I use the desktop in the shop." She hooked her thumb in that direction.

The chimes over the front door jangled. Chloe left to tend to customers.

I revisited Mission Control and viewed the other opened documents. The Calendar reflected appointments for the theater foundation donors' meeting last Friday and the tea scheduled for Saturday. Sunday was blank. On Monday, Marigold was scheduled to have lunch with Evelyn Evers, her second-in-command for the theater foundation. On Tuesday—today—she'd planned to have coffee with Oly Olsen, who owned the Brewery. Why would she have needed to meet with him? Was he a donor?

I clicked on Contacts and saw the *D* page was open. Lo and behold, Oly's contact appeared. The company noted on it was Due Diligence, not the Brewery. Odd name for a parent company. "Due diligence" was a legal term that typically meant conducting research, an analysis, and an investigation to verify facts about a particular subject. Had Marigold called Oly the morning she died or the evening before? I dialed his number on my cell, put the call on speaker, and waited.

He answered on the second ring. *"Ja?"* A hint of his Danish heritage was ever-present in his accent, even though he'd relocated to the States as a boy.

"Oly, it's Allie Catt. You knew Marigold Markel, right?"

"Ja."

"Did she call you the other day?"

He didn't respond.

"A Contact page is open on Marigold's computer, with you listed as the point person for a company named Due Diligence. We're trying to figure out if and why she reached out to you. You were scheduled to have lunch with her."

He remained silent for a long time. Tegan gestured, urging me to squeeze him for an answer.

"Oly? Are you there?"

After a long moment, he said, "She wanted to hire me."

"To do what? To make a private batch of beer?" I couldn't imagine Marigold ordering suds for the theater foundation event, but odder things had happened. Personally, she preferred champagne or wine.

"To look into something for her. I investigate things occasionally," he said obliquely.

"I see," I murmured. "That explains the company name. Due Diligence is a detective agency."

"*Ja.* Years ago, my uncle brought me into the business. He said it would keep me out of trouble when I wasn't brewing. I was a hellion as a teenager."

"Did Marigold give you a hint of what she wanted you to investigate?"

"She asked if I had read *Pride and Prejudice.*"

Hmm. That was odd. "Have you?"

"Indeed. With my girls. When they were in high school. Their mother and I both did. I don't understand the fascination. Marigold said she had a case of pride that needed to be handled. But that was our last phone call. She was going to send me an email explaining, but she didn't. Sorry I cannot be of more help."

I thanked him, ended the call, and slung my arm over the back of the desk chair. "A case of pride? What the heck? Why was your aunt so enthralled with the darned book?"

"Pride could be a code word," Tegan said.

"True, but it doesn't give a hint as to whom she wanted Oly to look into."

"It's time to call Zach. Tell him everything. He'll be open to our thoughts." She jutted a hand.

I tapped in his number. When he answered, I said, "It's me, Allie."

"I've got eyes." He chuckled.

If my name came up on his screen, it meant he'd added me to his contacts. That pleased me. I told him about Marigold's search history being erased and about the phone call to Oly, who happened to be a part-time PI, and about the mission she'd planned to assign him—something that might have to do with *Pride and Prejudice*—but Marigold didn't follow through.

He sucked in air but didn't say a word.

Then I plunged into the rest, ending with the hundred thousand dollars that Marigold took from the bank. "I think she put the bank's envelope into the 'Private and Confidential' one."

"That's conjecture," he said. "However, if she did, it supports my theory that her death was a result of a robbery gone wrong."

CHAPTER 13

She was convinced that she could have been happy with him, when it was no longer likely they should meet.

—Jane Austen, *Pride and Prejudice*

When the shop cleared of customers, another thought occurred to me. I joined Tegan. "Your aunt was going to have lunch with Evelyn Evers on Monday. But what if after she withdrew the money from the bank on Friday, she put the bank envelope into the other envelope and met with Evelyn that evening? She could've kept the 'Private and Confidential' envelope to recycle."

"Meaning nothing was stolen."

"Yes." That would only solve one question about the crime scene, but any little bit helped, right?

Tegan moved to the primary computer and opened the Contacts app. She found the theater foundation's telephone number and punched it into the store's telephone keypad. When someone answered, she gave her name and asked if Evelyn was in. She covered the mouthpiece. "The receptionist is getting her."

I'd met Evelyn on numerous occasions. An ob-gyn until she retired, the successful Black woman had been one of Marigold's best friends. She was intelligent and well-read and a dynamo in the African-American community in Asheville.

"Yes, Evelyn, hi. It's Tegan Potts. Marigold's niece." Tegan paused, and I could see her shoulders shake ever so slightly. She was stemming fresh tears. "Thank you. That's very sweet of you. Yes, she will be missed." Tegan tapped her foot, listening. "Yes, she was a grand, wonderful lady. Um, Evelyn, I have to ask a sensitive question. Did you meet with my aunt Friday evening?" She listened to the response. "You didn't?" Tegan made a face at me. "What's that, Evelyn? Why do I ask? Because Auntie withdrew a large sum of money from her bank account that day, and I met with the attorney for her estate this morning, and he said she was going to leave that same amount of money to the theater foundation." She paused, listened again, then proceeded to speak. "One hundred thousand dollars."

Evelyn reacted so loudly with shock and gratitude even I could hear her from the other end of the telephone call.

"Yes, it's a lot of money," Tegan said, "but my aunt appears to have amassed a significant fortune." She nodded. "Of course. The attorney will make sure the distribution reaches you. It could take a little time." More nodding. "Yes, I know the foundation needs the funds. Tickets? Why, sure, I'd be happy to accept season tickets from you. Thank you for your time. Good-bye." Tegan hung up the phone. "She was crying."

"To be expected. They were contemporaries. For years, they worked together on the foundation."

Tegan sagged and tears trickled down her cheeks.

I threw an arm around her. "Buck up. Hold it together a few more hours. I have to finish up at Dream Cuisine, but afterward I'll make dinner for you at my house, if you want."

"Can't. Sorry. I agreed to have dinner with Mom and Vanna . . . and Rick." Her nose wrinkled with displeasure.

"Any word from your soon-to-be ex?"

"Crickets. Which is fine by me. If he finds out about my inheritance—"

"I told you, he can't touch it. Also you have the right to initiate the divorce, you know. It is not a one-way street."

She wiggled her mouth right and left.

"You'll need to secure an attorney," I said.

"It appears I can afford one now." She folded her arms across her chest.

"Winston is a slug."

"A creep."

"A fool."

"An imbecile, jerk, loser," she said.

"He brings everyone joy when he leaves the room," I quipped.

That made her snort. "That is why I love you." She jutted a finger at me. "You have some of the best comebacks." She knuckled my arm. "Go. Do that thing you're brilliant at. And save me one of everything you make."

"Tomorrow you should show me the ropes here. Teach me what I'll need to do to support you."

"You already know how to do everything better than me." She hugged me. "Love you."

"Love you more."

The weather had grown cooler since I'd entered the bookshop. A stiff breeze was whipping along the street and cut through me. Teeth chattering, I protected my core with my arms and hustled to my Ford Transit. Luckily, I'd invested in seat warmers.

When I arrived at Dream Cuisine, I queued up some jazz music. I didn't want to listen to an audiobook while cooking. I might miss a step in a recipe. The first in the lineup, Kenny G's "Songbird," piped through the Bluetooth speaker. There was nothing like cool jazz to put me in the mood for spending time in my happy place.

For the next hour, dancing slowly in time with the music, I made the batter for the extra scones and cookies I'd need for the memorial and froze it all; then I packaged up the cowboy cookies, inserted the appetizers for the office party into eco-friendly containers, and arranged the scones on pretty party trays, which I would retrieve the following day. After I stowed everything into the walk-in refrigerator—I would deposit it all into the catering van in the morning—I decided to make a detour before heading home.

Wind was whisking through town and kicking up leaves and debris as I drove. I wasn't sure why I wanted to swing by Marigold's house again. Was I silly enough to hope the last few days were all a bad nightmare and I'd see her in her living room nestled in her favorite chair?

Yeah, no such luck. The house was dark and dreary. No exterior or interior lights had switched on automatically. I wondered if Vanna had spoken to a Realtor. If she had, keeping the house dark until it was up for sale could be a tactic. If that was the case, however, why wouldn't she have mentioned it to Tegan when they'd exchanged text messages? Perhaps she would tell her at dinner tonight.

As I passed by, Graham was sitting on a rocking chair on his porch, puffing on a cigarette while peering at a cell phone. The light from the phone's screen illuminated his face. He did not look happy. Not keen to have him think I was spying on him, I sped out of sight.

At home, I slipped on my favorite leggings and a soft hoodie sweatshirt. I didn't have much of an appetite, so I ate a quick snack of cold salami, sliced carrots, and Manchego cheese, and served Darcy a gourmet salmon treat. Then I poured myself a glass of Pinot Noir, set it on the table beside my oversized armchair, and switched on the gas fireplace in the living room. I snuggled into the chair, and Darcy hopped up and curled into my lap. His purring gave me comfort.

I took a sip of wine, set the glass aside, and picked up Christie's *The Murder of Roger Ackroyd* from a stack on the book table. I opened to page one. Minutes later, I realized I hadn't read a word because my mind was too preoccupied with Marigold's death. Though I enjoyed stories featuring Hercule Poirot, I set the book aside and tried to organize my thoughts.

The money. What if the murderer knew Marigold made a withdrawal? Perhaps that person had seen her at the bank and followed her and, like Zach theorized, robbed her. Did that mean it was a random killing? No, that didn't make sense. The timeline wasn't correct. Marigold picked up the cash on Friday. She didn't give the money to Evelyn, and nobody mugged her on the way home, or she would have mentioned it to me when we'd spoken Saturday morning. Of course, that didn't rule out that a thief could've killed her after our phone call. I recalled the previous theory that I'd contemplated. Did Marigold withdraw the money to pay off someone?

Darn it. If only the town's traffic cameras had been operational that morning, then the police could've seen who'd secretly slipped into the shop.

Darcy mewed and pleaded with his eyes for me to refocus.

Who were the likeliest suspects? Katrina's coworker Wallis said Katrina warned Marigold not to divulge a secret. What if Marigold had been researching the topic they'd argued about that morning on her computer? What if Katrina caught Marigold in the process of browsing? Would she know how to erase an Internet search history? Or what if Wallis got the story reversed? What if Marigold was the one with the secret? I recalled the opening of her historical novel. Had she written it to give expression to that secret? What if she'd planned to pay hush money to someone who knew something private about Noeline, Tegan, or Vanna? Would a contemporary like Evelyn know what skeletons Marigold had in her closet?

I picked up the glass of Pinot.

At that moment, something outside went *clack,* followed by a soft *thump.* The sound startled me. I lost hold of the wineglass. It toppled to the floor and, miraculously, didn't break, but the wine splattered.

Darcy yowled.

"Sorry, kitty," I whispered, and petted his head. "It's okay." But was it? My heart was hammering. Was someone on the front porch?

While listening hard, I plunked Darcy on the floor, hurried to the kitchen for a paper towel, and blotted up the mess by my chair. When I didn't hear anything more, I settled down, telling myself the sound must have come from a shutter I hadn't repaired a week ago when a storm had nearly ripped four of them off the front of the house—conceivably, the same storm that had taken out the town's traffic cameras. I'd fixed three of the shutters, but I'd run out of wood screws. I'd made a note to swing by the hardware store for more, but I hadn't gotten around to it.

Darcy mewed. Concerned.

"You're right," I whispered. I was being too lackadaisical. My friend had been murdered. I ought to inspect.

As if on cue, the front door flew open and banged against the wall.

I couldn't see the foyer from where I was sitting, but I wasn't going to be caught unarmed. Adrenaline chugging through me, I leaped to my feet, grabbed the fireplace poker, and hurried to the foyer. No one was there. My tote and keys were on the table, where I'd left them. The doors to the bedrooms were closed. Was it only the wind that had caused the disturbance? Leaves were swirling in a frenzy on the porch.

I rushed to the door, closed and locked it, and set a chair from the parlor against it to act as a barricade. Next I toured every room in the house and peeked outside through the breaks in the curtains. The streetlights were on. I didn't see anyone lurking about.

Even so, I shivered and took the fireplace poker to bed.

"It was nothing," I assured my cat. "Nothing."

I slept fitfully. On Wednesday morning, I decided to check out what I'd been too afraid to examine last night. I dressed in a long-sleeved T-shirt, down vest, jeans, gloves, and Timberland boots, fetched a screwdriver, and went outside. Indeed, the offending shutter was hanging by one screw, and a stool I kept on the porch had toppled. I righted it and climbed up to remove the shutter altogether until I could purchase more screws. My breath caught in my chest when I glimpsed down and saw a partial muddy footprint on the porch, where the stool had been. Male or female, I couldn't tell. Was it mine? I had big feet. In grammar school, Tegan had meanly dubbed them water skis. I'd countered that they'd gotten me where I needed to go. I studied the markings. The imprints didn't match the soles of my Timberlands, not to mention I hadn't donned these particular shoes in over two weeks. I'd worn my REI boots for the hike with Zach.

Had someone been outside last night, after all? Did they bump into the stool when attempting to peek through the window? Was that the thump I'd heard? Had that same person opened the front door but lost control of it in a gust of wind? The notion made me reel. I teetered and grabbed hold of the rickety shutter for support. It couldn't bear my weight and gave way. I toppled to the porch, shoulder first. Luckily, I didn't hit my head or break any bones. However, when I scrambled to a stand, I saw that I'd landed smack-dab on top of the footprint, making a mess of it. There went the evidence. *Shoot.*

Shaken and feeling vulnerable, I scuttled inside and closed and bolted the door. Breathing high in my chest, I made a pot of coffee, fed the cat, warmed a scone, and applied a pack of frozen peas to my shoulder. While I ate my mini breakfast and nursed my bruise, rotating my arm occasionally to keep blood flowing, I tried to figure out who might have visited me last night.

Had Graham seen me driving through his neighborhood and followed me home?

Evelyn Evers couldn't have had an inkling that I'd been standing beside Tegan when Tegan reached out to her yesterday, unless she'd called back and Tegan mentioned my name. Even if she had, why would Evelyn see me as a threat?

Katrina came to mind. If she found out Wallis told Zach and me about her argument with Marigold, would she wish to do me harm? That was a stretch, though. Zach was a much scarier prospect than I was.

What about Piper Lowry? I'd phoned her and let slip that I was looking into Marigold's murder.

"Hey, cat, the footprint could be the gardener's."

Darcy didn't give me a side glance. He was too busy lapping up the meal I'd dished into his bowl.

I didn't need his agreement. I was right. I knew I was. The gardener must have come out to clean up the muck from last week's mini storm. "Except that doesn't explain the front door flying open," I muttered. "I suppose it could've been due to a faulty latch." One more thing to add to my repair list.

My reasoning should have made me feel better, but it didn't. Desperately needing to find my calm before I made my deliveries, I dialed Tegan. "How about a quick cup of coffee, and I'll give you a ride to work?"

She answered groggily, "I could use some caffeine."

"Late night?"

"Yeah. Mom talked my ear off."

"About?"

"Me. Winston. My failed marriage. Of course, Vanna had to offer her two cents. Spare me!"

"Are you dressed?"

"Enough."

"I'll pick you up in fifteen," I said, and promised Darcy I'd be home soon. Time was relative. He twitched his tail and retreated to his cat bed beneath the kitchen table.

The Blue Lantern was a bed-and-breakfast designed in the Gothic Revival style, a variation of the Victorian architectural style, with steeply pitched roofs and pointed-arch windows. The peacock blue exterior color was a lovely contrast to the extravagant white vergeboard trim along the roof. The front porch spanned the entire width of the house. Multiple lanterns hung from shepherds' hooks. The gardens were just coming into bloom. Tulips in various shades of pink, orange, and yellow abounded. Years ago, when Montford was offering run-down historic buildings for twenty thousand dollars, Noeline Merriweather purchased the place for a song. Quickly she fixed it up to be one of the premier inns in town.

I swung into the semicircular drive and spied Tegan standing on the porch with her mother. Both had bundled up for a brisk day.

Noeline waved to me as Tegan clambered into my van and yelled, "Feed her! She's cranky."

"Will do."

Minutes later, I parked in a public lot on Elm Street, and Tegan and I jogged up the terrace steps toward Ragamuffin. "Did Vanna secure a Realtor?"

"She did."

"Did you tell her about the safety-deposit box items and cash?"

"I did."

"And?" I asked.

"She continues to harp about you getting a portion of the bookshop."

It wasn't my fault. Marigold could make up her own darned mind. I let my peeve go and held the door to the café open for Tegan to enter. Ragamuffin was packed. The aroma of cinnamon muffins was intoxicating.

"Are you clearheaded enough to answer a question?" I asked. It was one that had been plaguing me ever since I woke.

"I'm as clearheaded as a . . . as a . . . There is no idiom for that. I'm good. What's up?"

The line to order was eight customers long.

"Did Evelyn Evers call you after you and she spoke?"

"How'd you guess? She was crying and wanted to tell me how much she loved Auntie."

"What did you say to her?"

"I agreed that Auntie was special. Why?"

"Did she ask if anyone else was listening in on your conversation with her yesterday?"

"Actually, she did, which I thought was weird, but decided she simply liked privacy."

All right, it was a given that Evelyn's favorite foundation was due to receive a tidy sum of money, and yes, perhaps Marigold let slip to Evelyn about the hundred K she had on her person and Evelyn coveted it, but did that make her a murderer?

Stop, Allie. You know Evelyn. She's a nice woman. Larger than life and at times bossy, but nice.

My rational brain did battle with my irrational one for about ten seconds.

"Allie?" Tegan prompted.

"Call me suspicious, but would you phone Evelyn and sort of, you know, ask where she was Saturday morning?"

"You can't possibly think she killed my aunt."

I tilted my head.

Tegan frowned. "Can I touch base later? It's early. She's a theater person."

"Please."

"Let's take it outside." She left the line. I followed. She pulled out her cell phone and selected a recent contact. "Evelyn," she said when someone answered. "It's Tegan Potts. Yes, I know. I'm sorry to bother you so early, but, um . . . what's the next production?" she hedged, reluctant to launch an interrogation. She listened. "Really? *Annie Get Your Gun*? I love that show." She crooned, "'Anything you can do, I can do better.'" After a long pause, she snickered. "Oh, thank you, but no, I won't audition. I've got severe stage fright. I can barely look at a microphone without fainting. I only sing in my shower or in my car."

"Tegan," I whispered, reining in my frustration, "get to the point."

"Um, Evelyn, where were you Saturday morning?"

She held the phone away from her ear. Evelyn was squawking so loudly that I could hear every word. She was chastising Tegan for questioning her integrity.

When she quieted, Tegan pressed the phone to her ear and said, "No, ma'am, I'm not accusing you of anything. I was wondering because, see, we—" Tegan listened. "Yes, Allie and me. We're trying to establish where everyone who knew Auntie was."

Evelyn spit out a response.

Tegan flinched. "Yes, ma'am." She received another earful of Evelyn's diatribe. "No, ma'am. Allie is not close to her parents. What's that?" She positioned the phone between both of our ears.

Evelyn said in a dramatically husky voice, "That's good to hear, because Fern Catt is a vagabond."

"That's harsh," I whispered to Tegan. "My parents like to travel. They are not drifters." As much as my parents' globetrotting ways bothered me, I was not about to let anyone bad-mouth them.

"Never in her life has Fern been able to put down roots," Evelyn went on, "let alone raise a child."

How well did she know my mother? Could Fern shed light on Evelyn as a person?

"Evelyn . . ." Tegan looked flummoxed as to how to proceed.

I said, sotto voce, "Go back to why we're inquiring."

"Ma'am, we were curious because, well, we'd like to help the police rule out everyone we admire. My aunt's murder is such a mystery."

"For your information, young lady," Evelyn said in a condescending tone, "I was at the theater erecting sets. There were ten crew persons and a handful of actors around to verify. As for the offer of free season tickets, it is now rescinded." She ended the call.

Tegan sighed and pocketed her phone. "I hate you, Allie. She didn't deserve that."

"You didn't deserve to be dismissed, either. And don't forget, Sherlock Holmes said, 'Once you eliminate the impossible, whatever remains, no matter how improbable, must be the truth.' We're trying to rule out suspects."

We stepped inside Ragamuffin again, and when we reached the front of the line, I treated my pal to a muffin and latte. We sat at a bistro table and chatted about Winston for a nanosecond, just to rehash what her mother had doled out last night about her pending divorce, and then I let her carp about how overbearing her half sister was. When she had exhausted her anger, I drove her to work and fetched my wares from Dream Cuisine.

For the next three hours, I delivered goodies to clients, starting with the cowboy-themed cookies and office party treats. Then cream cheese muffins to Blessed Bean. Chocolate crinkle cookies to Milky Way. Raspberry-chocolate tarts to Perfect Brew. Two pumpkin pies and a dozen scones to Pinnacle Lodge, a log-cabin–themed inn with cottages. Each concern was pleased with my work. Each paid on the spot, as I required. I'd been stiffed by my very first client and swore I'd never accept late payments in the future. I couldn't run a business on credit.

Pulling into my driveway, I checked my cell phone. I'd missed a call from Zach.

CHAPTER 14

"When I have a house of my own, I shall be miserable if I have not an excellent library."

—Caroline Bingley, in Jane Austen's *Pride and Prejudice*

I did a quick perimeter of the house and, seeing no errant foot-prints, dashed inside and closed and locked the door. Darcy warbled hello. I scooped him up, nuzzled his nose, set him on the floor, and dialed Zach.

"Hi, it's me," I said when I reached him. "Were you calling about Marigold? Have you solved her murder?"

"Sadly, no." He sounded as exhausted as I felt. "We're working the case. Don't worry."

"Did you talk to Oly Olsen?"

"Not yet."

"Did you find out what secret Katrina might be hiding?"

"No."

"Then why did you reach out?" I asked, somewhat exasper-ated.

"I wanted to see how you were doing with the menu for the memorial."

I grunted. Really? He hadn't called to be forthcoming about the poison in the water bottle theory?

"I made white soup that turned out well," I said. I didn't tell him about the footprint outside my window, seeing as I'd demolished it, plus after musing to Darcy about the gardener, I'd convinced myself that an intruder had not left the print.

"What's white soup?"

I explained. When he said he hadn't read *Pride and Prejudice,* I was surprised. No wonder he wasn't curious about why Marigold had been holding that particular book. Sure, it was possible it had no significance. On the other hand, it had been one of her favorites, and as I'd suggested previously, a heftier coffee-table–sized book would have been a much better shield if that had been her intent. How I wished she could speak to me from the Great Beyond and give me a clue.

"I also baked Maids of Honor." I described them and realized I hadn't offered Zach one when he'd come to the bookshop Tuesday because I'd been too preoccupied with the details of Marigold's will, not to mention Vanna had forced us to move the cart of treats to the side of the room.

"Do you have any left over?" he asked.

"I'll make a new batch soon. You should touch base with Lillian if you plan to come in costume for the memorial," I said.

"I will. Say, do you want to . . ." He stopped and let the question hang.

Want to what? I wondered. *Talk about the case? Make him his own private stash of pastries? Accompany him to question Oly in person? Go on a date?*

I waited, but he didn't continue. After a long bout of silence, I said, "I've got to pick up Tegan. I drove her to work this morning."

"Okay. Talk to you soon."

I urged myself not to take affront at the abruptness of his good-bye. If I was honest, ever since ending my relationship with my ex-fiancé, I wasn't the best at reading men. Zach might have received another call he had to take, or Bates could have been signaling him to confer about the case.

I fed Darcy and freshened his water bowl and hurled a cat toy to distract him. Then I drove to the bookshop, rehashing the short-lived conversation with Zach. When I arrived, however, I pushed all thoughts of him aside. Our friendship was fairly new, and the murder investigation was definitely taking top priority in his world.

I parked and hopped out of the van and strode toward Feast for the Eyes. Lillian was cleaning the display window of her shop. I waved. She blew me an air-kiss.

A gust of wind kicked up around me. I shivered from the onslaught and pushed into the shop. Tegan was finalizing a sale at the counter. She'd braided her hair and had outlined her eyes in charcoal, making her look no older than the anime girl on her T-shirt. Chloe, clad in a red dress with a swing skirt and sweetheart neckline, was discussing YA novels with a young woman.

When Tegan's customer departed, I crossed to her. "I'm ready for my training session."

"Like I said, you already know everything you have to do. You've rung up sales when I've been too busy. You've even unpacked shipments of boxes."

"Are there any book clubs on the schedule?" I asked.

"Yes. I'm going to postpone all of this week's events, and . . ." She eyed me. "Will you lead them going forward?"

"Me?" I clapped a hand to my chest. "Uh-uh. You do it."

"No way. I'll freeze up. You remember that time in high school."

She'd had to give a book report in front of the English class. She'd stuttered over the opening sentence, which sent the others into hysterics and made her so flustered, she broke into tears. For a month, she didn't tell me that two girls continued to taunt her out of a teacher's or my earshot. When I found out, I took them to task.

"I'm daring when it comes to antics," Tegan went on. "I'll

short-sheet anyone's bed. But I've never gotten over my fear of public speaking."

"Or confronting your sister."

"That's a whole other story."

I knew she wouldn't budge on the book club decision and moved on. "Tell me about the end-of-day procedure in the shop."

"We tally receipts and stow them in the safe. I'll give you the combination." She ticked off the to-do items on her fingertips. "We roam the aisles to make sure the recommendation tags are hanging in their proper places. One of us examines the bath-rooms to make sure they're clean. We double-check that the doors are locked and the coffee is switched off. And we power-down the main computer."

I pulled my cell phone from my pocket and started to type the items in the Notes app.

"You don't need to do that," Tegan said. "Auntie made a checklist and hung it on the pegboard behind the computer so we don't mess up. Oh, and you need a roster of our clients and their phone numbers and emails. Chloe made a group of con-tacts and sent it to me. I'll forward that to you." Her voice caught. "You don't think one of our customers . . ."

"Killed your aunt?" I finished. Honestly, I didn't know what to believe. I brushed her arm.

"I miss her so much." She whirled into me and hugged me. Her chest shuddered.

I patted her back. When she was once again calm, I said, "What's on your agenda for tonight?"

"I invited Dennell to dinner at the B and B. Want to join us? You should get to know her. She's quite intense, but she's very gifted. You should see some of the jewelry she makes."

"I could eat." I'd skipped lunch. "How's she doing?"

"She joined AA, and she found an outpatient doctor who will help her with her problem. Fortunately, her business partner is none the wiser. Dennell plans to ask out of their deal in a couple of weeks."

"That's great news. Tell me, why haven't I met her before now?"

"I didn't keep you two apart on purpose. I guess . . ." Tegan hitched a shoulder. "I guess I didn't think you'd have much in common. We met at a plasticware party."

I wrinkled my nose.

"Yeah, you and plastic are not pals. Only glass can hold your precious leftovers."

I knuckled her arm.

"By the way"—Tegan regarded Chloe and me—"Winston called. He wants to meet so he can console me about Aunt Marigold."

"What did you say?"

"Bite me."

I snuffled. "You didn't."

"No." She crossed her arms as if to steady herself.

"What you should have said was, you thought about him today, which reminded you to take out the trash."

She snickered. "Good one. Actually, I told him to bug off and said I'd reach out when I was good and ready."

"How'd he take that?"

"Super well. *Not.*"

For the next few hours, I familiarized myself with all things *bookshop.* When the wall clock above the computer read six p.m., I jangled my keys. "Ready to close up?"

"You bet," Tegan said. "Chloe, finalize any sales. I'll tend to the stockroom and restrooms. Allie will see to the book tags."

Chloe's customer said cheerily she'd return tomorrow, and the three of us went about our tasks.

At ten past seven, I drove Tegan to the Blue Lantern. A man and woman were entering ahead of us, the woman pausing to admire the pair of brass lanterns that flanked the entryway.

Helga, the B&B's cook and housekeeper, a woman in her sixties with a good-natured spirit and a keen eye for whatever needed attending, greeted the pair and accepted their overcoats. She hung them on the coatrack in the foyer and turned to us. "Welcome, Miss Tegan," she said. I couldn't remember a time when I hadn't seen Helga in her pale blue uniform with broad white lapels and white cuffs. "And Miss Allie, so lovely to see you."

"You too, Helga."

I'd never stayed at the Blue Lantern, but occasionally Noeline invited me to enjoy one of Helga's legendary breakfasts. Her menu included a variety of egg dishes and some of the most delectable Belgian waffles and French toast I'd ever tasted.

"Tegan." Dennell, bundled in a midcalf coat over a light turtleneck sweater, jeans, and boots, was standing in the parlor to the right. The silver-and-gold hook earrings and heart-shaped pendant she was wearing looked like art. She was holding a glass of sparkling water. "Over here."

"Be right there," Tegan said.

Some guests were convening in the parlor's various seating areas. Many were enjoying the cheese-and-wine spread that the inn set out every evening. I saw Rick and Noeline mingling with them. The knot of Rick's tie was loosened slightly, as if he'd slackened it on purpose after a long day of working on securing bonds. Noeline, pretty in a cream silk blouse over slim black pants and short heels, was pouring the wine and chatting up its qualities. A piano sonata was playing softly in the background.

Tegan fetched herself a glass of Perrier with lime from the handsome mahogany sideboard, while I accepted a glass of white wine from Noeline, and then we moseyed to Dennell.

Tegan hugged her and reintroduced us. "Dennell, you remember Allie, my best friend since kindergarten?"

"I do. Nice to see you." Dennell's smile was strained. I wondered if she would have preferred staying home but was forcing herself to be social.

"Will my having a glass of wine bother you, Dennell?" I asked.

"No. I've never been a wine drinker. Scotch is . . . *was* my weakness."

"Your jewelry is gorgeous," I said. "Your designs?"

"Mm-hmm."

"I told you she's talented," Tegan chimed. "Every item has *class* written all over it."

She guided us to a furniture arrangement that included a settee and an antique Louis XV–style upholstered chair. The two of them sat on the settee. I took the chair.

"Tell me everything you've learned so far about your aunt's murder," Dennell said.

Of course, she'd want to know. Everyone in town did.

"The police haven't told us much," Tegan said.

"Who do you suspect?" Dennell sipped her beverage.

"My half sister," Tegan said acidly.

I reached over and flicked her thigh.

"Just kidding. But she's such a pain in the—" She swallowed the next word along with a sip of Perrier. "Allie, I meant to tell you, Vanna did not find that ring Ms. Ivey mentioned. There was other jewelry, she said, but it was all costume stuff."

I wondered if the police had searched Marigold's car. If she had taken the diamond-and-ruby target ring to be cleaned, as I'd quietly theorized, she might have kept the jewelry store ticket in the glove box.

"Also Vanna invited a member of the Antiquarian Booksellers' Association of America to appraise the rare books at the shop and the ones at Auntie's home. They're coming to town next week."

"Was Vanna at the bookshop when you found your aunt?"

Dennell asked, segueing to the murder. "I heard there was quite a mob waiting to go inside."

"No, she wasn't," Tegan answered.

I listed the people who were there: Piper, Graham, some people I hadn't recognized—tourists, most likely. "Noeline and Rick were at the front. Chloe arrived late. Vanna showed up after that."

"Do you think someone in the crowd killed her?" Dennell asked.

"A customer suggested that Piper killed her," I said, "but Graham Wynn's neighbor intimated that Graham has been acting suspicious. Maybe drugs are involved."

"Graham's letter carrier saw him arguing with Marigold," Tegan offered.

"Hey," I blurted as something dawned on me. "Graham has a bandage on his arm."

Tegan raised an eyebrow. "Explain."

"It might be covering a fresh tattoo, but what if it's not? What if he struggled with Marigold, and she scratched him and drew blood?" I recalled asking Zach about that when we went on the hike and him remaining mum.

"Could the police match the DNA?" Tegan asked hopefully.

"I don't know. Maybe." I wasn't an evidence expert. "There's also Katrina Carlson, the bartender at the Brewery. She and Marigold exchanged words. But she wasn't in the mix on Saturday morning."

"Come to think of it, Allie," Tegan said, "I might have seen Quinby in the crowd."

"Quinby?" Dennell asked.

"Quinby Canfield, the customer who believes Piper is the killer," I said. "FYI, I don't think Piper did it. She's one of the nicest women on the planet."

"Nice people kill." Dennell sipped her drink and held the glass between two hands. "Your mom looks happy, Tegan," she said, pivoting to a lighter subject. "Do you like the guy she's dating?"

"Rick? He's okay."

"Are they, you know . . ." Dennell waggled her eyebrows.

"Intimate? Yeah, I'm sure. In fact"—Tegan glanced over her shoulder and again at us—"Rick looked pretty disheveled Saturday morning. My guess? He and my mom spent the night together. Helga, do you know?"

Helga, who was carrying a tray of caprese appetizers on skewers, stopped beside us. "That is not for me to say."

"C'mon, Helga," Tegan urged. "Spill the tea."

"All I know is Mr. O'Sheedy left for a business meeting on Saturday."

Tegan snickered. "Nah, he didn't go to a business meeting looking like he did."

"He did not stay for breakfast," Helga said.

"Maybe he ducked out early," I suggested, "so tongues wouldn't wag."

Helga exited the room without acknowledging my theory.

Tegan pursed her lips. "I wish . . ." She didn't finish.

"Wish what?" Dennell asked.

"I wish my mom happiness."

I threw my pal a knowing look. That was not at all what she was wishing. She hoped Rick would disappear.

Dinner was served in the communal dining room. There were eight rectangular tables covered in white linens. Candles and small vases of fresh flowers adorned each table. Guests could sit wherever they chose. Helga had cooked a resplendent menu that included a choice of rack of lamb, Dover sole, rosemary roasted chicken, or beef stew, potatoes prepared three different ways, petite vegetables in a butter-lemon sauce, and a number of desserts. I opted for the beef stew, garlic mashed potatoes, and the petite vegetables—a person needed one's greens. I would finish with the flan. Tegan and Dennell both selected the chicken, scalloped potatoes, and decadent gluten-free chocolate cake.

Over the course of our meal, Dennell regaled us with stories about the jewelry business. She was funny and sincere and at peace with her decision to stay sober. When there was a lull in the conversation, I once again reflected on the jewelry Marigold had acquired over the years and the missing ring. I asked Dennell how one priced items. Why did a certain piece cost fifty thousand while another might draw a meager thousand? She explained that the name of the designer mattered—she hoped to be a big deal in the next decade or two—and the cut and weight of the gems were crucial. However, in the long run, it was all about demand.

I polished off my flan and glimpsed my watch. "Oh, my. I have to get going. I have a few loose ends to wind up at Dream Cuisine for tomorrow's deliveries. This has been lovely, Tegan. Thanks for inviting me."

I sped to my professional kitchen, where I began finalizing tomorrow's deliveries. I was behind, but right now, with all that was going on, sleep was highly overrated.

With a soothing tune playing in the background, I made six dozen lemon-raspberry scones for Ragamuffin. Every summer, I froze fresh raspberries so I would always have some on hand. While the scones were baking, I mixed the batter for four dozen coffee lace cookies to deliver to Whispering Winds, a bed-and-breakfast not far from the Blue Lantern. The cookies were crisp delicacies that I drizzled with melted chocolate, but they were difficult to box up until they were completely cool because they couldn't be stacked on top of one another when warm. Patience was required.

After removing the last of the scones and putting the first batch of cookies in to bake, I studied the recipe I had for pound cake. It required twelve eggs—six whole eggs and six egg yolks. Luckily, I bought eggs in bulk. The cake would be dense—as it should be so it could absorb the juices of the fruits in the trifle—but it would also be melt-in-your-mouth good.

I greased and floured a loaf pan. Next I whisked the butter and added the sugar. When they were fluffy, I set them aside and attacked the eggs. Using a digital scale, I weighed the dry ingredients. Measuring properly was vital to the success of any baking enterprise. I combined the ingredients, poured them into the loaf pan, and placed the pound cake in the oven to bake.

With an hour-plus to fritter away, I opened my laptop computer with the intent of playing a word game. I paused when I glimpsed the empty search bar. Instantly I pictured Marigold's computer and the last search she'd done: *gaslight.* The search made sense, given the historical aspect of the book she'd started. Were all her previous searches related to her budding writing career? What if she'd cleared the history on purpose because something she'd researched could be considered incriminating?

I could be grasping at straws thinking that someone other than Marigold had wiped it clean. On the other hand, a gamer like Graham Wynn would be computer savvy, and a junior-college professor like Piper Lowry would be computer literate, too. Was it possible one of them hacked Marigold's computer and cleared the history from afar?

Tegan said only she and Chloe knew the password, but Marigold might have written it down. Also she'd died clutching *Pride and Prejudice.* What if her murderer got a clue from her shield, guessed the password, and erased the search history after murdering her?

How lucky could one killer get?

CHAPTER 15

"Do not consider me now as an elegant female, intending to plague you, but as a rational creature, speaking the truth from her heart."

—Elizabeth Bennet, in Jane Austen's *Pride and Prejudice*

The next morning, I donned a long-sleeved white shirt, black jeans, ankle boots, and lightweight puff jacket. I fed and snuggled Darcy, kissed him good-bye, and ventured out. It wasn't raining—the sun was shining and the aroma of new flowers perfumed the air—but it was chilly.

While making deliveries, I decided to resume listening to Sherlock Holmes's *The Sign of the Four.* I was at the part where the police were arresting Thaddeus Sholto, when I spied Fair Exchange, the pawnshop where I'd purchased my Celtic knot. I parked in the lot on Holly Street and hoofed it to the sidewalk. I wanted to pick the owner's brain about where Marigold might have taken the ring she'd removed from her safety-deposit box. She wouldn't have pawned it. She hadn't needed the money. But perhaps he knew jewelers who were good at cleaning antique pieces.

Nearing the pawnshop, I drew to a halt. Of all people, Rick O'Sheedy was entering Fair Exchange, an overcoat slung over his left arm. In his right hand, he carried a messenger bag-style leather briefcase.

Something niggled at the edges of my brain warning me to be wary. Why, I couldn't say, but throughout my childhood years, my parents had urged me to listen to my intuition. If I was going to be in charge of my fate, they said, I had to be alert. So I lingered and observed Rick's transaction through the pawnshop window. J.J., the owner, a bald man with a scruffy beard and spectacles—he'd probably come out of the womb looking withered and tired—was on a moving ladder, pushing himself to the right as he dusted the top shelf of books.

Rick sauntered toward him, pulling something from his breast pocket while speaking. I couldn't see what it was, but J.J. descended the ladder and held out his hand. Rick passed it to him, and J.J. placed the item on the sales counter. He let the spectacles, which were attached to a chain, fall to his chest and lifted a loupe. He held it to his right eye. Waiting, Rick rubbed his arms nervously, as if eager to conclude the business deal as quickly as possible. Why? Had he brought in a stolen ring? To be specific, Marigold's ring?

Don't leap to conclusions, Allie. And don't judge the man based on your pal's misgivings.

J.J. said something to Rick, which seemed to put Rick at ease. He stopped rubbing his arms and started idly twirling his key ring on his index finger. J.J. jotted out a receipt on a pad, tore the top sheet off the pad, went to the antique cash register, and rang up a sale, or, in this case, a purchase. He pulled out a few hundred-dollar bills and gave them and the receipt to Rick.

Business concluded, Rick gestured a two-fingered salute and left, and J.J. stowed whatever Rick had sold him in a drawer, to the right of the cash register.

Though curiosity was ticking my insides like crazy, I waited a few beats before wandering in. When I did, I said, "Morning, J.J."

He squinted at first before realizing he needed his glasses. After putting them on, he said, "Well, I'll be. It's the alley cat." He snickered. When I'd first told him my name, he'd laughed so hard, which led to a conversation about our ancestry. His family had come from the same part of Ireland that mine had. "What would be bringing you in today, lass?"

"I wanted to ask you about jewelers who might be good at cleaning antique jewelry."

"I do fine work, if I don't mind bragging, but there are plenty in town. It depends on what type of jewelry you need cleaned."

"A diamond-and-ruby target ring, circa 1920."

He whistled. "I'd like to see that."

"So the man who was just here didn't bring you something like that?"

"Ha!" J.J. chortled. "Nah, he was getting rid of his wedding ring. Seems his wife divorced him. Heartbroken, he decided not to hold on to it."

Rick didn't strike me as the heartbroken type. Had he acted up a storm so he could soak J.J. for more money than the ring was worth? Maybe that was what I'd sensed when I'd spotted him at first. He'd looked cagey because he was in need of cash.

"He said he wanted to clean the slate so he could make room in his heart for someone new."

Like Noeline? I wondered. "He sure opened up to you."

J.J. smiled, baring his tobacco-stained teeth. "I'm like a father confessor."

"Could I see the ring?"

He pulled it from the drawer and held it out to me. "Plain, with a simple inscription inside."

Love always, it read.

He clucked his tongue. "Love isn't always, in his case. It's good quality and generic enough that I can resell it easily. I gave him top dollar. Now"—he leaned forward on his elbows—"if you'd like to show me that 1920s beauty you're touting, I'll be interested."

I promised I'd bring it in when I found it. "I didn't lose it," I added hurriedly. "It belonged to Marigold Markel."

"The lady who died."

"The same." I explained how she'd removed it from her safety-deposit box, and it was missing.

"If you'd like, I can send you a text with the list of jewelers she might have taken it to."

I thanked him and left.

Over the next few hours, I finished up my deliveries. The sisters who owned Whispering Winds cooed over the coffee lace cookies and instantly ordered more, adding that they would recommend my wares to all of their friends, including Blessed Bean. I assured them I'd already snagged that account and would pitch the cookies to the owner myself.

By the time I arrived at Feast for the Eyes, it was close to noon. I strolled in and held the door for two entering customers. I said hello to Chloe, who was helping a young woman in the YA aisle, and greeted a customer who was browsing the endcap by the mystery aisle, after which I went in search of Tegan. I found her in the office, sitting at the desk, the Internet browser open on the laptop computer.

Yet again, she'd donned the black-colored, thigh-length anime sweater that was three sizes too big. She was deep in concentration. Her forehead had creases, and she was sucking on her lower lip with her teeth.

"Hello," I said.

She looked up, startled.

"Sugar for the weary." I set a box of assorted cookies on the desk and nudged them toward her.

"Thanks." She took a coffee lace cookie and bit into it. "Delish."

"What are you up to?"

"I'm doing a deep dive on Graham Wynn. Have you ever been in his store, GamePlay?"

"Nope." I didn't play video games. I liked crossword puzzles and sudoku. "You have, I'm presuming," I said, given her fascination with comic books. I'd lost my interest in them around the age of ten, too enthralled with novels to find time to read anything else.

"It's a great place, packed with Funko collectibles, bobble-head dolls, and board games."

I enjoyed board games, in particular, Clue.

Tegan swiveled the laptop slightly so the link she clicked on was easier to read. "Here's an article about when he first opened the shop ten years ago. The *Tribune* interviewed him. He comes from humble means. No father. His mother worked full-time as a nurse, but she passed away. He didn't say what happened to her, although he said, because she worked nights when he was a boy, he pretty much found himself playing games to stay out of trouble. He's never been married. He doesn't outright say he's a virgin, but he refers to himself as a 'monk for life.'"

"That might explain his interest in clerical fiction," I kidded.

"Be serious."

I sobered. "Did you find anything criminal in his past?"

"He's a fiend for double-parking."

I had tried to skirt the law in that way a few times, until I'd grasped it wasn't worth the financial penalties I'd incurred.

"He was in a bar fight during college. No arrest was made. And he likes to gamble."

"You found all that online?"

"Yep. He posted pictures of himself in Atlantic City on a video game junket, but the pix weren't from the conference. They were all taken at blackjack tables."

I thought of the missing hundred K Marigold had withdrawn from the bank and how Celia Harrigan hinted that Graham's business was suffering. Was it possible he killed Marigold to get his hands on the money? "Can you pull up info on his finances?"

"No. I'm not that savvy. I also couldn't come up with anything pertaining to a drug habit."

Which left us no closer to the truth.

"Before digging into him, I was looking into Rick," Tegan said.

"Why?"

"To protect my mom. He doesn't have a social media footprint."

"Lots of people don't."

"Sure, but get this. My friend at the hospital—she's the one I help out at the blood bank—doesn't have a clue who he is."

"Being a financial consultant, he probably doesn't mingle with the regular staff. Funny you should mention him, though. I saw him at the pawnshop this morning." I told her what J.J. said, that Rick was trying to clean the slate so he could start fresh with someone new, probably Noeline. "Between you and me, I think Rick might be a decent guy."

"If you say so."

I patted her shoulder. "Let's leave it for now and handle the customers. You want to rack up a ton of sales, don't you? Tell me what to do."

"Actually, we have some orders to gather and tag. I printed the list. It's sitting by the computer in the showroom."

"On it." I fetched the box of cookies, returned to the main shop, and placed it on the counter. "Chloe, I brought cookies. Enough for everyone."

"Bless you," Chloe said.

While she and each of the customers partook, I nabbed the

list of books Tegan had printed and roamed the store to pull them. I returned with an armload and began to tag them. Three books for Lillian, all pertaining to costuming. Two YA novels for the septuagenarian who owned Mosaic. She had adorable teen granddaughters. One thriller by Harlan Coben for Zach's partner. A theater-themed mystery for Evelyn Evers titled *A Fatal Finale,* which took place at the cusp of the twentieth century in Manhattan. I'd read it a couple of years ago and had delighted in the intrigue. Two books for Rick O'Sheedy, a thriller and a Deputy Donut Mystery with the cute name, *Survival of the Fritters.* The latter seemed totally out of character for him.

The door to the shop opened and, to my surprise, Rick entered. Noeline wasn't with him.

Tegan met him halfway. "Hi, Rick. Lunch break?"

"No lunch today. I'm in and out to get my books and then off to meetings."

"Good timing," I said, joining them. "I pulled the titles moments ago. I noticed you set aside a cozy mystery. For you?"

"What's a cozy mystery?"

I chuckled. "Yeah, I thought it might be for Noeline." She and I had similar reading tastes. "It's a mystery that most often doesn't have bad language. There's rarely any sex. And usually the murder occurs off the page."

He grinned. "That sounds perfect for her. She said someone recommended the donut mysteries. She loves donuts."

"Well, she won't be disappointed. The series is wonderful, with recipes, to boot. She can suggest Helga make some of them." I fetched the books I'd pulled, slotted them into a Feast for the Eyes gift bag, and handed the bag to him. "By the way, I saw you at Fair Exchange this morning. You appeared to be in a hurry, so I didn't call out to you."

"Were you spying on me?"

"No, I—"

"Relax. I'm just joshing you." The corners of his mouth curved up. "This is a small town. Everywhere I go I'm seeing people I've met."

I breathed easier. I didn't want him to think I was nosey. Curious, perhaps. Interested, definitely. But not a snoop. "I happened to be heading to the shop myself because I bought this there." I fingered my necklace. "And I wondered whether J.J.—he's the owner—might know the best jeweler for cleaning something like it."

"Ahh." Rick nodded, accepting my explanation.

"J.J. is quite a talker, isn't he?"

"Interrogator, you mean. The police should hire him. Better yet, the FBI." Rick winked. "If I'd stayed any longer, I'm pretty sure I would have revealed my entire life story."

I laughed.

"You revealed enough," Tegan blurted. "He told Allie you were married before."

"Did he?"

I stared at my pal. *Really? So much for keeping a conversation confidential.*

Rick said, "It's true. I was married. For fifteen years. It wasn't a good fit. I traveled too much. After a while, she didn't trust me, mainly because her father was a traveling salesman and stepped out on her mother. I never did. And I sure as heck wasn't a salesman. But . . ." He raised a hand. "But she couldn't get past it. Today, when I spotted the pawnshop, I decided it was time to sell the ring. Put the memory behind me."

"What're your intentions with my mother?" Tegan blurted.

"That's none of your business, young lady," Rick said.

"Actually, it is," she countered.

"Fine." Rick clicked his tongue in his mouth, another smile appearing. What he must think of the two of us. "For the record, your mother likes me, and I like her. We've been talking about traveling together. She wants to see Italy, and I'm game. It's one of the few countries I've never visited. Does that about cover it?"

"Almost." Tegan crossed her arms. "I asked about you at the hospital, and nobody seems to know you."

I winced. I knew my friend could be blunt, but this was so direct even I was stunned.

Rick's gaze narrowed. "You asked about me, and you"—he regarded me—"have been following me?"

"I told you, I wasn't—"

"Just teasing you again," he said. The way his eyes twinkled with mischief, I could see why Noeline was falling for him. He had a feistiness about him.

"My friend is one of the head nurses," Tegan went on, undaunted. "She knows everyone, and she's never heard of you."

Rick smoothed the hair along the right side of his head, trying and succeeding to tamp down exasperation. "I've only been in town a short time, Tegan. Previously I lived in Charlotte and before that in Raleigh. I've moved around a lot. I rarely mingle with the nursing staff."

Which corroborated my theory.

"Do you intend to stay in Bramblewood?" Tegan asked.

"I'm considering buying a condo or a small house, if that's saying anything. I'd like the Asheville area to be my home base. It's the nicest place I've ever lived. Quaint but cosmopolitan. Lots of outdoor activities. Plenty of good theater. And the best craft beer in the US." He spread his hands. "Look, if you're worried about my bona fides, ask the kids at the hospital how they feel about me. I read to them a lot."

"You read to the children?" Tegan tilted her head.

"Yes."

"So the volunteers know you."

178 / DARYL WOOD GERBER

"Some certainly do." He held her gaze.

My cell phone pinged. I'd received a text message from J.J. I stepped aside and reviewed the list of jewelers he'd sent. It was so long, I didn't know where to begin. I made a mental note to ask Noeline if she knew the name of her sister's favorite jeweler. With all the jewelry Marigold had purchased over the years, she must have had one.

CHAPTER 16

"I could easily forgive his pride, if he had not mortified mine."

—Elizabeth Bennet, in Jane Austen's *Pride and Prejudice*

By the time I got home, I was dog-tired, but I couldn't go to bed. Not only because it was early—seven p.m.—but because Darcy wouldn't let me, considering the way he was pacing the floor. He wasn't starving. He was in need of attention.

"Really, sir?" I grumbled, picking him up and staring into his eyes. "Sometimes I swear you are a dog. Feline lesson number one: Cats aren't supposed to mind that their humans go away for hours at a time."

I carried him to my bedroom and told him about my day, filling him in on what Tegan had uncovered and complaining that I was frustrated with the police. Why hadn't they come up with the killer's identity by now?

My cell phone chimed. Zach was calling. Had he sensed my dismay? Were we that in tune? *No, not possible. Like Tegan would say, "Cool your jets, Allie."*

I answered after one ring. "Evening. Got the killer?"

He sighed. "Allie, murder investigations take time."

Did they? I'd never known anyone who was murdered. On TV, the cases were solved within days, and in nearly all the mysteries I read, the killer was brought to justice by the final page. Not the cold cases, of course. Those could take years. I prayed that wouldn't be the situation this time.

"What's up, then?" I asked, quelling my disappointment.

"I wondered if you'd like to get something to eat at the Celtic Festival. It's not super cold out. We shouldn't freeze. But if you'd rather not—"

"I'd love to." Though I was tired, I did want to spend time with him, and yes, I hoped I could pick his brain and give him a clue he hadn't thought of. For instance, I hadn't told him about Quinby Canfield accusing Piper of killing Marigold, and I wasn't sure I'd mentioned the historical suspense story I'd found on Marigold's computer. I said, "I'll meet you in front of the rec center in thirty."

I placed Darcy on top of the comforter, did a quick cleanup because I smelled like a baker who had delivered goods and sold books all day—an odd combo, to be sure—and slipped into a sage-green turtleneck and light sweater. Darcy watched me with obvious displeasure. I pulled a similar face and stuck out my tongue. "Feline lesson number two: You may be judgmental but don't gloat."

He trilled something.

I trotted to him and scrubbed him under his chin. "Yes, I know. You are the love of my life, too. You make me feel treasured."

Without budging his body, his tail flipped up and plopped down on the comforter.

"I'll be home soon," I said, and went on foot to the Bramblewood Park and Rec Center.

Like a Renaissance fair, the Celtic Festival would include live music, food and beverages, face painting, arts and crafts, and organized chats to help attendees learn about Celtic history and traditions. As a girl of Irish descent, I'd often wondered if being a Celt was the same as being Irish, but I learned in my teens that wasn't the case. The Celts were a group of people, while Ireland was a nation, not to mention that the Celts once spanned Eastern and Central Europe, but many were wiped out by the Roman Empire, or they conformed to other cultures. The traditionally Celtic nations now included Wales, Scotland, and Ireland, as well as Brittany in France and Catalonia in Spain.

I approached the rec center, an auditorium-sized space where the town often held concerts, and I paused to drink in the festive atmosphere. White tents, open-air booths, and pop-up dining stations were everywhere. Cheerful bagpipe music was droning through speakers. People in colorful folk dance costumes were swirling around a maypole. Attendees were roaming about in traditional kilts and tams or in period costumes, the women's clothing quite similar to dresses worn during the Regency Era.

Seeing all the costumes made me wonder how Lillian was doing with orders for the memorial. Right then, as if I'd conjured her out of thin air, I spotted her near the pop-up Nectar Café chatting with the same twenty-something actress she'd dined with at the Brewery the other night. They were standing near an outdoor heater. Lillian sported a kilt, a puffy-sleeved blouse, knee stockings, and a tam. Her friend was in a lovely blue gown and shawl.

"Lillian, hello!" I called as I approached. I didn't see Zach and decided I'd stay put so he could find me.

Lillian introduced me to her friend Yvonne, who was slim and winsome, with a Cupid's-bow mouth and loose updo that enhanced her cheekbones. Both women were sipping a golden liquid, with cinnamon swizzle sticks poking from their glasses. Cider, I determined.

"Your costumes are gorgeous," I said.

"Thanks," Yvonne replied. She had a slight accent, which I

couldn't place. Eastern European was my guess. "I'm going to play Hermia in *A Midsummer Night's Dream* next month, and I'll wear this."

"I'll have to come see it." I enjoyed Shakespeare's plays, in particular the comedies.

"How are you holding up, Allie?" Lillian asked. "I heard the scuttlebutt. You're now part owner of the bookshop?"

I wondered who'd told her. Not Vanna. She would have been mortified to share that tidbit. Possibly Chloe, without guile.

"Busy lady." Lillian's face grew grim. "Any word on . . . you know . . . Marigold's murder? Have they found who did it?"

"No. I'm meeting Detective Armstrong in a few minutes."

"Oh?" She gave me a sly smirk. "Are you two an item?"

"We're friends," I said flatly. *For now.* Who knew what the future might hold?

"Are you feeding him theories? Tegan said you and she were batting around ideas."

Aha! Tegan was Lillian's source. We'd have to chat. "No. I'm not feeding him anything, except the occasional cookie."

Lillian laughed and grew serious again. "Tegan mentioned something about Katrina Carlson and Marigold having an argument."

Tegan needs to zip her lips, I mused. Whatever clues we dug up were for the police—and only the police.

"I know Katrina pretty well," Yvonne remarked. "I cannot imagine her arguing with anyone, but if her boyfriend, Upton— I should say her ex-boyfriend—was involved, it is likely." She made a dismissive sound.

"You know him?" I asked.

"Oh, yes. He is a photographer. He takes all the photos for the theater productions. She used to come to the theater to watch him in action."

"Upton has done some work for me, too," Lillian said. "For my website."

"I do not wonder that Katrina has broken up with him," Yvonne went on. "He is stuck on himself, if that is the term. He thinks he is the next Florin Ghioca."

"Who?" Lillian and I asked in unison.

"A renowned theater photographer in Romania."

"That's a thing?" I asked.

"Indeed," Yvonne said. "Theater photography is quite unique. Ghioca knows everything about how to work with dim lighting, angles, and live action. He also has photography exhibitions and gives master classes. He is brilliant. Upton Scott cannot hold a candle to him."

Yvonne's assertion rang true, making me wonder if Katrina's secret had something to do with her ex. Maybe she'd wronged him or hurt his career, and Marigold found out. Thinking about theater people made me also reflect on Evelyn Evers and her alibi for Saturday morning.

"Say, Yvonne, do you know Evelyn Evers?" I asked.

"Yes, of course!" She beamed and clapped a hand to her chest. "She is the glue that holds the theater together. A marvelous woman. A mentor to many. Why do you ask?"

"She told our friend Tegan"—I motioned between Lillian and myself—"that she was working on set design early Saturday morning."

"We all were. We worked through the night. The production of *Annie Get Your Gun* goes up next weekend. We were falling behind. I do not sing or I would have auditioned for it."

Well, that settled that. Yvonne's testimony exonerated Evelyn. The young woman had no reason to lie.

A bell chimed, signaling the beginning of a musical session inside the rec center.

Lillian said, "Allie, listen, if there's anything other than the costumes that I can do for the memorial to help Tegan or Noeline or you, you have to tell me."

Gratitude clogged my throat. I croaked out, "Thank you. By

the way, how are the costumes going? Are many people getting in the spirit?"

"Honey, you have no clue. So far, there are over fifty who want to dress up to honor her."

"That's great to hear. She would be so pleased."

"*Ooh!*" Lillian snapped her fingers. "I almost forgot. I'm having a soiree in two weeks. At my house. A dozen people. Will you cater it? They're not fussy, but they're clothing reps that I'd like to impress."

"Allie!" Zach was wending through a knot of silent bag-pipers filing out of the hall.

"I'll send you the details," Lillian said, and blew me a kiss.

Yvonne flicked her fingers as a good-bye, and they went inside.

Zach looked as handsome as ever, his cheeks ruddy, his gaze direct and warm, though I could see he'd been concentrating. Hard. His forehead was creased, and the lines between his eyebrows were deep. "You didn't don a costume?" he teased.

"Gee, if only I had a costume at the ready," I said, making a mental note to ask Lillian if I could purchase the sage-green one she was altering for me. "Have you decided whether you're dressing in costume for Marigold's memorial?"

"I'm considering it." He clasped my elbow. "How about a beer?"

"I'd love a tasting of scotch." I saw a vendor across the way and steered Zach in that direction. "I seldom drink hard liquor, but it sounds like a perfect match for tonight's cool weather."

"Why, Miss Darcy, I do declare you're taking my breath away."

"Wrong," I chided. "I'd be Miss Bennet. You'd be *Mr.* Darcy." I squinted at him as we waited to purchase two tastings of single malt scotch. "I know you're well-read. How did you miss out on *Pride and Prejudice*?"

"In high school, if it wasn't required reading, I didn't do it. I was a B student who dreamed of being an A student, but I didn't have the dedication to work harder."

"And now?"

"I'm as hard a worker as anyone you'll meet, and nobody since college has ever asked me my GPA." He grinned and purchased our drinks, which were provided in disposable shot glasses, and then we continued on through the arts-and-crafts booths, browsing various wares, like hand-tooled leather belts and hand-carved pipes. "So tell me why you're enthralled with the story."

"I'd say it's because of the theme of classism."

"Explain."

"The novel suggests that though class determines one's social standing, it's arbitrary and doesn't account for one's behavior."

"I can agree with that."

"Jane Austen emphasized how rules and prejudices influenced people's lives and decisions. For example, Mr. Darcy was disagreeable and awkward in social situations and considered himself above the fray when it came to others not of his class."

"Thus, he was proud."

"Exactly. Therefore, to Elizabeth and her family, the charming Wickham was a better catch. However, in the end, it appeared Darcy was misunderstood."

"How so?"

"He was honest and truthful, he helped Elizabeth's sister out of a prickly situation with no fanfare to himself, and he was intensely amiable when it came to Lizzie, while the duplicitous Wickham turned out to be a cad of the lowest order."

Zach studied his scotch. "I've known a few cads over the years."

That intrigued me. I sipped my drink and said, "I don't know much about you. Care to explain."

"How about over dinner?"

"Yes, please." Was this a date? An official date? I was reluctant to ask.

We passed a booth offering an array of Celtic jewelry. One necklace looked similar to mine. The vendor tried to sell me a matching ring. I declined.

At the pop-up food site named the Pint House, we perused the handwritten menu.

"I'd love shepherd's pie," I said, adding it to the list of foods I intended to make for the memorial. It was a hearty dish that originated in Ireland and the UK, consisting of ground meat, onions, potatoes, and carrots, all baked in a mashed potato crust.

"I'll try the mac-and-cheese pie," Zach said, "and I'll share if you'll give me a bite of yours."

"Done, but I'm warning you, I make a killer mac 'n' cheese, and this one won't compare."

"You'll have to cook me dinner someday."

"When you grill me a steak," I countered.

He purchased our meals and two bottles of water, and we sat at one of the common seating wood-plank tables, alongside a pair of musicians resting from their bagpiping duties. They were holding a private conversation that sounded heated and scooted to the far end of the table.

I took a bite of the pie and swooned. The mashed potato crust was laced with cheddar cheese. "Zach, earlier you said you've known a few cads. Care to explain? Were you married and some loser ran off with your wife?"

"No. Nothing like that. I . . ." His face pinched with a painful memory. He stirred his mac-and-cheese pie with his fork, but didn't eat. He pushed the dish away and leaned forward on his elbows, hands folded on the table. "I was married. You were right on that count, but she passed away fifteen years ago."

"I'm so sorry."

"We met in high school. The day after we graduated, we

married. I was eighteen. A year later, she died of COPD complications."

"How awful." I reached over to touch his arm. "Did you know she was sick?"

"Yes. We decided whatever time we had together would be worth it. Six months after her death, I joined the army. As for the cad comment"—his shoulders rose and fell—"my younger sister dated more than her share of losers over the years. With my dad gone, I was in charge of shooing them away. She hated me for that, until she met her current husband. Husband number two." He pulled his arms from beneath my hands and dug into his food. "Carpe diem. Seize the day," he said between bites. "Life is too short to waste a moment of it."

"Your father—"

"Passed when I was sixteen. He was a heavy smoker. I've never lit up in my life."

"And your mother?"

"She rebounded after Dad died and put all her efforts into opening a restaurant. She owns Jukebox Joint."

"No way. I thought she was a farmer."

"Grandpa was the farmer. Mom couldn't wait to leave the nest and forge her own path. When Dad was alive, she managed a couple of restaurants, but she couldn't find the courage to start one of her own."

I'd been to the Joint, as locals called it. It was known for its tasty barbecue. I looked at Zach harder, trying to see the resemblance. Like him, his mother had dark hair and bright eyes, but she was petite and delicate. He must have gotten his strapping physique from his father.

I said, "I've been trying to land the Joint as a customer. The desserts menu is limited."

"I know," he said sheepishly. "She plans to call you soon."

A bard in a Tudor flat cap, brown cape, canvas pants, and ankle-high leather boots jauntily strolled past our table playing a tune on a lute. He wasn't singing, but he was humming in a throaty baritone voice. He tipped his head and winked at me.

"Seems someone has forgotten the words," Zach said, mock-jealousy in his tone.

I laughed. "Don't worry. I don't date anyone who wears a feather in his cap."

Oops. I'd said the forbidden word . . . "date." What was I thinking?

We both grew quiet and ate our meals.

After a long moment, I said, "What more have you unearthed about Graham Wynn? By the way, he has a bandage on his arm. Did Marigold scratch her killer?"

Zach's gaze grew flinty. "You're going there? Really? You want to hear about the investigation? We were having such a good time."

I grinned, but my smile faded quickly, because he wasn't kidding. He was ticked off. His cheek was twitching the same way my father's would when I didn't complete a homework assignment. I held up both hands. "Please don't be mad. I simply wanted to tell you what Tegan dug up on him."

"Why was Tegan looking into him?"

"Because she wants her aunt's killer to be brought to justice as much as I do, and he's on her suspect list. After his neighbor mentioned that he might be into drugs—"

"You never told me that."

No, I didn't, because I hadn't taken the accusation seriously. Years ago, a friend in college had been into drugs, and his eyes were always rheumy, as if he'd checked out. Whenever I'd talked to Graham, his eyes had been clear. On the other hand, if he wasn't doing drugs, but he was selling them . . . *Hmm.* "Have you questioned Celia Harrigan?" I asked.

"Bates did. Like me, he thinks she's a rumormonger."

Why dismiss her out of hand? I wondered, but let it go.

"FYI, there was no scratch on Graham Wynn's arm," Zach said. "He got a new tattoo."

Like I'd first surmised. Rats. "What about the people who had keys to the bookshop, you know, security people and such?"

"All cleared. All have alibis."

"Ruling out suspects is important, right?"

"Allie."

"As for Tegan," I said to divert him. "She's an ace researcher. It's the almost librarian in her."

"Almost?"

"She intended to become one, but when she started working at Feast for the Eyes, she fell in love with bookselling and working alongside her aunt. Even so, she never lost the skills she honed in her undergraduate library science studies." I took another bite of my meal and offered Zach a taste. He declined. "If Graham is somehow involved with drugs, does that put him back on your radar?"

"Let's discuss Tegan," he said.

The way he said it made my blood go cold. "Okay."

"You should know she's the one on my radar."

"What?" I squeaked. "Why? You heard Dennell on Tuesday—"

"The delivery guy for Big Mama's Diner didn't see or hear her at Ms. Watkins's apartment."

"But he brought two cups of coffee."

"Which Ms. Watkins could have ordered."

"Tegan doesn't lie."

"Maybe not. Or perhaps you don't know her very well."

"Only all my life!" I retorted, taking umbrage.

Zach grew quiet.

I would not—*could* not—think Tegan was guilty of murder. The sheer notion made me shudder.

"Cold? Want my jacket?" Zach asked.

"No thanks. I was remembering . . ."

How mad was he going to be if I spilled the beans about me driving through Marigold's neighborhood? Plenty, I decided, but I laid it all out, including the bit about Graham having a smoke on his porch. "He might have seen me, and he might have thought my presence meant I knew something, and he might have come to my place to frighten me."

"That's a heck of a lot of *mights*, Allie. Why are you taking risks? It's my job to investigate—" He sucked in air. "Wait! Hold on. He came to your place?"

"I'm not sure. Later that night, I heard a *clack* and *thump* outside my house, and then my front door flew open. I figured it was the wind and shut and barricaded the door. I did a tour of the house, peeking out windows. I didn't see anyone lurking about. However, in the morning, I saw a muddy footprint on the porch that wasn't mine, and my first thought was that Graham must have spotted me in his neighborhood and followed me home." I waved a hand. "I've tried to dismiss the footprint, telling myself that my gardener left it, but I can't shake the feeling about Graham."

"You think he came to silence you because you were spying on him?"

"I wasn't spying."

Zach worked his tongue inside his cheek. "I could have my team take a look at the print."

"I'm afraid that's a bust, because I obliterated it. Accidentally. Not on purpose," I added quickly. "I didn't notice the print until I was on a ladder fixing a shutter, and seeing the print spooked me, and I tumbled off." My shoulder still smarted, though icing it had been the best course of action.

Zach's nostrils flared. With anger? Frustration? Concern? He collected his barely eaten food, strode to the nearest garbage receptacle, and tossed it in.

I followed and threw away my trash. "Zach, I've been meaning to ask why you sent me a frowning-face emoji when I texted you asking whether the poison that killed Marigold was found in the water bottle taken from the crime scene."

"Look, Allie"—he whirled around—"I don't want you butting in where you shouldn't. I need you to stand down. You and, most particularly, Tegan." His tone was crisp. Official. "Understood?"

I nodded, but I didn't agree to his terms.

"By the way, you were right," he said.

"About the water being laced with poison?"

"The mac-and-cheese pie wasn't very good." He glanced at his watch. "I'm heading home. Want me to walk you to your place?"

"No, I'm fine on my own. I'd like to catch more of the music."

I watched him walk away, hands shoved into his pockets, and a sinking feeling formed in the pit of my stomach. Would he and I ever date again? If this really had been a date. Was I now persona non grata?

From behind, a woman hollered, "Allie!"

Expecting to see Lillian and Yvonne, I swung around. Vanna, in a faux-fur–collared navy plaid coat, slacks, silk blouse, and high-heeled ankle boots, was storming toward me. Her blue tam looked jaunty over her tresses of long blond hair, but her expression was filled with venom.

What did I do now? Dare to exist?

CHAPTER 17

"We all know him to be a proud, unpleasant sort of man; but this would be nothing if you really liked him."

—Mr. Bennet, in Jane Austen's *Pride and Prejudice*

Cool breath ballooned between Vanna's bright red lips. "What are you doing here?" she demanded. "Are you trying to steal one of my clients?"

"Huh? What are you talking about?"

"You're a sly one, Allie Catt. I know what you did regarding my aunt. You cozied up to her and made her trust you. That's why she gave you a quarter of the—"

"Stop, Vanna!" I held up my hand like a righteous Cher in *Clueless* might, *Clueless* being the movie reboot of *Emma*. "Why don't you like me? Ever since I met you, you've been mean to me. Is it because Tegan is my friend and not yours?"

"She's my sister."

"But not your friend. The two of you have never been warm to one another and that makes you mad, doesn't it? In fact, it makes you jealous of anyone who is her friend."

"Get real."

"She could use your support right now. She really misses your aunt."

"So do I." Her lower lip pushed forward.

"Then start acting respectful. Of me. Of Tegan." My friend

was *not* guilty. *Not, not, not.* "And vis-à-vis your clients, I will never poach them. You've got your style of catering and I have mine. Never the twain shall meet. Now, feed your own ego. I'm busy."

"Allie, be assured I've got my eye on you."

"Ouch! That must hurt." I mimed plucking it off me. "Would you like it back?"

She bristled.

"FYI, if you're willing to help, Vanna, we could use some eyes on a certain someone who lives across the street from your aunt."

"Who?"

"Graham Wynn. Since you're going to be around there with the Realtor, take notes . . . if you know how to write."

I didn't wait for her response and hurried away from the festival. The thought of listening to cheery music with Vanna anywhere in the vicinity was turning my stomach sour, not to mention I was kicking myself for hurling such a petty response. Yes, I liked to be witty, but not cruel.

In bed, I struggled to sleep, not because I was rehashing my encounter with Vanna—I'd apologize the next time I saw her—but because I was wondering how I could have handled the conversation with Zach better. Needless to say, I couldn't come up with an answer. He didn't want me prying. I didn't want a murderer to go free.

When I awoke at five a.m., Darcy growled at me. Positioned by my feet, he was plainly not pleased with my nightlong non-stop movement.

"Go to sleep," I muttered. "I'm not going to Dream Cuisine. I'm going to cook here. You can be a lazybones, if you want."

After dressing in sweats, a long-sleeved T-shirt, and my comfy moccasins, I prepared Darcy's meal, set it by the dining table, reentered the kitchen, and closed the Plexiglas door. I donned an apron and queued up Taylor Swift's "A Place in This World." By the time she reached the second verse, I was singing along full blast, which helped eliminate the tension in my shoulders.

Shortbread cookies were fairly easy to make. Some I would deliver to customers. Others were tests for Tegan's approval, because I'd be serving them at the memorial. I began organizing ingredients on the counter, and my cell phone pinged. It was my mother, paying no mind as to what time it was in the US. Granted, she knew I kept bakers' hours, but texting someone at the crack of dawn was rude.

Fern: **Checking in. Your father says hello. Any progress on the case?**

I bit back a smile. The case, meaning the investigation?

Me: **The police aren't sharing.**

I didn't want to go into detail about Zach shutting me down. I was still shivering from his icy good-bye.

Fern: **See? I was right. Are you looking into it?**

Me: **In my own way.**

Fern: **Be dogged, cookie. That's the single most effective way to accomplish anything. Ta-ta.**

Ta-ta, meaning *so long, I am busy-busy.* Where was she now, anyway? South Africa? India? Bali? Or still in Timbuktu? I didn't reply.

While mixing the butter and sugar in a stand mixer, I wondered how dogged I could be without losing Zach as a friend. Not very, I determined, but I wouldn't let up. Marigold deserved justice, and Tegan was once again on his radar. I reviewed my conversation with him and realized I hadn't mentioned Quinby's accusation to him. Did he consider Piper a suspect? Of course not. Why would he? She'd had no obvious beef with Marigold, and all I had to offer was hearsay from a disgruntled father of a student. On the other hand, Lillian claimed Piper could be secretive. She'd seen Piper embracing a young man. And Chloe said Piper came into the shop and asked to see the spot where Marigold died.

Curiosity was one thing. Morbid curiosity was another.

I switched off the mixer and sifted flour and salt into a separate bowl, reflecting as I did that Zach hadn't given me a chance to ask whether he'd had a conversation with Katrina or discovered why Marigold had wanted to hire Oly Olsen as an investigator. Had she wanted Oly to search for the missing ring? Or to dig up some dirt on a competitor? Or to suss out juicy or damaging information about someone on the community theater foundation board?

Darcy put his nose to the Plexiglas door.

"*Oho!* Now I can be of service to you, sir?" I teased. "Fine. Are you still hungry?"

Silly question. Of course, he was.

I scooped tuna into his bowl, then returned to the kitchen, washed my hands, and continued with my baking. I added the flour blend to the butter mixture, while musing that piecing together clues of an investigation was akin to baking. You had to add ingredients gingerly, and you couldn't try to speed up the process or you could spoil the whole thing.

My stomach grumbled. I turned out the dough onto a piece of parchment paper, which I'd dusted with flour, pressed it into a flat round, wrapped it in plastic, placed it in the refrigerator to chill, set my black cat–themed kitchen timer to thirty minutes, and pulled out items to make myself breakfast.

First I brewed a pot of coffee. I liked it strong, almost twice as strong as anyone I knew. I poured myself a cup—I'd have two—and drank it as I made a batch of scrambled eggs and a slice of toast. The aroma of bread browning reminded me that I had an order for twelve extra-long loaves of sourdough bread to be delivered to Big Mama's Diner a week from Saturday— the same day as the memorial. The diner was offering free slices of hero sandwiches to the donors of a fund-raiser that would honor the firemen of Bramblewood. I peeked in on the sourdough starter, which I stored in a glassware mason jar in the fridge. I kept another at Dream Cuisine. This one had the right color and consistency.

Sitting at the kitchen counter, I dug into my meal and reviewed messages on my phone. I'd received a couple of new orders for tomorrow. No last-minute ones for today, thank heavens. I saw a message from Tegan to call her, and out of the blue, a memory of Marigold came to me. Tegan and I, both twelve, were sitting in Marigold's backyard, drinking iced tea and dining on sugar cookies, while boning up for a book report that Tegan and I had to give in tandem. The book was *Murder on the Orient Express.* Marigold urged us to think about the clues and the suspects' motives. She wouldn't feed us any of the answers. By the end of our session, we knew for certain which motives were correct. To drive the point home, Marigold said mysteries were life lessons. Paying attention to clues and attributing motives would help us solve problems throughout our lives.

The memory made me refocus on her murder. Tegan did not kill her, but I was not going to loop my friend in on Zach's recent reveal. She didn't need the stress.

Therefore, I was on my own. Who were the suspects? So far, all I had come up with were Graham, Katrina, and Piper. I didn't like Vanna as a person, but I was certain she hadn't killed her aunt, and Evelyn Evers had a solid alibi.

"Hmm," I said to Darcy, who was staring intently through the door at me, "like Tegan, I might need to do a deep dive on the three on my list."

He mewed disdainfully.

"Can you come up with a better idea?"

His tail swished the air.

"Yeah. Didn't think so."

I dialed Tegan. When she didn't answer, I left a message, and then preheated the oven and moved to my laptop computer, which I kept on the island in the kitchen. I opened the lid and brought it to life. I perched on a stool, created a new Word document, and typed in the basics Tegan had discovered about Graham Wynn: *GamePlay, his place of business, his parking ticket record, no father, his mother was a nurse, he liked to gamble, he had an altercation in college, he had never been married.* I added what I knew about him: *gamer, reader of clerical fiction, smoker, argued with Marigold.* I'd bet dimes to dollars that the argument was not about the way he trimmed his hedges. I doubted it was about his home's color scheme, either. Had they argued about his drug use? What else might give him motive for murder?

I launched the Internet and typed Graham's name into the search engine bar. I added *GamePlay* plus *owner.* Myriad links and images materialized. Two links led to articles. One about GamePlay's opening day ten years ago. Another about the set-to Graham had in college. I clicked on the article and read what Tegan must have seen—Graham giving the specifics about how he was raised, which made him spend lots of time playing video games. There were dozens of photographs included with the article of teens, as well as adults, primarily of the male persuasion, eager to enter the store. Each customer was holding a golden ticket, like the ones tendered in *Charlie and the Chocolate Factory.* Graham, who must have been about thirty at the time, looked as gleeful as Willy Wonka himself.

The second article told the story of Graham and another boy going at it with fists. Graham, being a hothead, had started the fight, but the other boy did not press charges. Why had they fought? Had the boy teased Graham for his fresh-faced looks? I re-read the notes I'd written regarding Tegan's search and paused at the mention of Graham's mother. A nurse might have known tetrahydrozoline was poisonous. Had she clued Graham in before she died?

I focused on Katrina Carlson. A single article emerged. The Brewery had featured her in one of its public-relations profiles for its waitstaff. The article claimed Katrina was one of the most popular bartenders the Brewery had ever had, adding that she delighted in listening to people's stories, which I already knew. What I didn't know was that she'd always wanted to become a therapist, but she hadn't finished college. When asked why, she said her mother had suffered from mental issues and had needed Katrina's round-the-clock care. Though Katrina had no website or major social media presence, there were pictures of her at the Brewery and others of her and her ex-boyfriend, Upton Scott, a scruffy-looking heartbreaker, at a theater production. One photograph showed her at a party held at Feast for the Eyes for historical-romance aficionados. Marigold had loved posting snapshots of get-togethers. I zoomed in on some of the pictures and noticed Katrina was wearing a bracelet I hadn't seen her wear. Like Marigold, she adored her bling, though I doubted any would claim the price tag of Marigold's pieces. What did she and Marigold argue about? What secret was she hiding?

The timer jangled. I needed to roll out the dough. I stood up and stretched my arms and hands before setting to work. I preferred using two pieces of parchment paper when rolling out dough, one below and one on top. That way, dough didn't stick to the rolling pin. In a matter of minutes, I shaped the dough to the half-inch thickness I preferred. Using a smooth-edged shortbread cookie cutter, I cut out twenty-four cookies, rolling the scraps of dough once more and cutting those into shapes to make the tasting batch. Rolling scraps didn't harm the flavor of the dough, but sometimes the cookies wound up firmer. For my purposes with Tegan, I simply wanted her to approve the taste. For the memorial, as for my clients, I'd make sure the texture was perfect. I arranged the cookies on the cookie sheet and placed the sheet in the preheated oven.

After resetting the timer for eighteen minutes, I went to my computer and typed Piper Lowry's name in the browser's search line. Why had she wanted to see the crime scene at the bookshop? Was she the killer and worried she'd left a clue?

She was quite active on social media. I assumed that was because she was a teacher and wanted to stay up-to-date with her students' activities. Most of her posts were on Facebook, with photographs of school events, like plays and track meets. Was she an athlete? I didn't see any pictures of her in running gear. She owned a gray-haired cat, which she obviously treasured. Two-thirds of her images were of her kissing that cat. There were a few snapshots of her with her arms around what I presumed were students—both boys and girls. None of the students seemed perturbed or uneasy. Piper also shared images of books she'd read. Many were from the Golden Age of Detective Fiction. There were a few books that, based on the cover art, I would peg as YA novels. I hadn't read them. She'd posted a few images of books about dance, but I wasn't familiar with any of them, except *Dance to the Piper*, written by Agnes de Mille, the famous choreographer. Had Piper read that one because her name was cited in the title or because she'd once aspired to be a ballerina?

I searched the links for interviews that might shed light on her personality and found one written by another teacher who wanted Piper to share her tricks of the trade. In the Q&A, Piper said that her mother, an English teacher, had given her invaluable advice over the years, and her father, an elementary-school principal—not hers, fortunately, she'd added glibly—had been one of the kindest men in the world and always had something positive to tell a student. I gathered from the use of the past tense that both parents were deceased. She had two sisters, who became teachers. It was in the family blood. She'd been married once, but she and her ex, also a teacher, parted amicably. She had no children. In view of everything I'd read, I couldn't wrap my head around Piper being a killer, but as Dennell said at dinner the other night, *Nice people kill.* Piper would be alert to students misusing drugs. She might know which over-the-counter items were deadly.

Darcy meowed. He was gazing at me with such seriousness.

Was he tapping into my mind and questioning my reasoning? Was he trying to tell me there was someone I'd overlooked? To be honest, I felt as stumped as I had when reading *And Then There Were None.* There had been lots of suspects, but not one had a clear-cut motive to kill.

Think outside the box, readers, Marigold would urge us at book club discussions.

"Okay," I muttered, as if she was in the room with me.

Was it possible Marigold's murder was, as Zach theorized, a robbery gone wrong?

Katrina didn't finish college because her mother needed round-the-clock care, but perhaps funds had been the real issue. If Graham's business was suffering, he, too, could use an influx of money. What about Piper? Was she flush or in need?

Hercule Poirot claimed, "In conversation, points arise! If a human being converses much, it is impossible for him to avoid the truth."

"That's it!" I said. "I need to get these suspects to talk to me, but how?"

Darcy rose on his hind legs and batted the door with one raised paw. Was he giving me a high five in agreement?

Out of the blue, I remembered Marigold advising Tegan and me, after our friend's mother died in a tragic accident, to reach out to our friend, adding, *No one needs to mourn alone.* I could call Katrina and sympathize with her about losing Marigold in hopes of getting her to chat, but the ploy hadn't worked on Graham when we'd conversed at the bookshop. Quite the contrary.

Deciding Katrina, given her work schedule, probably slept in until noon, I opted to call Piper again, to *bat around theories* as she'd suggested before she'd cut me off last time. I hadn't memorized her number, so I opened the file Tegan had sent me with the shop's customers' emails and phone numbers, found her contact, and dialed.

Her phone rang three times before she answered. "Hello?" She sounded breathy.

"Hi, Piper, it's Allie Catt."

"Oh, Allie," she said, her tone instantly sorrowful. "I've been meaning to call you back, but I've been so busy. I haven't come up with any theories as to who might have killed Marigold, if that's why you're calling. It just doesn't make sense."

"Actually, I was calling to console you," I fibbed. "Chloe said you swung by the shop Sunday. You seemed grief-stricken." It felt too bold to mention that she'd wanted to see the crime scene. "I wish I could've given you a hug." I nearly choked on the word "hug," remembering how Lillian had seen Piper embracing a younger man. "How are you holding up?"

"Like you, I miss Marigold something fierce. She was so wonderful. Her leadership on the theater foundation board was remarkable. I wish . . ." She sniffed. "I wish I'd come to the shop earlier Saturday morning, instead of staying home to grade papers. If I had, maybe . . ." Her voice trailed off.

"We all wish we could have saved her."

She exhaled softly, but didn't add anything more.

"Were you home alone that morning?" I asked, and silently berated myself, knowing Hercule Poirot would have clicked his tongue at my lack of finesse. But how else could I coax out the answer?

After a long moment, Piper said, "Yes, I was alone. I'm not married."

Did she think I cared if she spent the night with a boyfriend?

"Alone," she repeated, to drive home the point.

That was when I knew she was hiding something.

CHAPTER 18

"I wonder who first discovered the efficacy of poetry in driving away love!"

—Elizabeth Bennet, in Jane Austen's *Pride and Prejudice*

I checked the updated list of orders on my Notes app, made sure I didn't forget anyone, and in a matter of two hours, baked the scones and muffins I needed to deliver, packed each delivery in the appropriate boxes, left the dishes to soak in the sink, and dressed in jeans, white blouse, and peacoat. I threw on my scarf, too. The sun was shining, but the weather report said the temperature would be chilly. Before heading out, I assured Darcy I'd check in on him at midday. With a twitch of his tail, he bounded to the bay window and nestled on the sitting bench to soak in a beam of sunlight.

While tootling around town, Zach came to mind, but I forced myself not to text him. He was miffed at me. I didn't know him well, but I could imagine his response if I begged for mercy being akin to what my father's response would be—my mother's opinion about me investigating, notwithstanding. *Drill it into your stubborn head,* my father would say. *You are not to get involved. End of story.* If I knew what Zach's favorite cookie was, I could make him a couple dozen to win him over.

At noon, after all the deliveries were made, I went home. I gave Darcy a ten-minute hug-and-petting session, fixed myself a toasted English muffin topped with mozzarella cheese, sliced tomatoes, and chopped basil, and headed out again, this time to purchase supplies. It was impossible to shop at only one store for my goods. I picked up fruits and veggies at a farmers' market. Eggs were a specialty purchase at Garden Greene Farm. Their eggs were unparalleled, and they claimed it was the organic, homegrown feed they gave their chickens that did the trick. The best butter, however, was sold at Butting Heads Farm. They raised cows and sheep and churned butter daily. For flour and sugar, which I bought in bulk, I had to drive to Baker's Club, located at the eastern end of Main. The club was a warehouse setup for restaurants and concerns like mine. I tried to make any shopping trip in less than four hours but always failed.

After I'd unloaded all the perishable items at home—I'd cart them to Dream Cuisine in the morning—I dialed Tegan again. This time she answered, sounding depleted. When I asked why, she went into a tirade about Winston, who'd had the temerity to harangue her. I offered to bring takeout to the B&B. We could eat in her room, she could bend my ear, and I could tell her about my deep dive. Maybe, in person, I'd reveal that she was once again on Zach's persons-of-interest list. *Maybe.*

"I'd love a burger," she said. "From the Brewery. And potato skins. If you don't mind, bring enough for Mom . . . and Rick," she murmured, resigned to his presence in her mother's life. "Helga has been on a fancy-food kick, and Mom is craving good old diner food."

At dusk, the Brewery was hopping with activity. I perched at the bar and slung my coat onto the back of the swivel chair. Katrina and a male bartender I'd never met were on duty. She sashayed to me, and I gave her my order.

"Anything to drink while you wait?" she asked.

I requested an Audrey Hopburn beer and paid up front, adding a hefty tip.

Lickety-split, she placed my beer on a napkin on the bar. "Here you go."

"Nice bracelet." Today's beauty was handsomely made with jasper beads and a turquoise centerpiece.

"Like it?" She tapped her finger on the stone. "The seller said the combo is to promote ultimate healing and encourage calm and balance. Plus it's supposed to make me feel like a goddess."

"And does it?"

"I'm crossing my fingers. I'll put in your order now."

How could I get her to talk about the secret she wanted Marigold to keep?

While working on a conversation starter, I swung my chair around so I could observe the crowd. I spotted Lillian's friend, Yvonne, sitting with a trio of women and two men, one older, one younger. Yvonne looked fresh-faced and natural. The three women were wearing a lot of makeup, not the typical style in Bramblewood. I decided they were actresses in the upcoming musical and had come from a dress rehearsal. The younger man had a surly expression and longish hair that fell over the collar of his leather jacket. He looked familiar, but I couldn't place him. Repeatedly he checked his watch. The silver-haired man was regaling the others with a story.

From the far end of the bar, Katrina signaled my order was being prepared, then she began to wipe down the counter with a wet towel. Suddenly the surly man appeared and hissed her name.

Katrina jolted. The half of her face that I could see blazed with anger. "What d'you want, Upton?"

Upton. Of course. Her photographer ex-boyfriend. I'd seen his face in the photos when I'd researched Katrina online.

He pulled a manila envelope partway out of his jacket, whispered something I couldn't make out, and snickered. With the speed of a viper, Katrina flicked him with the towel. The distraction gave her an opening to snatch the envelope.

"Don't get cocky, babe. I've got more." Cackling, Upton swaggered to the theater group.

More what? I wondered.

Katrina pivoted, giving me a full glimpse of her face. Tears were pooling in her eyes. Her chin was trembling. She said something to her fellow bartender, ducked under the hatch, and raced through the saloon-style doors into the kitchen. The doors swung shut with a *swoosh-clack*.

Call me crazy, but something was not right, and I intended to find out what was up. Was her ex trying to buy his way back into her life, or had he involved her in some kind of nefarious scheme? Did whatever was in the envelope she'd seized have to do with her secret? Was I correct earlier when I'd guessed Katrina could use an influx of cash?

Katrina's coworker Wallis overheard Katrina warn Marigold, *If anyone finds out, I'll know it was you who told them.* Did Marigold figure out what angle this Upton jerk was working? I could see her taking the same tack she'd often employed with me and Tegan, giving advice and being the voice of reason, telling Katrina the guy wasn't worth it and to get out while she could. I could also imagine Katrina resenting Marigold's counsel, but would she have killed her to keep her from meddling?

Pretending to need my takeout in a hurry, I pressed through the swinging doors into the kitchen. I spied Katrina exiting out the rear entrance. The sous chef, who knew me because she also worked at one of the cafés I supplied with baked goods, said, "Allie, your dinner's up next."

"Thanks. I'll be out there with Katrina." I hooked my thumb.

When I stepped outside, I regretted having left my coat on the chair. Cool breath billowed from my mouth in puffs.

Katrina was pacing, muttering to herself, an unsmoked cigarette in one hand. "Stupid, stupid, stupid."

"Hi, Katrina," I said. I didn't have a match. I didn't offer a light. "I hope you don't mind sharing your space with me. I needed some fresh air. Long day. Lots of baking." I was prattling, but figured if I talked up a storm, I could persuade her to do the same. "You okay?"

"Yeah." She tossed the unlit cigarette on the ground and jammed it with her heel.

"You sort of, um, ran out after that guy—"

"I don't want to chitchat. Your dinner should be up. Go away."

"Is he your ex-boyfriend?" I asked, knowing he was.

She swiped her pinkies beneath both eyes to mop away tears.

I dared to proceed. "You and Marigold argued. Was it about him?"

Her face went dark. "Who told you we argued?"

"I can't remember."

She folded her arms across her chest. "It's none of your business."

Her tone made me feel like I'd been hit by an arctic freeze. "I'm sorry. I—"

"Leave me alone." She strode into the kitchen and shouted, "I'm heading home. I'm not feeling well."

Nobody stopped her. She marched into what I presumed was the employee locker area without a backward glance.

When I returned to the bar to fetch my coat, my order was sitting on the counter.

The Blue Lantern was aglow in warm ambient light when I arrived. I parked in the lot and strolled to the entrance. Guests were mingling in the parlor, chatting excitedly about the activities they'd shared during the day. A few were discussing the Celtic Festival. Others were talking about hikes they'd taken. I found Tegan sitting in a far corner with her mother, drinking red wine. The blue sheath Noeline was wearing matched her eyes. Tegan was dressed in leggings tucked into ankle boots and a cropped sweater that almost covered her midriff. *Almost.* A glimpse of skin made me shiver. The heater in the van hadn't eliminated the cold that had seeped into my bones while standing outside with Katrina.

"I've got dinner." I hoisted the bag. "Will Helga be upset?"

"Now you ask?" On cue, Helga bustled into the room with a tray of canapes. Her hair was knotted into a bun, but wisps of hair fell around her aging face. "I am the best cook in town, but you order in from the Brewery, of all places. No, I am not upset. Bah!"

Tegan sat taller. "You don't make burgers."

Helga scoffed. "Burgers are for riffraff."

"Then I guess we're riffraff." Tegan hopped to her feet and took the bag from me. "*Mmm.* Potato skins. Yay! Let's go to my room now. Mom, you too."

"Isn't Rick joining us?" I asked, scanning the crowd for him.

"Rick is off being noble." Noeline gathered the glasses they'd been sipping from and the bottle that sat between them.

"Reading to the kids at the hospital," Tegan replied.

"He usually does it on Saturday mornings and Thursday nights," Noeline said. "Tonight is an extra volunteer session. Isn't that wonderful?"

"Wonderful," Helga repeated, and harrumphed. I wasn't sure if she was commenting on our dinner plans or she didn't like Rick. I supposed she could be protective of Noeline. I didn't get a chance to ask. She left to serve the others in the room.

"Can you tell Mom is smitten?" Tegan teased as she tramped up the stairs.

"Noble is as noble does." Noeline trailed her daughter and knuckled her on the shoulder. "He's a good soul helping hospital communities thrive."

"Woot, woot, woot!" Tegan said, but her accompanying fist pumps were unenthusiastic.

Noeline thwacked her again. "Give him a chance."

On the second floor, decorative lanterns hung outside each door offering soft illumination. Tegan's room was situated at the far end. We stepped inside.

"It's magical," I said, shrugging out of my peacoat. I'd never been inside one of the guest rooms.

"Thank you," Noeline said. "I worked with a designer."

The view from the window was of the rear yard, which extended for quite a ways and was planted with graceful trees. The expanse featured a babbling fountain and seating areas designed so guests could sit in the shade while enjoying nature.

The interior of the room was white with blue trim. Paintings of Victorian homes and gardens adorned the walls. The drapes featured multicolored hanging lanterns. The linens on the queen-sized bed were a soft blue. The pillow shams matched the drapes. Furniture included a quaint blue table, with two scroll-back chairs, a mahogany dresser and armoire, and a small settee and coffee table. A hurricane lamp sat on a bedside table. An antique lamp with a lantern motif stood on the dresser. Both were turned on, by Helga, I presumed. Guests didn't relish walking into dark rooms.

"All of Mom's ideas made the final cut," Tegan said.

"And some of your aunt's," Noeline added, her voice catching. "Marigold had lots of good ones. The lamps. The hall fixtures. The drapes. She was superb at finding things online for me. I'm not computer savvy."

"I could teach you," Tegan said.

"You're sweet to offer, but I'm really not interested."

Tegan put the bag of food on the small table and pulled out

the containers. The Brewery had supplied paper plates and plastic utensils. "Allie, you take the settee. Mom and I will pull these chairs over. You each want something of everything, right?"

"Yes, please," I said.

Noeline fetched another wineglass from the dresser and poured some red wine into it. "It's Chianti. I hope you like it." She handed it to me. "I heard you saw Vanna last night, Allie."

Oof. What had Vanna told her? "I, um, yes, we . . ." I realized I hadn't mentioned the altercation to Tegan.

"Vanna said she improperly accused you of stealing clients," Noeline went on.

"She what?" My voice squeaked. Vanna told the truth? Well, I'll be.

Tegan said, "The nerve of her. You? Filch her clients?"

"She didn't mean it," I said quickly, cutting Vanna some slack. After all, I'd delivered the final barb. "I mean, she did . . . accuse me . . . but she was ginned up from the music at the festival. It was rowdy." Oh, wow, could I weave a yarn. "Please tell her I'm not mad at her."

The corner of Noeline's mouth started twitching, leading me to believe she knew the whole story. "Don't worry," she whispered, confirming my suspicion. "She has a short fuse, but she gets over her miffs just as fast."

I sipped my wine, not believing her for a minute.

"She's so like her father," Noeline added. "The man could be such a hothead. Vanna leaps before she thinks. Why, that's the very reason she accused you of murdering your aunt, darling."

"Tegan . . ." I began, earnestly wanting to inform her that Zach considered her a person of interest again.

"Yes?"

I couldn't speak. My mouth felt as if I'd swallowed alum. I licked the inside and started again. "Nothing." Changing gears,

I said, "Noeline, I've been meaning to ask. Do you know which jewelry store your sister frequented to have her jewelry cleaned, possibly the one who brokered her deals?"

Noeline shook her head. "She was circumspect about her purchases. I think she worried that I might chastise her for spending so much money."

"I thought her long-lost lover gave her the jewelry," Tegan said.

"Some of it," her mother replied, "but not all."

Tegan set our plates on the table and passed us each a napkin. "Dig into the food, and then, Allie, spill. What have you drummed up?"

"Detective Armstrong would prefer if I didn't."

"Don't listen to him," Tegan said. "It's not like the police are breaking any speed barriers solving Auntie's murder."

"Who do you suspect?" Noeline asked around a mouthful of potato skin topped with sour cream and chives.

I told her the three names and why, adding that Marigold might have discovered Katrina's secret regarding her ex-boyfriend. I recapped how Upton hounded Katrina at the Brewery earlier, but she wouldn't talk to me about it.

"Do you think Auntie wrote down what she knew?" Tegan asked.

"Good question. We should look through her computer tomorrow and review any notes she might have jotted down."

"Tell Mom about Graham."

I did, adding that we weren't sure about the specifics of his argument with Marigold.

"As for Piper Lowry," I said, "Quinby Canfield is convinced she's a killer."

"Quinby Canfield." Noeline wrinkled her nose. "That man could kill a fake plant."

I detected some history between them, but didn't have to ask because Noeline continued.

"I interviewed him to redo the inn's gardens. I wanted to add more azaleas. He said azaleas didn't do well here. *Ha!*" She coughed out a derisive laugh. "They are the most populous plant in the Asheville area other than Indian hawthorn and mountain laurel. So I checked out his references and not one former client had anything good to say about him. Plus don't get me started about his Yelp reviews."

I recalled Stella Burberry claiming Quinby lived frugally. Perhaps being bad at his job was the cause. Was there a reason he might have held a grudge against Marigold and pinned the crime on Piper to deflect suspicion from himself?

"Back to Piper." Tegan sighed. "I can't believe she's a killer."

"Lillian said Piper is secretive," I said. "She saw Piper hugging a younger man. She thought the boy was over sixteen, but what if"—I swallowed hard—"he wasn't?"

"No way," Noeline said. "Besides, she was at the bookstore when we all arrived, so she couldn't have done it."

"Mother, are you as naïve as toast? Anybody who was there could have done it. There are more than two hours unaccounted for after Graham saw Auntie that morning, and Allie talked to her on her cell phone." Tegan paused. "I think the killer lay in wait outside her house, followed her to the shop, sneaked inside, did the deed, and left out the rear, avoiding being picked up by any CCTVs—"

"Those weren't working in the area," I said.

"Right," Tegan continued. "Do you think the killer knew that?"

"Hard to say."

"No matter what, the killer avoided being seen by anyone in the area. Since there was no blood at the crime scene, the killer didn't need to go home and change. Feeling cocky, he—"

"Or she," I cut in.

"He or she came to the shop at the regular opening time to establish they were as innocent as apple pie."

"Innocent as a lamb," I corrected.

"I mix metaphors. Sue me." Tegan took a bite of her burger. Sauce squirted out of the bun onto her lap. She wiped it off with a napkin.

"The doors were locked," I stated.

Noeline set her fork down with a *clack*. "I'm losing my appetite. This is why I don't like reading murder mysteries. I can't handle the gory details."

Tegan patted her mother's leg. "That's because you're a visceral reader. You read as if it's happening in real time. That's how I read, too."

"And yet," Noeline said, "you can digest those kinds of books with ease."

"I read all genres, Mother. I like to experience a range of emotions, not suppress them like you."

Noeline glowered at her daughter.

"I'm sorry," Tegan said. "That was rude of me. I . . ." She pressed her lips together.

"I forgive you. We're all tense."

Tegan turned to me. "What about Piper's alibi?"

"I spoke to her on the pretense of consoling her. She says she was at home alone, but there was something off about the way she said it."

"And do we know what Graham's alibi is?"

"No."

"I think we should go to his house," Tegan said, taking another bite of her burger. "And keep watch."

"Don't you dare," Noeline warned.

"Mom, we won't approach him. We won't even talk to him. But his neighbor Mrs. Harrigan said she saw someone suspicious hanging around more than a week ago. Maybe the killer is a person who lived near Auntie and staked out her house from across the street so they could follow her. C'mon, Allie, what do you say?"

Throughout our childhood, though Tegan was not an extrovert when it came to public speaking or taking charge of something as simple as a book club, she had been a sly scamp, able to talk me into all sorts of hijinks. Ride bikes to the mall on a busy street to buy éclairs. Jump off the top of the roof into a pile of leaves. Steal through a graveyard while whistling for ghosts.

I never said no.

CHAPTER 19

"I had not known you a month before I felt that you were the last man in the world whom I could ever be prevailed on to marry."

—Elizabeth Bennet, in Jane Austen's *Pride and Prejudice*

Noeline tried to deter us, but Tegan was adamant about doing reconnaissance. I didn't dissuade her. Something about Graham bugged me, too. His prickly attitude the other day at the bookshop before Quinby accused Piper of murder grated on me. Granted, I'd put him on the spot because of what Celia Harrigan had said, but how could I not press? If I could prove he killed Marigold, Tegan was in the clear.

"I'll drive," Tegan said.

I climbed into her MINI Clubman and strapped on my seat belt. "What exactly do you hope to see when we get there?"

"Not sure. A lurker? A drug lord? A neon sign saying, *I'm the killer!* We'll pretend we're going to Auntie's. I've got a key. We'll observe his place from the living room."

"Didn't Vanna change the locks for the Realtor?"

Tegan shot me a look. "She'd better not have."

Oh, but she had. There was a lockbox on the door and a FOR SALE sign plugged into the lawn.

"Crud," Tegan muttered under her breath. "If we sit in the car, he'll spot us. I know what we can do." She drove on and parked around the corner. "We'll sneak to the front of my aunt's house and hide in the bushes."

"Tegan—"

"*Shh.*"

We returned on foot. The cool night air nipped my cheeks. I drew my peacoat tighter around my body.

Hugging the side of Marigold's house, Tegan skirted the corner. I trailed her. She ducked into the evergreen bushes in front and pulled me to her. Luckily, they weren't thorny bushes.

An hour passed without incident. No comings. No goings. My fingers grew numb. I said, "Let's leave. I'll buy you a hot cocoa."

"No. You heard Mrs. Harrigan. I want to know what's up." Without giving me a warning, she darted across the street.

"Wait!" I rasped, loath to follow, but I had to. I couldn't let her go off half-cocked.

She flattened herself against the wall of Graham's house and inched along the side until she reached the corner near the rear. I remembered a time when we were girls and Tegan sneaked to a neighborhood at the south end of Bramblewood. She wanted to peek inside the witch's house. The old woman who owned it wasn't a witch, but the woman had straggly hair and bony hands and her Victorian home was gray and shabby, so Tegan often joked that the old crone ate children for breakfast. Tegan had wanted to see what the witch was cooking for supper. She'd hoped it would be Vanna.

"See anything?" I whispered.

"Nothing," she said, peeking past the corner.

I peered around her. Graham's house was laid out like Marigold's, with the kitchen facing the rear yard and a screened-in porch jutting off the kitchen's dining area. The porch was dark. "It's quiet. No loiterers. Case closed. Let's scoot."

"Wait. A light went on. I see a shadow moving inside the room."

"For all you know, Graham is practicing dance moves.

C'mon, Tegan, let's skedaddle." I clasped her shoulder. "We're trespassing."

But she didn't heed my advice. She wrestled free and tip-toed toward the porch.

Suddenly a dog snarled. In an instant, a huge, ugly thing barreled through a dog portal, which neither of us had noticed carved into the porch door.

"Tegan, run!" I clutched her elbow and steered her toward the street. When I'd played basketball, we'd had to practice sprints, but we'd never trained by running away from a vicious mutt. I was surprised by how fast I was . . . and how Tegan was keeping pace.

The dog barreled after us, grunting and slavering. To be fair, I couldn't be sure it was slavering, but the foamy sounds it was making led me to believe it was as dangerous as all get-out and eager to taste our blood.

In record time, we reached Tegan's car. She flicked it open with her key fob. We barreled inside and closed the doors.

The dog landed its paws on the driver's-side window. Tegan yelped. I shrieked.

Upon second glance, the dog wasn't as big as I'd imagined. In fact, it most likely weighed forty or fifty pounds, but it was a pit bull, and as a girl I'd had a run-in with a pit bull, the kind of encounter that had left a half-inch scar on the underside of my chin, so I wasn't a fan. I loved golden retrievers and Labradors and, well, any kind that was gentle—"gentle" being the operative word. *Don't hate me, pit bull owners.*

Tegan pressed the button to start the Clubman and jammed the car into gear. The dog dropped to all fours, squealed its displeasure, and cut around the corner, out of sight.

When we arrived at the Blue Lantern, Tegan's fingers were clutching the steering wheel so tightly her knuckles were white.

"S-sorry," she said, rubbing her hands to restore circulation. "I will never put you in danger again."

I patted her shoulder. "Yes, you will. You love living on the edge as long as it doesn't require public speaking."

She grunted.

I gazed sideways at her, fear for my friend simmering within me. "Tegan, I've got to tell you something."

Needless to say, Tegan was upset to hear the diner's delivery guy couldn't support her alibi, but she remained adamant that she'd been with Dennell. She described in detail holding Dennell's hands while she suffered the shakes and dry heaves. I believed her and vowed I would clear her.

Later at home, after double-checking that the doors and windows on my place were closed and locked, I received a special order from Blessed Bean for raspberry-chocolate tarts—the sisters at Perfect Brew had raved about them. Deciding to bake here in the morning, I put together some dough mixtures and refrigerated them. An hour later, I climbed into bed, stared at the darkened ceiling, and rehashed the trek to Graham's house. Was his pit bull a self-starter, or had Graham seen Tegan and me outside and sicced the dog on us? Darcy picked up on my unease and cuddled close to me. His purring helped me drift off to slumberland.

When I roused at five o'clock Saturday morning, I did the reasonable thing and peeked out all the windows. Seeing the coast was clear, I slipped on some leggings, a college sweatshirt, and a pair of UGGs, and stepped outside. Flashlight in hand, I made a tour of the house and breathed easier when I didn't find any suspicious footprints.

I went inside and fed Darcy, then made a slew of scones, cookies, and tarts, using the dough mixtures I'd put together before hitting the sack, and readied them for delivery.

At nine a.m., I changed into my work clothes and drove to Blessed Bean. To my surprise, Zach and his partner, Bates, were outside the café addressing a couple. Upon closer inspection, I realized the man in the denim jumpsuit was Quinby Canfield. His wife Candace, the singer with the shy, reserved voice, was standing by his side. She had huge, round eyes and a dimpled chin. Her coat was a mishmash of tweeds, like a throwback 1960s design. She held a guitar case in one hand and a to-go cup of something in the other. Had Zach stumbled upon Quinby and his wife on a morning coffee run, or had Zach known they would be there? Had he learned Quinby had accused Piper of murder? I'd missed the opportunity to tell him. Was he pressing Quinby as to why he'd say such a thing? Did Quinby have more to offer than he did the other day?

Zach caught sight of me and frowned. I parked on the street, retrieved the order of tarts, and, tray in hand, strode toward him.

"What are you doing here, Allie?" His voice was harsh. Cold. Clad in black, he looked ominous. To ease the tension that had crept into my shoulders and jaw just by being in the same vicinity as him, I imagined a cartoonish rain cloud hovering over his head and soaking him.

"I . . . I'm . . ." I sputtered. "I'm here on business. I'm delivering tarts." I held up the tray.

"Uh-huh," he said, but I could tell he didn't believe me.

"I'm not here to interrupt. 'It's not personal . . . It's strictly business.' "

"Are you quoting *The Godfather*?"

"As a matter of fact, yes. Are you impressed?" I offered a sassy grin.

He didn't react.

"See you." I reached for the door. With my hand on the handle, I said, "Hey, I've been meaning to ask, have you questioned Katrina Carlson? She—"

"Allie!"

Knowing my cheeks were blazing with embarrassment, I hurried inside and let the door swing shut. I didn't look back.

When I completed all my deliveries, I sped to Feast for the Eyes. I had one week until the memorial and needed to finalize the schedule for the event. While on my delivery route, Tegan had texted me to say Dennell and a couple of her friends were going door-to-door in Dennell's neighborhood to see if any of them had seen Tegan entering her home last Saturday morning. Giving her a thumbs-up, I then messaged her with a few of the particulars for the memorial. The tea would start at two. A quarter of an hour later, despite her fear of public speaking, to honor her aunt, Tegan would muster the courage to welcome the attendees. Noeline would say a few words about her sister. Vanna wanted to participate, so Tegan suggested she read a passage or two from *Pride and Prejudice,* but Tegan would moderate. She didn't want her sister to have an open mic to air grievances.

Now I needed to pin down when I would set up and determine how many servers and cleanup crew I'd need to hire. I also wanted to know who would say the closing words. Perhaps Tegan should invite the pastor from Marigold's church to speak.

When I entered the shop, Lillian was standing by the mystery aisle with Stella Burberry. There were people lingering in all of the other aisles, too, and a few were perusing books in the reading nook. Tegan and Chloe were at the sales counter, assisting customers.

"I brought a few goodies for taste testing," I said quietly to them as I placed pastry boxes on the desk behind the sales counter. I hadn't brought enough for all the customers.

"Yum," Tegan said. "Exactly what we needed."

"For us, too?" Lillian asked as she and Stella made a beeline for me. Lillian had dolphinlike hearing, I decided. She offered a *pretty please* smile.

"Sure, okay, but keep it to yourselves." I opened the boxes and motioned to the shortbread cookies, pound cake, and the fresh batch of Maids of Honor. I'd also included some of the raspberry-chocolate tarts. To Tegan, I said, "By the way, I saw the police questioning Quinby Canfield this morning."

She took a piece of pound cake and bit into it. "*Ooh,* so good and rich. Saw them where?" she asked, nibbling more of her treat.

"Outside Blessed Bean on Mountain Road."

"I love that place." Stella unbuttoned the single button of her tailored jacket and brushed a crumb off her silk blouse. "Quinby's wife sings there."

"Oh?"

"She entertains at three other places, too," Stella added.

I must have been wrong about her being allowed to perform merely because she was a relative. I supposed my hearing could have been off, and the woman's voice was better than I'd remembered. I said, "Didn't you say Quinby was strapped for cash? If they're a two-income family, they should have plenty coming in."

"Folk singers don't make a lot," Stella said. "It's a gig job. Very iffy."

Tegan took a tart and bit into it. "Golly, Allie, your best yet. These will be a hit at the memorial."

"I'm not sure chocolate tarts are appropriate for the time period."

"Really?" she muttered. "Wasn't chocolate brought to Europe in the late 1500s?"

"Yes, but—"

"Back to Zach," she said, cutting me off. "Do you know what he was asking the Canfields?"

"I got the impression he'd stumbled upon them," I said. "Right place, right time."

"No handcuffs involved?" Lillian waved a shortbread cookie as she posed the question.

"No. Quinby isn't a suspect, as far as I know," I said. "He

liked Marigold. It's Piper he wants to malign. I guess Zach was asking him why he suspected her."

Tegan said, "Allie spoke to Piper yesterday. She doesn't have an alibi for last Saturday morning."

"Why would she need one?" Stella asked. "There's no way she murdered Marigold. Like I started to say when I was here the other day, when Quinby rudely cut me off"—she sniffed—"I saw her that morning around seven thirty. In her house. With someone."

"She told me she was alone." I recalled how she had reiterated the word "alone," which had set off alarm bells.

"That doesn't track," Stella said. "She was definitely with someone. And that someone was a man. Piper is no slouch, and the other person was a head taller."

"Could you make out his features?" I asked.

"I only saw shadows through the sheer drapes. They were moving about the room as if they were pacing."

"Why do you think she would she lie about being alone?" I asked.

"Maybe the person she was meeting was married," Tegan suggested.

"Or . . ." Lillian clicked her tongue. "Or it was a student."

CHAPTER 20

"Vanity and pride are different things, though the words are often used synonymously. A person may be proud without being vain. Pride relates more to our opinion of ourselves, vanity to what we would have others think of us."

—Mary Bennet, in Jane Austen's *Pride and Prejudice*

"No," I said firmly. "Don't go there."

"An of-age student." Lillian raised both hands to ward off my wrath.

"Why don't you ask her?" Stella said. "She's volunteering at Alta Barlow Hospital today."

"How do you know that?" I asked.

"Because I donate my time there, too. I usually greet people and steer them to the elevator or the proper floor. It's not easy walking into a hospital. Nearly everyone's pulse rate spikes. Having a guide makes them feel comfortable."

"What does Piper do there?" I asked.

"She plays with children who are in the waiting room when the grown-ups need to visit or have checkups. You know, she never had children of her own. I think it makes her feel needed."

"That's so nice of both of you," Lillian said. "I should get involved."

"Let me tell you about the opportunities." Stella and Lillian moved to the side to chat.

"I'll go see Piper and ask her about Saturday morning and why she lied," I whispered to Tegan.

"Tell Zach. Let him do it."

"I'd rather it was a friendly visit."

"Then I'll go with you."

"But the shop—"

"Chloe can handle it for an hour."

I gawked at her. "You sure? Look around. It's a full house. I think we need to cull the crowd."

At one thirty, when the throng thinned to two customers, Tegan grabbed her purse and offered to drive.

The Alta Barlow Hospital reception area was bright and white. Fresh flowers adorned the counter. I asked the cheery receptionist where I might find the children's playroom, and she directed us to the right.

The playroom was filled with paraphernalia appropriate for children of all ages: books, chalkboard easels fitted with pastel chalk, stuffed animals, and a desk with art supplies, where some projects were already in progress. A janitor in a uniform was emptying a trash can by the watercooler. Piper, clad in jeans, a plaid blouse, and red canvas Keds, was perched on a tot-sized chair, reading a book to a trio of children, who were sitting, cross-legged, on an interlocking, foam, multicolored play mat. One boy, who I pegged at around five years of age, was plucking something off his striped T-shirt. The girl beside him—his sister I was pretty sure because their coloring was identical—was fiddling with one of her braids. The other boy was opening and closing the Velcro straps on his shoes.

Piper glanced in our direction, probably expecting a parent to be entering with a child, and blinked. "What are you two doing here?"

"We'd like to chat with you for a sec," I said.

She pursed her lips, then closed the book she was reading—

an A to Z Mystery titled *Detective Camp.* "Children, go finish up your art. I'll be over to help in a few minutes."

They scrambled to their feet and raced to the art table. The boy in the striped shirt pushed the girl out of the way. She squealed that she'd "tell Mom," which meant I'd correctly assumed she was his sibling. The other boy plopped into a chair and scooped a project toward him.

Piper rose, smoothed the front of her blouse, and moved to the watercooler, where she poured herself a mini cup of water. "Want some?"

We both declined.

"What's up?" she asked after taking a sip.

"When I talked to you yesterday," I began, "you said you were home Saturday morning."

"That's right."

"Alone."

"Yes." She brushed her dark hair over her shoulders. "Look, I know it doesn't provide me with an alibi, which apparently I might need because I'm getting the feeling you suspect me of murder—"

"No," I protested.

"Yes." She threw me a peeved look. "But I was grading papers. I have those to show for my time."

"Piper, I have it on good authority that you weren't alone. Someone saw a man in the house with you."

"What?" Her eyes widened. Her chin began to tremble.

"Piper." I reached out, but didn't touch her. "I don't think you harmed Marigold, but someone has fingered you, and that someone is talking to the police."

"Who?"

"I can't tell you his name."

"*Aha.* It's a he."

"The witness saw you peeking in the bookshop's windows a few days before the murder, after the shop closed."

"I needed some YA books. The YA aisle is the one facing the window."

That sounded reasonable.

Tegan said, "You also came to the shop Sunday when we weren't open and asked Chloe if you could see the crime scene."

Piper studied the cup she was holding, as if formulating a response. After a moment, she raised her gaze to meet ours. "Being at the shop that morning, knowing Marigold had been murdered, rocked me to my core, and . . ." She gulped down the rest of her water, crushed the paper cup, and tossed it into the refreshed garbage can. "And I've been shaky ever since. I hoped seeing the site, making sense of it in my mind, might help." She paused, looking as if she wanted to say something more.

I waited.

"Okay, that's a lie," she said with a sigh. "I came to the shop Saturday morning at seven a.m., and I met with Marigold."

Tegan and I exchanged a glance.

Piper continued. "She wanted to talk to me about something in private. I brought my cat with me, and Marigold held him."

"What did she want to chat about?" I asked.

Piper shook her head once, not willing to cough up that particular answer, but she pressed on. "I was in the shop less than five minutes. Marigold and I worked out the issue, and I left." She screwed up her mouth. "After she was killed, I got to thinking . . ." Her shoulders slumped. "I got to thinking someone could have seen me and believed I killed her. I've read enough mysteries to know the smallest clues might lead to an arrest. So I returned, after the fact, to check out something."

"What?" Tegan and I asked in unison.

"See, every spring, my cat sheds like crazy. The thick layers he grew for the winter come out in clumps. I worried that the police might find his hair in the shop and on Marigold's clothes." Her face pinched with pain. "I didn't kill her. You've got to believe me. I went home and came back later, when others were already there. I didn't do it."

"Tell us who was with you in your house that morning," I coaxed. "He's your alibi."

Piper regarded the children at the art table and returned her focus to us. "You can't tell the police."

I almost said I wouldn't, but stopped short, because if I needed to, I would.

"A homeless student has been staying with me. That's what Marigold wanted to discuss. She knew." Piper wheezed as if all the air was leaving her lungs. The relief on her face after uttering the truth was palpable. "She was concerned about the impropriety of it. My reputation."

"Go on," I said.

"College students are struggling right now. Leasing an apartment is expensive, especially with no credit record. Some students are able to rent rooms, and many find RVs to live in, but a few don't have the funds and decide they need their education more than housing, so they wing it."

"Wing it?" Tegan asked.

"They live on the street. In tents, if they can afford them." Piper worried the sapphire gem on her necklace with her thumb and forefinger. "One of my former students is now a junior at UNC Asheville. He knew a young man who was in such a situation. He would have taken him in and hidden him in his dorm room on campus, but if he got caught, he could be ousted and didn't want to risk it. He asked if I could help out."

"How old is this young man?" I asked.

"Nineteen."

Of age. I breathed easier.

"He's a good student, and he gets excellent grades. I invited him to stay at my place for a few weeks while we figured out where else he might be able to live. He's been very helpful with fixing a few plumbing issues and painting a bedroom. I've kept the drapes closed so neighbors wouldn't get the wrong idea, but apparently someone has." Her gaze went from me to Tegan. "I'm guessing it was Stella Burberry."

We didn't respond.

"Stella has a keen eye," Piper said. "She doesn't miss a beat. She's a regular at the bookshop, if I'm not mistaken."

"So, in sum, you were not alone that morning," I said. "You admit you lied."

"To protect him."

"You were seen hugging a young man last week. Was it the same one?"

"Who told you? Lillian Bellingham? I saw her passing by. I wasn't sure if she saw us."

I nodded.

"Yes," Piper continued. "He was so grateful for my offer, he broke down in tears. I was consoling him."

"Piper," I said, "I suggest you reach out to Detective Armstrong. He's a good guy. Maybe he will know people who can help place the boy with a family for the duration of the school year."

She thanked me profusely, and before returning to her wards, she said, "By the way, I like Graham Wynn, and I'm not trying to throw suspicion on him, but he and Marigold exchanged words last week. I couldn't make out what they argued about. It was after a book discussion. I did hear him say, 'Mind your own business.'"

On the way to the shop, I asked Tegan to stop at Ragamuffin. She idled at the curb, and I purchased three vanilla lattes, the extra one for Chloe.

Minutes later, I climbed into the car and positioned the carry pack on the floor. "You know, I've been haunted by a few lines of the novel your aunt was writing." I recited them: " 'She knew the truth, but she dare not tell anyone. She couldn't. If she did, her family would be a target.' "

"Good memory."

"Her words make me wonder whether she, Marigold, was the protagonist in the story, and someone was threatening to harm you or Noeline or Vanna."

Tegan cut a look at me. "I hadn't thought of that. That could have been why she wanted to hire Oly Olsen. To spy on, say, Graham."

"Like I said last night, I think we should take a peek at her computer again and see if there's something we can discover about Graham or anyone else."

"I'm with you. Also Oly might have gathered new info since we last spoke to him."

I wasn't sure how that was possible, but I didn't dissuade her of the notion.

Chloe was checking out three customers at the counter when we returned. A mother and her brood of children were browsing the children's and YA aisle. Two senior citizens were sitting in the reading nook, books open.

"Here." I handed Chloe the latte, and she blessed me.

"We'll be right back," Tegan said to her, and stepped through the doorway leading to the stockroom. I followed.

In the office, Tegan wakened Marigold's personal computer, pulled up the Contacts page for the letter *D,* and poised the cursor arrow over the Due Diligence listing. "Ohmigod, did you see these?" She giggled.

With a finger, she referred to two other contacts: Dates and Places, and Detective Darcy.

I knew which one had made her laugh. "Detective Darcy?" I snickered. "Honestly? She really was obsessed with *Pride and Prejudice.* Click it."

She did and a contact for Fitzwilliam and Sons materialized. "Get out of here!" she exclaimed. "Call him."

I pulled my cell phone from my trouser pocket and dialed. I waited and then heard an answering machine for Fitzwilliam and Sons, a detective agency. I informed Tegan.

"Another one? Leave a message."

I waited for a *beep*. "Hi, this is Allie Catt, and my friend Marigold Markel has your contact in her files. I was wondering, sir, if she hired you for an assignment. She's . . ." I pressed my lips together. I didn't want to say the word "deceased."

"Could you return my call?" I rattled off my number and ended the call.

Tegan said, "Do you think she picked that agency because of the name?"

"Possibly."

"She must have listed it under *D* for detective."

"Or maybe Mr. Fitzwilliam's mother was an avid Jane Austen fan and actually gave him the first name Darcy." I tapped my chin with a fingertip, deliberating why Marigold had reached out to not one, but two detectives. "Marigold knew Katrina's secret. And Piper's. What if she knew others?"

"You're not suggesting she blackmailed anyone."

I fanned the air. "Far from it. She was a caring person. She would have wanted to help anyone who was in trouble, like she did Piper."

"Man, I hope her story pans out."

"Me too."

Tegan picked up a pen and rhythmically rapped it on the edge of the desk. "You know, it bothers me that Auntie was arguing with so many people this past week. She wasn't the quarrelsome type. Something must have been bugging her."

"I agree."

"Do you think she was sick?"

"I don't have a clue."

Tegan said, "That waitress at the Brewery thought Auntie knew Katrina's secret. What if she knew others? Customers and friends confided in her all the time. What kind of secrets would be worth killing over?"

"A woman having a baby out of wedlock."

"Or a woman running away from an abusive husband."

"Or a man on the lam."

Tegan flicked the pen aside. "I don't trust Rick."

"Whoa!" I threw up both hands. "That came out of left field. Why don't you? Because he's courting your mother? He's not running from the law."

She grunted. "What if he's phony-baloney? What if he's one of those guys who has two families in two states? If I ask my friend to dig into the employment records—"

"Rick is an independent contractor, so she'll find nothing. Relax." I patted her shoulder. "I seriously doubt he'd pawn his wedding ring if he was hiding another family. Let your mother have some fun. If he's not the right guy, she'll figure it out."

Tegan picked up the pen again and resumed tap-tapping as she theorized about what other secrets her aunt might have known. "How about a married man with a clandestine lover? Or a woman with an obsession that's embarrassing?"

That notion gave me pause. A few weeks ago, when I was browsing the bookshop for a new mystery to read, I heard Katrina ask Marigold to order a special book for her, *The G-String Murders,* written by none other than Gypsy Rose Lee. It was an odd choice, although Katrina did like historical romances, and the famous striptease artist, by all intents and purposes, was a person of history, with a somewhat-romantic past. Was it possible Katrina was performing or had performed at a gentlemen's club? Did Marigold figure it out because of the strange book order? Did Katrina's boyfriend catch her doing so? He was a photographer. What if he'd taken compromising photos? He said he had *more.* What if he threatened to show the pictures to her boss at the Brewery?

No, that would have been a reason for Katrina to want him dead, not Marigold. Even so, after we closed the bookshop, I decided to chat with her one more time, not that I could consider the last time we'd interacted a chat.

CHAPTER 21

"When she is secure of him, there will be more leisure for falling in love as much as she chooses."

—Charlotte Lucas, in Jane Austen's *Pride and Prejudice*

Tegan and I drove separately, knowing we'd both head home after our inquiry.

The lot in front of the Brewery was full. We parked in the side lot and hoofed it to the front entrance. Once inside, we realized there wasn't a seat to be had, although there were a few spaces at the standing-only tables. Tegan and I secured two spots, and I scanned the restaurant for Katrina. I glimpsed her working the bar with the same guy as last night.

Wallis, her blond hair swept into a messy bun with tendrils gracing her cheeks, laid down two napkins on our table. I'd been hoping she'd be working tonight's shift. On the way to the Brewery, I'd formulated a plan, and Wallis had a starring role in the execution of it.

"Hello again, Allie," she said. "You're becoming a regular. Spruce Goose?"

"Sure," I said.

"An Ugly Pig," Tegan said.

"Who are you calling ugly?" Wallis joshed, and winked.

"A side of your house fries, too," Tegan added. "With all three sauces." The sriracha aioli was my favorite. Tegan preferred the cumin catsup. We both liked the chutney mayo.

"Wallis, before you go, I've got a question for you." I lowered my voice. "Katrina's ex-boyfriend—"

"Scum."

"Yeah, I got that vibe. I saw him here last night. He and Katrina exchanged words. I asked if she wanted to talk about it, but she told me to butt out. Do you know"—I decreased my volume even further—"if he's blackmailing her?"

Wallis cut a look at Katrina and returned her gaze to me. Matching my tone, she said, "You'll have to ask her."

"Did she and Marigold argue about pictures Upton took?"

"You know about the pictures?"

Bingo! I was right. "Yes. He's a creep."

"To the max."

"Tell her to talk to me. I think I could help her."

"She didn't kill Marigold," she stated with authority. "I asked her."

I swallowed hard. That was bold on her part, but how would she know whether Katrina was lying? I didn't think they were best buds. "Even so, tell her. Please."

"I'll be back with those beers," she said in her full voice.

In minutes, she returned, set down our drinks, and said, "Katrina will talk to you, Allie, but *only* you. Alone. Outside. Behind the kitchen."

She wouldn't dare lay a finger on me, not with Wallis and Tegan knowing where I was. I had to risk it.

Zach entered the Brewery with Bates and made a beeline to the hostess. He said something. She gave a curt nod and headed away as if he'd sent her on a mission. Bates was viewing something on his cell phone. Zach did the same.

In a flash, I sneaked through the kitchen and out the door to the rear of the building.

Katrina was, once again, pacing with an unlit cigarette in hand. She flicked the cigarette to the ground and crushed it with the toe of her shoe. "So you figured things out, huh?"

"Upton is blackmailing you. With what? Does he have photos of you at a gentlemen's club?"

"A gentlemen's . . ." Her mouth dropped open. "What gave you that idea? Do I look like I can pole dance?"

"You're fit."

"Ha! That's sweet, but no I'm not. I don't work out a stitch. However, you were close with your guess. Upton took some compromising photos."

Of the two of them? In the act? Ew.

"He threatened to post them on social media."

"What a slime bucket."

"Yeah, he's a vindictive SOB and super angry that we broke up."

I waited. When she didn't proceed, I said, "Marigold and you argued. Was it about him?"

She nodded. "She wanted me to leave him."

"Did she learn about the photos, or did you tell her?"

Katrina fell silent.

"You were heard saying to her, 'If anyone finds out, I'll know it was you who told them,' which, I'm guessing, meant Upton would keep quiet about the photos if you paid him off. Except he reneged on your deal, didn't he? He came around last night wanting more money."

"No, he . . ." Katrina pulled her hair free of the decorative clasp holding her curls off her face. "Look, Marigold's heart was in the right place. She wanted to mother me, like she did everyone else, but she was making me feel bad about what I was doing."

If Katrina was a willing participant in the photos, it was none of Marigold's business. Why would she butt in? Katrina wasn't her daughter or even a relative.

Katrina went on, "I have low enough self-esteem without someone holding up a mirror."

After the breakup with my fiancé, my ego suffered. Therapy

and a few self-help books prodded me into getting my head together. One book advised me to chant: "I am a good person. I am worthy. I don't need a man to love me to bolster my self-esteem." I chanted for three months until I convinced myself I was not only worthy, I was great.

Katrina refastened her hair in the clasp. "I know Wallis is the one who blabbed to you, as well as to that hunky Detective Armstrong. He came in earlier today and asked me my whereabouts on Saturday morning."

"He did?" My parting question outside Blessed Bean must have spurred Zach to immediate action. So, why had he returned now?

"I informed him I was with a friend. We spent Friday night and into the next morning bad-mouthing our exes, but my friend is out of town and can't be reached. She's on a three-week unplugged camping trip. When she gets back, she'll touch base with him."

The friend thing sounded iffy, but there was no way to disprove it.

I wished Katrina well, said I hoped she and Upton could work things out to her satisfaction, and went inside. To my surprise, Zach and Bates were questioning the owner, Oly Olsen. He was a sixty-something bear of a man with thinning hair, rosy cheeks, and a nose that had withstood a pounding or two.

Zach caught sight of me, held up a hand for Oly to sit tight, and waved me over. "I wanted to tell you that Piper Lowry reached out to me." His voice was monotone. His gaze official, not warm. "I am able to help her because my mother, a do-gooder by nature, knows lots of folks willing to assist, so thanks for getting me involved."

"You bet. And did the student confirm her alibi?"

"He did."

"That's great." I smiled, but he didn't return the gesture. "I heard you spoke with Katrina Carlson, too."

Oly's ears perked up. "Why did you need to speak to my best bartender, Detective?"

Zach said, "She was a person of interest in the Marigold Markel murder, but she's cleared."

Is she? I wanted to ask, but kept mute. I certainly didn't want to receive a chillier reception from Zach than the one I was getting. If he accepted her unsubstantiated alibi, then I would, too.

"Good to know," Oly said. "That means my job for Marigold is done."

"What job was that, sir?" Zach asked.

"Marigold wanted to hire me. Just this morning, I received a delayed email from her. It was weird getting it after, you know, she died, but the Internet . . ." His laugh was gravelly and gruff. "It's amazing it works at all."

"What did she ask you to do?" Zach pressed.

"She wanted me to dig into Katrina's problem and sort out her pride."

" 'Sort out her pride,' " Zach repeated, and gazed at me as if I had the answer.

I shrugged, clueless.

"That was the message," Oly said. " 'Sort out her pride.' I figured it was why she'd asked if I'd read that book, Allie. Like I told you, I did. When my girls were in high school, me and my wife read everything they did. In the story, Elizabeth Bennet is clever and can talk circles around anyone, but her hasty judgment—her pride—leads her astray. I suppose Katrina is much like Elizabeth. But if she is no longer a suspect, and I am happy to hear she is not, then my investigation is not necessary."

No longer curious why Zach and Bates had come to see Oly, I bid the detectives and Oly good night, then I returned to Tegan and filled her in on the conversation about the delayed email from her aunt.

"'Sort out her pride?'" Tegan raised an eyebrow.

I nodded. "Do you think she reached out to Fitzwilliam and Sons to investigate someone's prejudice?"

Tegan narrowed her gaze. "Do not kid about this."

"I'm being serious."

After she and I finished our fries and were heading to our respective vehicles, I glimpsed my cell phone. No one from Fitzwilliam and Sons had reached out yet.

"If and when they do," Tegan said, "text me."

Darcy was awake when I entered the house, waiting at the door like an anxious parent checking up on an errant teen.

"Good evening, sir," I said. "I had a long day. How about you?"

He chuffed his response.

"You have food. Water. You even have a llama."

He complained again.

I bent and nuzzled his nose. "I'm sorry. I forget that you're a weird cat. You get lonely. I'm going to read for a bit in bed before going to sleep. You game?"

He meowed.

I grabbed my copy of *The Murder of Roger Ackroyd,* tucked Darcy under one arm, and carried him through the house as I got ready for bed.

Later, after reading four chapters of the book, I switched off the bedside light and snuggled beneath the sheets thinking I'd fall asleep in seconds, but to my dismay, I couldn't get Katrina's words out of my head. Her friend was on an unplugged vacation. Maybe I needed to do the same. But how could I take time off? I didn't have a business partner, and now I was part owner of a bookshop. My mother often carped that I needed to prioritize *me* if I was going to have a life. She could be right.

When the morning sun glared through the break in the curtains and stabbed my eye like a sword, I lurched to a sitting position. Had I overslept? How could I have forgotten to set the alarm? *Yipes!*

Church bells chimed, and I leaned back on my pillow, chuckling.

"It's Sunday," I said to the cat. "Yay! I don't have to bake, and I don't have any deliveries."

He mewed his support.

Like many towns in North Carolina, Bramblewood had its share of churches. The Congregational church, built in 1905, was the one nearest to me, and the place where my grandmother had attended services until her death. Nana and I had been close, much closer than I ever would be to Fern and Jamie. I'd gone with her a few times to services, but after her passing, when my parents didn't force me to go, I stopped.

"However, I do have to go to the bookshop," I said to the cat.

He tilted his head and swiped the air with his tail.

"Because." That ought to be enough explanation for him, but it wasn't. He bounded onto my stomach and glowered at me. "Because," I continued, "Tegan is counting on me. There might be shipments of boxes to unpack or recommendation tags to hang or a book club to arrange." How had Marigold managed it all?

Darcy grumbled and hunkered down.

I stroked his ears and cooed, "I'll be home before you know it."

Who was I kidding? My furry companion had an internal alarm clock that Apple, if it was smart, ought to clone. Without glancing at a wristwatch, he knew when it was time for me to feed him and usually—not today, for some reason—if I'd overslept. How many times had I awakened with a paw brushing my nose? *Hello, sleepyhead, wake up!*

I clambered out of bed, washed up, did a quick stretching session, and fed Darcy. In less than twenty minutes, I was out the door.

When I strode into the bookshop, which wouldn't open officially until noon, I found Chloe arranging preordered books at the sales counter.

"Book clubs," I said. "Have we rescheduled them?"

"Good morning to you, too." Dressed in a red jumper over a white blouse, knee socks, and black Mary Janes, she reminded me of a character out of a children's novel. "As a matter of fact, we have one tomorrow night, Monday, for our Amateur Sleuths group. We've been reading *Twelve Angry Librarians* by Miranda James, which, if you didn't know, is the pen name of Dean James."

"I do know, and I've read that book." The series featured interim library director Charlie Harris and his highly intelligent and animated cat, Diesel.

She tapped a sheet to the right of the cash register. "This is the list of attendees."

I perused it and recognized many of the names, like Stella, Lillian, and Piper.

Tegan waltzed from one of the aisles, her arms laden with books.

"Tegan, I really think you should lead the first book club since . . ." I faltered. *Since your aunt won't be able to.* "It would be good for you to confront your fear before the memorial."

"Nope. You're taking the helm." She placed her treasures on the counter and began to sort them by genre.

"But I bake at night."

"Excuses, excuses. The club lasts two hours. You can make the time. Auntie created book club questions for every book in the shop that didn't have author-prepared questions and saved them in a file drawer in the office. It'll be easy-peasy."

"Zach Armstrong is signed up," Chloe said. "So is his partner."

I eyed her curiously. "I didn't know they read books starring amateur sleuths."

"Men can surprise you," Chloe joked.

"Chloe," Tegan said, tapping a stack of three cookbooks. "These are the other books Vanna requested."

"Oh, I forgot to mention." Chloe gently rapped her temple with her knuckles. "She came in earlier to pick up her partial order and said she'd return later."

Tegan's mouth curved up in a grin. "*Phew.* That means I don't have to see her." She threw me a sly glance. "You either."

I didn't want to admit I was relieved and quietly moved to the pegboard to review Marigold's instructions for daily duties.

"Vanna was talking up your mother's new boyfriend," Chloe said.

"Talking up, as in, she approves of him?" Tegan arched an eyebrow.

"Apparently, he's been super helpful handing out her business cards to 'muckety-mucks at the hospital.' Her words, not mine." Chloe bound the cookbooks with raffia ribbon and affixed a Post-it note with Vanna's name on it. "How are you getting along with him?"

Tegan shrugged one shoulder. "I rarely see him. He's a busy guy. On Friday night, when Allie and I met Mom for dinner, he was at the hospital reading to kids. Today he can't make church because—"

"He was reading to them at night?" Chloe asked, stacking a pair of romance novels. "That's odd. Volunteers only read to kids in the afternoon."

"How do you know?" I asked after landing on the chore of cleaning up the reading nook.

"I entertain the kids there a couple of times a month. It's my way of giving back to the community, and . . ." She giggled. "And a way to convince myself I don't want to ever become a mother. Don't get me wrong. The kids are sweet, but I'm constantly reminded that I don't have enough patience to repeatedly answer the question 'Why?'"

Tegan exchanged a glance with me. "Rick also said he was

reading to them last Saturday morning. He told my mom Thursday nights and Saturday mornings are his slots."

"Uh-uh." Chloe shook her head. "Not possible. Only afternoons," she repeated.

"Why would he lie?" Tegan asked. "Is he two-timing my mother? Is he lying about his career? Is he not really a bond guy? Maybe he's a grifter."

"Tegan," I cooed, "chill. He must have a good reason."

"You said he hawked a ring at the pawnshop. I'll bet he needs the money, and now he's after my mother's. He's a con artist." Her voice was rising by decibels. "What if he killed Auntie so he could get his hands on the hundred thousand—"

"Tegan, stop!" I barked. "You're making yourself crazy. Your mother is a sane and sober woman. She's not stupid. And Rick is not a killer. He's simply got to account for his—"

"I was convinced the business meeting Helga said Rick had last Saturday morning was actually reading to kids, because they wouldn't have cared if he'd come rumpled, but it was a lie," Tegan hissed. "A lie!" With short intakes of air, she tried to calm herself, but couldn't.

I fetched her a glass of water and shoved it into her hands.

Chloe said, "I thought after you ruled out Piper that Graham Wynn was your main suspect in your aunt's murder."

"Graham." Tegan gulped down the water. "Right. We have to go to his house again."

Chapter 22

"Again?" Chloe asked.

"We went there Friday night," Tegan replied, and focused on me. "Remember Graham's neighbor Celia Harrigan said she saw someone? It wasn't at night. It was during the day. We were wrong to case his place in the dark. Let's go prepared this time. We'll pick up some dog treats and a leash."

"Dog treats and a leash?" Chloe echoed, clearly confused.

Tegan didn't wait for me to dissuade her. She swanned through the stockroom and out the exit.

I said to Chloe, "We'll be back soon."

Like we did Friday night, we parked around the corner from Marigold's house. However, in the light of day and the sun directly overhead, it was impossible to hide in the bushes in front of her place. Instead, Tegan suggested we act like we were waiting for the Realtor to appear. She stood next to the FOR SALE sign and regarded her watch. An actress she was not, but Graham didn't step onto his porch to check us out, and his dog didn't attack us, so the validity of her playacting wasn't in question.

"There's Celia Harrigan's house," Tegan said. "Down the street. The yellow-and-white Craftsman."

The woman was standing at the opening on her porch, holding binoculars to her eyes. She caught sight of us and disappeared inside.

"There's nothing like having nosey neighbors," Tegan said, adding, "Hey!" She hitched her chin in the direction of Graham's house. "Who's that pulling up?"

A black Kia Sportage parked in front of Graham's place. Seconds later, a linebacker-sized person in a dark brown anorak exited. Face obscured by the hood, the person—I presumed by the sheer size it was a man—strode to the rear of Graham's house.

"He's dressed a tad warmly for spring, don't you think?" Tegan asked. "Let's follow."

"No way." I grabbed her elbow. "Are you—"

"Look. There's another car coming," Tegan rasped.

An old blue Chevy Tahoe parked behind the Kia. A figure in a sweatshirt hoodie and jogging pants exited, a cell phone pressed to his or her ear. It was hard to tell which sex this one was. The slimness and height could lean either way, and the boots were generic. Whoever it was followed the same path as the previous visitor.

Tegan said, "Celia Harrigan told us the person she saw was wearing a hoodie."

The recent visitor could be the person, but so could a thousand other people who were out for a stroll in Bramblewood on this fine day.

Within a minute, a third person arrived in a silver Mercedes E-class sedan. A fourth in a green BMW SUV. They, too, rounded Graham's house.

"We've got to follow and see what they're up to," Tegan urged.

"Pal, c'mon. For all we know, these people are going to a prayer meeting."

"You think? Then why are they doing everything they can to hide their faces?"

"They parked their cars right in front of the house." I jutted a hand.

"We should call the police."

"And tell them what? Graham has guests who enter through the back entrance? That proves nothing. His front door could be busted," I suggested.

"What if Celia Harrigan is right and Graham is dealing drugs?"

Rowf! Grr!

The pit bull charged around the corner of the house and barreled across the street, teeth bared. My adrenaline spiked.

Tegan clenched my arm and anchored me to my spot. "Don't. Move." She cooed, "Here, doggy. Treats. C'mon. Treats." She pulled the recently purchased bag from her pocket, plucked a peanut butter bone from it, and held it out.

The dog snarled and ran faster, ready to pounce.

Tegan waggled the treat. "I have more, sweet doggy. Sweet, sweet doggy. Treat." She wiggled it furiously.

The dog came to a halt, visibly perplexed that we weren't hightailing it to our car like we had on Friday. Sniffing suspiciously, he slinked toward Tegan. Deciding that whatever she was offering wasn't poison, he snarfed it down. Tegan had a second treat at the ready. While the dog chewed, she hooked the leash onto the loop of his leather collar.

"Who's a good boy?" she said. "You are. Yes, you are."

"Omigosh! Your volunteer work at the veterinarian's office during junior high really paid off," I said, astonished.

Growing up, she'd wanted a dog, but her mother said if she needed one so badly, she had to donate her time at the vet for one full year. After twelve months of cleaning up poop and vomit, Tegan had been pretty much cured from ever wanting a pet full-time, but she'd loved hanging out with them and teaching them tricks. I, on the other hand, had helped out at a birds-of-prey sanctuary feeding owls and raptors because at the time, I was reading fantasy fiction and had become enamored with creatures with wings.

Tegan scratched the dog's ears. "Let's go for a walk." She began to guide him to Graham's.

"What are you doing?" I said, panic surging in my gut.

"Bringing him to his owner. Graham will reward us for rescuing his prized mutt. But before we ring the doorbell, let's take a peek through a window and catch him and his guests unaware."

"No."

Of course, she didn't listen to me. She continued on, moseying toward the rear of the house. We neared the screened-in porch, and the dog let out a high-pitched yelp.

"Traitor," Tegan mumbled.

In a flash, Graham rushed out the door. The person in the hoodie trailed him, but stopped short of exiting. "What the heck are you doing here?" Graham demanded.

"Your dog got loose," Tegan said. "I'm being a Good Sam—"

"He's free to roam." He snatched the leash from Tegan.

"Oh, gee," she said, vamping. "We thought as vicious as he is—"

"He's not vicious," Graham spat. "He's ardent."

Ardent? Honestly? I scowled. The dog was a brute, except when bribed with a treat.

"I repeat, what are you doing here?" Graham asked, his voice gruff.

"Graham, relax," the person in the hoodie said.

I'd heard the soft female voice before. It was Quinby's folk-song–singing wife, Candace. She stared at Tegan and me with big, round eyes. Scared eyes, actually. Had we caught Graham in the act of dealing drugs? Was Candace a user or a distributor for Graham? Or was I, like Tegan, blowing things out of proportion? Perhaps Graham invited her to his house to discuss an employment opportunity, like singing at GamePlay.

Get real, Allie. Singing at a game store? And what about the other guests? Are they all gamers?

"Mrs. Canfield," I said, "what are you doing here?"

"You know m-me?"

"I'd have thought you'd be performing somewhere today. Sundays are big coffeehouse days."

"Yes, well, I'm taking the day off." She tugged at the strings of her hoodie.

The linebacker-sized visitor cut around her and barged outside. "What the heck is going on? Are we finishing this deal or not, Graham?"

"Told you," Tegan whispered. "It's drugs."

"I've got pocket aces, man," the guy said, "so you're not getting away with folding the hand on account of your dog running amok."

Deal? Pocket aces? I tamped down a giggle. "Are you hosting a private poker game, Graham?"

" 'Private' is the key word. *Leave.*" He made a shooing motion with his hand. The pit bull growled.

Tegan pulled a treat from her pocket and held it out to the dog, who snatched it before Graham could tell him no.

"Are you participating, Mrs. Canfield?" I asked.

She stepped outside. "Yes, but you can't tell my husband."

Why not? Did she have a gambling addiction? Was she losing regularly, thus draining the family coffers of much-needed cash?

"Celia Harrigan told you, didn't she?" Graham stated.

"Not about the poker game." I didn't repeat her theory that he might be a drug dealer. "But she did mention someone stealing to the rear of your house a week ago. She was concerned."

"Ha!"

"Do you host other games?"

"Yes," the other poker player answered before Graham could respond. "Mornings only. No nights." He stared accusingly at his host, as if he would prefer evening games.

"As you very well know, mornings are more convenient for me," Graham said sharply. "That way I can open GamePlay at eleven a.m. And mornings give you, and others like you, the ability to keep your penchant for cards a secret. Nobody pays attention."

Except Celia Harrigan, I thought.

"As for Sundays," Graham went on, "you're lucky I have a game at all, seeing as it's a holy day."

I wondered if having private games was against state law, but decided not to pursue that angle. Celia Harrigan could take up the cause if she so desired. I eyed both of Graham's guests. "Mrs. Canfield, were you playing poker here a week ago yesterday—"

"Early Saturday morning," Tegan said to clarify.

Candace Canfield's eyes widened. "How could you possibly know that? Have you been spying on me?"

"No," I said. "Celia Harrigan gave a description of the person she saw. Gray hoodie, hiking boots. Like the items you're wearing. What time did the game end?"

"Eight thirty."

Given the timeframe, I doubted Graham could've managed to kill Marigold and elude being spotted by the crowd that was gathering in front of the building.

When Tegan and I returned to the shop, I told her I had to go home and bake. She advised me that Lillian was stopping by for costume fittings later in the afternoon and suggested I return. I said I would show up close to four, and I'd bring the fixings for tea.

Darcy stirred in his spot in the bay window as I breezed into the house. He hadn't polished off the kibble I left out for him to nibble on. His breakfast tuna must have filled him up.

"Hello, handsome, miss me?"

He made a sound that I deciphered to mean, *More than you could possibly know.* At least, that was how I preferred to interpret it.

I nuzzled his nose, entered the kitchen, closed the Plexiglas door, washed my hands, and pulled out the items I needed to make a sample trifle, which would be a perfect addition for our tea and a good taste-testing experiment for the memorial. Yes, a trifle should chill at least six hours in the refrigerator, but today, I'd make an exception. On a whim, I decided to put together a second one. I could bring it to the book club tomorrow night.

The idea made me think of Zach, which once again triggered memories of Marigold's murder.

"Darcy," I said, "who killed my friend?"

The cat pounced onto the barrel of the llama, his ears perked, but his expression was puzzled.

"Yeah," I mumbled. "I feel the same way. Piper Lowry is out and so is Graham Wynn. That leaves Katrina Carlson." I liked Katrina. I didn't want her to be guilty. But her alibi of being with a friend who might or might not corroborate her whereabouts nagged at me. Was it possible she was stalling for time while figuring out a discreet way to get out of Dodge?

If only I knew who was on Zach's radar, but he was definitely keeping me at bay. No text messages. No invitations to go hiking. I liked him, but I was slightly miffed. I mean, what was so wrong with me wanting to help him solve the crime? Sure, I understood why the police wouldn't want an amateur sleuth sticking her nose where it didn't belong, but Marigold was my friend and Tegan's aunt. I cared. Shoot me.

"Trifle," I muttered.

I needed to keep focused if I wanted to make the dessert correctly. It wasn't hard to construct, especially once the pound cake was baked—let's hear it for planning ahead—but the stirred custard could be tricky and could curdle if one wasn't careful.

First I prepared a bowl of ice water and set it aside. This was crucial. Next, in a saucepan, I whisked together the egg yolks, milk, and sugar, and turned on the burner to medium. Stirring continuously, I watched as the mixture simmered to the de-sired texture. Once it was cooked, I removed it from the heat, added the vanilla, and put the pan in the ice water, again swirl-ing the mixture constantly. When the custard was sufficiently cooled, I poured it into a bowl and covered it with plastic wrap. This would prevent a skin from forming on top. I placed the bowl in the refrigerator, then checked on the strawberry freezer jam, which I would use when assembling the trifle. Freezer jam was exactly what it sounded like—jam that did well in the freezer and could be used at any time to enhance a dish. It was runnier than typical jam. I often added a room-temperature dollop to a warm scone.

For the next two hours, I decided to make mini tarts, using a lemon curd filling that I would top with fresh fruit. I always had frozen mini tart crusts, in their tart tins, ready to go. Once a week, I made lemon curd that I jarred and preserved.

I slid the tarts into the preheated oven and rinsed the rasp-berries, blueberries, and strawberries.

Minutes later, the timer pinged. I removed the crusts from the oven and slid the pans, one by one, into the countertop multi-tiered rack to cool. One pan tipped and the tart tin slipped off, causing the tarts to spill out and crumble.

"Drat." I needed an assistant. I was going too fast. "Slow down, Allie."

Darcy mewed his agreement.

"Hush." I cleaned up the mess and wondered if I'd ever be able to expand my business. I could ask someone like Chloe to assist. She had free time on her hands. But she wasn't a baker, by any stretch of the imagination. I mean, get real. She burned coffee. Maybe I could put feelers out to some of the bakers at cafés and restaurants around town. They'd have to be subtle feelers, like a clandestine business card palmed off after a delivery. I didn't want anyone to get fired for taking a second job.

On the other hand, I didn't need to expand. I managed what clientele I had, and I would be working in the bookshop and earning an income from my portion of the partnership that would cover expenses. Or would it? Did Feast for the Eyes make money? I hadn't thought to ask Tegan. What if Marigold had covered the shop's losses with her own funds, meaning I would be working simply for the fun of it?

Another timer jangled. The custard was ready, and the remaining tart shells were cool. I assembled one of the trifles in a pretty glass bowl by drizzling the inch-square pound cake pieces with triple sec, topping the cake with custard, adding a layer of freezer jam, and then repeating the process. I whisked the cream and stored it in two containers, one of which I'd take with me so I could decorate the trifle with it right before serving. Then I assembled the tarts.

At ten to four I arrived at Feast for the Eyes, and Tegan helped me take the tarts and trifle, plus the assortment of teas, teacups, and plates I'd brought, into the conference room. She had draped the table with a white tablecloth and added pretty napkins.

Lillian was already there in the stockroom, hanging the dresses Chloe, Tegan, and I had selected. She looked primed for the tea in an ankle-length blue floret dress with lovely blue bows. "Here's your hat, Allie," she said, handing me the sage-green bonnet I'd tried on.

Tegan locked the shop's front door, flipped over the OUT TO LUNCH sign, and returned to the stockroom to change. "That will give us a little privacy," she said, and giggled nervously.

"What's wrong?" I asked.

"Are we . . ." She ran her lip between her teeth. "Are we dishonoring Auntie's memory by having too much fun?"

I clasped her elbow gently. "Your aunt would be so proud of you for handling the tragedy with aplomb. I remember her telling me about losing the love of her life. She scraped herself off the floor and put one foot in front of another. 'Life,' she said, 'never promises us anything. We have to make of it what we can.'"

Tegan threw her arms around me. "You're so right." Tears pooled in her eyes.

When we were all dressed in our costumes—Chloe in a red Empire dress with back buttons, and Tegan in a dusky blue dress festooned with cream-colored flowers—the four of us convened at the table.

Just as I was serving the trifle, the door to the conference room flew open.

"Tegan!" Winston Potts barged in, his face flush with rage. Sweat dripped down the sides. "How dare you consult an attorney!"

Tegan popped out of her chair. "Don't you 'how dare' me! How dare *you* let yourself in with the spare key? Don't Closed signs matter to you? And more importantly, how dare you have an affair? How dare *you* make me feel like garbage? Why, Mr. Wickham, you disgust me."

Her soon-to-be ex-husband stammered, "W-Wick—"

"You are the one who sullied our marriage," Tegan continued. "You are the soul who is at fault. I shall not be blamed, and I shall not be dissuaded from my resolve."

I gaped at her. Had she referred to her husband as Mr. Wickham? Had she actually used the words "shall" and "sullied"? Was she roleplaying, or was she channeling Elizabeth Bennet? Whatever was going on was working because Winston's mouth opened, but no words came out. He yanked on the lapels of his too-tight jacket. He hadn't put on weight. It had been an ego purchase, for sure, and would never fit him.

Finally he found his voice and croaked, "I love you." He dropped to one knee and pressed his hands together in a pleading gesture.

"I don't care," she said.

"We can work this out."

"No, sir, we cannot. You forsook me. You broke up *this*." She wagged a finger between the two of them. "You drove me away. You cannot beg forgiveness. Give me that key and take your leave." With that, she lifted her teacup and, pinky extended, took a sip.

Winston scrambled to his feet and puffed out his cheeks. He reminded me of a blowfish I'd seen on an aquarium visit. An ugly, mad blowfish. "Now you listen here—"

"Key," Tegan demanded.

He fished it from his pocket.

"Winston." I stepped between him and Tegan and took the key from him. "Stupidity isn't a crime. You're free to go. And don't come back unless you want the cops to intervene."

CHAPTER 23

"Happiness in marriage is entirely a matter of chance." . . .
*In spite of his asserting that her manners were not those of
the fashionable world, he was caught by their easy playfulness.*

—Charlotte Lucas, in Jane Austen's *Pride and Prejudice*

W inston banged the conference room door as he exited.
Tegan exhaled, set her teacup on its saucer, and sank into her
chair. Chloe, Lillian, and I applauded.

"You were masterful," I said. "Brilliant."

"Your aunt would be so proud," Lillian said.

"Elizabeth Bennet too!" Chloe cried.

Tegan pressed her burning cheeks with her palms. "It was
the dress. I felt Jane Austen's style of speaking churning inside
me, and I couldn't stop it from popping out."

"Bravo!" I exclaimed.

When we were all sufficiently calm, I served up the trifle,
and we dug in. Maybe it was the electric energy in the air, but I
had to say it was one of the best I'd ever made.

At dusk, after changing into our regular clothes, packing up
the dresses and bonnets Lillian provided, and taking dishes
and leftovers to my van, I helped Chloe and Tegan close the
shop, and we tallied up the day's receipts. Then I followed

Tegan, who was rattled by Winston's appearance, to the Blue Lantern to make sure she arrived safely.

The lanterns hanging on the shepherds' hooks were all illuminated. The brass ones by the entry were, too. In the parlor, to the right, guests had gathered for the nightly wine tasting. Noeline wasn't in attendance. Helga was serving mini-quiches laced with rosemary. I bit into one and hummed my approval. They were divine.

"Where's my mother?" Tegan asked, nabbing a second quiche.

"In her office," Helga said.

Tegan steered me to the room that was situated left of the kitchen and opened the door. Like the guest rooms, the office was decorated in white and blue with a lantern motif. The antique furniture pieces included a secretary's desk and chair, a bookshelf filled with hardcover classics, a pair of oak file cabinets, a large vintage floor safe, a beautiful blue brocade divan, and a pair of scroll-back side chairs. Noeline was bent over the desk, which was as messy as all get-out, with pens, pencils, receipts, and paper clips scattered hither and yon.

"What's going on, Mother?" Tegan asked. "Did a hurricane hit?"

"I've lost my keys."

I flashed on Marigold's wild search for hers a couple of weeks ago.

"I've rifled through every drawer in here." Noeline sounded as frantic as her sister had. "This is the only place I leave them, unless I'm on my way out. Then they're by my purse."

"I left mine in the laundry room last week," Tegan said.

"I don't do laundry," her mother snapped.

Tegan raised both hands in defense.

"I'm sorry, darling," Noeline said, her cheeks flushing as florid as her rose-colored sheath. "I simply don't misplace things. I don't. I'm a creature of habit. Losing things isn't normal for me."

"Are these the same keys you said you left home last Saturday?" I asked.

"Yes. I haven't required them since then and forgot to look for them until now, but I need one to open the wine cabinet, and—"

"Helga doesn't have a set of keys?" Tegan asked.

"Not to the wine cabinet. It's not that I don't trust her. I do. With my life. The cabinet is a recent acquisition. I just never got around to making one for her." Noeline grunted in exasperation. "Shoot! I always place the keys in the top drawer of this desk. Helga said the last time she saw them, they were by my purse in the kitchen. Shoot!" She spanked the desktop.

Tegan said, "Let Allie and me help you look."

"I've searched everywhere!"

"Breathe, Mother." Tegan poured her a glass of water from the pitcher on the mahogany bar trolley. Noeline gladly accepted it.

For a good fifteen minutes, Tegan and I rummaged through the cushions of the divan and rifled through every file in the cabinets. Tegan removed and replaced book after book from the shelves. I got to my knees and searched under all the furniture.

When we'd exhausted every possibility, I said, "Let's go through the desk one more time." I told them about Marigold's quest.

Five minutes later, just as when I'd helped Marigold, I found a ring of keys stuffed into the rear corner of the topmost-right drawer of the desk. "Voilà!"

Noeline bounded to her feet and gripped them in her fist. "You're a magician."

"Sometimes things get jostled when opening and closing drawers." I reiterated what I'd said to Marigold about how many times I'd lost a measuring cup or cookie cutter in the far corner of a kitchen drawer.

Even though I was offering reassuring words, a nagging sensation tugged at the corners of my mind. Was it possible someone had moved Marigold's keys to make her question her sanity? Was that same person toying with Noeline? No, it didn't make sense. To what end?

"Do you keep a lot of cash on hand here, Noeline?" I asked.

"No. Most of our transactions are credit cards."

I eyed the vintage floor safe. To open it, one needed a combination, not a key. "Do you lock the office door when you leave?"

"Yes. Our records hold a lot of personal information. Why?" Tegan gave me a questioning look.

"I was wondering if a thief might have taken your keys and made a copy so they could access the office."

Noeline gasped. "Heavens." She pressed a hand to her chest. "None of our lodgers has complained about being hacked."

"That's a relief," I said.

Dream Cuisine was robbed a year ago. No records were stolen, but my favorite stand mixer and an autographed first-edition cookbook were taken. For the longest time, I couldn't figure out who would've done it until it dawned on me that the cleaning crew I'd hired had worked for me on only one occasion before claiming they really weren't kitchen-type people. The police retrieved my items from them within a week.

"Mother, are you in here?" Vanna flounced into the office and caught the toe of her four-inch heel on the area rug. She stumbled forward, the hem of her flowing silk skirt snagging on the corner of the floor safe. "Oh, crap. Help me."

I ran to her rescue, telling her to stand still so she wouldn't tear the fabric. When I'd freed her, she adjusted her skirt and tugged the hem of her knit top down.

"Thank you, Allie. That was very kind of you."

Oh, my word. Had I heard correctly? She wasn't chiding me? "You're welcome."

"Mother said she resolved things between you and me." Using a finger, Vanna daintily smoothed the right side of her hair, which was swept into a chignon. "I hope that's so."

"It is. No bad blood. All is forgiven."

For now. I wasn't gullible enough to believe Vanna would change her ways. She would verbally assail me at some point in the future. I'd be prepared.

"Are we dining together?" Vanna asked. "I heard Helga is serving her famous roast lamb."

"I'm heading home," I said. "I came over because Tegan—"

My pal knuckled me and shook her head sharply.

"Because Tegan wanted to show me the office. I've . . . been looking for a vintage floor safe for the longest time," I improvised, instantly wishing I could take the inane response back.

Vanna accepted my explanation. "Another time," she murmured.

"Evening, everyone." Rick strolled in and tossed his briefcase on the desk chair. The breeze the motion stirred up caused the loose paper items on the desk to scatter. "What a successful day I had." He sidled to Noeline and bussed her cheek.

She blushed. "Not in front of the girls."

"They're grown women." He chuckled. "Certainly, a little public display of affection is allowed. Now, ask me what made today a success."

Noeline smiled indulgently. "What made—"

"Rick," Tegan cut in. "I have a question for you first."

Uh-oh. I knew that tone. Winston had primed the pump. She was feeling her oats and gearing up for a fight. "Tegan," I cautioned.

She waved me off. "Rick."

"Fire away," he said, grinning at Noeline as if he couldn't wait to hear what her daughter wanted to ask.

"A friend of mine told me about the reading schedule for volunteers at the hospital." Tegan didn't identify Chloe. A friend was general enough. "They only read to kids in the afternoon. If I'm doing the math correctly, you couldn't have been reading to kids on Thursday and Friday nights."

The color drained from Rick's cheeks.

"Are you stepping out on my mother?" Tegan asked.

Noeline gasped. "Tegan, take it back!"

"No." Tegan folded her arms, not willing to budge an inch. She reminded me of a moody teen. I was pretty sure Noeline had seen the defiant pose before.

Rick gave Noeline a sorrowful look and shoved his hands into his pockets. "You're right, Tegan. I was not reading to children. I was covering my sorry behind because I was browsing properties and didn't want your mother to know. As I revealed to you and Allie confidentially the other day when I picked up the books you'd set aside, I want to settle here. I had a full slate of houses to see, so I went house hunting those nights." He eyed Noeline. "I didn't want to tell you my plans, sweetheart, until I made a firm decision."

She reached for his hand and squeezed. "I'm so excited. You're moving here? For good?"

"Were you doing that a week ago Saturday, too?" Tegan raised a skeptical eyebrow.

Rick gave the type of indulgent smile an adult might give a petulant child. "Yes. Curb appeal matters to me. I told my Realtor I wanted to tour the first set of homes we'd looked at on my own. In the daylight. That way, I could rule things out. Here are the addresses I viewed, if it matters."

He opened the Notes app on his cell phone and flashed the screen at Tegan. I peered over her shoulder. Indeed, there was a list of over twenty addresses. One was on my street.

Conflict deflected, Tegan convinced me to stay for dinner,

and I was glad I did. Helga's roast lamb was as good as Vanna had promised. Served with a savory rosemary jus, I could cut it with a fork, and each bite melted in my mouth. The garlic mashed potatoes were a perfect accompaniment. Dessert was a knockout triple-chocolate trifle that Helga proudly said she'd concocted with premade brownies, pudding, and crushed candy bars.

During dinner, Rick regaled us with stories about the houses he liked. He was partial to a Craftsman he'd viewed in Montford, not far from the inn. Noeline knew the area. She said he couldn't go wrong with that choice. Throughout dinner, she leaned into him, her shoulder brushing his. Occasionally he swept a stray hair off her face and pecked her cheek.

When leaving the inn, stuffed to the gills and not having the energy to venture to Dream Cuisine to bake, I decided I could make all the scones and cupcakes I needed for the morning's deliveries at home. Darcy zipped to me the moment I entered, his tail lifted in distinct displeasure.

"Sorry," I said. "If you could read a text message, I would've clued you in as to my whereabouts." I petted his ears. He meowed, his eyes blazing with curiosity. "No, I wasn't investigating anything. I was with my friend's family. It was nice to see them enjoying one another in the wake of all the sorrow."

Even Vanna had contributed to the conversation. At first, her stories had been about her challenging clients, but upon hearing the address of a house on Rick's list, she warned him to steer clear. The house was owned by a woman who claimed there might be ghosts in it. Rick pooh-poohed her. Noeline ribbed him, telling him he should believe, because she'd had an encounter.

While I mixed my batters, paying close attention to these ingredients, I resumed listening to my audiobook recording of *The Sign of the Four.* By the time I got to Sherlock donning a disguise to track down the *Aurora* launch, all the prep work was done. I would awake early to bake everything. Yawning, I clicked off the story and dragged myself into bed.

At four a.m., I rose, pulled on a pair of jeans and a long-sleeved blue Henley shirt, and started baking and icing.

At six, I received a text message from Tegan. Chloe wanted our two cents about the decorations for the memorial. The printer could have them done by Friday, but only if we delivered our decisions today, Monday.

After agreeing to swing by, I decided it might be a long day and Darcy should accompany me. He would do well at the bookshop, and as long as I put his kitty crate on the floor in front of the passenger seat, so none of his hair would contaminate my wares, I could take him on all my deliveries.

I swapped out my now-covered-in-flour Henley for a white blouse, spruced up my hair and makeup, and hurried to the van. It took no time at all to tootle around town. Tourists didn't come out in droves on Mondays, and many businesses had gone to a four-day workweek, with Mondays as the day to work remotely, if possible. I delivered five dozen cupcakes to Perfect Brew, two dozen scones to Ragamuffin, three cheese-filled coffee cakes to Big Mama's Diner, and an extra-large chocolate fudge cake to Legal Eagles. It was the boss's birthday.

When I arrived at Feast for the Eyes, some school-aged kids, all under the age of seven, were roaming the children's aisle with their mother, and a pair of teenaged boys were studying the YA literature. One was holding the latest Neil Gaiman novel.

"We've been busier than all get-out with kids and teens today," Tegan said. "It's a town-wide teacher conference day so educators can meet with parents, one on one." She took Darcy's kitty crate from me, pressed her nose to the window on the crate, and cooed hello. She led me to the office and switched on the overhead lights. They flickered. "*Grr.* That's been going on all morning. I'll need to hire an electrician." She placed Darcy's crate on the desk and twisted the rod for the blinds to provide a view of the main shop. "Darcy, will you be a good boy and stay in here? I don't want any complaints from those who might not be cat people." He meowed his assent, and Tegan beamed. "I knew you'd get it, you handsome boy." She released him, and he leaped to the top of the bookshelf abutting the far wall and instantly curled into a ball for a snooze.

I removed a bowl from the crate and filled it with water. While setting it at the foot of the bookshelf, I remembered the female officer at the crime scene putting the teacup into a glass container. Had the killer laced the tea with poison? Was that how Zach had figured out tetrahydrozoline had been used, or had the coroner deduced it by testing the contents of Marigold's stomach? The teacup had looked full, so I didn't think Marigold had drunk any of the liquid, but possibly the poison was so lethal one sip would have killed her. My insides ached at the notion of how she must have suffered.

I rejoined Tegan in the main shop. She was poring over a list of quotes Chloe had gleaned from *Pride and Prejudice*.

"I like this one," Tegan said. She showed us the selection: *"Do you prefer reading books to cards?" said he; "that is rather singular."*

Chloe laughed. "Good one, Tegan. Marigold would agree wholeheartedly with the sentiment."

"And this one," Tegan said. She pointed at: *"Nothing is more deceitful," said Darcy, "than the appearance of humility. It is often only carelessness of opinion, and sometimes an indirect boast."*

I nodded. "Truer words were never said."

"Here's one Vanna might enjoy," Tegan said, giggling. She

motioned to: *"Nobody can tell what I suffer! But it is always so. Those who do not complain are never pitied."*

Chloe cackled.

So did I but instantly felt bad about it. "Tegan, we can't hang that one."

"Auntie would have found it amusing."

"Okay," I said, "but let's put it in an aisle Vanna won't browse."

Tegan fanned a hand. "We're safe. She won't peruse any books other than cookbooks."

For the next half hour, we selected another dozen quotes. Chloe marked them off to take to the printer. Then we decided on the artwork—still images from the *Pride and Prejudice* series—that Chloe had downloaded from the computer and had printed in black-and-white samples.

"They're publicity photos," she said. "No rights required. Besides, we're not selling them. We're purely using them for decoration."

"Fitzwilliam Darcy is dreamy, isn't he?" Tegan sighed, putting a checkmark on six of the images Chloe had downloaded. "I like these. Let's have the printer make sixteen-by-twenty posters."

Chloe collected them into a file folder and set off on her task.

"Tegan," I said, "speaking of Fitzwilliam Darcy, I haven't heard diddly from that detective agency."

"Maybe Auntie didn't follow through with them?"

"But she had with Oly Olsen, as I told you."

"What if . . ." Tegan spun around. "What if the police haven't solved Auntie's murder by Saturday? It will cast a pall over the proceedings."

"A memorial is already sad, my friend. There's nothing we can do about that." I patted her shoulder. "But we'll do our best to make it a celebration of your aunt's life, even if there isn't closure. We'll tell stories about how she started the bookshop and how she donated her time and energy to worthy causes."

She rounded the counter and sank onto the ladder-back chair. I sat in the one beside her. "If Graham didn't kill her, and Piper didn't do it—"

"Katrina is my bet."

"But she has an alibi."

"Not confirmed yet. I wish we knew who might be savvy about poisons."

"Poisons?" She arched an eyebrow.

I wanted to kick myself. Until now, I'd kept my promise to Zach and hadn't told my best friend I knew the method of murder.

"Auntie was poisoned? With what?"

"A decongestant that comes in nasal sprays and eye drop forms and might have been administered in the bottle of water or cup of tea the police took for evidence."

"Was that why you were asking about which of our customers might be doctors or scientists?"

"*Mm-hmm.*"

"Did you know that Evelyn Evers was a doctor?"

"Yes."

"A doctor would know about poisons."

"She has a solid alibi. An actress friend of Lillian's confirmed it."

"What if the poison was, indeed, in the water bottle, and Evelyn gave that bottle to Auntie on Friday? You heard Auntie when you chided her. She said others had warned her to hydrate, too. I'd bet dimes to dollars Evelyn did."

Oh, my! Tegan was spot-on. The killer, learning Marigold was seriously into hydrating herself since the fainting incident, could have dosed the water the prior day, which would mean all alibis regarding Saturday were null and void.

I was about to text Zach the theory when the front door

opened. To my surprise, Katrina, clad in a sunny yellow dress, sandals, and bright colorful jewelry, stepped inside. Her floral purse was slung over one shoulder. She held a key chain in one hand. Her hair was hanging in soft curls over her shoulders. The whole look screamed *Spring has sprung!* but she didn't seem cheery. In fact, her mouth was downturned, her gaze grim.

In barely a whisper, she said, "I lied."

CHAPTER 24

"Undoubtedly, there is a meanness in all the arts which ladies sometimes condescend to employ for captivation. Whatever bears affinity to cunning is despicable."

—Fitzwilliam Darcy, in Jane Austen's *Pride and Prejudice*

Katrina sagged slightly. I dashed to her and guided her to a chair by the sales counter. Tegan fetched her a glass of water and gave it to her.

"You lied?" I asked.

Katrina sipped the water and nudged the glass aside. "I . . ." She gulped in air. "I can't do it any longer. Guilt is eating at me."

I exchanged a glance with my pal. This was it. Katrina was going to confess to murder. Tegan was free. Case solved. We waited. The teens were still browsing YA books, and the mother had settled her brood into the reading nook and was showing them pictures in an alphabet book.

"My friend who's supposed to corroborate my alibi . . ." Katrina twirled a hand.

"The one on the three-week camping trip," I finished.

"Yes. Her. Even when she returns, she won't be able to confirm my story because I wasn't with her the night before or even on the morning Marigold died. But I do have an alibi."

My pulse started to race so fast that I was sure Katrina and Tegan could hear it churning. "Go on," I coaxed.

"See, when I'm not working at the Brewery, I'm a hostess."

I gawked at Tegan, who shrugged her shoulders, as in the dark as I was.

"A hostess . . . online." Katrina wheezed as if it was taking all her effort to form words. "With clients. Male clients."

My mouth opened, but no words came out.

"I don't have virtual sex with them," she rushed to add. "I'm a listener."

"A listener," I echoed.

"Like a therapist?" Tegan asked.

"No. I'm not a therapist. I can't be. I'm not licensed to be one."

I recalled the Brewery article saying Katrina had wanted to become a psychiatrist, but hadn't been able to finish college because her mother had needed full-time care and funds were scarce.

"I'm more like a friend. A confidante. See, sometimes they . . . my clients . . . ask me to say things to them. Not to turn them on," she rushed to add, "but to bolster their ego. It's easy for me. I've always been good at listening. When I was dating online, I learned to keep it neutral, you know? Dates and places—"

"Your boyfriend Upton Scott figured out the truth, didn't he?" I cut in. "He threatened you."

Her face pinched with pain. "Yes. He hacked into my account. He took pictures of my clients' profiles. Some are well-known people. He wants to out them. He thinks they're perverts, but they're not. They're simply lonely." Tears pooled in her eyes. Tegan handed her a tissue. She took it. "I've decided to pay off Upton to make him bury his story. And I'll quit the business. I can get by on less money. But before I do, I wanted to tell you about the client I was befriending on the Saturday morning Marigold died."

Befriending. What a curious word.

"Saturday morning seems like an odd time to be talking to . . . clients," I murmured.

"It was the only time he had available. He's a workaholic." Katrina licked her lips and took another sip of water. "If he'll talk to the police, that should help me, right? That'll prove I didn't kill Marigold."

Not if our theory about the bottled water lying in wait for Marigold was correct, but for now, that was only a conjecture, and Katrina seemed so earnest that I wanted to believe her.

"Could this client see you?" I asked.

"He saw me, all right. I was dressed like a schoolmarm in glasses and a high-necked blouse. That's what he asked for. It wasn't kinky. He said he would take instruction better if I didn't look sexy. Many of my clients ask me to dress up. It's no big deal."

I said, "Katrina—"

"Katty," she cut in. "They know me as Katty. It's a nickname for Katrina."

I could've palm slapped my forehead. Wallis told Zach and me that Marigold had said to Katrina, "Don't be catty," and that was when Katrina threatened her. "Marigold knew what you were doing," I said. "She knew your secret identity."

Katrina nodded glumly.

"How did she find out?"

"She caught me. Behind the Brewery. Having a session. I was in my car on my cell phone. I hadn't driven away. I was . . ." Katrina toyed with a tendril of hair. "I was in a nun's habit."

Katty the nun. I couldn't picture it.

"The next day"—Katrina's shoulders rose and fell with defeat—"Marigold approached me and begged me to stop. She told me to reenroll in school and get my degree so I could become—"

"A real psychiatrist."

"Yes, but that takes a lot of cash, which I didn't have. She offered to pay my way. I told her no." She wadded the tissue in the hand that was clinging to her key ring. "My pride wouldn't let me. I had to earn the money myself."

Aha! That was why Marigold had wanted Oly to sort out Katrina's pride.

"Will you help me smooth things over with the police?" Katrina asked. "I've written down all the dates I've met with people online."

The word "dates" joggled something in my mind. "Katrina, you mentioned that you'd learned the ropes when you were dating online, and you were about to say something more, but I interrupted after you said 'dates and places.' Marigold had a contact in her directory for something named Dates and Places. Is it a business?"

She nodded. "It's a dating app. It's how I finally grasped how to interact with guys—what to do and what not to do."

Tegan said, "Allie, do you think Auntie decided to look for love again after all these years?"

"It's feasible."

"She asked me about it," Katrina said. "I told her I hadn't had any success. After a few encounters, I realized I didn't want to get involved with anyone."

Not in the romantic way, I mused.

"But it was that experience that made me figure out I could make money listening to guys like them, so I created my website KattyTalks, and then I touched base with a few previous dates to spread the word, and voilà."

Aha. I hadn't found any social networking presence for her when I'd researched her online because I hadn't known her alias.

Katrina lifted the hand holding the wadded tissue and key chain. "See this fob?" It was red and curved, with a jagged edge.

"Dates and Places gives them to its clients. It's half of a heart. It's what you show someone when you're meeting them on a blind date. The app owner says it's like getting the license plate of your Uber driver to make sure you climb into the right car."

Tegan pointed at the key chain. "Hold on. Rick has that same fob. I saw him twirling his keys the other day. The red thingy caught my eye. He is cheating on my mother, Allie. I told you!"

I remembered seeing the fob and thinking it reminded me of something on a dog's collar.

"Auntie knew it!"

Did she? Was that why she'd asked Katrina about Dates and Places? Had she discovered Rick had a profile on the app? Had she planned to tell Noeline what she'd uncovered? Would Rick have killed her to keep the secret? That seemed far-fetched. For all we knew, Rick and Noeline might have met through the app, but Noeline fibbed to her daughters, claiming they'd bumped into each other at a grocery store, so they wouldn't worry.

I said, "Katrina, would it be possible to get your profile info so we can sneak into the app and scope out Tegan's mother's new boyfriend?"

"Sure. Give me your phone, Tegan."

"Mine's in the office," Tegan said. "Use yours, Allie."

I handed my phone to Katrina. She uploaded the Dates and Places app and then entered her user name and password.

"Here." She gave it back to me. "You can explore by first name, if he's using his real first name, as well as by zip code and age range. There are even filters for ethnicity. Some people are really lame about only dating someone who has the same skin tone, so that's required for all profiles. Photos too, though lots of those have been photoshopped. Believe me, I know."

"What about by profession?" I asked.

"If he's honest about it, sure."

I typed in as many keywords as I could think of: *Rick, Rick O, Rick O'Sheedy, white male, banker, financier, investor, money-man.* I added our zip code and the descriptors: *sixty to seventy* and *silver hair.*

"Are his eyes blue or green?" I asked Tegan.

"Blue, I think."

Not being certain, I left eye color blank and hit Enter. There wasn't one *Rick O'Sheedy*, but there were twenty *Rick O* listings, and well over one hundred profiles for *Rick*. Some of the names merely matched one keyword. I started with any *Rick O* in our zip code but didn't find one that resembled Rick O'Sheedy. Most of the men were in their forties. None did any work related to money matters. I moved on to the selections of *Rick,* with no initials, who were living in or near our zip code.

"Ma'am, we're ready to check out." The teenaged boys approached the sales counter.

Tegan excused herself and handled the sale.

Katrina rose to her feet. "I should go. I have an appointment."

An online appointment, I surmised by how anxious she was becoming.

"Thank you for listening," she added. "Will you, you know . . . with the police?"

"I suggest you go to them directly and tell them everything."

"I was hoping you'd smooth it over for me before I did. You and Detective Armstrong seem to get along so well."

The singsong way she said it made me uncomfortable. Had I been giving off a way-too-interested vibe? Was that why Zach had cooled to me?

I rested a hand on her shoulder. "I'll text him and tell him that I believe you, but you have to do this yourself."

She lifted her chin. "You're right. It's time to bite the bullet."

Or *suck it up,* as my father would say.

When Katrina left and Tegan, who'd finalized the sale, moseyed to the aisle by the front window to advise an elderly woman who was waving for help, I texted Zach. I didn't see the ellipsis symbol hovering like he was planning to respond, so I closed Messages and resumed browsing the profiles.

Before I'd scrolled through three, the mother and her children arrived at the sales counter. The children were clearly restless. The oldest, who looked to be about seven, was doing her best to quiet her siblings, but to no avail.

"I'm sorry," the mother said, wearily setting down ten children's books and *Lost Luggage,* a humorous mystery I'd thoroughly enjoyed.

"These are good selections for your children," I said. On occasion, I riffled through picture books, dreaming of the days when my mother, acting like a mother should, had taken me to a library. "The artwork in the alphabet book is super, and this mystery"—I tapped the book's cover—"is written by one of my favorite authors. The protagonist, Cyd Redondo, is a hoot. There are more in the series, if you enjoy it."

"Thanks." She paid with a credit card. After I bundled the books into one of the shop's tote bags, the woman shepherded her squirming children to the front door.

"Found anything on Rick yet?" Tegan asked me when she returned.

"Zilch."

"Let me have a go."

I gave her the cell phone.

Fingers tapping and swiping, she landed on Rick's profile within minutes. She grunted. "Honestly? His nickname is Ricochet? How cheesy."

Ricochet. Get real! "Um, do you think your mother has a profile, too?"

"I sure hope not." She keyed in her mother's name and,

finding no one, not a single person named Noeline or any facsimile of the name, she breathed easier. "I've got to tell her he's doing this."

"You don't know that he's active. This could be an old profile."

"Except he still has that fob on his key chain."

"So does Katrina, and she's no longer using the app."

"I suppose."

"Let's table it for the rest of the day," I said. "We have the book club to prepare for. After that, you'll come up with a way to break it to your mother. She might find it funny."

"Hardy-har." Tegan grimaced. "Not."

CHAPTER 25

"But disguise of every sort is my abhorrence."

—Fitzwilliam Darcy, in Jane Austen's *Pride and Prejudice*

At noon, I ran out to pick up some turkey-salami sub sandwiches for us. I ate mine in the office and fed Darcy a can of his favorite chicken pâté. He purred his delight, happy as a clam at being a guest at the shop. About midafternoon, I saw him walking along the desktop in the office, peering out through the picture window. He wasn't necessarily a *people* cat—other than me and Tegan, and yes, Zach—and he was most certainly not a *child* cat, but he did like to know what was going on. By end of day, Tegan murmured it was a good thing all three of us had been on board to ring up customers. Sales had exceeded expectations.

At six, leaving Darcy snoozing peacefully in the office, I sped home to fetch the goodies I'd made to serve to the book club. When I returned, I offered to make coffee—heaven forbid I allow Chloe to do so—and Chloe set out the food. I teetered when I saw the bottles of water she'd placed on the snack table.

"Chloe, where did you get those?" I rasped.

"From the refrigerator in the stockroom. We'd run out, so I picked up a case this morning on my way to work. I stowed them in the refrigerator to chill."

They were fresh. Untainted. Phew.

At six thirty, attendees started to arrive. Five could sit on the L-shaped couch and a few might take the beanbags or mid-century modern chairs, but there would be close to fifteen, so Tegan had put out folding chairs. Stella and Lillian, dressed to the nines, put their purses on the couch and ambled to the table of scones, cookies, and dishes of trifle. Their appreciative oohs and aahs for the trifle made me proud. It would go over well at the memorial. Piper, in a short-sleeved silk blouse and trousers, sneaked up behind them and poked them. Startled, the two women turned and laughed.

Piper said, "Nice to see you, ladies."

"You too, Piper," Stella and Lillian chimed.

I spotted a bandage on Piper's arm, which I hadn't noticed before. She'd admitted to coming into the bookshop the day Marigold died. Did they argue? Did they struggle? Did Marigold scratch her?

Stop, Allie. She told Zach her alibi, and the student confirmed it. She's not a suspect.

The three women group-hugged and moved to the reading nook, each expressing how sad it was Marigold wouldn't be here to guide them in the discussion.

A few more people arrived. Zach and Bates showed up in tandem. Bates made a beeline for the coffee. Zach slowed near the book island. He was studying his cell phone.

For a new lead, I prayed. I approached and he smiled, but the smile didn't meet his eyes. My insides snagged as I realized my feelings for him might never be reciprocated.

"Hi." Keeping my tone breezy, I said, "Did Katrina Carlson touch base with you today?"

He pursed his lips. "She did, but for the record, whether or not you believe her—"

I held up a hand to stop him. "My opinion doesn't matter. Got it. I just hope her story pans out. What about my other text regarding the water bottle?"

His brow furrowed. "I didn't get another text from you."

Of course, he hadn't. I'd forgotten to send the text because I'd been distracted by Katrina's reveal. Quickly I told him what Tegan and I had theorized, that the water bottle could have been tampered with earlier than Saturday, and the killer could have left it for Marigold, who had been consciously re-hydrating.

"Allie, stop." Zach paused as if to prevent himself from blurting something he didn't want to say. "I like you. You've got a good head on your shoulders. But you're not—"

"All right, everyone, let's get started!" Tegan cried, clapping her hands. "Convene in the reading nook. Allie Catt will be our moderator. Let's go. Chop-chop."

I stared at Zach. *What had he been about to say? You're not seeing the forest for the trees? You're not a professional investigator? You're not my type?* I pushed the niggling thoughts from my mind and settled onto one of the folding chairs. "Welcome, everyone."

The book club went off without a hitch. A few hadn't finished reading the book, and I told them what Marigold would have said, that it was okay. Not everyone read at the same speed. There would be no spoilers tonight. We dove into the character of Charlie and his relationship with Diesel. We discussed Charlie's former classmate, a best-selling author who was an arrogant jerk. We mulled over the setup of the suspects and their motives. By the time the book club ended, everyone had contributed, much to my delight.

Zach and Bates said good night in synch and headed for the exit. Zach stopped by the door as Bates ran something by him. I doubted they were discussing the book. Neither of them had shared the enthusiasm that the others had for an amateur sleuth handily solving the crime.

Idly Zach bounced his key chain in his palm. Seeing the action made me think of Marigold's missing keys, which were ultimately found, and I revisited a previous theory. Was it possible a customer stole the set and made a copy of the shop's keys and then, forgetting where they'd found the keys, stuffed them into a random drawer? I continued to stare at Zach's movement, the rabbit's foot attached to the key chain dancing merrily with each bounce, and thought of Katrina's key fob. Marigold had asked her about Dates and Places. Truly believing Marigold never wanted to date again after she lost the love of her life, I wondered if she'd purposely asked for the information so she could do a deep dive into Rick, aka Ricochet. Had she found something incriminating? Neither Tegan nor I had scrolled far on the app. Was there more to learn about him?

When the book club participants left the shop, I edged to one side and pulled my cell phone from my jeans pocket. I opened the Dates and Places app and pulled up Rick's profile again. I scrolled down to below where Tegan had stopped and continued reading. He touted himself as an investment banker, which wasn't a lie. He said he worked with hospitals. Also true. He claimed one of his great loves was money, saying one could never have enough. That was blatantly honest. He gave his age as sixty-two. I doubted he'd fudged that. He admitted he was divorced.

In answer to a standard app prompt, *Previous employment,* he wrote that he used to work in banking telecommunications and had also served as a sales rep before breaking out on his own to raise funds for hospital bonds. The sales rep mention made me laugh. He'd told Tegan and me that his ex-wife couldn't handle his being on the road because her father had been a traveling salesman, but then Rick had joked that he sure as heck wasn't a salesman. Wasn't a sales rep the same thing?

I read further and froze. Rick had repped pharmaceuticals. Someone who had worked in the drug industry might know a thing or two about poisons. As Tegan had glibly asserted, had he killed Marigold? Tegan patently did not like him. Was there more to her aversion than being overly protective of Noeline?

I thought again about the misplaced keys. What if Rick stole Noeline's set of keys from the B&B, made a copy of the shop's keys, and used one or both of them to access the bookstore on Saturday morning? In order to cover his intended duplicity, with malice aforethought, he swiped Marigold's keys and deposited them in a desk drawer so it would appear that she, like Noeline, had a tendency to misplace things. The theory was a stretch but sounded plausible.

Something else occurred to me. At the pawnshop, Rick had rubbed his arm as if eager to conclude his business transaction and get a move on. Was it possible his arm had a scratch on it? Inflicted by Marigold?

My cell phone buzzed. I didn't recognize the number but answered.

"Miss Catt?" a man with a genteel Southern accent asked.

"Yes."

"I'm Frank Fitzwilliam, Fitzwilliam and Sons."

Frank, not Darcy. Either Marigold had dubbed the agency's contact as Detective Darcy in jest, as Tegan and I had speculated, or she'd done so as a diversion to ensure someone wouldn't realize what she was up to. "Did Marigold Markel hire you?" I asked.

"She did."

"Did you hear that she was murdered?"

"Yes. What a shame. I didn't reach out with my condolences. Our matter was concluded well before that time."

"Could you tell me why she hired you? I'm a dear friend and a partner in the bookshop."

He hesitated.

"Sir, please. Did it have anything to do with"—I made a wild guess—"prejudice?"

"Prejudice?" He made a clicking sound with his tongue. "I can't say it did, but I won't say it didn't. She wanted me to find out about a man she didn't trust."

"Rick O'Sheedy?"

"That's correct. I delivered my findings."

"In writing?"

"In a PDF file."

When I'd browsed Marigold's personal computer, the Adobe Reader app hadn't been open. I hadn't thought to peruse it. Was the file still on her computer? Or did Rick, who I was now certain killed my dear friend, delete it after he hacked into her computer to erase her Internet search history of him? Noeline said he was savvy in all things technical. If he did a slapdash job, the PDF file might still be in Trash.

"Can you give me a few hints as to the contents?" I asked.

He hummed.

"Please," I prompted.

"I don't see the harm. Sure. The man is broke. He has a lot of outstanding debts. I won't say he's a gambler, but he hasn't been frugal, if you catch my drift."

I thought of the book Marigold had been holding when she died, *Pride and Prejudice,* and it all became clear. She'd grabbed it as a clue to warn her sister that Rick was not all he appeared to be. He wasn't a nice guy making room for Noeline in his heart when he'd pawned his wedding ring. He was, as Tegan theorized, targeting Noeline in hopes of gaining access to her deep pockets. He was Wickham, not Darcy.

I thanked Mr. Fitzwilliam as a scenario took shape in my mind. Marigold found out Rick was active on a dating site. She had him investigated. What if, armed with her findings, she told Rick to leave her sister alone or else she'd tell Noeline the truth? What if, as a last-ditch effort, she offered to pay him one hundred thousand dollars to go quietly?

One of the lines in Marigold's manuscript read: *The killer's threats had been real, she had no doubt.* What if Rick, seeing an opportunity to make out like a bandit, agreed to Marigold's demands and asked to meet at the bookshop Saturday morning before the event? Naively believing she had the upper hand, she agreed. But using the keys he'd copied, he sneaked in before her and was lying in wait. He pushed her, poisoned her, took the money, and created a phony alibi of house hunting. Would the photographs on his cell phone of the homes he was considering be time-stamped?

I saw Zach standing outside the shop with Bates. Both were studying Zach's phone. Would he listen to me if I shared my theory? Doubtful. I didn't have any hard facts, only suppositions. It dawned on me that if Rick hadn't disposed of the shop's keys that he'd copied, they might be hidden in his room at the inn. If I could find them, they would be solid evidence of his guilt.

Tegan swept past me, carrying a tray filled with used cups and saucers. Chloe was tending to the water bottles and plates.

"Tegan, *psst.*" I motioned her to join me.

She did, tray in hand. "What's up?"

I told her.

Her jaw dropped in disbelief. "Zach's still outside. Tell him."

I explained how he didn't want me butting in. "Plus it's only a conjecture."

She considered that for a moment. "Here's what we'll do. I'll go to the inn. Rick is there with Mom. A bit ago, she texted asking when I'd be back. They're in the backyard and would like to spend time with me. Before I join them, I'll search his room for the keys. If I find them and they match mine, I'll take a picture. That's enough proof, right?"

CHAPTER 26

"Believe her to be deceived, by all means.
You have now done your duty by her, and must fret no
longer."

—Elizabeth Bennet, in Jane Austen's *Pride and Prejudice*

"I can't let you do this on your own," I said. "It's not safe. I'm going with you. I'll sneak into Rick's room." She started to argue. I lifted a finger to quiet her. "You'll distract him and your mother."

After we finished cleaning up the shop and dousing the lights, I packed Darcy into his crate, got into my Ford Transit, and followed Tegan to the Blue Lantern. I left the cat in the van, window rolled halfway down.

Guests were in the parlor enjoying dessert when Tegan and I entered. Helga was clearing empty dishes from the various tables.

Tegan approached her. "Helga, where are Mom and Rick?"

"They are sitting in the backyard, enjoying the night air. Would you like me to announce you?"

"No," Tegan said. "Thanks." She turned to me and whispered, "They're still outside. Perfect. You'll need a key to his room. Unlike you, we still lock our doors at the inn." She beckoned me to follow her to the front desk, where she tapped a code into the security panel of the key cabinet. She swung the door open and located the duplicate key on a fob for Rick's room. "Mom hasn't advanced to the twenty-first century. No magnetized door keys yet," she confided. "You have to return this. If she finds it missing, I'll be in hot water. Only Helga, Vanna, and I know the code to this key cabinet."

"Which is?"

"Four-three-zero-zero."

Tegan fetched a cup of tea from the parlor and, shaking tension from her neck and shoulders, proceeded to the rear porch. I tiptoed up the stairs.

Rick's room was at the end of the hallway. Like Tegan's, it faced the backyard. I sneaked inside, not surprised that the layout was also similar to Tegan's. The hurricane lamp and lantern-motif light were on. The bed had been turned down. A wrapped Godiva chocolate sat on each pillow. Through the break in the drapes, I spied lanterns hanging from shepherds' hooks in the yard. They created a magical ambience. I dared to step closer to see if Rick, Noeline, or Tegan might be sitting on a bench where they could have an angle to view inside his room. They weren't, and I breathed easier.

Swinging around, I studied the space. Where would Rick have hidden a couple of keys? I scoped out the bureau and went through the drawers. I inspected the nightstand. I checked beneath the coffee table. Nada.

I spotted Rick's briefcase on the couch. I rummaged through the outer pocket, but didn't find any keys. I peered into the interior and paused when I spotted an envelope embossed with Bramblewood Savings and Loan poking from the computer slot. I gingerly plucked it out. It had been sealed at one time but was now open and empty. Was this the envelope that had held Marigold's one hundred thousand dollar withdrawal? Would Rick have been brazen enough to deposit the money in his personal account, or was the money in the room somewhere?

Perhaps hidden between the mattresses or in the closet? I went to peek in the latter, but froze when I heard Tegan say loudly, "Allie went home." It sounded as if she was projecting to the last row of a theater. Was she trying to warn me? Had Rick caught sight of me in his room? Maybe Helga had stepped outside and asked my whereabouts.

"Yes," Tegan went on. "She was here because she wanted to make sure I got home safely. I've been so frazzled since Auntie died, and with Winston hounding me . . ." Her voice drifted off.

I tiptoed to the drapes and peeked out. Rick had moved from the shadows and was standing beside one of the lanterns, but he wasn't looking in the direction of the inn. He was staring up at the stars.

Quickly I snapped a picture of the bank envelope with my cell phone and reinserted the envelope into the briefcase. I slipped out of Rick's room, returned the room key to the key cabinet, as instructed, and hustled to the van. Darcy let out a low rumble. I shushed him, flicked on the ignition, and sped down the drive while peering into the rearview mirror. I didn't see Rick or Noeline come into view. I was in the clear.

Minutes later, as I was doing triple duty—transmitting the image of the envelope to Zach, while rounding the corner to my street and unzipping Darcy's carry crate so he knew freedom was seconds away—my Apple Watch buzzed my wrist. On the screen blinked a security company notification that an alarm was going off at Dream Cuisine. Someone had breached the rear door. It was probably a false alarm, but if I didn't clear the problem, the police would come, and I'd be charged a fee. I made a U-turn and told Darcy to hunker down.

I arrived at Dream Cuisine in under three minutes and parked in the alley behind the building. I slung my tote over my shoulder and lifted Darcy in his crate. The rear door wasn't ajar, but it was unlocked, which gave me pause. I always bolted it. *Always.*

Glancing right and left, not seeing anyone lying in wait for me, I eased the door open. I didn't detect movement, but that didn't mean anything. I wouldn't be able to hear someone creeping about with the alarm system blaring. A prowler could be hiding. Darcy didn't make a peep, however, which calmed me. I flipped on a light that illuminated the area—I was alone—and tapped in the four-digit code. Miraculously, the alarm switched off on the first try.

I made a tour of the site, hoping nothing had been stolen. Everything appeared in order, but I wanted to count items, in case I needed to file an insurance claim. My cell phone jangled. The security company was calling. I answered and told the woman the passcode: "I love books." I apologized for the mistake. She told me it was no problem. Things happened. The police would not be dispatched.

I closed the door and bolted it, tossed my keys onto the desk, and placed Darcy's crate on the floor. He poked his head out. I petted his ears and cooed that it was all right. He could get out if he liked. I wasn't going to be baking. He mewed his relief and scrambled out. In a couple of sprightly leaps, he landed at the top of a set of shelves affixed to a wall and nestled down. I fetched a clipboard and a pen and retraced my steps, counting the pans hanging from hooks and the knives on the magnetic rack.

Something went *creak.*

Darcy caterwauled. I whirled around, my tote swinging wildly, and saw the door to the pantry opening.

Rick O'Sheedy emerged with a Beretta aimed in my direction. He was twirling a ring of keys in his other hand—quick-release keys like mine—and I wilted. He'd swiped a duplicate key from my key ring. *When?* I wondered, until it dawned on me. It had to have been the other night when the shutter clacked and thumped the side of the house. Seconds later, the front door blew open. Rick must have raced in, swiped the key, and darted out before I could grab the fire poker and catch him in the act.

"Why are you here?" I asked, doing my best not to sound scared spitless. "Didn't Helga offer you dessert?"

"I saw you sneaking out of the inn. I followed you the moment you left."

If only I'd checked the rearview mirror.

"You continued toward home," he continued, "giving me just enough time to come here, trip the alarm, and slip inside the pantry." He smirked. "You're smart, but you're too curious for your own good, young lady."

Darcy hissed.

"My cat hates when anybody calls me a 'lady,'" I quipped.

Rick's mouth curled up in a sneer. "Ha ha." He wagged the gun. "Walk into the refrigerator."

"I forgot to wear my anorak. I'll pass."

"I said go."

"Actually, you said 'walk.'"

"Don't make me shoot you," he growled.

I sized up what weapons I had at my disposal. A kitchen was full of them, like knives and sauté pans. But he'd shoot me before I could grab one of them. Then I remembered my tote. It was as heavy as an anvil, I reasoned. Ask my mother.

"Marigold hired a detective to investigate you," I said.

"So I heard."

"You read the PDF?"

"What PDF?"

He didn't know about that? Then how had he learned about the probe? I flashed on his Dates and Places profile and wanted to palm slap my forehead a second time. Before being a sales rep, he'd worked in banking telecommunications. Had he bugged the bookstore, perhaps setting up the surveillance when he was supposedly using the bathroom in the stock-room? Had he listened to Tegan and me discussing our next move? For that matter, had he tapped my cell phone and eavesdropped on my conversation with Frank Fitzwilliam? I hadn't thought to look for reconnaissance equipment in his room at the inn.

"Move."

"The police will figure out you used to sell pharmaceuticals. They'll realize you're savvy enough to have poisoned Mari-gold."

"With you gone, I doubt it."

"One question."

"Shoot." He snickered. "Oh, gee, you can't." He waggled the Beretta. "I've got the gun."

"Why did you trigger the alarm here?" I took a small step toward the refrigerator while getting a firm grip on the strap of my tote. "Why not kidnap me at my house? You felt comfort-able stealing in the other night."

"*Aha.* You figured that out. Clever girl."

Darcy yowled.

"My cat doesn't like when someone calls me 'girl,' either," I said.

"To answer your question, why did I come here? I thought it would be easier to contain you. The space is limited, and let's face it, sealing you in the refrigerator is, in a word, brilliant. When someone finds you days from now, they'll think how careless you were to let the door close. Keep moving."

Rick had to know there was a safety lock on the inside. He wasn't just going to put me into the refrigerator. He intended to knock me out. I'd freeze before I roused.

I took another baby step. Had Zach seen the text I'd sent him with the image of the empty bank envelope? Would he re-alize what it signified? I said, "Marigold offered you a hundred K to walk out of Noeline's life, didn't she?"

Rick didn't respond, meaning *yes.*

"Why didn't you take it and go?" I pressed.

"Because I fell in love with Noeline."

"As if."

"It's true. I decided to stick around."

"How long do you think you can hide the truth?"

"A long, long time."

"Tell me this," I said, rounding the granite island, judging the distance between us. I'd only get one chance to swing my tote. "Did you also take Marigold's ring?"

"What ring?"

"A diamond-and-ruby target ring, circa 1920, value seventy-nine thousand dollars."

Rick whistled. "Alas, no, that evaded me. Oh, well. C'mon, now, don't dally any longer. I told Noeline I was going out for coffee. I need to pick it up before I return."

I made eye contact with Darcy. He was standing on the shelving, ears pricked, tail bristled and stiff. *Good boy,* I tried to transmit via ESP. I took one small step and then, giving the command like I would for a game of Pounce, I raised my chin and nodded.

Darcy leaped to the floor. The action startled Rick.

At the same time, I whacked Rick in the arm with my tote. He dropped the Beretta. I kicked it away and hit him again. The tote connected with his ear. He groaned and fell to his knees.

I whooped. *Let's hear it for recipe cards, books, e-readers, and to-do lists.*

Darcy leaped onto Rick's neck and clawed. Rick let out a shriek.

Someone pounded on the rear door. Remembering I'd locked it, I raced to it, threw the latch, and swung it open.

Zach was standing there with Bates. Zach's gun was aimed.

Gratitude and relief caught in my throat. "How did you—"

"The security alerts filter through the station. Yours rang for quite a while. After seeing your text with the photo of the bank envelope, I decided to check this place out, even though you used the proper code to disarm the system. Are you all right?"

"I am now."

Chapter 27

"Till this moment I never knew myself."

—Elizabeth Bennet, in Jane Austen's *Pride and Prejudice*

I'd never been inside the police precinct. I'd never even received a speeding ticket. Being debriefed took much longer than I expected, but Zach was as gentle as he could be, and Darcy, confined to his crate, was as patient as a saint. Words of explanation poured out of me. The money. The keys. The key fob. Rick's dating profile. His being a sales rep for a pharmaceutical company, meaning he'd know about poisons. I mentioned that Rick might have a scratch on his arm. Zach assured me he'd check it out. Skin tissue, he finally admitted, had been found under one of Marigold's fingernails.

Tegan and her mother came to the station to support me. Noeline was a bundle of tears, for the loss of her sister, for learning that Rick was the killer, for realizing she'd been bamboozled. After I was released, the three of us went to my house for a much-needed brandy. We didn't talk a lot other than to discuss Noeline's plans to cremate her sister tomorrow. The warmth of the gaslit fireplace soothed us. Darcy, free to roam, tiptoed from one to the other, mewling for affection. Tegan and her mother obliged. Tearfully, at midnight, they left.

The next morning, after a few hours of sleep, I managed my orders. I had to do all the baking at home. Dream Cuisine was off-limits until the investigative team released it. Darcy, like a sergeant at arms, micromanaged me by pacing outside the Plexiglas door. I assured him I wasn't in any more danger, but he didn't believe me. In fact, if he could, he would have barked orders at me to stay in bed.

At the end of the day, the police informed me I was once again allowed to enter Dream Cuisine. I headed there and finalized everything I needed for Marigold's memorial. While I organized and baked, I couldn't tamp down how pleased I was that the pall of having an unsolved murder had been lifted. We could celebrate Marigold's life knowing who had killed her and why. Her friends, customers, and family wouldn't be suspects any longer.

On Friday, I picked up my gown from Lillian. She hugged me and told me how relieved she was that I hadn't been hurt. She added how proud she was to know someone who would risk her life to solve the murder. I wasn't sure I had. On the other hand, whenever I approached the walk-in refrigerator at Dream Cuisine, I shivered. If Rick had prevailed, would I have survived?

At noon on Saturday, I arrived at Feast for the Eyes. Tegan and Chloe helped me wheel in the cart with all my goodies. The three of us had on the same dresses we'd worn to our mini tea. Vanna showed up a half hour later with the items Tegan had assigned her to make. She'd donned an embroidered teal gown with a plunging neckline and a Celtic cross.

"Pretty necklace," I said.

"I purchased it at the festival," she replied, touching the charm. "I might not be of Celtic heritage, but I would have liked to be. I really dig the music and the magical aspect."

I told her what I'd learned as a girl about the migration. "For all you know, you might have some Celtic blood in your veins."

Her eyes twinkled with delight. "Thank you, Allie. That's very sweet of you to say."

I opened my mouth and pressed it shut. Vanna sure was trying hard to be civil to me.

"I'm sorry Mother's boyfriend trapped you at Dream Cuisine," Vanna went on. "You must have been frightened to death."

"It was pretty scary."

"What a toad he turned out to be."

A toad was putting it mildly.

"Where should I lay out the petit fours?" she asked.

"On the rectangular table by the book island."

Chloe had done a bang-up job of decorating the shop. She'd hung the images of *Pride and Prejudice,* as well as the quotations, everywhere. There was one long table near the book island covered in a white tablecloth and adorned with daisies, tulips, and daffodils—Marigold adored yellow flowers. All the sweets would be served there. By each of the endcaps, Chloe had arranged smaller tables. I intended to place the savory dishes, like the poached salmon and white soup, on those. We would pass the mini quiches. A beverage table was stationed by the sales counter. We'd decided to offer beer, gin, champagne, and a couple of wine selections, including claret, Marigold's favorite, as all on the list were Regency Era drinks. Of course, tea, coffee, and water were available as well.

Through a speaker, instrumental music was playing softly. We'd discussed having a string quartet, but ultimately nixed the idea. There simply wasn't room for them and all the guests. I'd sent Chloe a list of titles to queue up.

At one, the four servers I'd hired to help pass hors d'oeuvres and clean up after the memorial arrived.

At one forty-five, Noeline and Helga shuffled into the shop, letting the door swing shut behind them. Noeline looked elegant in a pale yellow gown with a lace neckline and lace overskirt. The train made it quite dramatic. She'd tamed her bobbed hairdo with a hairband made of rhinestones, pearls, and fake leaves. Helga was in her blue uniform—did she ever dress in normal clothes?

"How are you holding up?" I asked.

Noeline forced a smile. "I'll manage." She raised the floral Cloisonné urn she was carrying and confided that her sister's remains were within.

Battling tears, I told her to set the urn by the lectern we'd positioned beside the sales counter.

Noeline complied. When she returned, she said, "How can we help?"

"Put me to work," Helga said.

"Don't do a thing, either of you," Tegan said, joining us and kissing her mother's cheek. "We hired staff. Just be present for everyone else. Go. Mingle."

As they moved off, Tegan's friend Dennell entered in a lavender frock. She was carrying two large bottles of spring water. I was glad to see she looked rested. Her eyes had lost the haunted look.

Tegan clasped Dennell's hand. "Thanks for coming." She guided her friend to the beverage table.

Lillian, Stella, Piper, and Evelyn arrived at two.

Evelyn, a larger-than-life woman who towered over the others, and made herself even taller with the coiled updo she always sported, excused herself and made a beeline for me. She clutched my elbow. "All is forgiven." Her tone was low, with a definite edge.

I swallowed hard. "All is—"

"You believed me to be a murderer."

"N-no." I tried to break free.

Evelyn held on tight. "Oh, yes, honey, you did." Her dark brown eyes were as stony as onyx, but then her gaze softened. "Under the circumstances, it was understandable. Everyone was presumed guilty, and well they should have been. Marigold was a sweet soul and deserved justice. You did right by her." She released my arm and smiled warmly. "If you have time, why don't you volunteer at the theater foundation? The powers that be have recently invited me to take over Marigold's job. I'd like to get to know you better."

My knees, which for a second had turned to jelly, grew steadier, and I decided that, yes, to honor Marigold, I'd give volunteering a try . . . in my spare time.

"Allie!" a woman called from the front of the shop.

I was shocked to see my mother and father strolling in. "Fern. Jamie." I hurried to them and kissed each of them on the cheek. We didn't embrace. Neither was a hugger. "Why are you here?"

"We came to pay our respects," my mother said. "Tegan texted me."

Fern was shorter and slimmer than me, and had straight, dark hair. In keeping with her wish to never draw attention to herself, she'd donned a cargo jacket over a beige blouse and slacks. My father, as slim as my mother, although a tad taller, had worn similar nondescript clothing. I could easily see the two of them, the moment the memorial ended, jetting off for another adventurous trek.

"Everyone's in costume," Fern said, stating the obvious.

Not everyone, I mused, which was fine. Tegan and I knew many wouldn't get into the spirit.

"Yes," I said. "Some are in costume because we thought the celebration should be an homage to Marigold's favorite book, *Pride and Prejudice.*" Apparently, Tegan hadn't mentioned that aspect of the memorial to my mother. I gestured to the posters and quotations.

"Never read it," Fern said. "But the shop is lovely. And you're lovely. Your sage-green dress matches your eyes." She patted my cheek, which jolted me. I couldn't remember the last time she'd touched me tenderly. "Tegan said you were trapped by a killer. I can't imagine. You are so brave. We're so very proud of you."

That sent a seismic shock wave through me. Never, not once in my life, had my mother said she was proud of me. I supposed standing up to a murderer set the bar.

"I knew you'd solve the mystery," Fern continued. "Didn't I tell you, Jamie? Our girl is as bright as a spark. No one holds a candle to her." She turned back to me. "I hope the police were appreciative of your service."

Actually, Zach did thank me for sending him the image of the bank envelope that I'd found in Rick's briefcase. That led the police to search Rick's room at the inn. They found the stolen money stuffed into a sock, along with a half-empty bottle of eye drops, the solution of which matched the poison used to kill Marigold, and they'd discovered surveillance equipment in the closet.

"Quiche?" a server asked as she drew near with a tray of appetizers.

My father reached for one and popped it into his mouth. "You made these?" he asked me around a mouthful.

"I did."

"Delicious." He winked at my mother. "I told you it was a good thing you didn't teach her to cook."

Everything I'd learned had come from a book or a cooking show.

"Be nice." Fern batted his arm, but she was smiling. "Oh, Jamie, there's poor Noeline. Let's give our condolences."

My mother breezed past Evelyn Evers, and I heard Evelyn whisper her name to Lillian. My mother must have heard, because she lifted her chin proudly and continued on without a glance.

Tegan joined me with a plate filled with sweets. She was nibbling on a Maid of Honor. "Why did your mom snub Evelyn?"

"Got me." I recalled the telephone conversation in which Evelyn had bad-mouthed Fern. What was their story? Would either confess?

"Petit four?" Tegan offered me one from her plate. "Vanna really does knock these out of the park."

I couldn't resist.

The pastor of Marigold's church entered the shop, chatting with Graham Wynn, who had dressed in clerical garb appropriate for the Regency period. I bit back a smile. The look suited him.

Katrina Carlson stepped inside next and paused by the first endcap. Oly Olsen sauntered in after her. Neither had dressed in costume. The two studied the growing sea of faces. Oly whispered something to her and gave her a nudge.

She tripped over her feet, but recovered and crossed to Tegan and me. "Hi. Um, I'm glad you were able to, you know . . ."

I embraced her. "Without your help, we wouldn't have figured out what Rick did. It took a lot of courage for you to come forward." I released her.

"It was the least I could do," Katrina murmured. "Detective Armstrong has been wonderful. He helped me get all the negatives from Upton, free of charge."

"That's great news."

"Katrina, I told my mother about your situation," Tegan said, "and she would like to offer you a loan so you can go to school and get your degree. She'll give it to you at a really low interest rate." She leaned forward. "Between you and me, I'll bet she forgives the loan, as long as you finish school. She would want to honor what Auntie intended to do for you."

"You're kidding." Tears sprang to Katrina's eyes. "Really?" She glanced over her shoulder at Oly, who was beaming.

"Yeah, he knows," Tegan said. "Mom clued him in as to her intention to make sure you'd come by today."

"That's so generous I can barely breathe." Katrina pressed a hand to her chest. "Yes. I accept. Thank you."

Katrina rejoined Oly, and the two walked to the beverage table, where he poured her a celebratory glass of champagne.

"Look who sneaked in," Tegan said. "It's Zach. Go." She nudged me.

The moment I saw him, my jaw dropped. He looked stunning in a black tailcoat over brocade vest, his trousers tucked into black riding boots. He hadn't gone so far as to wear a top hat, but *wow!*

Heart racing, I had to tell myself to walk at a slow pace until I reached him. "Thank you for coming."

"I wouldn't have missed it. Marigold was one of my favorite people. This shop"—he motioned to it—"has been my solace since I moved back to town."

I ushered him through the crowd to the table filled with treats.

"You made all these?" he asked, amazed.

"All but the petit fours and cream puffs."

He took a raspberry-lemon cookie and bit into it. "I'm definitely a cookie guy."

"What's your favorite flavor?" I asked, desperately wanting to know the answer.

"Good old chocolate chip. Double chocolate, if possible." After polishing off a second cookie, he leaned in. The woodsy scent of him was heady. "Listen, Allie . . ."

I held my breath.

"We haven't had a chance to talk since the debriefing," he went on. "Wrapping up this case has taken all my attention, but I've been wanting to apologize for being gruff with you."

"Gruff?"

"And for inadvertently hurting your feelings."

"You didn't."

"I did, but I had a job to do, and you were, let's face it, getting in the way."

"By offering you clues?"

"By . . ." He worked his tongue inside his cheek and managed to smile. "I care about you."

From his tone, I gathered that it was the *concerned* kind of care, not the *let's fall in love* kind, and resigned myself to be okay with that. "I care about you, too. Friends." I jutted my arm to shake hands.

He took my hand between both of his. "Yes, friends. But I'd like it to be more than friends if . . ."

I held my breath. What were the conditions? Could I comply?

"If you like me," he said. "I'm not sure you do. Not in the way I mean. Maybe you were showing interest because you wanted information about the investigation."

"No," I blurted. "I like you, too. I do."

"In that case, I want to ask you on a date if . . ."

There was another stipulation? Honestly? I tilted my head, waiting.

"If you don't get involved in any more murder investigations." He offered a lopsided grin.

I smiled, too. Perhaps a memorial wasn't quite the place to be flirting, but I felt Marigold might approve. "I think I can make that promise." At least, I hoped I could, because I really did like him. A lot.

"Everyone," Tegan said, microphone in hand. She was standing at the lectern. Her hand was shaking with nervous tension, but when she glanced at me and I mouthed, "You've got this," she plowed through her discomfort. After all, she'd practiced the speech a dozen times with me as her audience. "I can't tell you how much my aunt appreciated all of you. How much she loved this bookstore. How much she enjoyed sharing her appreciation of books with you. Take a moment to remember her fondly, and in her honor, continue reading as much as you can. Open your minds to the wonderment of a good story. Talk to others about what you read. Spread the word."

"Hear! Hear!" Zach said.

"And now, before I get maudlin, remember my aunt's favorite quote of all times. 'Vanity and pride are different things, though the words are often used synonymously. A person may be proud without being vain. Pride relates more to our opinion of ourselves, vanity to what we would have others think of us.'"

Many said "Amen," in chorus.

Noeline spoke next. Vanna followed and read a few lines from *Pride and Prejudice.* Tegan regained the microphone, looking more composed than she had at first—maybe she was conquering her stage fright—and said if any would like to share stories about Marigold, now was the time.

Two hours later, after sixteen speeches from guests, a heartfelt sermon by the pastor, and one rousing chorus of "Danny Boy"—Marigold's all-time favorite song—the memorial disbanded. There wasn't a dry eye in the bookshop.

Later, after cleaning up, I was on my way out the door with Tegan when Vanna stopped us.

"You know, this was such a success, I think it would be a great idea to have more costume parties related to books at the bookstore. Don't you?" She was brimming with enthusiasm. "Lillian can do the costumes."

Heart, be still! Vanna actually had a clever idea?

"Tegan," Vanna went on, "you'll pick the book, because you're the reader in the family. Won't this be fun? I'm thinking books like *The Great Gatsby,* or—"

"Or *The Thin Man,*" Tegan chimed. "Or *Lord of the Rings.* Or *Murder on the Orient Express.* I love the idea."

"Allie and I could make food that matches the theme," Vanna said, applauding in genteel fashion. "Allie, are you in?"

"Yes, I . . ."

Hold the phone! Did Vanna just say *we,* as in *she and I* would make the food together? My head started to spin. No, not possible. We could never work together. I regarded her and saw tears of joy pooling in her eyes. Was she a changed woman? Could we be a team?

"Allie?" Tegan squeezed my arm.

A few days later, Tegan asked me to come with her to Marigold's house. She, Vanna, and Noeline were going to go through her clothes and household items and give whatever they didn't want to charity. Vanna's Mercedes and Noeline's RAV4 were in the driveway. Tegan pulled up to the curb and parked.

"Vanna is going to be ticked off," I said as I walked up the porch steps.

"She has no say. You're here at my mom's request. In case you see something you like." Tegan plucked a stray hair off her *Book Lover* T-shirt before opening the front door and motioning for me to enter first. "She knows how much Auntie treasured you."

I stepped across the threshold and took in my immediate surroundings. I'd visited Marigold on numerous occasions, but now it all seemed so museum-like. A Chagall hung on the wall above the foyer table. A trio of small Miró paintings were mounted on the opposite wall. In the parlor, to the right, stood a piano and a grouping of antique furniture. The living room, on the left, was plush with an oversized sofa and equally cushy chairs. A portrait of Marigold as a young woman with her beloved hung above the fireplace. It was going to be her gift to him on their wedding day. On the mantel stood the urn containing her ashes. To the right and left of the fireplace were bookcases filled with books. There was also one freestanding hermetically enclosed case, similar to the one in the office at Feast for the Eyes.

"You're going to keep the first editions, aren't you?" I asked.

"Absolutely. Auntie couldn't part with any of them, and neither can I."

"We'll need the books appraised," Vanna said, striding into the foyer from the kitchen at the rear of the house, her four-inch heels clicking on the hardwood floors, her pencil skirt—honestly, why did she insist on wearing uncomfortable clothes?—straining with every stride. She eyed me. "What are you—" She jammed her lips together. Her restraint impressed me.

After her suggestion to host costume-food-book parties at the shop, she had been doing her best to play nice. In a prickly moment, I'd wondered whether her catering business was floundering, thus making her more eager to partner up with me, but then I'd reminded myself that couldn't be the reason, considering what she would inherit from her aunt. I did need someone to assist me, but was she the right person? Would I need to invest in a pair of boxing gloves?

"By the way," Vanna went on, "the Realtor has three offers on the house. She's coming here to present them. Okay?"

Tegan nodded.

"Mother is upstairs." Vanna pointed to the staircase. "She'd like to start there."

She led the way. Tegan followed. Small masterpieces adorned the walls. Persian runners lined the floors.

We found Noeline in the primary bedroom, her face tear-stained. She was standing beside the bed, where an array of sweaters, skirts, and blouses were lying in a pile. Others were folded, stacked, and assorted by color. Hanging in the walk-in closet were trousers, winter coats, arty smocks, and T-shirts. Like Tegan, Marigold had delighted in wearing fun, whimsical clothing. She would don her more tailored, classical styles to impress foundation bigwigs.

"Evelyn reached out and asked if we could donate some of Marigold's things to the community theater." Noeline lifted a silk blouse. "What kind of character would wear this?"

"Anyone in a courtroom drama," Tegan said.

Noeline nodded absently.

Vanna ambled to the bureau near the window. Sunlight graced her face as she opened a mahogany jewelry case. "The other day while I was waiting for the Realtor to arrive, I went through this box. I think most of it is paste." She hooked a pinky around a necklace and displayed it to us. "There are similar containers in the closet."

Tegan said, "Allie, help me bring everything out here." She walked into the closet.

I followed.

She gathered smocks and T-shirts in her arms. "Grab the coats," she said.

I lifted three, but paused when I spied a wall safe behind them, the kind you'd see in a hotel, with an electronic digital code. I plunked the coats on the floor. "Tegan, did you know about this?"

Tegan joined me and gawked. "Mom! Vanna! C'mere."

The two joined us. It was crowded, but we managed.

Noeline gasped. "Is that—"

Tegan nodded. "Would you know the combination?"

"No clue."

"Vanna?" Tegan asked.

"Me neither," her half sister replied.

"Ms. Ivey might know," I suggested.

Tegan pulled out her cell phone and dialed the bank manager, who said she didn't have a record of a wall safe and apologized. Tegan exchanged a look with me and a grin spread across her face. "What do you bet . . ." She stared at her cell phone and said, "Allie, tap in seven, seven, three, five, eight, three, four, two, three."

I did as told and the electronic lock released. "What the—"

"Those are the reciprocal numbers for *p-r-e-j-u-d-i-c-e,*" Tegan said. "Auntie really was obsessed with the book."

I swung the door open and Vanna stepped forward, but I blocked her progress, to let Tegan have the first look. She whistled.

"What's inside?" Vanna demanded.

"Baggies."

"Filled with marijuana?" Noeline asked.

"No, Mother, get real." A laugh burbled out of my pal. "It looks like valuables." Tegan pulled out the items and said, "This is for you." She handed Noeline a bag with a note addressed to her on it.

Noeline opened the bag and found a pretty turquoise ring. She read the note. "'Turquoise has always been your favorite, Sis. I bought this with you in mind. Don't worry. It's not too expensive. Wear it often. Love you always.'" Tears flowed freely from Noeline's eyes now.

"This is for you, Vanna," Tegan said, handing her half sister a baggie.

Vanna opened it and found a handful of gold coins. Confused, she read the note Marigold had written: "'Vanna, my dear girl, don't rely on your clients to determine your value. You are worth more than all the gold coins in the world, if you would believe in *yourself.*'" Her voice cracked on the last word. She clutched the bag to her chest, and whispered, "Oh, Auntie."

"Allie, this one is for you." Tegan held out a third bag.

"Me? But—"

She jiggled it. "Take it. Open it."

I did and inside found a Celtic knot ring that matched my necklace. I, too, read my note aloud. "'Dearest Allie, treasure your roots. Treasure your good heart. Treasure your gift of curiosity. They will not fail you as long as you live. And whenever you read a good book, think of me.'" My fingers trembled as I slipped the ring onto my finger. *Marigold, thank you,* I prayed silently. *I'll treasure you forever.*

"What's in there for you, darling?" Noeline asked Tegan.

"There's nothing more." She sounded disheartened but mustered a brave face. "Auntie gave me the bookshop. That's enough."

I picked up the coats I'd dropped on the floor, and silently we all moved into the bedroom. I tossed the coats onto a Queen Anne chair and something in a plastic bag flew from one of the pockets. I retrieved it, and my spirits lifted. It was tagged with a note to Tegan. Within was a beautiful ring. A diamond-and-ruby target ring, to be specific.

I handed the bag to her and she read the note. "'Tegan, my sweet, you always admired this ring. It is yours. If it hasn't been cleaned by the time you receive it, please do so. It will sparkle as you do and bring you joy, as you bring joy to me.'"

Tegan began to sob. Noeline swept her into a hug. Vanna joined the twosome.

I kept my distance. This was a family moment, and as much as I felt they were my family, I didn't want to intrude.

"Knock-knock," a woman said from the hallway. She stepped into the bedroom. "Am I interrupting?" She was wearing a blazer over a silk blouse and trousers. In one hand, she held a tooled leather briefcase. In the other, she carried what looked like contracts. "The front door was unlocked. I hope you don't mind that I let myself in."

"Mom, Tegan," Vanna said, "this is Ms. Richards, our Realtor."

They greeted her warmly.

Ms. Richards explained that she had three offers. "However, I have to say, ladies, one offer stands out above the rest. I think that person really wants the house and will cherish it the most. Would you like to hear it first?"

Vanna said, "Yes, please." She clutched Tegan's hand in sol-
idarity. "We're ready."

"Tegan," Ms. Richards said, "would you like to tell them?"

Tegan released her sister's hand. "Vanna, you have your Victorian. Mom has the inn. I'm done with Winston. I really, really
want this house. I'm willing to pay top dollar to have it. Please
say yes, Sis. *Please.*"

"*Sis?* Did you call me *Sis?*" Vanna's cheeks tinged pink.

"I did."

Vanna clasped Tegan in a hug and then held her at arm's
length. "I'll say yes, as long as you and Allie consider my idea
about the parties at the bookshop."

"We already have," I said, grabbing Tegan's hand. "We
agree. We're in."

RECIPES

Chocolate Butterscotch Cookies

(Yield: 20–24)

1 cup unsalted butter, room temperature
1½ cups packed brown sugar
½ cup granulated sugar
2 large eggs
2 teaspoons vanilla extract
3¼ cups flour
1½ teaspoon baking powder
1 teaspoon baking soda
1 teaspoon salt
1 cup butterscotch morsels
1 cup chocolate morsels
Sea salt, if desired

Preheat oven to 350 degrees F. Line 2 baking sheets with parchment paper and set aside.

In a stand mixer, cream the butter, brown sugar, and granulated sugar until blended, 2–3 minutes. Add eggs and vanilla extract and mix well.

In a separate bowl, whisk the flour, baking powder, baking soda, and salt. Slowly add the dry ingredients to the butter mixture.

Stir in the butterscotch morsels and chocolate morsels. If you feel the mixture is dry (it might be), you may add 2 tablespoons water.

If you want large cookies, drop large spoonfuls (about 2 tablespoons each) on the prepared baking sheets, 6 to a sheet. These do spread. If you want smaller cookies, drop small spoonfuls (about 1 tablespoon each) on the baking sheets, 12 to a sheet. If desired, sprinkle with sea salt.

Bake cookies for 10–12 minutes, until lightly brown. Remove from oven and let stand on the baking sheet for 5 minutes. Transfer the cookies to a cooling rack.

Chocolate Butterscotch Cookies
Gluten-free Version

(Yield: 20–24)

1 cup unsalted butter, room temperature
1½ cups packed brown sugar
½ cup granulated sugar
2 large eggs
2 teaspoons vanilla extract
2 cups sweet white rice flour
1 cup + 2 tablespoons tapioca flour
2 tablespoons whey powder
1 teaspoon xanthan gum
1½ teaspoon baking powder
1 teaspoon baking soda
1 teaspoon salt
1 cup butterscotch morsels
1 cup chocolate morsels
Sea salt, if desired

Preheat oven to 350 degrees F. Line 2 baking sheets with parchment paper and set aside.

In a stand mixer, cream the butter, brown sugar, and granulated sugar until blended, 2–3 minutes. Add eggs and vanilla extract and mix well.

In a separate bowl, whisk the sweet white rice flour, tapioca flour, whey powder, xanthan gum, baking powder, baking soda, and salt. Slowly add the dry ingredients to the butter mixture.

Stir in the butterscotch morsels and chocolate morsels. If you feel the mixture is dry (it might be), you may add 2 tablespoons water.

If you want large cookies, drop large spoonfuls (about 2 tablespoons each) on the prepared baking sheets, 6 to a sheet. These do spread. If you want smaller cookies, drop small spoonfuls (about 1 tablespoon each) on the baking sheets, 12 to a sheet. If desired, sprinkle with sea salt.

Bake cookies for 10–12 minutes, until lightly brown. Remove from oven and let stand on the baking sheet for 5 minutes. Transfer the cookies to a cooling rack.

Delightful Trifle

(Serves: 8)

Needed for the recipe:
1 recipe stirred custard
½ loaf pound cake
⅓ cup triple sec or orange juice
1 cup strawberry freezer jam
1 cup heavy whipping cream, whipped with 1 tablespoon sugar
   and ½ teaspoon vanilla
Fresh strawberries

How to make stirred custard:
5 egg yolks, beaten
1½ cups milk
¼ cup sugar
1½ teaspoons vanilla

In a heavy medium-sized saucepan, stir together egg yolks, milk, and sugar.

Prepare a large bowl filled with ice and cold water. Set aside.

Cook the egg mixture over medium heat and stir continuously until the mixture coats the back of a clean spoon, about 5–6 minutes. Do not boil. Remove the pan from the heat and stir in the vanilla.

Quickly cool the custard by placing the saucepan in the large bowl of ice water for 1–2 minutes, stirring repeatedly.

Pour the custard into a small bowl. Cover the surface with plastic wrap to prevent a skin from forming. Chill the custard for 2 hours or until serving time. It will be runny. Stirred custard does not "set."

How to make strawberry freezer jam:
2 cups fresh strawberries, sliced
2 cups sugar
1 package dry pectin or 1 package gelatin
¾ cup water

In a medium bowl, mix strawberries and sugar. Let stand 10 minutes.

Meanwhile, stir the pectin or gelatin into the water in a small saucepan. Bring this to a boil and boil for 1 minute.

Add in the strawberries and, using a potato masher, crush the berries. Allow the mixture to stand for 3 minutes and then pour into clean jars, leaving space at the top for expansion.

Let stand for 24 hours at room temperature before freezing. *This may be used immediately in the trifle recipe if you didn't have time to freeze it, but it must be cooled completely.

To construct the trifle:
Pound cake may be store bought or homemade. *For recipe for perfect gluten-free pound cake, see below.

Cut half a loaf of pound cake into slices about ½-inch thick and then cut the slices in half or cubes. Measure out the triple sec and jam.

To assemble individual trifles in bowls, layer:
Cake
1 teaspoon triple sec
1 tablespoon strawberry freezer jam
2 tablespoons custard
Cake
1 teaspoon triple sec
1 tablespoon strawberry freezer jam
2 tablespoons custard

To assemble a large trifle in a clear glass bowl that will serve 8:

Layer:
Half the cake slices or cubes
Sprinkle with 8 teaspoons triple sec
Top with ½ cup strawberry freezer jam
Top with 1 cup custard

Repeat:
Half the cake slices, cubes
8 teaspoons triple sec
½ cup strawberry freezer jam
1 cup custard

Chill trifle(s) for at least 8 hours. *This is a must.* The cake will
sop up the moisture.

When ready to serve, make the whipped cream and garnish individual dishes with the cream and fresh strawberries.

Helga's Super Easy Triple Chocolate Trifle + Homemade Caramel Topping

(Yield: 8 portions)

1 brownie mix, prepared and cooled, cubed (*may be gluten-free)
1 4-ounce chocolate instant pudding, prepared
½ cup caramel topping, store bought or homemade *see recipe below
2 Snickers candy bars, chopped
2 Heath Bars or Skor Bars, chopped
1 16-ounce frozen whipped topping, thawed

In a large glass trifle dish or a glass bowl, layer ⅓–½ of the cubed brownie, then half of the pudding, then half of the caramel topping, then 1 of the chopped Snickers bars, and 1 of the chopped Heath or Skor bars. Top with half of the whipped topping.

Repeat the layers in the same order, reserving a few bits of the Snickers and Heath or Skor bars for decoration on top of the final layer of whipped topping.

Refrigerate at least 6 hours.

Homemade Caramel Topping

(Yield: 2–3 cups)

2 cups brown sugar
1 cup dark corn syrup
1 can sweetened condensed milk
½ cup margarine
1 teaspoon vanilla extract

In a heavy saucepan, combine the brown sugar and corn syrup. Cook over medium heat until the mixture reaches 235 degrees F on a candy thermometer.

Remove the pan from the heat. Stir in the sweetened condensed milk, margarine, and vanilla.

Return the pan to the stove and cook, over medium heat, stirring frequently until the mixtures comes to a boil. Remove the pan from the heat and let the mixture cool slightly.

Store unused caramel topping in a jar in the refrigerator. Heat before reusing. May be heated in the microwave on medium low level. Do not boil.

Maids of Honor

(Yield: 12)

1 recipe for pastry for a single-crust pie
¼ cup raspberry jam
¼ cup unsalted butter, softened
¼ cup white sugar
1 egg
½ cup flour
¼ teaspoon baking powder
¼ teaspoon almond extract
2 teaspoons confectioners' sugar for dusting

Put the oven rack at the bottom and preheat oven to 375 degrees F. You may use a silicon 2-inch tart pan that doesn't need greasing, but if you use metal, lightly grease it.

Roll out the pastry and cut 12 circles, 2 inches each. Fit 1 circle into each of the tart forms.

Spread 1 teaspoon of raspberry jam into the bottom of each tart.

In a medium mixing bowl, cream together the softened butter and sugar until fluffy. Mix in the egg. Add flour, baking powder, and almond extract. Mix until combined. Drop 1 tablespoon of the batter on top of the raspberry jam that is already in the tart shell.

Bake in oven for 20 minutes. They will rise and become firm, like a muffin. Remove from oven. Let cool slightly. Dust with confectioners' sugar.

Maids of Honor
Gluten-free Version

(Yield: 12)

1 recipe pastry for a single-crust pie (*see below for a no-fail,
    gluten-free pastry recipe)
¼ cup raspberry jam
¼ cup unsalted butter, softened
¼ cup white sugar
1 egg
½ cup sweet rice flour
1 dash xanthan gum (about 1/8 teaspoon)
¼ teaspoon baking powder
¼ teaspoon almond extract
2 teaspoons confectioners' sugar for dusting

Put the oven rack at the bottom and preheat oven to 375 degrees F. You may use a silicon 2-inch tart pan that doesn't need greasing, but if you use metal, lightly grease it.

Roll out the pastry and cut 12 circles, 2 inches each. Fit 1 circle into each of the tart forms.

Spread 1 teaspoon of raspberry jam into the bottom of each tart.

In a medium mixing bowl, cream together the softened butter and sugar until fluffy. Mix in the egg. Add sweet rice flour, xanthan gum, baking powder, and almond extract. Mix until combined. Drop 1 tablespoon of the batter on top of the raspberry jam that is already in the tart shell.

Bake in oven for 20 minutes. They will rise and become firm, like a muffin. Remove from oven. Let cool slightly. Dust with confectioners' sugar.

No-fail Gluten-free Pastry Recipe

(Yield: 1 crust)

8 tablespoons unsalted butter, cut into tiny pieces and *frozen* for 10 minutes
2½ tablespoons ice water
1½ tablespoons sour cream
1½ teaspoons rice vinegar
¾ cup sweet rice flour
⅔ cup tapioca flour
1½ teaspoons white sugar
½ teaspoon salt
¼ teaspoon xanthan gum

Cut and freeze the butter.

In a small bowl, combine ice water, sour cream, and vinegar. Set aside.

In a food processor, blend the sweet rice flour, tapioca flour, sugar, salt, and xanthan gum. Pulse for 5 seconds. Sprinkle the frozen butter on top and pulse the mixture about 10–15 times.

Pour half of the sour cream mixture over the flour mixture and pulse 3 times. Pour the rest of the sour cream mixture over the flour and pulse again until the dough comes together.

Set the dough on parchment paper and flatten into a 5-inch circle. Wrap tightly and set in refrigerator for about 40 minutes.

When ready, remove dough from refrigerator. Top with another sheet of parchment paper and roll to a thin circle about ¼-inch thick.

Dough may be made 2 days ahead. Dough may also be frozen and thawed.

Perfect Pound Cake
Gluten-free Recipe

(Yield: 8 slices)

1 cup (2 sticks) unsalted butter, softened
1¾ cups granulated sugar
3 large whole eggs
3 large egg yolks
½ tablespoon vanilla extract
½ teaspoon salt
1¾ cups gluten-free flour, less 2 tablespoons
2 tablespoons whey powder
1 teaspoon xanthan gum

Preheat oven to 350 degrees F and grease and flour a loaf pan. You must use gluten-free flour. Shake out any excess.

In the bowl of a stand mixer, whip the butter until fluffy, about 1 minute. Add the sugar and whip again until fluffy, about 1 minute.

On low, add in the eggs, vanilla extract, and salt. Once incorporated, turn mixer to medium and whip for 1 minute.

In a separate bowl, mix the gluten-free flour, whey powder, and xanthan gum. Add half of the gluten-free flour mixture to the egg mixture and mix on low. Add the other half of the gluten-free flour mixture to the egg mixture and mix on low. Scrape down the sides.

Pour the mixture into the prepared loaf pan. Bake for 55–60 minutes, until a toothpick comes out clean. Set on a wire rack to cool for 20 minutes. When ready, loosen the pound cake with a knife around the edges, and then turn the cake out on the wire rack to cool for another 20 minutes.

Delicious served with sliced fruit or ice cream.

Poached Salmon

(Serves: 4)

2 tablespoons unsalted butter, softened
2 large filets salmon, skin removed, each cut in half (4 portions)
1 lemon
½ teaspoon salt
2 large sprigs dill, diced, more for garnish

Preheat oven to 400 degrees F. In a 13 x 9 baking pan, lay out 1 piece of parchment paper.

Add the butter and smear across the center of the parchment paper.

Set the salmon filets on the butter. Cut the lemon in half and squeeze both halves over the salmon. Sprinkle the salmon with salt. Top with the diced dill.

Seal the parchment paper by bringing up the sides, covering the salmon completely. Twist the ends of the parchment paper.

Bake the fish in the preheated oven for 18–20 minutes. Serve hot.

Shortbread Cookies

(Yield: 24–30)

¾ pound butter, softened
1 cup sugar, plus extra for sprinkling
1 teaspoon vanilla extract
3½ cups flour, plus extra for rolling the dough
¼ teaspoon salt

Preheat oven to 350 degrees F.

In the bowl of an electric mixer, mix the butter and sugar until combined. Add the vanilla.

In a separate bowl, sift together the flour and salt and add them to the butter mixture. Mix on low until the dough comes together. Dump the dough onto parchment paper dusted with extra flour and press into a flat round. Wrap the round in plastic and chill for 30 minutes.

Roll the dough out with a rolling pin to ½-inch thickness and then cut the dough into 1-inch wide pieces about 2 inches long.

Place the cookies on an ungreased baking sheet or a sheet lined with parchment paper. Sprinkle with the extra sugar.

Bake for 20–25 minutes until the edges are slightly brown. Cool on a wire rack.

*These may be drizzled with melted chocolate or dipped in melted chocolate, if desired.

Shortbread Cookies
Gluten-free Version

(Yield: 24–30)

¾ pound butter, softened
1 cup sugar, plus extra for sprinkling
1 teaspoon vanilla extract
2½ cups sweet rice flour, plus extra for rolling the dough
1 cup, less 2 tablespoons, tapioca flour
2 tablespoons whey powder
½ teaspoon xanthan gum
¼ teaspoon salt

Preheat oven to 350 degrees F.

In the bowl of an electric mixer, mix the butter and sugar until combined. Add the vanilla.

In a separate bowl, sift together the sweet rice flour, tapioca flour, whey powder, xanthan gum, and salt and add them to the butter mixture. Mix on low until the dough comes together. Dump the dough onto parchment paper dusted with extra sweet rice flour and press into a flat round. Wrap the round in plastic and chill for 30 minutes.

Between 2 pieces of parchment paper, so the gluten-free dough doesn't stick to the rolling pin, roll the dough out with a rolling pin to ½-inch thickness. Remove the top piece of parchment paper and cut the dough into 1-inch wide pieces about 2 inches long.

Place the cookies on an ungreased baking sheet or a sheet lined with parchment paper. Sprinkle with the extra sugar.

Bake for 20–25 minutes until the edges are slightly brown. Cool on a wire rack.

*These may be drizzled with melted chocolate or dipped in melted chocolate, if desired.

White Soup

(Serves: 6–8)

3 pounds veal chops, bone in
1 small chicken, cut up, bone in
1 large onion, chopped
3 celery ribs, chopped
2 carrots, peeled and chopped
1 bundle of herbs wrapped in cheesecloth (parsley, sage, thyme, bay leaf)
¼ teaspoon mace
½ teaspoon white pepper
12 whole cloves
2 teaspoons salt

Place all of the ingredients into a large stockpot and cover with water. Place the pot on a burner set to medium high. Bring the mixture to a boil.

Reduce the heat and simmer the stock for 2 hours. The meat should be falling off the bone. During the process, scoop any scum off the top of the liquid and discard.

Remove the pot from the heat. Take out the meat and set it on a cutting board. When it cools, shred it into small pieces, bones removed. Store the meat in a glass container in the refrigerator.

Strain the stock into a large bowl, removing all the bits of meat, vegetables, and herbs. Cover the bowl and refrigerate overnight.

The next day: Remove the stock from the refrigerator. Any fat will have risen and become solid. This is easily removed and discarded.

Ingredients to finish making the stock:
4 quarts meat stock
1 fresh bundle of herbs wrapped in cheesecloth (parsley, sage, thyme, bay leaf)

½ cup white breadcrumbs (*may use gluten-free breadcrumbs)
½ lemon, juice only
⅛ teaspoon mace
1 teaspoon salt
½ teaspoon white pepper
½ cup unsweetened almond milk

Place all the ingredients except the almond milk in a large stock-pot. Using a whisk, break up the breadcrumbs. Over medium-high heat, bring the mixture to a boil. Reduce the heat and simmer, covered, for about 20 minutes.

Remove the pot from the heat and strain out all the bread-crumbs and herbs. Return the strained liquid to the cooking pot and add the almond milk.

Ingredients to finish making the soup:
Soup stock, from above recipe
Shredded meat reserved in first recipe
1 pint of cream
1 teaspoon salt
½ teaspoon white pepper
Small dinner rolls, warmed, as an accompaniment

Add the shredded meat, cream, and salt and pepper to the mix-ture of stock and almond milk in the pot. Set the pot over medium heat and cook the mixture until heated through, approximately 20 minutes. Do NOT boil.

Serve with warmed dinner rolls and butter.

ACKNOWLEDGMENTS

The more that you read, the more things you will know. The more that you learn, the more places you'll go.

—Dr. Seuss

What wonderful support I've had as I pursue my creative journey. Without all of you listed below, I would have stopped writing years ago. I can never thank you enough!

Thank you to my family. Thank you to my talented author friends, Krista Davis, Hannah Dennison, Janet Bolin (Ginger Bolton), Kaye George, Marilyn Levinson (Allison Brook), Peg Cochran (Margaret Loudon), Janet Koch (Laura Alden), and Roberta Isleib (Lucy Burdette). You are a wonderful pool of talent. I treasure your creative enthusiasm.

Thank you to Facebook mystery groups for giving authors a place to share their work. I love how willing you are to read ARCs and post reviews. Thank you to all the bloggers who enjoy reviewing cozies and sharing these titles with your readers. Thank you to Lori Caswell for leading the pack when it comes to virtual book tours.

Thanks to those who have helped make this first book in the Literary Dining Mystery series come to fruition: my publisher, Kensington Books; my editor, Elizabeth Trout; my copy editor, Stephanie Finnegan; my agent, Jill Marsal; my cover artist, Patrick Knowles. Thanks to Madeira James for maintaining constant quality on my website. Thanks to my virtual assistant,

Christina Higgins, for your clever ideas. Thanks to my wonderful nephew, Bryce, for giving me a tour of the Asheville area and the Blue Ridge Mountains. I love you a ton. And many thanks to my lifelong cheerleader and sister, Kimberley Greene. You are the best!

Special thanks to my Fiverr mampmaker, Melissa @mnash884. You did a wonderful job.

Last, but not least, thank you, librarians, teachers, bookstore owners, and readers, for sharing the fun and colorful world of a bookstore that celebrates with book parties. I hope you enjoy the literary-loving, food-loving, fun-loving world I've created. Bless you all.